THE TROPHY KILLER

An absolutely gripping crime thriller with a massive twist

MICHELLE KIDD

DI Nicki Hardcastle Series Book 2

JOFFE BOOKS

Joffe Books, London
www.joffebooks.com

First published in Great Britain in 2023

Cover art by Nebojša Zorić

ISBN: 978-1-80405-973-9

CHAPTER ONE

Thursday 27 December 2018
The Theatre Royal
Westgate Street, Bury St Edmunds

Hugh Maxwell bit his lip, feeling the sweat breaking out on the palms of his hands. At that precise moment, standing in the corridor outside the Sir Isaac Newton box in the dress circle of the Theatre Royal, he was ashamed to say that he had no idea what to do.

For all the hours upon hours of major incident training he had received in the wake of the rise in the country's terror threat level — the numerous emails, video conferences and PowerPoint presentations he'd had to endure in order to 'tick that box' and make him 'competent in a crisis' — everything deserted him in an instant.

I don't know what to do.

Voices clamoured for his attention, but all he heard was a muffled collection of incomprehensible words as though he were underwater, drowning in the very air that should sustain him. With his vision swimming in and out of focus, his heartbeat reaching a crescendo, he merely stood rooted to the spot; paralysed.

I don't know what to do.

After what seemed like an eternity, the moment passed and a clarity of sorts returned. With his vision clearing, he noticed one of the newest members of his team standing opposite, a look of bewilderment on his young, pale face.

Clearing his throat, Hugh wiped his clammy hands on the sides of his neatly pressed trousers and beckoned the young employee forward.

"Take Mr Fisher to my office." He gestured towards an elderly gentleman standing to the side, the old man's ice-white hair almost the same colour as his face. "Set him up with a cup of tea, and I'll be along in a moment or two."

The employee dutifully took the old man by the elbow and guided him back along the corridor. Two elderly ladies hovered in the background, one clutching a souvenir programme, the other a packet of mint humbugs. Hugh tried a smile. "And why don't you both go along, too? A nice hot cup of sweet tea?"

The women didn't need asking twice and soon scuttled off out of sight.

Alone in the corridor once again, Hugh Maxwell took in a deep breath and brought the two-way radio to his dry lips.

"Carlton?" The radio gave a faint crackle in response. "Block off all the access corridors to the dress circle. Let nobody else through." He paused, his eyes straying towards the closed door of the Sir Isaac Newton box. "On second thoughts, let's get everyone outside. Tonight's performance is cancelled."

* * *

The Farmhouse

The last sinewy tendon divided cleanly beneath the sharpened blade. It always amazed him how little blood there was when the heart had already been stilled.

Clean.

Neat.

Just how he liked it.

Lucie had been her name — not that it really mattered much anymore. Adjusting the overhead lamp, he focused the beam of light on to the woman's exposed forearm and sighed contentedly. It was a near-perfect job, even if he did say so himself. Textbook, even. Gripping the sharpened scalpel in a steady hand, he sliced through the remaining tissue with ease.

The procedure itself had been straightforward enough — severing a hand took little or no skill when it really came down to it — but he had taken his time with her anyway.

Lucie deserved that at least.

They all did.

Briefly, he let his eyes wander towards his watch, his stomach muscles clenching in anticipation. Very soon his first offering would be discovered — if it hadn't been already. The play was due to start in half an hour. The thought made his usually steady hand begin to tremble.

The game was about to begin.

Part of him wished he could be there to see the shock and horror for himself, but Lucie needed him right now. So, with another twitch of his lips, he steadied his hand once more and turned his attention back towards the table.

With the wrist joint now exposed, all tissue, nerves and tendons skilfully dissected, he reached for the saw.

Beneath the flickering overhead light, Lucie's exposed bones gleamed the most eerie, creamy white. Gently scraping the remaining congealed blood and tissue away, he placed the blade of the saw against her radius. With his free hand, he turned the volume up on his phone and closed his eyes as Camille Saint-Saens' *Danse Macabre* filled the silence. A thin smile spread across his angular features as contentment filled every crevice of his being.

As the music intensified, he drew the saw across the surface of the bone, etching a tiny groove. The sound of grating bone joined that of the violins as he began to press deeper. Blade on bone, bone on blade — one of the most exquisite sounds to reach the human ear.

With the radius neatly severed, he turned his attention to the ulna. The same sweeping strokes soon resulted in the bone snapping beneath the blade. Taking a step backwards, saw in hand, he took a moment to marvel at his handiwork.

He could easily have taken a meat cleaver to the woman's wrist — one hefty downward chop and the job would have been done in an instant. But that wasn't what he wanted for Lucie — there was no skill in merely butchering her.

Lucie's left hand now lay completely separated from her limp and lifeless arm. He'd decided to amputate the hand several inches above the joint — the small butterfly tattoo etched into her skin needed to be preserved. It was one of the first things he'd noticed about her. And when he'd then spied the second inking — a tiny, delicate rose just beneath the base of the thumb — he had hardly been able to contain himself.

Such a beautiful, *beautiful* hand.

Taking a cleansing wipe, he carefully removed any traces of congealed blood and tissue from the outside of the severed hand. There wasn't much — he'd been careful and the dissection had been neat. Professor Ferguson would have expected nothing less from his most talented student.

Top of the class,' he would have announced in his clipped, Edinburgh accent. 'Top of the class.'

Satisfied she was clean, he pulled off his surgical gloves and turned to pick up the polaroid camera from the bench behind. Angling it towards the severed limb, he took two quick snaps, his stomach muscles tightening as he waited for each one to be developed.

Such a brilliant invention — the camera. His grandfather had given him his old Polaroid camera many years ago. He'd since upgraded to a more modern version — but he still preferred it over the point and shoot digital varieties.

Once the images were dry, he stepped soundlessly across to where he'd pinned a life-size scale drawing of the human body. His body map. Taking a piece of tape, he secured one of the Polaroid pictures of Lucie's hand to the paper, feeling

4

the familiar trickle of anticipation as his eyes roamed across the rest of the life-size drawing.

He had made a good start.

But there was still so much more to do.

* * *

Detective Inspector Nicki Hardcastle glanced at her watch and sighed. With the day being so overcast it was difficult to tell exactly when morning had turned into afternoon — and then evening. That dull, gloomy light that only late December could bring had settled over the town and was refusing to budge. Thick clouds which had threatened snow all day were, for the moment at least, holding on to their frozen cargo — but their pale pink hues were sending out a distinct warning of what was to come. Now night had fallen, it was only a matter of time.

Nicki shivered in front of the window and pulled the blinds shut. Christmas had been and gone, but its tired legacy still clung to the walls of the incident room. There'd been a half-hearted attempt to drag festive frivolity into the station — tatty pieces of red and green tinsel still skirting the edges of several of the whiteboards. A plastic Christmas tree had appeared from somewhere and still sat forlornly in the corner like a naughty child. The fairy lights had fused when they'd been switched on, but nobody had the energy or inclination to try and fix them.

It all looked rather tired and sad.

The Lucas Jackson case had drained the team's reserves, and the Christmas break couldn't have come soon enough. With the trial unlikely to start until well into next year, for now all the investigation papers had been boxed up and stored away.

A few days off over the festive period was what everyone had needed — everyone, that was, except Nicki. She had politely declined the offer from DCI Malcolm Turner to take leave over the holidays, preferring instead to seek solitude in the half-empty station, and plough through the mind-numbing paperwork that continued to build up on her desk.

She had eventually given in and spent a few hours at home on Christmas Day — a microwaved turkey dinner for herself, a pouch of duck liver pâté for her Russian Blue cat, Luna. They'd sat together on the sofa, Luna contentedly snoozing while Nicki scrolled through the banal offerings that constituted Christmas Day TV. As a child, she remembered watching endless cartoons on Christmas morning, plus festive editions of all her favourite programmes. She would spend hours poring over the *Radio Times*, highlighting what she wanted to watch during the holidays. But now all she could find was yet another repeat of some Disney film she'd seen several times before, or the Top of the Pops Christmas special.

It hadn't taken long for her to scrape the remains of her turkey dinner into Luna's bowl and head back to work.

The somewhat stilted and brief conversation she'd had with her parents on Christmas morning had taken a while to fade into the background. It was the same every year. Her parents would make a less than enthusiastic invitation for her to join them for Christmas lunch, to which she would predictably and politely decline, citing work pressures that they all knew to be a lie — but a necessary one. It was a ritual they danced through every year.

Despite the awkwardness, she still looked forward to hearing their voices. Her father's deep tones never failed to transport her back to the happier times of her youth. Christmas in the Webster household was always a magical time — her father lifting her on to his shoulders to place the angel on top of the tree. On Christmas Day itself, the aroma of sizzling turkey and roast potatoes would fill the air, her mother singing along to festive tunes on the radio while sipping a glass of sparkling wine. Presents would cover the living room floor beneath the Christmas tree, opened to a multitude of shrieks and cheers.

But all that had been before Deano.

In days gone by, when they'd actually tried to go through with the ridiculous performance of the annual Christmas get-together, Nicki couldn't help but see the distant look in her mother's eyes. She no longer sang along to the radio, or sipped her sparkling wine — the magic of Christmas was no longer present in the Webster house. Her father always tried to smile and hug her like before — but it was never quite the same. Something was missing.

And they all knew what that was.

Deano.

But thankfully Christmas, and all its pretence, was over for another year.

Sighing once again, Nicki snapped off the incident room lights and made her way back to her office. She could easily put in another couple of hours before heading home. Luna would be asleep on the sofa, her furry belly full; nobody else would miss her.

As she neared her office door, she caught a brief glimpse of a figure heading towards the stairs — a figure she instantly recognised.

"Graham?" Hesitating with one hand on the door handle, she stared at the now empty corridor. "Is that you?"

Several seconds passed before DS Graham Fox shuffled back into view, a sheepish look on his face.

Nicki waved him forward. "What on earth are you doing here? Come inside for a coffee."

DS Fox, walking with the aid of a wooden cane, dutifully followed Nicki back into her office.

"You should be at home with your feet up," she commented, reaching for two mugs and the emergency flask of coffee she'd made earlier.

"So should you," quipped Fox, gingerly lowering himself into the chair closest to him.

Touché, thought Nicki as she poured the drinks. "How have you been?"

Although he did look better, better than he had from the end of his hospital bed at any rate, Nicki saw that the detective had lost weight and his skin sported a waxen, pallid tone. Gone was the customary sparkle to his eyes. Maybe coming within an inch or two of death did that to you.

Fox accepted the mug handed to him across the desk, instantly wrapping his fingers around it. "I feel a lot better," he replied. "My stamina's improving every day. I can get up the stairs here without stopping halfway now." He tried a smile and sipped his drink.

"That may be so, but I'm still sure you should be resting at home. It's only been a couple of months since the accident."

Fox shook his head. "I'm done with resting. Being cooped up inside my flat's doing my nut in. I need to get out."

"And the first place you thought of coming to was *here*?" Nicki raised her eyebrows in jest, suppressing the spreading smile behind her mug. She had a lot in common with Graham Fox — each of them trying to escape the intense loneliness of Christmas, and each similarly ending up within these same four walls. It said something about them — but Nicki wasn't quite sure she wanted to know exactly what that was.

"I'm fit for work," he added, cradling the coffee mug in his lap. "I'll go out of my mind if I have to stay home any longer. I can at least do desk stuff."

"How was your Christmas?" Nicki decided to divert the subject away from his fitness to work, then instantly wished she hadn't. Graham hadn't long split from his wife, and this would have been his first Christmas away from his family.

The detective's tired shoulders slouched. "It was OK. Different. I went round to see the kids on Christmas morning — watched them open their presents." A sad, yet accepting look entered his eyes. "I guess it is what it is. You?"

Nicki placed her mug in front of her face as she considered her response. "It was quiet," she eventually replied. "Just me and Luna. Some turkey and Christmas TV."

Before she was forced to elaborate any further, the desk phone trilled. "DI Hardcastle?"

As Nicki listened to the voice on the other end of the line, Fox watched her expression change from mild annoyance to concern, her eyes widening by the second. "OK. Give me ten minutes."

As she placed the receiver back in its cradle, she bit her lip. "You know you said you wanted to get out and about?"

Fox nodded, cautiously. "Uh-huh."

"How do you fancy a trip to the theatre?"

CHAPTER TWO

The Theatre Royal
Westgate Street, Bury St Edmunds

The Theatre Royal sat opposite the Greene King Brewery on Westgate Street, and was a perfect example of a true Regency theatre. Nicki knew it well, standing not a stone's throw away from her own one-bedroom town house on College Lane.

Pulling her coat around her, Nicki left the car parked on a double yellow line and stepped out into the freezing night air. Her breath billowed out in front of her as she jogged across the street. Snow was definitely in the air; you could almost smell it. DS Fox joined her, his walking cane tapping on the icy pavement.

The road outside the theatre was alive with uniformed bodies. Someone had had the foresight to stretch a piece of 'police — do not cross' tape across the theatre entrance and two patrol cars had parked across each end of the road preventing vehicular access. Several cars were already performing three-point-turns, looking to find an alternative route through this particular part of the town. Thankfully, on a chilly Thursday evening just after Christmas, traffic was light.

Nicki ducked under the police tape and acknowledged the officer with the attendance log. Both she and Fox were immediately handed a protective suit to wear. As she pulled it on, Nicki was quietly impressed as to how quickly everything had been put in place to preserve the scene.

Stepping inside she looked around the foyer, her attention immediately drawn to a figure she recognised. Crime Scene Manager Faye Armstrong was already heading in her direction, her white paper suit going some way to disguise the tall, athletic frame beneath. As she approached, she tucked a few strands of blonde hair beneath her elasticated cap.

"Sorry to call you out," greeted Faye, snapping off her gloves. "Everyone else seemed to be on leave."

Nicki knew Faye well — always finding the experienced crime scene manager a bundle of enthusiasm, no matter what the time of day or circumstances she found herself in. But as she greeted her, Nicki noticed that even Faye seemed subdued. "No problem," she replied. "I was at the station anyway."

"I don't doubt *that* for a second," replied Faye, a tired half-smile on her lips. She turned towards DS Fox. "And good evening to you, too, Graham. I hear you've been in the wars recently. How are you doing?"

Fox gave a curt nod. "I'm fine. As good as new."

"Hmmmm." Faye briefly looked him and up and down, the smile still playing on her lips. "If you say so. Right, well, if you'd both like to follow me, I'll show you what we've got."

Faye slipped on a fresh set of gloves and motioned for both detectives to follow. Fox left his cane in the foyer, and did his best to keep up — the sound of their plastic overshoes shuffling along the stone floor the only sound they could hear.

The lighting in the corridor was subdued. The walls were bare, except for the occasional framed picture charting the theatre's history of past productions. Faye took them past the entrance to the pit. "This is what you might otherwise know as the stalls," she remarked, gesturing towards the door. "But we need to head along this way."

They followed the signs towards the Dress Circle — more corridors; more stone floors; more framed pictures on the walls. The chill from outside had crept in behind them, and Nicki gave an involuntary shiver as they turned the corner to arrive at the entrance to the Dress Circle.

In contrast to the rest of the building, this corridor was full of white-suited bodies. Metal stepping plates had now appeared on the floor to create a common pathway — the sound of scraping metal on the stone beneath was akin to nails on a blackboard. It quickly set Nicki's teeth on edge.

Despite the extra bodies, there was still an overriding sense of calm. Faye led the detectives towards the only box with its door open — the Sir Isaac Newton box. As Nicki approached, she thought back to the brief telephone message she'd received at the station. Very few details had been given — but what she'd been told immediately chilled her to the bone.

Surely there had to be some mistake? A hoax maybe?

Faye stepped to the side, allowing Nicki to enter the box. It didn't take long for her to register that the call had been no hoax. Resting on the faded fabric of one of the seats was a pair of human eyes.

Nicki turned back towards the open door where Faye and DS Fox were hovering. "And when were they discovered, exactly?"

"I'm told the doors opened at around quarter past six. Not long after that, a gentleman made his way towards his seat in this box when he . . . well . . . found the eyes."

Nicki shuddered. "Poor man. We have his details I take it?"

Faye nodded. "As far as I know he was taken to the manager's office for a cup of tea. He may or may not still be there."

"Do we think anyone else came near them? Touched them?" Nicki looked around her. There was hardly enough room to swing the proverbial cat inside the box itself.

"Not that we know of. As soon as he saw what it was, he managed to gain the attention of an usher who was just outside in the corridor. The manager was called — a man by the name of Hugh Maxwell — and very quickly the area was sealed off. People were evacuated from the building and they called it in."

Nicki nodded. At least that was something. Less people meant less contamination of the scene. She peered across to the adjacent box, and then over the edge and down towards the pit below. "And nothing else has been found as yet? Just the eyes?" Nicki felt herself shudder once again.

"Nothing else so far. We'll obviously give the place a thorough search, though."

As Nicki backed out into the corridor, she spotted someone hovering at one end — a person she presumed to be the theatre manager. The man's face was pale and drawn. Keeping to the stepping plates, she headed in his direction.

"Mr Maxwell? Hugh Maxwell?" The man gave a faint nod. "I'm Detective Inspector Nicki Hardcastle. I'm so sorry you've had to deal with this tonight. Can I ask how often this area is cleaned? When would someone have last been inside that box?"

Hugh Maxwell cleared his throat, his eyes still wide with shock. "This was the first performance of the day. The whole theatre would've been cleaned this morning."

"And what would that involve?"

The theatre manager looked panic stricken for a moment. "Well, I'm . . . I'm not quite sure. We use an outside cleaning company, you see. I . . . I can put you in touch with them, if that would help?"

Nicki nodded her thanks. "That would be great. Do you use the same people each day, for the cleaning?"

Maxwell hesitated. "Well, we use the same company, but I can't say for sure who exactly comes into the building to do the job."

"I understand. If you could let me have their details, and those of your own staff, too."

Hugh Maxwell nodded. "Of course, of course. Anything to help."

"I'll also need the contact details of everyone working tonight, and anyone who was here during the course of the day. And also, a list of any advance ticket holders — anyone who'd purchased a ticket for tonight's show."

The theatre manager continued to nod. "I can go and get that sorted for you right now. It'll only take a moment." He turned to go, remembering at the last minute to place his feet on the strategically spaced stepping plates as he did so. Nicki couldn't blame him for wanting to get as far away as possible — what lay behind the door to the Sir Isaac Newton box would turn even the strongest of stomachs.

"Go with him, Graham. He looks a bit green around the gills."

DS Fox set off as quickly as his legs would allow without the support of his cane.

Returning to the box, Nicki steeled herself once more. She'd seen dead bodies before, more times than she'd like to admit. The first one had, predictably, been the worst. People said you never forgot your first dead body — and they'd be right. Nicki could remember it as if it were yesterday. He'd been a young man, no more than twenty years of age, found on a railway line just outside Ipswich. His body had taken the full force of the train, and they'd needed to resort to dental records to identify him.

It was a vision that never left her.

The ones that came after were no less horrific, but somehow the brain adapts — learning to lock away distressing images into the mind's deepest, darkest corners. They would always be there — hidden beneath the surface — but thankfully just out of reach.

It was the only way.

She returned her attention back to the eyeballs. There was very little blood — just a speck or two clinging to the tissues around each one as they stared emptily towards the ceiling. Nicki felt herself shiver once more — praying that whoever the poor soul was, they weren't conscious when their eyes had been gouged out of their sockets.

The box was starting to feel cramped so Nicki headed for the door, catching Faye's attention as she passed. The night would be long and hard for the forensics team — every inch of the theatre would be examined, photographed and swabbed. Routes in and out of the building checked, and then checked again. Bins would be emptied, their contents bagged up for later examination. Everything scrutinised meticulously for even the slightest shred of evidence. It was an unenviable task.

Once back out in the corridor, Nicki exhaled the breath she'd been holding inside, and found DS Fox heading back in her direction waving several sheets of paper in the air.

"I've got all the staff details, plus the cleaning company. And a list of the customers who'd bought tickets in advance. There's also the contact details of the poor fella who found the eyes. Goes by the name of Ernest Fisher — lives in the town. He's given a brief statement to one of the uniforms, but someone took him home a few minutes ago."

"Well, that gives us something to start with." Nicki began to head towards the exit "Let's get out of here."

They soon arrived back in the foyer and began to shrug out of their protective suits. Stepping outside, Fox collected his walking cane and followed Nicki across the road. The chill of the night air hit them full in the face as they made their way across Westgate Street to where Nicki had left the car, the odd frozen snowflake dancing before them.

"You ever seen anything like that before, Graham?" Nicki half-turned towards the detective sergeant, nodding back over her shoulder towards the theatre.

"Never. I'm not even sure what to say. But one question does spring to mind, though."

Nicki pulled open the driver's door. "And what's that?"

"Well, we've found the eyes . . ." Fox paused, his own gaze lifting over the top of Nicki's head and back towards the crime scene. "But where's the body?"

CHAPTER THREE

The Theatre Royal
Westgate Street, Bury St Edmunds

Faye snapped off her gloves and headed through to the foyer. Her team were hard at work and it was unlikely any of them would be going home tonight. Hugh Maxwell had opened up his office for them to use as a base, and it was there that she sank gratefully into one of the leather chairs by the side of a huge mahogany desk.

She had sent Maxwell home, along with the rest of his employees — there was nothing they could do to help tonight. And, to be brutally honest, they were just getting in the way.

The man hadn't needed asking twice; scuttling out of the door like a frightened rabbit.

Faye didn't blame him — theatre managers, on the whole, wouldn't have expected to find something like this on a cold, December evening.

The Sir Isaac Newton box was being processed as much as was possible. They would move their attention to the corridors shortly, and the likely escape route of the perpetrator. Faye had noticed a fire exit not far from the Dress Circle, Hugh Maxwell sheepishly admitting the alarm wasn't currently working. She instantly placed it towards the top of her list. The exit led out into a courtyard behind the theatre — from there the offender could have gone anywhere.

And then there were the bins. They would all be thoroughly searched, contents bagged and logged. It wasn't anyone's idea of a pleasant job, but it had to be done — criminals could be surprisingly careless.

But Faye didn't really hold out much hope of finding anything useful to assist with Nicki's investigation.

Nicki.

They had known each other for years, and although their paths hadn't crossed much in the last few months, she could tell that something was wrong. Nicki looked tired, more so than usual, and her face looked drawn and lined. There was an air of despondency about her, as though she was balancing the weight of the whole world on her shoulders.

Faye glanced at the clock on Hugh Maxwell's office wall. Although it was getting late, she knew Nicki would still be awake — and, knowing her, possibly still be at the station. She pulled her mobile from the handbag she'd left on Hugh's desk.

They were long overdue a catch-up. Instead of calling, Faye sent a text.

'Catch-up needed. Join me on Monday for martial arts? You know you want to! F x'

Faye then poured herself a mug of coffee from the percolator Hugh had left for them. She blanched at the bitter taste, but then downed the rest of it in one go. She needed the fluids — and the caffeine — if she was going to make it through the night.

* * *

Bury St Edmunds Police Station

Nicki snapped on the incident room lights and immediately baulked at their brightness. Snow had started to fall as soon as they'd left the theatre — arriving thick and fast by the time they'd covered the short distance back to the station. And although there was precious little they could really achieve tonight, Nicki wanted to make a start.

As DS Fox followed her into the room, Nicki noticed how he was back to relying on his cane and seemed to wince with every step. Passing him the vending machine coffee she had picked up for them both on the way in, she frowned with concern. "You really don't need to be here, Graham — you do know that."

In the hunt for Lucas Jackson last month, Graham had placed his life on the line, and his car in the path of a speeding van, ending up in a hospital bed with a ruptured spleen.

"I'm fine." Fox placed his cane to the side and waved a box of paracetamol in the air. "I'll knock back a couple of these with this coffee and be as right as rain."

Nicki detected a hardened edge to his tone. Clearly, he was masking more pain than he was prepared to admit, but she let it go. Taking a sip of her black coffee she snatched up a marker pen and started to make her way towards the first whiteboard.

"Here, let me. You sit and have your coffee." Fox held his hand out for the pen. "You look knackered."

Nicki only briefly hesitated before handing over the pen, slumping gratefully into one of the vacant chairs. It was true. She *was* tired. Exhausted, even. "Cheers, Graham."

Fox threw a couple of painkillers into his mouth and dry-swallowed before approaching the first whiteboard. "So . . . what have we got so far?" He immediately answered his own question. "Not much."

Pulling the lid off the marker pen, he wrote *Theatre Royal* at the top of the first board — and beneath it *'blue eyes — Sir Isaac Newton box — Ernest Fisher'*.

"The manager seemed fairly certain on the timings — I had a brief chat with him in the office when he was printing the contact lists. The alarm was raised at 6.25 p.m." Fox added the time to the board. "And he was quite sure there would've been nothing there when the theatre was cleaned earlier that morning — someone from the cleaning company would've seen it. He estimates the cleaners left around midday." Fox added the second time to the board. "So that would appear to be our window of opportunity."

Nicki took a tentative sip of her drink, wincing at its bitter taste. "I've asked about CCTV and requested what there is. I'm not too hopeful, though. Although the foyer is covered, the system hasn't been working well of late. The rest of the theatre has no CCTV coverage at all. We'll see what it shows but I'm not holding my breath. We'll also need statements from the cleaning crew who were there that morning, plus any members of the theatre staff who were on duty."

Fox pulled out the sheets of paper Hugh Maxwell had given him earlier. "It's all here. A list of staff members who were on duty, plus the cleaning company employees. And, also, the list of theatregoers who had pre-booked their tickets for the show." He waved the sheets in the air. "There are a fair few names to check out — I can get started tonight, if you want?"

Nicki shook her head. "You can't possibly manage it all on your own. Darcie and Roy are both back tomorrow — as are Matt and Duncan." She paused, giving him a knowing smile across the rim of her coffee cup. "And, anyhow, you're not technically supposed to be working."

Fox took a mouthful of his sugary flat white. "Too late — I'm here now."

Nicki turned her attention back to the whiteboard, taking in the sparse details they had so far and sighed. "Look. We can't make much progress tonight without a full team. Plus, we're waiting on forensics and CCTV which won't be available until sometime tomorrow, at the earliest. We're both dead on our feet. Let's start again bright and early in the morning."

"It's no bother. I'm really not all that tired." The well-practised lie tripped off his tongue. "I can make a start on some of those numbers."

Nicki saw the hollow look in her fellow detective's eyes — and it was a look she both recognised and understood. She could tell he was avoiding going home — putting off heading back to a cold, one-bedroomed flat filled with nothing but empty memories and thoughts of what might've been. Nicki gave a sad smile, knowing just how that felt. "If you really want to stay and do something, start by collating those numbers into some sort of order. Get them on to the system so we don't have that chore to do in the morning. And look over that statement from the old man who found the eyes."

Fox eased himself into a chair and powered up the PC. "I'll do what I can."

"Just don't go phoning people out of the blue at this time of night, Graham. They won't thank you for it."

Nicki left him to it, taking herself and her coffee back along the corridor towards DCI Malcom Turner's office. Despite the late hour, she knew he'd still be in the station and want an update.

The DCI's office was larger than her own, but still managed to feel cosier — most probably due to the room having radiators that actually gave out heat rather than just an abundance of noise. The DCI made them both a fresh coffee and Nicki discarded her vending machine cup into the bin, wrapped her hands around the warm mug, and slipped into a chair.

"It's late — you should be heading home." Turner eased himself into his swivel chair and eyed her from across the desk. He knew Nicki better than he knew anyone — better than his own wife at times — so he knew his words were more than likely falling on deaf ears. Nicki Hardcastle wouldn't be going anywhere until she was good and ready. He decided to change tack. "Tell me about tonight."

Nicki inhaled the aroma of the coffee from her mug — a decent Colombian if she wasn't much mistaken. A million miles better than the bitter vending machine rubbish she'd just subjected herself and Graham to. She took her first sip, instantly feeling the intensely welcome caffeine hit, and began to fill the DCI in on the events so far that night.

Turner listened in silence, concern etched deep into his tired eyes. "This sounds like it could snowball into something much bigger, Nicki. You have all the resources you need?"

Nicki blew across the top of her coffee, releasing more of the rich aroma. "I think so. Darcie and Roy are back tomorrow. So are Matt and Duncan. I'll need a few more bodies to help with contacting the theatregoers and staff members. Maybe some more to do the house-to-house in the area."

"Then they're yours. Take whoever you need."

Nicki smiled gratefully over the rim of her mug.

"But don't run yourself into the ground. *Delegate.*" Turner fixed her with a knowing look. "You've just closed a massive investigation and it'll have taken a toll on all of you." *And you in particular*, he wanted to add. Instead, he said, "How have you been?"

"Fine," she lied, smothering the untruth with another sip of her drink. "I've been perfectly fine."

The DCI nodded, his eyes telling Nicki that he didn't believe a word of it, but was prepared to let it go.

"Well, I've heard there could be a commendation or two heading your way. Finding Lucas Jackson like that, and helping to close two unsolved child murders — those above are impressed."

Nicki batted away the compliment. "It was a team effort, sir." She wasn't a fan of commendations or awards — not when she was just doing her job. And there'd been so much heartache left behind in the wake of Lucas Jackson's abduction — being congratulated or praised didn't seem right in the grand scheme of things. She glanced towards the window where the blinds were not quite closed. Swirling snowflakes danced in the stiffening wind, battering themselves against the glass. "Looks like that's here to stay," she commented, nodding towards the window.

The DCI nodded, acknowledging the change of conversation. "And what about Christmas? Did you manage to get away?"

It was a merry dance the two of them performed every year. Turner already knew full well that Nicki had been at her desk every day over the Christmas break, even when he hadn't been physically within the building's four walls himself. He just *knew*. But he always asked the question anyway. And Nicki always responded in the same manner.

"I had a quiet one at home." Nicki avoided her senior officer's gaze, her own eyes flickering towards a framed photograph sitting next to the computer monitor on the desk. "Yourself? Manage to get some time with the family?"

The DCI's face immediately softened. "We were at home. Susie put on a big spread on Christmas Day, and my son came up with his girlfriend and her little boy." His smile widened. "It was nice."

Nicki hurriedly took another gulp of coffee. She knew the DCI wanted to ask whether she'd spoken to her parents over the holidays, but she was well practised in side-stepping that particular question by now. In any event, Turner was best pals with her father — so she was pretty sure that he already knew what limited and stilted conversations they'd had.

She delicately changed the subject. "Isn't your son's girlfriend expecting another soon?"

A proud gleam flickered in the DCI's eyes. "Indeed — due in March. Our first grandchild."

"That's wonderful." Nicki gazed down at her half-drunk coffee. "Something to look forward to — a spring baby."

Turner detected the edge in Nicki's voice and steered the conversation elsewhere. "How is DS Fox settling back in? Did I see him in the building earlier?"

Nicki swallowed the rest of the coffee. "He's doing remarkably well, considering."

Concern again clouded the DCI's gaze. "Well, don't let him do too much. And make sure all the paperwork's in order with HR if he's actually back on duty."

"I won't, and I will."

After a few more minutes of small talk, with Nicki skilfully managing to avoid any further questions about her family, she bid the DCI goodnight and took her leave. She needed to get home, even if it was just for a few hours.

Luna would be wanting her dinner.

CHAPTER FOUR

The Farmhouse

Two makeshift pathology trolleys sat where he'd left them. He called it his '*operating theatre*' but, in reality, it was the spacious old pantry which adjoined the farmhouse kitchen. Dried, canned and bottled goods had not graced the pantry's shelving for some time — replaced now with a variety of medical instruments, jars of antiseptic and anaesthetic agents.

Lucie looked peaceful enough on one of the trolleys, her left arm — now minus its hand — draped across her stomach. He'd carefully wrapped her severed hand in cloth, and it now sat on one of the pantry shelves.

Waiting.

He knew exactly what he was going to do with it, but that particular part of the game would have to wait a little longer.

His eyes strayed to the second pathology trolley — Jacqui. Such a pretty name — but she looked anything but pretty now. Her body was cold and rigid, and two cavernous hollows now replaced what had once been a pair of brilliant blue eyes.

He smiled and glanced towards the life-sized body map taped to the far wall. Even in the muted light he could see the

Polaroid of Jacqui's eyes staring back out. They really were the most vivid blue he'd ever seen.

Which was why he'd chosen them.

But he suspected they might have lost some of their lustre by now.

He swallowed back the chuckle he could feel brewing.

Not so beautiful now, my sweet.

Turning back to the trolley, he traced a finger around the deep gouges that had once hosted those oh-so-beautiful eyes. Although dried blood clung to the sides of the neatly sliced tissue, there really was nothing ragged about his work here.

As he gazed into the voids he had created, he wondered when her soul had truly departed. Was it at that distinctly delicious moment when the first eye had popped out into his hand? Or had her soul languished a little longer, releasing itself only when her heart had stilled and her blood had ceased to flow?

He gazed around the chilled pantry, wondering if any essence of her lingered.

Part of him hoped so.

Although only forty-eight hours had passed, he could remember each delicious moment when death had finally come knocking.

* * *

Tuesday 25 December 2018
48 hours earlier
The Farmhouse

Her body still felt delightfully warm beneath his touch.

Jacqui.

He had kept her sedated for the last three days — a slow, steady infusion of ketamine via the continuous syringe pump he'd set up was doing the job nicely. He often just sat by her side, watching. Minute after minute, hour after hour.

But today was the day — the day for Jacqui to wake up.

For there would be no fun for anyone if she remained asleep.

Satisfied that the video camera was switched on in the corner of the room, and seeing the red light blinking reassuringly, he began.

First, he disconnected the infusion pump, cutting off the supply of ketamine.

Then he sat and waited some more.

It took a while, the minutes ticking by agonisingly slowly, but he was in no rush. He contemplated putting on some Christmas carols to mark the occasion, but preferred the silence. Eventually, Jacqui started to stir.

To begin with there was only the very slightest of movements — the occasional flicker of an eyelid, a slight involuntary tremor in her fingertips. But as the minutes ticked by, he slowly and surely saw Jacqui's chest rising and falling more rapidly, her lips beginning to part — followed by more uncoordinated twitching of both eyelids. She started to gulp, trying to swallow the saliva that had collected inside her mouth.

"Come on, Jacqui," he whispered, his voice breathy in the stillness of the pantry. "Wakey, wakey. Rise and shine."

Jacqui was strapped to the pathology trolley by the ankles and wrists, something she would no doubt discover as her levels of consciousness increased.

An intense thrill began to bubble in the pit of his stomach.

Any moment now . . .

Any moment now . . .

Her lips were open wide now and both eyes began to blink. He saw her forehead start to crease as she took in her surroundings. Movement now spread to her limbs. He watched as she tried to raise each arm and leg, coming up against the restraints each time. The creases on her forehead deepened. Another moan choked violently inside her throat. She tried once again to move her legs, to kick out with as much force as she could muster, but her ankles were held fast.

He could only imagine the panic sweeping through her body, watching as her head started to thrash from side to side — only stopping when she saw the face grinning down at her from above. Horror could paralyse you like nothing else.

With her mouth agape, he could almost visualise the scream forming within — yet no recognisable sound emerged. She could have screamed at the top of her lungs if she'd wanted to — no one would hear. There were no houses for miles around. They were completely and utterly alone.

He had already prepared the rag and now stuffed it into her mouth, mid silent scream — only just pulling his fingers out in time to avoid her gnashing teeth. She was a feisty one, that was for sure. The thought gave him another unexpected thrill.

Once the rag was in place he focused once more on her eyes — after all, that was the reason she was here. He silently congratulated himself again on his choice. Fear made them even more perfect.

He had not performed an enucleation since his medical school days, but techniques like that never left you — not if you were a good enough surgeon. He'd done his research, like he always did, and knew his way around the anatomy blindfolded. And Professor Ferguson had always told him that he was his best student — a 'chip off the old block' had been his words on many an occasion. He wasn't going to resort to just gouging them out with a dessert spoon.

Not yet.

Before selecting his first scalpel, he reached for the head restraint. He'd made it himself — a cross between a wood-worker's vice and a head guard.

The restraint soon had Jacqui's head locked securely into place.

Feeling a dry coolness on his lips, he pulled the stainless-steel operating tray closer and selected a freshly sterilised and sharpened scalpel. The overhead lights reflected on the metal as he leaned in closer.

Jacqui continued to buck and thrust beneath the leather straps, her eyes widening in ever-increasing terror — but it was to no avail. The restraints held fast. Soundless screams built up behind the gag.

Bringing the scalpel closer, he decided to start with the left eye. In the end, it would make no difference. Sensing the woman's body tensing beneath him, he tightened the head restraint a further notch. The pain and shock would soon render her back into unconsciousness, so he didn't have long — but for now she was exquisitely alive.

He made the first incision.

Her chest began to heave uncontrollably, rising and falling faster and faster as her lungs sought more oxygen. He knew her body would now be flooded with adrenaline, preparing her for 'fight or flight'.

Neither of which were an option for Jacqui.

Not now.

The smile on his face widened.

Once again, he'd chosen *Danse Macabre* to play on his phone as he performed, turning the volume up high.

Jacqui soon began to choke on her own saliva, the screams buried so deeply inside her throat that she could no longer swallow. He could sense it wouldn't be long now — not long until the life in her was snuffed out like a dying candle. Her heart would eventually give up the fight, overwhelmed by pain and fear. He could almost feel it fibrillating beneath his touch — soon it would go into spasm, a cardiac arrest following on close behind.

And then Jacqui would be no more.

Not in this world, at least.

He craved to let the feeling linger, his hand pausing over her deathly white face, the bloodied scalpel glinting in the lights from above. Just a few more delicate incisions and his work would be complete. He could see her chest was rising and falling more sporadically now — her lungs finally accepting their fate, even if her brain would not.

The eyeball came away from its socket, almost as easily as popping a pea from its pod. As he stood with the bloody specimen in his hand, he watched Jacqui's last throes of life ebb away and her heart finally give up the fight.

Gazing down at the empty hole that had once contained a living, human eye, he searched for any signs of a departing soul. She'd been so finely balanced on the cusp of life and death — if her soul was to leave her body, it would be doing so now. He breathed in deeply, willing her soul to flood his senses.

And then she was gone, her remaining eye staring emptily towards the ceiling.

It wasn't the most peaceful of deaths, of that he was sure. But for him it had been one of the most exquisite. Bringing her round from sedation just in time to witness the whole delicious event — he'd enjoyed her immensely.

With a contented sigh, he flexed his grip on the bloodied scalpel.

He still had one more eye to go.

* * *

Thursday 27 December 2018
The Farmhouse

Jacqui.

Dragging his thoughts back to the present, he pushed the makeshift pathology trolley across the tiled floor, the wheels squealing. The trolley was a bit battered and tarnished in places, but it did the job. He'd tried to buy a proper one from the specialist suppliers in Nottingham, but they were surprisingly expensive for what they were and too many questions were being asked as to exactly *why* he wanted one. So, he'd had to look elsewhere. Amazon and eBay had been a dead end, so to speak, so he had eventually had to settle on something similar — a couple of second-hand retail trolleys from a cheap online supplier.

The infusion pumps and other medical equipment he'd acquired were easy enough to come by — if you knew where to look. No one raised so much as a digital eyebrow as he completed his purchases.

Wheeling Jacqui and her mutilated face into the boot room next door, he headed for the trio of chest freezers lined up against the far wall. He still called it the boot room, despite its lack of footwear. Back in the farm's heyday, it would have been full of Barbour jackets, muddied shoes and overexcited gun dogs. But now it was cold and empty.

Jacqui was fairly tall, but she was also slightly built, so he had no problem lifting her off the trolley and into the first freezer. There was plenty of room inside — which was just as well, because Jacqui wouldn't be alone for long.

As he lay her at the bottom of the freezer, he admired his handiwork once again. It never ceased to amaze him just how much difference the eyes made to someone's appearance — or in Jacqui's case, the absence of them. He really had made a good job of it. So much so that surely even Dad would be pleased — the eminent Mr Laurence Hemmingway Sr, trauma surgeon extraordinaire.

Maybe.

It took a lot to impress his father, something he'd learned at a very young age — but something like this just might do it. He gazed down once more at Jacqui's body lying in the bottom of the freezer and chuckled.

Once he'd popped out both eyes and tidied up the cavities, he had believed his work to be done. But just as he'd taken the saliva-soaked gag from her mouth, he noticed her swollen tongue.

He wasn't entirely sure what made him do it — no doubt some deliciously unseen urge from within — but it hadn't taken long to perform. A few good snips from a decent pair of long-handled scissors and her tongue had virtually come away in his hands. What blood there was — which wasn't much as Jacqui's heart was silent and still by this time — had merely trickled back down her throat.

As a boy he'd eaten ox tongue — fresh from the oxen his grandfather had kept on the farm. He could still visualise the slab of blood-red meat as it landed in the frying pan, sizzling in the hot fat.

He hadn't liked it, not really — but he would do anything for his grandfather. So, he'd eaten it up like a good boy.

But he wasn't going to eat this one.

Not Jacqui's.

He knew some people ate their victims — both raw and cooked. So, there was a part of him that was intrigued as to the idea — but he wasn't ready to succumb.

Not yet.

Anyhow, he already had plans for Jacqui's tongue — and time was marching on. He slammed the freezer lid shut and padded back through to the pantry.

Grabbing the second makeshift pathology trolley that contained Lucie's stilled body, he pushed it back towards the boot room. Once again, the wheels squealed across the Victorian tiled floor. Up close to the first freezer, he raised the lid once more and deposited her on top of Jacqui's rapidly chilling body. Lucie had already lost much of her warmth and her limbs were becoming stiff. Her arm, minus its hand, hung by her side.

A smile twitched on his lips. Two peas in a pod. At least they had each other for company now.

As much as he longed to linger, he knew he couldn't. Slamming the lid of the freezer back into place, he retraced his steps. Back in his operating room, his eyes skimmed the Polaroids that were now tacked to the surface of the body map. It was taking shape.

Jacqui's eyes shone out at the top, but were now joined by her bloodied tongue. A little further down, Lucie's neatly severed hand was pinned to the side.

A masterpiece in the making, he thought to himself as he reached for one of the two bloodied cloths sitting on the pantry shelves. Leaving Lucie's hand where it was, he placed Jacqui's tongue inside a plastic bag, and tucked it inside his pocket.

Although it was getting late, and the snow outside was beginning to fall with increased vigour, this part of the plan couldn't wait any longer.

CHAPTER FIVE

College Lane, Bury St Edmunds

Nicki pulled the tinsel down from around the mantelpiece and shoved it into a tatty-looking Amazon box. It wouldn't take her long to take everything down; she didn't have much — just a few pieces of cheap tinsel here and there, some festive scented candles surrounded by holly, and a hideous plastic Santa that lit up and *ho ho ho*'d when you touched him. The latter had been a present from one of the detective constables on Nicki's team — Darcie — who also happened to be the younger sister of Nicki's best friend, Amy. Both had badgered Nicki relentlessly to let some Christmas cheer into her home — so, eventually, she'd relented.

But she'd been itching to pack it all away as soon the big day had come and gone, eager to close the door on yet another Christmas. Santa and the rest of the tinsel quickly found their way back inside the box, but she decided to keep the candles out. They were a nice touch and gave the house a warm, inviting scent.

Thankfully there wasn't a lot of space in her one-bedroom townhouse for much more than a few strands of tinsel. With the roof garden above, there was no loft space for storage — which was an excuse she'd used many a time to explain her desire for a clutter-free life.

It was only partly true, though.

The accumulation of knick-knacks invariably came attached with memories — and it was the memories that Nicki found the hardest to deal with. You couldn't exactly box those away with the tinsel and shove them under the bed for another twelve months.

Memories stayed with you.

Despite the late hour, almost eleven-thirty now, she was still wired from the night's events — her brain still trying to process the shocking scenes from the theatre — so she decided to light the candles on the mantelpiece, and pour a glass of wine. The candles were nearly spent, just a few more hours burning left in them. She inhaled the warming clementine and mulled wine scent.

Candles were good.

Candles didn't have memories.

The first glass of wine hadn't lasted long — so she'd poured another and settled down on the sofa. Luna had barely raised a whisker at her tardy arrival home, and once she'd devoured the food in her bowl, she'd padded away upstairs.

Although she should try to get some rest, Nicki knew that if she tried to close her eyes, all she would see would be a pair of staring eyeballs congealed in blood. She inhaled the comforting scent of the candles once more, her own gaze coming to rest on the photograph nestled between them.

Deano.

For the last twenty-two years she had been wracked with a soul-destroying sense of loss, followed by overwhelming guilt at what had befallen him. At five years of age, he'd simply disappeared — here one minute, gone the next. In the briefest of heartbeats, her whole life, and that of the whole Webster family, had been turned upside down.

They had been at the local fair, and Nicki had taken Deano to queue up for a ride on the caterpillar. He was so excited, but she was more interested in the candyfloss stall opposite. She'd only meant to be gone for a minute, maybe two. But that was all the time it had taken for Deano to disappear. And Nicki had never forgiven herself. Not for one split second. Even the mere thought of candyfloss sent an immediate wave of stomach-churning nausea through her body.

Despite never actually saying it out loud, she knew her parents must blame her in some way. They had to. The once tightly knit Webster family had been ripped apart at the seams that cold November night in 1996 — and the pieces had never quite stitched back together again in the same way. The only way forward had been to leave her family and its name behind. Nicola Webster was no more. As Nicki Hardcastle, she could be someone else. Someone for Deano to be proud of.

Draining her glass, Nicki pushed herself up from the sofa and grabbed the Amazon box. The sooner it was out of sight the better. Climbing the stairs, she deposited the box outside her bedroom door and turned towards the ladder that led to the roof garden. Luna sat on the landing, watching as Nicki unhooked the latch, a look of derision on her whiskered face. Usually, Luna loved coming up to the roof garden, but tonight even she knew it was too cold. And Luna hated the cold. With one final look of feline disdain, the Russian Blue turned around, flicked her tail in the air and disappeared into the bedroom.

Nicki climbed through the hatch and pulled herself up on to the roof. It was one of her favourite places in the whole wide world.

Her garden.

Her roof.

Her space.

Nothing and no one could ever touch her up here. It was as if time could stand still.

The events of the evening so far had rocked her and she didn't need the plunging temperature to make her shiver — the thought of one's eyes being gouged out did the trick right enough. Whatever Christmas cheer she'd felt up to now — which admittedly wasn't a lot — had well and truly disappeared.

She gazed out across the town. With the sky dark and threatening, the air was already thick with mid-winter chill. Snow was falling fast, and it wouldn't take long for the stiffening wind to create a blizzard to soak her to the skin.

Stamping her feet on the ground, she willed the blood to flow towards her frozen toes. She knew she should go back inside — if she stayed out here any longer, she'd more than likely catch her death, and then she'd be no use to anyone.

'You'll catch your death'.

A silent chuckle caught in Nicki's throat. It was an expression her mother had used constantly when she was young — chastising her for going outside in the pouring rain in nothing more than a T-shirt and shorts.

A pang of heartache gripped her as Anne Webster's face floated into view and Nicki thought back to this year's Christmas phone conversation. Maybe it'd been her imagination, but she thought her mother's voice hadn't sounded quite so frosty as in previous years. There had been something in her tone — a softening, almost. A chill that had almost thawed.

For a split second, Nicki had felt the urge to throw caution to the wind and announce she would, in fact, make the journey back home for Christmas after all. She ached to see her mother's face break out into a smile.

After all this time.

But the moment had gone as quickly as it had appeared, and Nicki briskly hung up the phone after wishing them both a Merry Christmas.

Hot tears began to sprout from her eyes, freezing on contact with her wet skin. She rubbed her face and headed for the hatch.

Back in the warm, she pulled off her wet clothes and stuffed them into the washing basket in the bathroom before padding through to the bedroom. Luna was curled up asleep on the duvet, and after rubbing her wet hair with a towel, Nicki slipped on a fresh pair of pyjamas and crawled under the covers, careful not to disturb the sleeping cat.

Still too wired for sleep, her eyes strayed towards the bed-side table — and the business card propped up against the lamp.

Caspar Ambrose — Private Investigator

Just thinking of the man's name caused Nicki's stomach to jolt. Something akin to anger, tinged with more than a dose of embarrassment, jarred her. Ambrose had crashed into her life only last month, but then disappeared just as quickly. One minute he was there, the next he was gone.

Just like Deano.

He'd given her the most cryptic of messages — *'I know where he is'* — together with a photograph. Although not coming out and saying so explicitly, Nicki had interpreted the message as referring to Deano. Somehow, Caspar Ambrose — whoever he was — knew where her brother was. As absurd as that sounded.

But the man had then vanished without a trace. Any phone numbers he'd given her, disconnected and untraceable, which spoke volumes.

She'd been had.

Ambrose was nothing more than a conman. To believe that Deano was alive, and somehow this man Ambrose knew where he was, was nothing short of fantastical. Feeling the tears start to prick in the corners of her eyes once more, Nicki reached for the business card and flung it across the room.

Also on her bedside table was the photograph Ambrose had left for her. Squinting through her wet fringe, she studied the image once again. She'd looked at it dozens of times — hundreds even — and she was convinced now, more than ever, that this too was a fake.

It wasn't him.

It wasn't Deano.

The hair, the eyes, even the dimples — they could all so easily be someone else. She was looking at a stranger — not her five-year-old brother as a man.

One of the cruellest jokes to play, she'd fallen for it far too quickly — despite all her police training. And that was what hurt the most. How could she have been so naive?

She wouldn't be so gullible next time.

Flinging the photograph across the room, she turned on to her side and reached out to stroke Luna's soft fur. The cat remained fast asleep, purring softly. And just when Nicki thought she might try and close her eyes, make a half-hearted attempt at sleep, her mobile trilled.

Grabbing the handset, she saw it was DS Fox. Frowning at the hour, she stabbed the 'accept' button. "Graham? What's up?"

Fox sounded breathless. "Boss? I'm on my way to pick you up. I hope you're decent." He paused, and Nicki heard a car door closing. "We've got another one."

CHAPTER SIX

Friday 28 December 2018
Southgate Street roundabout
Bury St Edmunds

The journey only took a few minutes, barely enough time for Nicki to strap herself into the passenger seat of Fox's car. She didn't ask why he'd still been at the station to take the call when it came through — the haunted look in his hooded eyes told her all she needed to know.

And when he'd told her the reason for his late-night phone call — '*We've got another one*' — she hadn't quite believed it. It sounded like some sort of practical joke — something for April Fool's Day.

Except it was December.

And Fox's voice had been unnervingly sincere.

With the time now past midnight, they weren't the first on the scene. Patrol cars had already blocked off each entrance and exit from the roundabout, their flashing blue lights reflecting eerily in the snow which was now falling with increased ferocity. Several officers were out of their vehicles, ready to move along any inquisitive onlookers if they decided to come out of their houses — which, given the time and weather conditions, was distinctly unlikely.

Nicki and Fox abandoned their car at the end of Southgate Street and made their way towards the first uniformed officer they saw. As they trudged across the frozen ground, all Nicki could hear was the creaking of impacted snow beneath her feet. Not used to particularly heavy snowfall in this part of the world, she could already see the chaos looming for the morning travel to work.

"Where is it?" Nicki buried her chin into the collar of her coat as the ice-cold wind bit into her skin.

The officer pointed towards the roundabout, where two of his colleagues were hastily trying to erect a section of 'police — do not cross' tape. "Just there. Found by a local lad out on his skateboard." The officer nodded back towards one of the patrol cars where, even through the developing blizzard, it was just about possible to make out a figure hunched in the back. "Told him to wait as you'd probably need a word."

Nicki nodded her thanks and headed towards the roundabout, while Fox headed towards the boy in the patrol car.

As she ducked beneath the police tape, another uniformed officer took her name for yet another attendance log and Nicki felt a distinctly uneasy sense of déjà vu prickling beneath the collar of her coat. Two crime scenes in one night. First the theatre, now this.

A team of crime scene investigators were busy setting up the common pathway with a series of stepping plates — for all the good that would do. Nicki glanced up at the heavy skies above, her face instantly covered in falling snow. As far as crime scenes went, this one was going to be difficult to preserve.

Reading her thoughts, Crime Scene Manager Cassie Mills headed in her direction. With Faye still busy with her team at the theatre, and likely to be there throughout the night, Cassie and her team had been mobilised.

"Nicki," greeted Cassie, hurrying across the snow. "Good of you to make the trip out — it's an awful night."

"It is that." Nicki wiped melted snow from her eyelashes. "What can you tell me?"

Cassie paused, then beckoned Nicki to follow her. "Let me show you what we've got. But you'd better put this on first."

After pulling on her protective suit, thankful for an extra layer against the elements, Nicki dutifully followed the crime scene manager towards where another section of tape was being unfurled to mark the inner cordon. Nicki came to a halt.

Gracing the roundabout since 2013, and made of solid oak, the wolf sculpture stood around two metres tall — depicting the animal that legend said guarded the severed head of King Edmund until it could be reunited with his body. Nicki had never really paid much attention to it before — with the Police Investigation Centre just a short distance away, she could drive past the roundabout several times a day without so much as acknowledging its presence.

She saw the tongue almost immediately, wedged into the wolf's open mouth. A pinkish stain to the surrounding snow told Nicki all she needed to know.

Blood.

"Do we think it's human?" The thought made Nicki's stomach lurch.

Cassie gave a faint shrug, barely detectable beneath her protective suit. "Maybe. We'll test the blood first then it'll be quite easy to see if we're dealing with an animal or a human."

"Did he touch it?" Nicki glanced back over her shoulder towards the parked patrol car housing the skater boy, noting DS Fox leaning in through the open side window.

"He says not." Cassie shrugged again. "Saw what he thought might be blood, then apparently went and told his mum. She's waiting inside the house."

Nicki stepped to the side to allow the crime scene investigation team to start taking photographs and whatever samples they could from such a challenging scene. Nicki wasn't holding out much hope there would be much.

Her attention then turned to the surrounding area. The access roads leading off from the roundabout were all deserted and silent. Whoever left the bloodied tongue on display could have come along any one of them — and disappeared just as quickly. The lack of snow covering the tongue suggested that maybe it hadn't been in situ all that long — although the wolf's mouth could have sheltered it from most of the flurries. Or maybe the tongue had been too warm for the snow to settle, melting on impact.

Nicki gave another involuntary shiver. If it *was* human, then a warm tongue meant a warm body.

Could someone still be alive without their tongue? If they could, then maybe they weren't looking for a victim.

Yet.

First eyes, now a tongue.

Nicki felt an acute sense of foreboding.

Turning back towards Cassie, she didn't bother to mask the shudder that followed. "Can we get that fast tracked? And the eyes from the theatre, too? If the tongue is human, I need to know if they come from the same person."

The crime scene manager nodded. "Of course, top of the list. I'll liaise with Faye in the morning — we'll get what we can to you as quickly as possible."

"Cheers."

"Happy Christmas."

Nicki gave a wan smile and began to retrace her steps. She pulled the elasticated hood from her head and felt melted snow begin to trickle down the back of her neck, seeping underneath her collar. It didn't take long for her hair to become sodden and plastered flat to her scalp. Noticing DS Fox was now back at the car, she negotiated the stepping plates and headed in his direction.

"You get much from skater boy?" she enquired.

Snowflakes tumbled from Fox as he shook his head. "Not the most talkative of beings. Goes by the name of Tommy McCrae. You might know him — most of the uniforms do. Says he was just passing — saw blood in the snow

40

and went to tell his mum. I said we'd catch up with him again tomorrow. He only lives on the corner over there. I've told him not to go anywhere."

Nicki pulled open the passenger side door and slipped inside. "Let's get going. I'm freezing to death out here."

Fox flicked snow from the shoulders of his jacket before climbing into the driver's seat. "You don't think we'll get a pair of ears next, do you?" he said, slamming the door shut and shoving the keys in the ignition.

"Ears?" Nicki's breath billowed out in front of her. The inside of the car was no warmer than the outside. "Why ears?"

"Well, you know." Fox snapped his seatbelt on. "See no evil, hear no evil, speak no evil. The three wise monkeys. We've had two out of the three tonight already."

Nicki whacked the heaters on full blast as the engine roared into life. "Don't even think about it, Graham. Don't even think about it."

* * *

The Farmhouse

Standing in the old boot room of the farmhouse, he peeled off his coat and hung it on one of the remaining pegs by the back door. He was certain no one had seen him — nobody but the boy — and he'd quickly dealt with that to his own advantage.

Knowing CCTV cameras were more than likely covering such a busy part of the town, he'd taken a circuitous route and parked on a minor side road some streets away. He'd dressed in black, avoided the busier residential streets and soon arrived at the deserted roundabout. The rapidly falling snow had masked his presence perfectly — Mother Nature had been curiously on his side tonight.

And what better stage for his art than one of the busiest roundabouts the town had to offer? Just thinking about how many people might see it — or at least see its picture once the vultures from the press descended — made him tingle. He could almost see the headlines now.

Turning away from the back door and his memories of the evening, he cast his eyes over the line of gently humming freezers where both Jacqui and Lucie would be silently slumbering, side by side inside their frozen tomb. Stepping forward, he ran a hand over the top of the first freezer, imagining their frozen faces looking up at him from beneath. He knew he could lift the lid and take another look — but he resisted the urge.

Sometimes the imagination was far more potent.

He felt his stomach rumble.

Just thinking about Jacqui and Lucie in the freezer was making him hungry.

Leaving the boot room and its frozen occupants, he padded through the pantry and on towards the farmhouse kitchen. As he entered, he immediately felt the welcoming warmth of the old range cooker. The farmhouse was cold at any time of the year, but in December it was especially so. With traditionally thick stone walls, the house had some natural insulation against the elements, but it wasn't uncommon to see ice forming on the insides of the windows, and his breath a constant fog in front of his face.

Winters in the farmhouse when he was a boy were *always* cold. And dark. Being buried deep in the countryside, the electricity would often fail and they would find themselves having to resort to candles and paraffin lamps.

But at least the range still kicked out enough heat to make the downstairs habitable. He'd toyed with the idea of upgrading to central heating — but he would need to spend more time here to make that worthwhile. Maybe he would — one day.

If he moved into the farmhouse full-time, he'd think about the central heating.

Maybe.

But part of him liked the chill.

He spied the half loaf of bread still sitting on the chopping board — a supermarket loaf that was already turning dry. Sawing off a chunk, he slid it on to a plate and warmed it over the range's hot plate while he retrieved butter and cheese from the fridge.

Covering the bread with a thick layer of butter and a wedge of cheese, he picked up the plate and turned towards the door. There was only one other room he inhabited in the farmhouse, after the kitchen.

The snug.

The snug was nestled at the rear of the farmhouse, reached via a narrow flagstone passageway just off the kitchen. As he entered, he was pleased to note that there was just enough wood stacked on the hearth for a decent fire — enough for tonight, at least.

Putting down his plate of bread and cheese, he quickly spread the cinders out in the grate and tossed several more roughly hewn logs on top. Screwing up some newspaper into balls, he stuffed them into the gaps between the logs and flicked in a lit match. It didn't take long for the flames to take hold.

Picking up his plate, he sat down on the battered leather sofa in front of the growing fire. He was still wired, his blood pounding through his veins, but tiredness would overtake him soon. He calculated he'd had no more than eight hours sleep in the last five days.

He sank his teeth into the bread.

Killing made you hungry.

The flames were jumping much higher now, casting an eerie orange glow around the walls. His grandfather had always called the room his snug — although it was really an office where he kept the accounts and paperwork for running the farm.

Back then, everything was done by hand; no computers or apps around to take some of the strain. Huge leather-bound tomes would sit on the desk — one for wages, one for the animals, one for the farm machinery, and one for the general upkeep of the farmhouse and other outbuildings.

Not blessed with much of a formal education, leaving school at just thirteen, George Frederick Hemmingway had taught himself to read and write — with just enough arithmetic to be able to do his own basic accounts. A simple man from a simple background. No airs and graces with George: what you saw was exactly what you got.

He only possessed one photograph of his grandfather — taken the summer before he died. And he'd looked the same as he did when they'd first arrived on the farm. Maybe it was the life spent outdoors that had turned his skin to a rough, burnt leather — the early mornings and late nights chiselling deep grooves into his face, the manual labour causing his hands to become gnarled and cracked.

After a long day's hard toil on the farm, paperwork complete, his grandfather would sit in front of the fire in his snug, pipe in hand, the smell of tobacco smoke lingering in the air long after the old man had retired to bed.

The air in the snug no longer smelled of tobacco — and hadn't done so for a long time. On his grandfather's death, more than twenty years ago, his father — the eminent surgeon Laurence Hemmingway Sr — had turned the snug into his own study and tobacco among many other things, was banned. The old leather-bound books were discarded and replaced with a word processor, and later a computer. The shelves were then crammed full of medical textbooks and journals. Gone also were the most wonderful photographs and drawings that had graced the snug's walls. Most had depicted farm scenes — men in flat caps and dusty boots, climbing aboard tractors and horse-drawn carts. A bygone age.

Slowly, George Frederick Hemmingway was erased from the snug — in his place, a hideous life-sized map of the human body.

A body map.

The map showed all the bones, muscles, veins and arteries of the human body — every image annotated with medical terminology and descriptions.

Then every night, after dinner, his father would take him to the study where he would be forced to learn countless anatomical body structures, endless diseases and diagnoses, medical definitions and terminologies, until he could recite them in his sleep.

And every time he made a mistake, a painful slap around the ear would follow. Soon the slap turned into a punch, and then the punch into a beating from a stiff, leather-tipped cane.

He could remember it as if it were yesterday.

* * *

Friday 14 May 1999
The Farmhouse

"Wrong!" The slap stung hard and Laurence felt his head snap sideways with the force of the blow. His ear smarted and soon burned red-hot. "How many times do I have to tell you, boy?!"

Laurence looked up at his father with suitably mournful eyes. He'd known the answer to the question — it hadn't been that difficult. So why had he given the wrong one on purpose? He wasn't quite sure. Getting the answer wrong hurt — it hurt a lot.

"Sorry," he mumbled, rubbing his ear.

"Sorry, what?!" thundered Laurence Hemmingway Sr.

"Sorry, *sir.*" Laurence Jr was kneeling on the floor beneath the huge body map, and steadied himself. "Let me try again? Please?"

The trauma surgeon stepped back and regarded his son. At ten years of age, he already knew the boy was destined for great things. He had an unusually retentive memory, akin to a sponge — but he needed to be taught discipline. And discipline was something Laurence Hemmingway Sr was very good at.

He gave a curt nod. "From the top, then. One more time."

Laurence felt his heartbeat quicken beneath his pyjamas. He could recite the bones of the human body in his sleep — but there was something curiously exciting about watching his father's anger soar to new heights. It gave him a perverse thrill — something his ten-year-old self couldn't yet understand.

Laurence Hemmingway Sr pointed his leather-tipped cane at the body map.

"Cranium," began young Laurence. "Orbit. Maxilla. Mandible." The names tripped off his tongue like velvet. He liked the way they sounded — much better than the baby words his friends still spoke at school. "Cervical vertebrae. Clavicle. Sternum. Scapula." The words kept coming, one after the other and, as each one escaped his mouth, he saw his father's expression change. A lightness entered his eyes, a glint of pride radiating towards him.

"Thoracic vertebrae. Lumbar vertebrae. Coccyx." Laurence began to smile. Any minute now. *Any minute now.*

"Humerus. Ulna. Radius." The young Hemmingway paused, trying to stop his smile from widening. "Tarsals."

That was it. The cane came crashing down once more, connecting with the side of his head. The force blew him from his knees, sending him sprawling across the tiled floor.

"They are *carpals*, goddam you! *Carpals*!" Laurence Hemmingway Sr's face burned hot scarlet, spit flying from the corners of his mouth as he raged. "How many more times?!" The cane came down again with another sickening crack, but Laurence Jr was already curled up tightly into a ball, his hands cradling his scalp.

Amid the pain inflicted by the cane, young Laurence smiled.

Tarsals.

* * *

Friday 28 December 2018
The Farmhouse

He brought a hand up to the side of his face, almost able to still feel the searing heat beneath his fingers. Night after night he'd endured that pain. He had very quickly learned his metacarpals from his metatarsals, his tibia from his fibula. His cerebrum from his cerebellum. All under the watchful gaze and heavy hand of his father.

It wasn't difficult.

But the perverse delight he felt when he made mistakes — getting to see his father so *angry* — made the pain from all the whippings worthwhile.

He'd initially thought about destroying the map, now that his father was no longer around — burning it and taking delight in reducing it to a pile of ash — but something had stopped him. A dark thought had taken root inside his head — and then it had grown.

So, he'd kept the map and hung it instead inside his own operating theatre — the farmhouse pantry — giving it a new lease of life. A new purpose.

He often wondered whether his father would be proud of what he'd achieved. He certainly knew his tarsals from his carpals now . . .

A dark chuckle vibrated within his throat as he swallowed the last of the bread and cheese. He'd long since abandoned any notion of earning the eminent surgeon's approval. Nothing Laurence did — even scoring a clean sheet of straight As in his exams and securing a place at medical school — was ever good enough to impress his father. Being a Hemmingway meant high standards and soon the name became a millstone around his neck. As soon as he was able, he ditched the family name and moved on — Laurence Hemmingway Jr was no more.

With the flames in the grate warming his skin, he began to feel sleepy. It was after 1 a.m. and the exertions of the past few days were finally catching up with him. Jacqui's eyes would have been found by now, of that he was certain. On his way back to the farmhouse, he'd noticed several roads cordoned off around the theatre, causing a thrill to ripple through him as he quietly drove past.

It was starting.

He didn't expect her tongue to be found just yet, though.

Not if the boy did as he was told.

But it would be soon.

Pulling an old tartan blanket across his legs, he curled up on the battered sofa and closed his eyes.

He needed to sleep.

Killing was tiring.

CHAPTER SEVEN

Friday 28 December 2018
Bury St Edmunds Police Station

The incident room was a hive of activity by the time Nicki entered at a little after 8 a.m. DC Darcie Butler had arrived early, connecting everyone's PC and arranging all the desk spaces. It didn't take much — the previous investigation had only just wound down. Nicki was pleased to note that she'd managed to hold on to the hot water urn and replenished the supplies of tea and coffee.

"Morning, boss!" Darcie's bright, sparkling eyes shone out beneath her jet-black fringe. "Got you a coffee on the go already!"

Nicki smiled and accepted the tall mug with '*BOSS*' written on the side. The coffee was much needed and she took a grateful sip. After getting home from the scene at the roundabout last night — or the early hours of the morning, to be more precise — she hadn't been able to sleep. The remains of the bottle of Chardonnay had been sitting on the kitchen worktop but, tempting as it was, Nicki knew that wasn't the answer to her insomnia.

She'd tossed and turned for a couple of hours before getting up and sitting by the window, watching the world outside turn white. At 5 a.m. she'd decided to go out for a run to try and dislodge the images of eyes and severed tongues from her thoughts. It had been pitch black and the streets covered with fresh snowfall, so the run had very quickly turned into a walk. A slow one. She'd returned home frozen to the bone, but the cold had sharpened her mind.

As she took a second sip, the incident room door opened and DS Fox entered. *You look as bad as I do*, she wanted to say — but, instead, she greeted him with a tired smile. He was carrying two greaseproof paper bags and, from the aroma wafting towards her, it looked like he'd been down to the local bakers to get them all breakfast.

Did the man never sleep?

Nicki already knew the answer to that particular chestnut. As she accepted a ham and cheese toasted sandwich, she noticed he was wearing a different shirt from last night — so maybe he had made it home after all. But his face told her he hadn't rested much.

"Cheers, Gray." Darcie flopped into one of the vacant chairs and sank her teeth into a warm pain au chocolat. "This is amazing!"

Although Nicki's stomach growled with hunger, her appetite had yet to return. She nibbled at the corner of her toastie. "How was your Christmas, Darcie? Did you manage to get away and see your parents?"

Darcie nodded, wiping a flake of pastry from her chin. "Amy and I went down the day before Christmas Eve. She came back on Boxing Day for a shift, but I stayed until yesterday." Darcie's older sister, Amy, was an A&E nurse at the town's hospital. "But it was good, thanks. Mum and Dad were chuffed to have us both in the house at the same time for once!"

Nicki smiled, feeling a pang of envy tweak her conscience. Hearing about Darcie's family gathering only reminded her how splintered and damaged her own family was. But before she could let the melancholy overtake her thoughts, the door burst open again and Detective Sergeant Royston Carter blustered in, his face hidden behind a towering pile of confectionery tins balanced precariously in his hands.

"Greetings all!" His wide smile lit up the room, and even Nicki felt herself buoyed in his presence. "A little something to keep us all going." He nodded towards the tins of sweets and chocolates, depositing them on to the nearest desk. "They're selling them off at half price in the supermarket this morning."

Behind Roy, DCs Matt Holland and Duncan Jenkins breezed in, Matt instantly grabbing one of the tins and ripping its lid off. "Great — I'm starving."

"Matt, you gannet!" exclaimed Darcie, giving his arm a playful slap as he headed past in search of a desk. "Share them around!"

Nicki patted the chair next to her. "Come and sit down, Roy. Tell me how you've been. I've not seen you since before Christmas."

Still grinning, Roy dutifully took his seat, DS Fox handing him a warm croissant as he sat. "All good, boss. Raring to go."

Nicki eyed him suspiciously, noticing the same haunted look in his dark eyes that she saw in Graham's. "How about your injuries?" Joining the team only two months ago, Roy had earned himself a fractured cheekbone, several cracked ribs, a concussion and multiple cuts and bruises during the Lucas Jackson investigation.

"Like I said, all fine," he replied, taking a mouthful of his pastry. "Fit as a fiddle."

Nicki didn't know how fit fiddles usually were, but she was pretty sure they didn't look like Royston Carter. Although he smiled and said all the right things, Nicki was no fool. The way he gingerly sat down and shifted his weight told her all she needed to know. But she smiled and gave him a nod. She had a good team — they didn't even let broken bones or brushes with death slow them down.

Coffee mug in hand, Nicki got to her feet and approached the first whiteboard. Annotated by herself and Fox last night, it still only provided somewhat sparse information about the find in the Theatre Royal. Thinking of enucleated eyeballs once more, her stomach gave a familiar lurch.

She noted that the second whiteboard had also now been annotated — giving details of the grim discovery in the wolf's mouth on the Southgate Street roundabout. Tommy McCrae was the only name written up so far, appearing above a crude map of the area and the location of the wolf sculpture.

"It's definitely a human tongue." Fox came to hover by the side of the second whiteboard. "The call came in earlier this morning. The blood came back positive — definitely not an animal."

Nicki nodded solemnly. As horrific as it sounded, she'd suspected as much. "Any idea when they might be able to tell us if it comes from the same person as the eyes?"

"I'm told both cases are being prioritised." Fox gave a slight shrug. "So, it's anyone's guess really. Regarding the theatre, I've collated all the names from the advance ticket holders and staff members. That performance was only booked out to fifty per cent capacity — and there's sixty-five names on the system as having bought tickets in advance."

Nicki took another grateful mouthful of coffee, willing the caffeine to do its work while she turned back towards her team. "Welcome back everyone. You've arrived just in time. I'll let Graham take a few minutes to update you on exactly what's happened over the last twelve hours — then it's a case of having to hit the ground running, I'm afraid."

Once Fox had finished giving a brief overview of both cases, Nicki took over.

"Matt. Duncan. I want you to follow up on the theatregoers, employees and then the cleaning company. I want to know exactly who was inside that theatre yesterday. And Darcie — I know it's a long shot, but run a check on any missing persons in the area, and maybe neighbouring counties, too. Highlight any with blue eyes or eye colour not recorded."

Darcie snatched up a fresh notebook and settled down into one of the seats closest to the whiteboards. "Surely someone would have seen something," she commented, firing up the computer. "Both at the theatre and the roundabout. I know there's no CCTV inside the actual theatre, but still — this is a small town. You run the risk of being seen, surely?"

"My thoughts exactly. That's why we need to focus on staff at the theatre, or anyone else who was inside for a legitimate reason — such as the cleaning company. Eliminate as many as we can."

"Perhaps he was just lucky." Roy moved seats, pulling out a chair next to Darcie, giving a faint wince as he sat down. "It happens. Maybe he's a chancer?"

Nicki rubbed her eyes, feeling the grittiness beneath her eyelids. *Great, that's all we need*, she thought. *A chancer.* "Roy, I want you and Darcie to go and visit our skater boy, Tommy McCrae, regarding the tongue. Graham had a few words with him last night, but I'm not sure he fully understood the significance of what he found. See if you can get anything more out of him. If he was skateboarding — although how that would have been possible with the conditions such as they were — then I want to know where he went and who he saw. Anything and everything. Even the tiniest of details might be just what we need."

Darcie and Roy gave simultaneous nods.

"I'll go out and see our Mr Fisher." Nicki glanced back up at the first whiteboard where the man's name had been written. "He found the eyes when he took his seat in the Sir Isaac Newton box. We need to find out if he was targeted specifically or whether he was just unlucky. The discovery would have been a shock for anyone, but at nearly ninety years of age it must be even more so. Graham, you're with me. Give me an hour or so to check my emails, then we'll get going."

Nicki picked up her coat, took her leave and headed back to her office. The churning in her stomach was telling her she should eat more of the toasted sandwich, but she couldn't get the thought of gouged eyeballs and severed tongues out of her head, which killed any appetite stone dead. She'd topped up her coffee mug before leaving the incident room, and took her barely touched ham and cheese toastie with her.

* * *

2 Old Railway Cottages
Dullingham, Nr Newmarket

Benedict Thatcher hauled the holdall out of the back of the taxi, placing it on the pavement while he fished inside his pocket for some cash. With the crisp notes in his hand, the taxi driver pulled the Lexus away from the kerb and headed back along the lane.

He hadn't meant to be away for so long. The few days away he'd been planning had quickly turned into weeks — long weeks, when all he could think about were the Brownings.

And what he'd found at the bottom of their garden.

Making his way to the front door, he glanced towards the house next door and caught sight of a face in the upstairs window.

The woman always seemed to be watching — staring, even — but ducking out of sight whenever their eyes locked. He'd done some digging, found her name to be Annette, and even went to introduce himself not long after they'd moved in. A tiny, bird-like woman, Annette Browning had barely raised her voice above a whisper, forever glancing over her shoulder back into the house as if worried they might be overheard. He got the distinct impression that she couldn't close the door and send him on his way fast enough.

They hadn't been moved in long — sometime in early spring — and they'd kept themselves pretty much to themselves since. But they seemed nice enough, from what he'd seen — which admittedly wasn't much. An occasional hello over the fence, or a nod when taking the bins out on a Monday morning.

There were two sons — one he knew worked at a local butcher's shop. He'd seen him lugging bags of meat out of his van, some of which Benedict suspected were of dubious history — but that was none of his business.

With the woman's eyes still trained on him, Benedict trudged up the short garden path that led to his front door, pulling the key from his pocket and ramming it into the lock. The house would be ice-cold, having lain dormant for so long. He prayed the boiler would fire up without too much protestation and that the pipes hadn't iced up in his absence.

Stepping inside, he snapped on the hall lights. A multitude of envelopes decorated the floor beneath his feet, but he merely stepped over them. There would be nothing of importance, he was sure — most likely just a collection of takeaway flyers, charity bags and adverts for funeral plans.

Walking through to the kitchen, he flicked the switch on the thermostat and waited to hear the welcoming 'whoosh' as the boiler kicked in. So far so good. Leaving his bag next to the washing machine, he pulled open the door of the fridge, knowing there'd be very little that was still edible inside. Leaving so suddenly, he hadn't had a chance to clean it out — and he'd been expecting to return much sooner — before Christmas at any rate.

His eyes scoured the meagre contents, his nose wrinkling at the sour aroma emanating from the shelves. The only items that were in any way still edible were a jar of mayonnaise, a slab of dark chocolate, and two bottles of Peroni. Pulling open one of the salad drawers, he recoiled at the mush that now swam in the bottom.

Grabbing one of the bottles of Peroni, he slammed the fridge door shut. He'd deal with that another time. Maybe one of the takeaway flyers on the doormat would come in handy for later tonight.

Pushing thoughts of food out of his mind for now, he wrenched the top off the bottle and took a gulp. It was after five o'clock somewhere in the world, so he didn't feel too bad. Immediately, his eyes gravitated towards the kitchen window and to the fence that separated his garden from the Brownings next door.

What he'd found there in October was still fresh in his mind.

* * *

Sunday 28 October 2018
2 Old Railways Cottages
Dullingham, Nr Newmarket

Benedict stood outside the back door and surveyed the damage.

The storm had caught him unawares — as it had the rest of the residents in the street by the looks of things. Fence panels had blown down all the way along the lane, guttering peeling away from walls like banana skins. Wheelie bins and plastic garden furniture were turned upside down and tossed around like boats on a rough sea. A sudden and unexpected change in air pressure had been the explanation from expert meteorologists in that morning's news — so 'expert' that they'd failed to see it coming.

Benedict slid his phone back into his dressing-gown pocket and drained his coffee. He'd gone out yesterday morning, leaving a load of washing pegged to the line. Arriving back home late last night, he'd decided to leave it where it was — even amid the near-hurricane blowing forcibly along the lane.

In hindsight, that possibly hadn't been the best decision. But he'd got off lightly compared to some.

He had been surprised to see the fence was virtually intact — just one panel had blown down and was now lying just inside next door's garden. He didn't keep much else outside, so there wasn't a lot to get battered by the gale force winds — except for his washing.

Which was currently decorating most parts of his garden.

He grabbed the laundry basket and began traipsing around the garden retrieving the garments from where they'd come to rest in various flowerbeds, bushes and even the compost heap at the very bottom. The grass was soaking wet and soon drenched the thin slippers on his feet. Having seen the carnage from his bedroom window, he'd not bothered getting dressed — just pulling a flimsy dressing gown around himself and heading straight outside in his slippers.

Not a great look.

But no one was watching.

After gathering up the wayward washing, he was making his way back to the house when he spotted them.

Bright red, they were clearly visible through the gap in the fence — hanging from the lower branches of a mountain ash tree in next door's garden. Ordinarily, he would have left them where they were — not being particularly attached to them — but they *were* underpants. And they just so happened to have a somewhat rude message printed across the front; a joke present from an ex-work colleague. It would be obvious to the Brownings who they belonged to, and he didn't want them coming across them the next time they went to do a spot of gardening — so for that reason alone Benedict decided he needed to get them back.

He headed towards the convenient gap in the fence — intending to dash towards the tree, rescue his underwear, and dash back again. The whole thing should take no more than ten seconds. Stepping into his neighbour's garden, he hesitated on the sodden grass, feeling his feet squelch inside his slippers. His toes were beginning to go numb from the cold. Should he go and knock first? What if the woman was up at the window again and saw him sprint across the grass in his flimsy dressing gown? It would be quite embarrassing — underwear or no underwear.

But there was no sign of anyone in any of the windows at the rear of the house, so he decided to continue in the direction of the mountain ash and his underpants.

As he neared the tree, he realised the offending garment was quite high up — higher than he could reach, anyway. Frowning, he glanced around the garden for something to help — his gaze falling on a pile of old logs and garden waste a bit further towards the end of the garden. If he could find a twig or a branch long enough, he'd be able to hook his underpants and be on his way.

With one last glance back at the house, he made his way towards the bottom of the garden and began to hunt for a decent-sized branch. Brambles and tangled thorns grabbed at his dressing gown as he rummaged.

As he pulled a particularly promising long branch towards him, he saw there was another section of garden behind the pile of waste — a hidden section — tucked away out of sight behind encroaching hedgerows. Momentarily forgetting the quest for his underpants, Benedict abandoned his search for a branch and pushed himself through the thick brambles. Much more overgrown, this part of the Brownings' garden had thick tufts of wet grass, ankle deep in places, which soon soaked into the bottom of his pyjamas.

Taking a glance around, his eyes quickly came to focus on something strangely out of place.

What on earth was *that* doing in the bottom of someone's garden?

Benedict stepped closer and knelt down in the wet grass. The headstone had weathered a little over time so, taking the sleeve of his dressing gown, he rubbed the accumulated thin layer of dirt and lichen away from the stone to reveal the inscription.

'Precious son and brother — taken too soon'

Although the date on the headstone was over twenty years ago, the earth around it looked freshly dug. The frown on Benedict's forehead deepened. Although it was completely legal to bury someone in your own back garden, it wasn't exactly a common occurrence.

Interest piqued, Benedict pulled out his phone and took several quick snaps.

Conscious he may have inadvertently stumbled across a sensitive family secret — with his underpants still to rescue — he turned away from the headstone and pushed his way back through the brambles.

Selecting the sturdiest looking branch he could find, Benedict returned to the tree and successfully hooked the underpants free, catching them as they fell.

With one last glance over his shoulder towards the hidden headstone, he slipped back through the gap in the fence and disappeared from sight.

CHAPTER EIGHT

Friday 28 December 2018
Abbott Road, Bury St Edmunds

Nicki and DS Fox were shown into a small but neatly kept front room. The small electric fire in the fireplace was kicking out some welcome heat.

Ernest Fisher was surprisingly sprightly for his eighty-eight years, Nicki noticed as he padded over to his high-backed armchair in his moleskin slippers. He gestured with a liver-spotted hand towards two further chairs by the window.

"Please. Have a seat. Can I get either of you a cup of tea?"

Nicki smiled gratefully and sat down. "No, thank you, Mr Fisher. We're fine."

Fox pulled out his notebook as they both sat.

The house was in a quiet part of the town, nestling in among several streets of retirement bungalows. The patterned carpet underfoot looked aged and worn — Nicki wouldn't be surprised if it was the original carpet from when the house was built. The walls were covered in a plain textured wallpaper, and adorned with an assortment of framed photographs. Every inch of wall space seemed to be covered.

Most of the pictures looked to be wildlife — birds, fish, an occasional butterfly. The others, Nicki assumed, were family photos — smiling faces turned towards the camera, dressed in their Sunday best.

Nicki loved looking at photographs; seeing images charting a family's evolution from babes in arms through to weddings and christenings — although not too many funerals, it had to be said. But the move towards digital cameras and cloud storage meant that real photographs were a disappearing art.

Turning her attention back to the job in hand, Nicki smoothed down the front of her coat, watching several flakes of melting snow fall to the carpet. "We won't take up too much of your time, Mr Fisher. It's about your discovery at the theatre last night."

Ernest Fisher settled back in his armchair and began to nod. He was a small man, his feet barely touching the floor as he sat. Dressed in an olive- green button-up shirt with a darker green waistcoat over the top, a pair of neatly pressed brown corduroy trousers completed the look. A thin face sported wire-framed spectacles, and a pair of inquisitive pale blue eyes stared out from behind the lenses. His pale skin looked freshly shaved, a smudge of shaving cream still sitting on top of one of his ears. An aroma of Palmolive soap hung in the air as he sat. At the mention of last night's theatre trip, his eyes lost their sparkle.

"Yes, yes of course." The old man knitted his gnarled hands together in his lap. "Such an awful business."

"Can you run through what happened?" Nicki watched Fox flip to a fresh page in his notebook. They already had Ernest's initial statement, taken at the scene by one of the uniformed officers, but it had been brief and Nicki was keen to hear what he had to say for himself.

Ernest sighed. "It was *An Inspector Calls* — the play we were all going to see. Me and the rest of the Old Codgers. It's one of my favourites, that play."

"The old codgers?" enquired Nicki.

Ernest managed a smile. "It's what we call ourselves. A friendship group really. We meet up once a fortnight for a cup of tea and a slice of cake, and sometimes we arrange little trips out. Anything from a trip to the museum, the theatre, or sometimes the coast. Anything to keep the old brain cells ticking over." He tapped the side of his head with a bony finger and gave a chuckle. "It was something I chose, actually. The play. I've watched it plenty of times before. It's very clever. Have you seen it?"

Nicki shook her head. "No, I don't think I have."

"It's about this well-to-do family who are visited by a police inspector one evening at their family home. The inspector informs them of the death of a young woman — Eva Smith. At first, the family deny knowing anyone by that name but slowly the inspector gets them each to admit that they did actually know her and may have played a part, albeit unwittingly, in her eventual demise." Ernest paused, giving another nervous chuckle. "It's a little odd if you think about it — with an inspector now sitting in my living room! Later, the family discover that the inspector wasn't an inspector after all." The old man eyed Nicki, somewhat warily, his voice hitching. "But that's where the similarity ends, isn't it? You really *are* the police."

Nicki tried a sympathetic smile. "I'm afraid so, Mr Fisher. We're very much real." Glancing at Fox and noting he had his pen poised, Nicki turned back to the old man. "Could you tell me what time you arrived at the theatre?"

The old man's gaze drifted towards the ceiling for a moment. "Must have been around six o'clock, maybe just before. Not too long before the doors were meant to open. We didn't want to arrive too early — it was bitterly cold out and looked like it might snow."

Nicki had read as much in Mr Fisher's statement. "Indeed, it was. So, you were only outside for a few minutes before the doors opened?"

"A bit longer than that. The doors didn't open on time — we probably waited around ten or fifteen minutes before we eventually got inside."

"And who was the 'we'? Who else was with you at the time? Just the members of your group?"

Ernest nodded. "It was just me, Edna and Maude this time. The others didn't want to come, didn't fancy coming out in the cold."

"Were there many people waiting outside with you?"

Ernest paused for a second. "Well, there were others, yes. But I can't really say how many. I don't think there were too many, though — due to the weather, you see. I didn't really take much notice of them, to be honest." He gave an apologetic shrug. "They were all around our age, though — mostly pensioners."

"And when the doors opened, did you see anyone coming *out* of the theatre?"

The old man thought for a moment before shaking his head. "Not that I recall — but, then again, I'm not sure I would have taken much notice of them if I had. The manager came out to apologise for the delay, but that's all I can remember. Sorry."

"No need to be sorry, Mr Fisher. You're doing fine." Nicki caught Fox's eye. "When you say the manager came out to apologise for the delay — what did he say the reason was?" Nicki searched her memory but couldn't remember Hugh Maxwell mentioning it to them last night. From the look on Fox's face, neither did he.

"I think he said something about a technical problem, and some staff sickness?" Ernest Fisher gave yet another apologetic shrug. "I'm sorry — I didn't really pay much attention. We just wanted to get into the warm."

"And then what happened — after the doors were opened?"

Ernest crossed his legs and brushed some invisible specks of dust from his trousers as he did so. He settled back once more against the cushions. "The three of us went into the foyer — glad to get out of that biting wind. We already had our tickets — I'd booked in advance to get a discount — so we didn't need to queue up."

"And you went straight to your seats?"

The old man started to nod, but then stopped. He brought a hand to his lips. "Oh, my — I think I might have told that lovely officer last night that we did — go to our seats straight away, that is. But now I come to think of it . . . I don't think we did. Not right away, anyway."

Nicki felt her eyebrows hitch. She exchanged another look with Fox who still had his pen poised over his notebook. "So, you *didn't* go straight to your seats?"

Ernest shook his head animatedly. "No, no we didn't. I remember now! Sorry, I think I must have been in shock or something when that lovely officer asked me. We stayed in the foyer for a few minutes because Edna wanted to buy a programme and Maude needed the ladies. When you get to our age, our bladders are a law unto themselves. Especially when you've been standing out in the cold for so long."

"Quite." Nicki managed another smile. "How long do you think you were waiting in the foyer?"

Mr Fisher scratched his freshly shaven chin. "It wasn't very long. Just a few minutes at a guess. Maybe five? Is it important?"

"Probably not. And while you were waiting, were other theatregoers making their way to their seats?"

Ernest Fisher continued to scratch his chin. "I guess so. I wasn't paying too much attention, but yes — the foyer wasn't very warm, so I expect they all wanted to get along to their seats."

"And what happened when you eventually made your way to your seats?"

Ernest swallowed, his already waxen skin paling even more as he gripped the edges of his armchair. "We've been to the theatre countless times before, so we already knew where to go. We were in one of the dress circle boxes — not in the pit this time. We made our way through the corridor towards our box. It only took a minute or so to walk, even for oldies like us."

"Who entered the box first, Mr Fisher?"

"That would have been me." Ernest Fisher's face went a shade whiter. "I pulled open the door and went inside. The ladies stayed out in the corridor looking at some of the framed pictures on the walls."

"So, you were on your own?"

Ernest gave a quick nod. "I made my way over to my seat. I was planning to sit at the front, so I could get the best view of the stage."

"And when did you first notice that something was wrong?"

The old man removed his spectacles and pinched the top of his nose, his hand shaking as he did so. "My glasses had steamed up from the cold outside. I took them off . . ." He looked down at the spectacles in his hand, giving an involuntary shudder before putting them back on. "I started to wipe them on my scarf as I went to sit down." He broke off, his voice starting to crack. "I almost sat on them," he finished in a whisper.

Despite the heat from the fire opposite, Nicki felt herself shiver beneath her woollen coat. "It must have been very distressing, Mr Fisher. Can we get you a glass of water?"

The old man shook his head, a weak smile crossing his face. "No, no need. I'd rather just get it over with." After receiving an encouraging nod, he continued. "As I bent down, I saw something on the seat. I wasn't sure what it was at first — I thought maybe someone had left something behind from an earlier performance. But . . ." He broke off to clear his throat. "When I put my glasses back on, I couldn't quite believe it."

"Are you OK to continue? Are you sure I can't get you a glass of water?"

Ernest shook his head. "No, no. It'd be something stronger than water I'd need, if I'm honest, and it's a little early in the day for that." He tried another weak smile. "It just shook me up that's all. It's not really something I expected to see."

"Quite," agreed Nicki. "So, what happened next?"

"Well, as I bent down to take a closer look, Edna and Maude came into the box. I think they wondered what I was doing." The old man gave a faint sigh. "I was trying to tell myself it was a joke. That they were false ones, like those you get for Halloween. But, in my heart, I knew. I've seen death before, Inspector. I know what dead human eyes look like. Once you've seen them, you never forget."

Nicki let her gaze travel over the old man's shoulder once more towards the wall full of photographs behind him. Walking into the room earlier, she had briefly registered the bank of happy, smiling faces alongside the birds and the fish, but she hadn't really noticed the series of black and white military photographs taking centre stage. Even from this distance, she recognised the face of a dashingly handsome Ernest Fisher in his British Army uniform.

"You were in the Army?" Nicki's tone was soft.

"I was." Ernest's chest heaved beneath his waistcoat. "In Korea — the battle of Imjin River in 1951. I'd just turned twenty-one. The things I saw. It's not something I'll ever forget — haunts me even now."

Nicki knew all about being haunted by the past. She tore her gaze away from the photographs. "This might sound like a silly question, Mr Fisher, but did you touch them at all? The eyes?"

Ernest Fisher's chest heaved once again, but he was already shaking his head. "No. The instant I knew what they were I took a step back. I told the ladies to retreat, too — to go back out into the corridor. I knew something was wrong — I knew something was very wrong."

"I know it might be difficult, thinking back, but do you recall anyone hanging around? Watching you as you made the discovery? Maybe from a neighbouring box or someone still out in the corridor?"

Ernest shook his head. "I'm sorry. I really don't recall."

"That's fine, you've been really helpful. Is there anything you'd like to ask us before we leave you in peace?"

The old man leaned forward in his chair, planting his slippered feet down on to the worn carpet. The heat from the fire opposite gave his pale face a warm glow. "There is something that's been on my mind. Whoever they are, did they choose that seat on purpose? Was *I* meant to find them?" The old man tried to hide the quiver in his voice.

Nicki tried to sound as reassuring as she could. "I really don't think that's the case, Mr Fisher. I think we're looking at a completely random act — a completely random seat. Nothing more significant than that. The fact that it was your seat was just an unhappy coincidence." Nicki hoped she was right. The alternative didn't bear thinking about.

Ernest Fisher shuffled along the carpet, showing Nicki and DS Fox to the door.

"And don't forget — if you think of anything else that might be relevant from last night, please get in touch." Nicki pressed a business card into the old man's hand. "And if you have any questions or worries, please give me a ring."

Ernest thanked them and pulled open the front door. As he did so, Nicki's eyes strayed to more photographs adorning the walls of the hallway. Just like the front room, there were a variety of animals — mostly birds and fish — the rest looking like family get-togethers in days gone by. Mostly in black and white, some had yellowed with age.

One photo in particular caught Nicki's eye.

"My grandchildren," explained Ernest, seeing where her gaze had come to rest. "Taken some years ago now."

The image was of two young children, maybe six or seven years old, standing in front of a big wheel at a funfair. Huge grins stretched across their faces, sticks of pink candy-floss in their hands.

Candyfloss.

Nicki's stomach heaved as the sickly, sweet smell filled her senses. Suddenly, her ears were filled with the sounds of the fairground — the rides, the incessant music, the shouts and screams of excited, sugar-filled children. It was as if she were transported back in time, not standing in the narrow hallway of Ernest Fisher's home.

"Boss?" Fox had clearly noticed how Nicki was steadying herself against the wall, her face suddenly paling. "You OK?"

Then, as quickly as it had appeared, the vision of Deano and the candyfloss disappeared into the ether.

"Yes, fine," she replied, clearing her throat. "Let's get some air."

* * *

Friday 28 December 2018
2 Old Railway Cottages
Dullingham, Nr Newmarket

With the radiators starting to get warm, Benedict headed upstairs for a hot shower. He felt chilled to the bone — and thinking about the Brownings, and what lay at the bottom of their garden, didn't do much to help.

Pulling off his clothes, he stepped into the shower and turned the heat up to maximum. Standing beneath the hot jets he heard the water pipes groan and clunk as if affronted at being woken from their slumber, but he closed his eyes and soon tuned out the noise

As the water pummelled his skin, Benedict's thoughts gravitated back to the headstone.

From the dates etched into the weathered stone, it had been a *child*.

Benedict shivered beneath the scorching water.

Ever since that windy day last October, he'd been desperate to find a reason to get inside number four and find out more.

As it turned out, he didn't have to wait long.

* * *

Wednesday 31 October 2018
4 Old Railway Cottages
Dullingham, Nr Newmarket

"I'm sure it's nothing, but . . ." Annette Browning looked sheepishly towards the floor. "Neither myself nor my husband are very good with technology — and our sons aren't home right now."

Benedict stepped into the hall. "No problem at all," he smiled, trying hard to mask his good fortune.

It had been three days since he'd rescued his underpants and seen the headstone. Three long days when all he could think about was finding out who was buried at the bottom of the garden.

Mrs Browning led them both along the hallway in the direction of the kitchen, but stopped outside a door beneath the stairs. "It's just in here." She pushed the door open to reveal a surprisingly spacious study.

"Nice room," Benedict commented, ducking his head as he entered. "Very cosy."

Annette gave a weak smile, her eyes still lowered towards the floor.

"Who's the artist?" Benedict nodded towards a drawing board set up by the window and a selection of intricate looking sketches.

"Oh, that's my eldest — Mason. He's the artistic one — I don't know where he gets it from." Annette's cheeks coloured a little as she spoke.

Sensing she was feeling uncomfortable, Benedict cleared his throat. "So, whereabouts is your router? I'll start there and see what's what."

Mrs Browning edged past Benedict and gestured towards a mass of cables by the side of a mahogany desk.

"I'm sure it's down there, somewhere," she replied, her cheeks colouring even more. "I'm sorry. Technology isn't my thing."

So you said, mused Benedict, bending down to take a look at the tangle of wires. "No worries. I'll soon be able to tell you if you've got a problem or not. It might just be a loose connection."

Annette scuttled out of the study, leaving Benedict alone. He could already see what the Brownings' issue was — or, at least, was likely to be. One of the cables looked to have popped loose from the back of the router — he'd seen it the very instant he'd bent down. A simple, two second job.

But instead of reconnecting the cable, Benedict stood up and glanced around the study. He suspected it was more Mr Browning's domain than his wife's. Maybe the son's, too. It had a man-cave type of vibe. Several clusters of pictures hung from the walls — mostly family, from what Benedict could deduce. He took a step closer.

One of the last pictures appeared to be Mr and Mrs Browning on their wedding day, surrounded by bridesmaids and confetti. From the hairstyles and clothing, it looked to be in the late eighties, early nineties. Circling this picture was a mixture of other photographs, most depicting two young boys sitting by a Christmas tree, climbing on playground equipment, running along a sandy beach.

The Brownings and their growing family.

All very ordinary.

As he turned around, about to reconnect the Brownings' Wi-Fi, Benedict noticed one of the drawers in the mahogany desk was open. Only slightly — but open all the same. An open drawer couldn't be ignored — it was just asking to be looked in.

With a quick glance towards the open door, through which he thought he could detect the sound of the kettle boiling in the kitchen, Benedict edged closer to the desk. Soundlessly, he pulled the desk drawer fully open. He wasn't sure why, but he held his breath as he began to rummage through the contents.

The drawer contained newspaper cuttings — lots of them. Hesitating only briefly, he picked up the topmost cutting, which had yellowed a little with age. It was a front-page article from the *Daily Mirror*.

Benedict frowned as he read the headline. Folding the cutting up, he reached for another. The same storyline, the same time frame. The year matched that on the headstone at the bottom of the Brownings' garden.

Coincidence?

More and more articles lay inside the drawer, from both national and local newspapers, each one carefully cut out and preserved. All reporting on the same news story.

Benedict detected a faint noise from the direction of the hallway, the front door opening and closing. Hurriedly he replaced the cuttings and pushed the drawer closed. Quickly turning towards the jumble of cables behind him, he grabbed the loose connection and slotted it home in the back of the router.

* * *

Friday 28 December 2018
2 Old Railway Cottages
Dullingham, Nr Newmarket

Benedict stepped out of the shower, his skin still tingling from the scorching water. Wrapping himself in a towel, he padded through to the bedroom and headed to the small desk space in the corner.

His laptop, together with all his research, was still there — several notepads bursting with thoughts and timelines. He'd worked on it ever since seeing the headstone. It had taken him a while, but he was sure now that he'd got to the bottom of exactly *who* was buried in the garden next door.

Water dripped from his hair on to the laptop's casing. He brushed the droplets away and fired it up. After lying dormant for several weeks, it took a while to load — but eventually Benedict pulled up the spreadsheet he'd created last October.

It was all still there. All his research. All his findings. Everything there in black and white.

Taking a seat at the desk, he made a list of things to double-check. Maybe even triple-check. He couldn't afford to get something as monumental as this wrong. His mouth turned dry at the thought of what the Brownings had done; at the secret that lay next door.

Clicking on the folder of pictures, he brought up the image of the headstone.

'Precious son and brother — taken too soon'

Leaving the image on the screen, he pulled on some clothes and headed out in search of food.

He was ravenous.

CHAPTER NINE

Friday 28 December 2018
West Suffolk Mortuary

It was an unusual request.

Used to seeing the human body in varying stages of decomposition, often mutilated beyond recognition, Dr Carolyn 'Caz' Mitchell of the West Suffolk Mortuary thought she'd seen it all.

Sixteen years' service had exposed her to more than her fair share of the violent acts that one depraved human being could inflict upon another — but nothing had quite prepared her for what greeted her on the steel examination table this cold December morning.

The pair of once brilliant blue eyes stared up emptily towards the mortuary ceiling. No doubt once full of love and laughter, they were now dulled, their light permanently dimmed. Caz watched intently as her assistant photographed the specimens from every conceivable angle, capturing even the minutest of detail.

Importantly, this gave the pathologist time to think. Time to think what kind of monster could possibly do this to another living creature.

Living creature.

One of the questions Nicki had posed was whether the victim had been alive when the eyes were removed — and whether there was any possibility that they were alive now. Tapping a gloved finger against her chin as she watched, Caz edged a little closer to the table.

It wasn't inconceivable that the poor victim had been alive when the eyes were removed — medically it was possible, although the thought was somewhat unpalatable. Caz decided to leave that question unanswered for now, and concentrate on the examination. With the photographs now complete, she began.

Picking up a scalpel from the instrument tray, she approached the specimen — her microphone already running, ready to capture her thoughts.

"Today is Friday 28 December — 11.55 a.m. — and before me is a pair of adult human eyes. Oculus dexter and oculus sinister — left and right. Both eyeballs appear intact, with no obvious damage or loss of vitreous humour." Caz nudged each eye with her scalpel, rotating them through three hundred and sixty degrees. "There is evidence of careful dissection on each specimen — surrounding muscles and tissues have been debrided and separated with care. The optic nerve in each eye is intact and has been severed with a sharp instrument." Despite the macabre spectacle before her, the pathologist's professional intrigue was piqued and growing by the second. She pulled her microscopic eyewear down and focused. "No visible damage to the cornea in either eye. The sclera is also intact. There are some signs of micro haemorrhaging in the conjunctiva in both eyes, more so on the right than the left."

"Other than that, both eyes, externally at least, look to be unexceptional." Caz paused, straightening up slightly. "Except that they are gracing my examination table minus the body they belong to."

It wasn't often that the job made Caz shiver, but she felt a distinct cold flood her spine as she took the left eye in her gloved hand. *Give me gunshot wounds any day*, she thought. Or stab wounds. Even a burn victim. *Anything.*

Anything but this.

Selecting an 18-gauge needle from the instrument tray, Caz carefully rotated the eye to the side. Inserting the needle through the tough exterior of the sclera, she felt only the slightest resistance. Pausing momentarily, she cleared her throat and gently pushed the needle in further.

"Inserting an 18-gauge needle into the vitreous humour." Satisfied the needle was in the correct position, Caz proceeded to draw out a sample of fluid. Clear and colourless, it aspirated easily. "Withdrawing the needle now."

She reached for a sterile tube and released the fluid inside. "Sample of vitreous fluid to be sent for the usual testing." Vitreous humour was ideal for post-mortem analysis as it resisted the body's usual putrefaction process. She handed the tube to the waiting technician who immediately labelled it and placed it in a separate steel tray.

Caz then repeated the process for the right eye — obtaining another 5ml of colourless fluid. The tube was taken by the technician and placed in the samples tray ready for processing. The pathologist then turned back to the eyes resting on the steel table.

"Comparing the external condition of both eyes, I can confirm there are no outward signs of injury or disease. The conjunctiva in both eyes are intact, with minimal signs of petechia — just the faint haemorrhaging mentioned before. The corneas in both eyes have started to cloud over, as would be expected. Tissue and fluid loss within the eyes is minimal." Caz paused, holding her voice steady. "Outwardly, it would appear that both eyes have been extracted fairly recently — more tests on the vitreous fluid may give an indication as to the approximate time of death, or at least the time of removal from the body."

Caz then spent several more minutes obtaining a sample from each retina for DNA analysis before re-examining the outside surface of each eye. Satisfied that her work was complete, she placed her scalpel down.

Catching the attention of the mortuary technician, the pathologist indicated that both eyes could now be returned to cold storage. The first part of her day was over. Stepping back from the table, she glanced towards the second steel trolley waiting in the background, knowing full well what lay beneath its protective cover.

Before she faced that, she needed a strong coffee.

* * *

Southgate Street, Bury St Edmunds

Tommy McCrae's house overlooked the Southgate Street roundabout, set back from the road behind a partial wall. With the roundabout itself still cordoned off and closed to traffic in all directions, Darcie parked the car directly outside. The tongue had long since been removed, but crime scene investigators were still working to gather the last scraps of evidence before the road could be reopened.

There was a peacefulness to the area that morning — whether due to the lack of through traffic, or something else, Darcie couldn't quite tell. Heavy snowfall could always swallow noise, smothering it in a protective blanket of whiteness — nature's own soundproofing. And with the skies above still heavy with cloud, it looked like nature wasn't quite finished yet.

A line of uniformed officers had performed a fingertip search of the surrounding streets, but Darcie knew the likelihood of finding anything useful was slim. The elements were against them — snow was particularly efficient when it came to cleansing a crime scene. If there had been any footprints last night, they would be long gone now, buried beneath the two or more inches of snow that had fallen overnight. A tent had been erected over the wolf sculpture, but enough snow had already fallen beforehand to make that a largely moot point. Retrieving any useful evidence from it would, most likely, be futile.

And if the perpetrator had arrived by vehicle, the same could be said for any tyre tracks — obliterated almost as soon as they were laid.

As a choice of dumping site, the perpetrator had chosen well.

Darcie kicked her boots against the kerbside to dislodge the snow and followed Roy along the short concrete path that led to number twelve. It took two rounds of knocking to rouse those inside and for the door to be opened.

A harassed-looking girl in her early teens stood in the hallway, a baby on her hip in mid-cry. The sound of a TV somewhere in the house filled the rest of the otherwise quiet morning on Southgate Street.

"Yes?" the girl frowned, jiggling the baby on her hip. "Shush, Freddie. I'll get you your bottle in a minute."

Darcie flashed her warrant card, as did Roy next to her. "I'm DC Darcie Butler — this is DS Royston Carter. Is Tommy at home?"

The girl's frown deepened, followed by her pale lips pursing. She looked Darcie and Roy up and down with a pair of wary eyes before turning her head to the side. "Tommy," she bellowed. "It's the cops. What've you been up to this time?"

"Maybe we could come in?" Darcie nodded towards the hallway. "It's a bit chilly out here and we're letting all the warmth out."

The girl continued to eye them both suspiciously, before shrugging and taking a step back. "Suit yourself." With that, she turned and walked away, presumably in the direction of the kitchen and the bottle the crying baby was hollering for.

Roy didn't hesitate, stepping across the doormat and into the hall. Darcie followed and shut the door behind them to keep away the gathering chill. The sound of the TV was much louder now, coming from the room to their right. Roy peered inside the open doorway to see a spacious front room, the carpet of which was buried beneath a sea of toys. In the middle of the mess sat two pre-school children, their wide eyes glued to the sixty-four-inch TV attached to the opposite wall. A quick glance told Roy that Tommy McCrae wasn't in attendance.

Rejoining Darcie in the hallway, he let his eyes drift towards the narrow stairs. Before he could say anything, the young girl came shuffling back towards them, a bottle of milk now firmly wedged into the baby's mouth. All that could be heard, apart from the blaring TV, was the contented gurgling and sucking as the baby took its comfort.

"You mind if we go upstairs?" Roy gestured towards the ceiling. "Is Tommy up there?"

The girl gave a non-committal shrug. "Do what you like. He's probably asleep or on that fucking Xbox."

"Is your mother around?" Darcie couldn't see or hear any evidence of Mrs McCrae's presence.

"Working," replied the girl, shifting the baby over to her other hip. "Back about three." With that, she pushed past the two detectives and entered the front room.

The stairs creaked with every footstep as Darcie and Roy made their way up. The small, cramped landing had four doors leading off from it. One was definitely a bathroom — the door wedged open by an abandoned towel, leaving an old fashioned avocado green bath and sink in full view.

Next to the bathroom was a large bedroom which looked to belong to Mrs McCrae — judging by the double bed and hanging rails rammed full of clothes alongside it. Moving along the landing, Roy nudged another door open with his foot. It revealed an equally good-sized bedroom, with a wooden cot by the window and a set of bunkbeds opposite. A further single bed was wedged up behind the door — the top of which was covered with teenage magazines and empty plastic cola bottles.

That left one more door at the end of the landing. It was shut fast and decorated with various skateboarding and heavy metal band stickers. Roy edged forward and tapped the outside.

"Tommy? It's the police. Can you open the door for me, please?"

Several seconds of silence followed. The sound of the TV had followed them upstairs, albeit now dulled to a minor roar. Roy leaned in closer, straining to hear any sounds coming from within. There were none. He gave a few more sharp raps to the wood, harder and faster this time. "Tommy." Roy's voice now had a stern edge. "Open the door. We need to speak to you about last night."

With his ear almost flush to the grain, Roy thought he heard movement, and maybe a muttered expletive, just managing to step backwards in time before the door was wrenched open.

Tommy McCrae stood in the doorway, bleary-eyed with his hair in tufted clumps. The beginnings of patchy stubble grazed his spotty chin.

"Tommy?" enquired Roy, pulling out his warrant card. The boy nodded, scowling. "I'm Detective Sergeant Carter, and this is Detective Constable Butler. We're here regarding the events of last night? Would it be possible to have a little chat?"

Tommy McCrae stood motionless in the doorway for several more seconds, as if the words had yet to infiltrate his brain and be processed. Eventually, he nodded again. "Sure."

Roy gestured towards the bedroom. "Could we step inside?"

The boy hesitated, looking back over his shoulder as Roy took in the mess strewn across every inch of the bedroom floor. The curtains were still closed and the unmistakable scent of weed lingered in the air. A look of uncertainty mixed with panic crossed the boy's pasty face.

"We'll only be a few minutes," added Roy, inching forward. "And we're only interested in what happened last night . . . nothing else." He gave the boy a knowing look.

Tommy appeared to consider the proposal for a moment, wiping his nose on the sleeve of his hoodie before stepping backwards to allow the two detectives to enter the bedroom. With three of them now inside, it felt cramped and suffocating. Smaller than the other two bedrooms, there was just enough room for a single bed beneath the window and a narrow wardrobe opposite. The carpet was hidden from view beneath mounds of clothes, dirty trainers, plates of half-eaten food, and an abundance of takeaway wrappers. Darcie wrinkled her nose as she breathed in the stale teenage aroma, resisting the urge to fling open the window.

Tommy stepped across to his bed, surreptitiously swiping an ashtray from the top of his duvet and stuffing it beneath the pillow. Roy stifled a smile. "Like I said, we're not interested in anything other than what happened last night. Can you tell us little bit more about it?"

"I've already spoken to you coppers about that." Tommy sniffed, sitting himself back down on his unmade bed. "Told 'em everything I know."

Roy nodded. "I appreciate that, Tommy. But sometimes it helps us detectives to hear it fresh. You're how old now, nineteen?"

Tommy nodded, wiping his nose once more on the sleeve of his hoodie.

"You working?" Roy watched the teenager shake his head.

"Nah, can't get nothin'."

"And you live here with your mum? And is that your sister downstairs taking care of the baby?"

Tommy nodded again. "Kelsey. She's fourteen. My baby brother is Freddie. Then there's Kane and Kieran, the twins. They're three."

"So, Tommy, tell me what happened last night. Where had you been before you found the tongue on the rounda-bout? Looked like you were out on your skateboard." Roy spied the upturned skateboard lying on the floor next to the bed, the wheels just visible beneath a greasy pizza box.

Tommy visibly stiffened. "Just hangin' around, you know."

"And what time was this?"

The boy shrugged and avoided eye contact, looking instead at an area of peeling paint on the wall next to the window. "Dunno. 'Bout half-ten I guess."

"Bit late to be going out on your skateboard, don't you think? It'd be dark. And it was snowing."

Another shrug. "I always go out at night. So do me mates."

"So, where do you usually hang out? You and your mates. Anywhere regular?"

"All over," replied Tommy, curtly, continuing to stare at the peeling paint. "It depends."

Roy could already sense it would be hard work getting anything new out of the boy, but he decided to persist. "Tell me what happened when you found the tongue. Where were you coming back from?"

"Like I said last night — I'd been down the skate park to see if anyone was there, maybe have a smoke. I didn't stay long. It was getting cold."

"That would be the snow. I'm guessing snow isn't so good for skateboarding?"

Tommy looked up with a blank expression.

Roy pressed on. "What made you go across to the round-about? If you were heading home from the skate park, you wouldn't need to cross the roundabout at all, would you?"

Tommy went to open his mouth, then closed it again. His eyes flickered to Darcie, who was still hovering in the doorway. He eventually shrugged a shoulder. "I already told you lot — I just saw something, then told my mum."

"You saw something?" Roy raised his eyebrows. "And what was it that you saw?"

A flash of colour entered Tommy McCrae's pallid cheeks. "Some spots in the snow. I dunno." Another shrug followed. "Looked like blood."

Roy glanced sideways towards Darcie, then slowly nodded. "OK. After you saw what looked like blood, what did you do?"

Tommy hesitated, a ghost of a frown flickering across his brow as he fiddled with the black silicone tunnel in his left stretched ear lobe — the hole almost the size of a two pence piece. Predictably, another shrug followed. "Like I said — I told my mum what I'd seen."

Roy watched Tommy avoid his gaze once more. "So, this would've been about ten-thirty, correct?"

Tommy nodded, wiping his hoodie sleeve across his nose again. "About that, yeah."

Roy watched the boy continue to fiddle with his ear lobe, a nervousness still haunting his eyes — possibly due to the contraband currently stuffed beneath his pillow. Or maybe it was more than that.

"Thing is, Tommy, we've got the call coming into the station at just before eleven-thirty. That's sometime *after* you said you'd arrived home. Why the delay?"

Tommy's hooded eyes widened a little, while more colour entered his pale cheeks. Several tense seconds passed before he answered.

"I dunno — like I said, I went home. I didn't know what to do. I told my mum when she got in from work."

"Ah — your mum wasn't there when you got home?" Roy's eyebrows hitched higher as he watched the boy start to nod. "And when she got home, you told her you'd seen something odd — some blood outside — and then what?"

"I took her outside to show her." Tommy paused and gave his nose another wipe with his sleeve. "Once we saw what it was, she said we had to call you lot."

"That's when you saw the tongue?"

Tommy nodded. "Yeah. In the wolf's mouth."

"Did you touch it? The tongue?"

"No way, man. Course I didn't. That'd be gross." Tommy's face took on a defiant look. "And I never put it there, if that's what you're thinking."

Roy eyed the teenager through the dimness of the bedroom. "That's not what we're thinking at all, Tommy."

Knowing that they probably had all that they would get from the young lad today, Darcie and Roy backed out of the bedroom and headed downstairs — telling Tommy he would need to call by the station to make a formal statement.

As they made their way towards the front door, they could hear baby Freddie's dulcet tones once again, even above the sound of the TV. Pulling the door shut behind them, they returned to the car — the sound of SpongeBob SquarePants following them all the way.

"What's your first thought, Darcie?" Roy pulled open the passenger side door.

"Well." Darcie unlocked the driver's side and slipped inside. "My first thought is that Tommy McCrae's lying through his back teeth."

CHAPTER TEN

West Suffolk Mortuary

Although her body had needed the caffeine hit, the coffee itself now swirled uncomfortably in Caz's stomach. Not usually affected by what she witnessed in her post-mortem room, the first examination of the morning had disturbed her — more so than she'd expected. There was something about eyes that unnerved her — especially eyes without a body.

Snapping on a fresh set of gloves and tying a fresh apron around her waist, she pushed back through the doors of the examination room, the sound of her rubber wellington boots squeaking on the scrubbed vinyl floor.

The mortuary technician had returned the eyes to the freezer units next door. In their place stood the second task of the day. Another examination table, another body part.

Removing the protective covering, Caz looked down at the small section of human tongue and felt the same sense of disquiet as before.

Clearing her throat, which had suddenly become curiously dry, she took a step forward and switched on the overhead microphone.

"Today is Friday 28 December — 1.35 p.m. Here we have a section of human tongue. At 5.75 centimetres in length, I'm confident that the majority of the sample is the oral part of the tongue." Caz leaned in closely beneath the harsh overhead lighting and took the severed tongue in her gloved hand. Examining the widest section, she began to nod. "Only a very small section of the pharyngeal tongue is visible."

Placing the tongue back down on the steel table, she took a series of detailed measurements, writing them up on the whiteboard behind her. She then turned the specimen over.

"On the base of the tongue, the rich blood supply is evident. The pharyngeal section has been severed with a clean cut — by a sharp instrument. I can see no outward damage to the tongue itself — no evidence of tongue biting, no scalloping, no lacerations or abrasions on either side."

That was something at least. Although she couldn't be certain, the chances were the poor person was dead when the tongue was removed. Or at least unconscious. The lack of damage to the tongue suggested its removal had occurred post-mortem. Moreover, if conscious, surely the victim would be trying to move their tongue out of reach of the knife? The chance of inflicting other injuries and abrasions to the surface of the tongue would be very high. If that were the case, Caz would expect to see additional injuries to the lips, the oral mucosa, even the gums.

Unless you couldn't move.

Caz shuddered once again.

"Acute haemorrhaging from the lingual artery would have followed if the victim was alive — but if the tongue was removed post-mortem, then the blood loss would have been much less severe. Blood samples have already been taken for DNA analysis, but I'll take further samples today."

The rest of the examination went without incident. Unable to glean much more from the table, Caz stepped away and dispensed with her gloves and apron. Nicki had wanted to know if the eyes and tongue belonged to the same person.

The DNA samples would no doubt confirm whether that was the case in due course but, in her heart of hearts, Caz hoped to God that it *was* the same person. As unpalatable as it was that anyone had to endure this level of torture — with both eyes and tongue removed in such a barbaric fashion — the thought that *two* people could have suffered was somehow worse.

If that were possible.

Pushing back through the examination room doors, she headed for her office, where she collapsed into her chair and heaved a great sigh of relief that the job was over. But before she could relax and go in search of a coffee, there was a call she needed to make.

She snapped her elasticated cap from her head and let an abundance of chestnut-red hair cascade to her shoulders. Reaching for the phone, her hand brushed against her desktop diary. Sighing, she let her eyes skim the day's appointments. She'd juggled her morning workload to accommodate Nicki's urgent request to examine the eyes and tongue, but that inevitably meant the rest of her schedule was running late.

The name Milly Darkins stood out in the centre of the page. Currently residing in freezer number four, the little girl was her next job of the day. Although she couldn't really admit to looking forward to any of her post mortems, this one was going to be especially difficult.

Killed in a hit-and-run RTA on Boxing Day, Milly's broken body had been transported to the mortuary from the hospital overnight. And the family were coming in later.

Caz always welcomed visits from the family of the deceased — they could view their loved one if they wished, or merely have a chat. Caz saw it as an important way of demystifying the post-mortem process. It would never be a pleasant experience for anyone, but Caz hoped she went some way to help relieve the colossal weight on the grieving family's shoulders.

And none more so than would be shouldered by Mr and Mrs Darkins.

Little girls should be able to cross the road in safety — they shouldn't get mown down on a pedestrian crossing in broad daylight. Caz had seen the photographs from the scene — the image of the little girl's bag of sweets lying scattered across the tarmac would stay with her long after the body had left the mortuary.

Knowing she couldn't put the rest of her day on hold any longer, Caz reached for the phone.

* * *

4 Old Railway Cottages
Dullingham, Nr Newmarket

"Come away from the window, Annette." Larry Browning stood in the bedroom doorway, a frown creeping across his brow. "People will talk."

"What people?" Annette Browning stepped back behind the anonymity of the curtain. "No one can see me."

"That man from next door can. I saw him pull up in a taxi earlier this morning. He's back."

"Is he? I didn't see him." Annette didn't know why she felt the need to lie. The words tripped off her tongue before she'd even realised.

"The boys will be back soon with the shopping and they'll be wanting their lunch. And what are we having for dinner tonight?"

Annette sighed and pulled her cardigan more firmly around her narrow shoulders. Lunch. Dinner. *Is that all I'm good for?* She pushed her way past her husband. "There are some pork medallions Adrian brought back from work yesterday. We'll have those tonight. The boys can have a sandwich for lunch."

Larry murmured his approval. "Good."

Making her way to the top of the stairs, Annette hesitated with one hand on the banister. Seeing the man from next door that morning had unnerved her. When she saw him from the window, he seemed to be staring right back at her. *As if he knew.* Shuddering, she turned back towards her husband.

"Why here, Larry. Why did you bring us here?" It was a question she'd asked many times over the last nine or so months — ever since their first day here. But she never got an answer. Not one she believed, anyway.

Larry gave a shrug, but avoided his wife's eyes. "Adrian needed us. We've been through this."

Annette almost snorted out loud. "Adrian? That's the reason you're giving for uprooting us all and bringing us here? We had a good life in Wales — we'd settled into the village and I'd started making friends. Why did you have to ruin it?"

"Like I said. The boy got himself into bother — *again*. We needed to come back for his sake."

"But *here*, Larry." A vulnerability entered her tone, her eyes sparkling with the promise of fresh tears. "*Here* of all places. Do you really want us to get caught? For everyone to find out what we did?"

Larry felt his jaw clench. *What you did*, he wanted to say — but he didn't. He never did. Instead, he found his face softening, as he reached forward to place a hand on his wife's arm. "Of course not."

"But it's so close, Larry." Annette's voice cracked. "*Too* close."

"Nonsense." Larry brushed past her and headed down the stairs. "You're imagining things, as usual. Come on — the boys will be back soon."

Annette hesitated on the landing, rubbing at her wet cheeks with the sleeve of her cardigan. It *was* too close, no matter what Larry said. Unless they were very careful, someone would find out — and everything from the last two decades would start to unravel before their very eyes.

And there would be very little anyone could do to stop it.

* * *

Bury St Edmunds Police Station

Nicki shrugged out of her coat, still damp with melted snowflakes, and hung it up to dry on the back of her office door. On the way back from visiting Ernest Fisher, she and Graham had called at the theatre. Faye and her team had now finished their business, but the theatre remained closed to the public. She'd wanted to ask Hugh Maxwell about why the doors were late opening last night — but the place was locked up and deserted. Leaving empty handed, they'd then swung past the Southgate Street roundabout scene before heading back to the station.

Crossing over to the ancient radiator beneath the window, she cranked the thermostat up as high as it would go. The pipes gurgled in protest but Nicki doubted they would elicit much more heat. Brushing the last of the snowflakes from her hair, she headed out into the corridor and towards the incident room. She'd missed a call from Caz, but before she returned it she wanted to find out where the team were at.

A hive of activity greeted her as she entered. DS Fox was already at the first whiteboard, updating it with the details they'd managed to glean from Ernest Fisher. The possibility that the perpetrator could very well have been waiting in the queue alongside him and his 'Old Codgers', made tracing the owners of the pre-booked tickets a high priority and also scrutinising the CCTV.

"Matt? Duncan?" Nicki crossed the floor. "How have you got on with that list of ticket holders?"

DC Matt Holland was staring intently at his computer monitor, a biro clenched between his teeth. "Getting there," he replied, the pen wobbling as he spoke. "We've spoken to a fair few already, but nothing's coming up. I've a list of names and addresses here if you want to take a look?" He tapped a sheet of paper by the side of his keyboard.

Nicki headed towards him and scanned the list of names.

"I got their dates of birth, too," continued Matt. "So we can see the age ranges. They're all pretty old. Looks like some kind of pensioners' night out."

Nicki put the list back down on Matt's desk. "Keep trawling. If anyone sounds shifty, or doesn't want to speak to us, flag them up. I don't fancy having to go and physically speak to each and every one of them — we don't have the manpower for that. So, let's try and eliminate who we can."

"I checked the CCTV from outside the theatre at the time the doors were opened." Matt brought up the images on his monitor. "Doors open at 6.15 p.m. — and no one comes out other than Hugh Maxwell."

Nicki peered over Matt's shoulder at the screen. "Well, that fits with what our Mr Fisher just told us. Maxwell apparently came out to apologise for the delay — saying it was due to a technical fault or staff sickness. We'll need to check that." Nicki watched the grainy images unfold. No one else left through the front doors until the first police patrol car arrived and theatregoers started emerging from the building once the discovery had been made. "OK. Have a look further back in the day. See what other comings and goings there were."

DC Duncan Jenkins held up a hand to catch Nicki's eye. "I've been checking out the staff members who were on duty that day. Again, nothing really flags up. They were short-staffed — three employees rang in sick that morning. I've spoken to the ones that were on duty, and they all sounded genuinely shocked. I'm just working on the cleaning company employees now."

"Get the names and contact details of the ones who rang in sick. We need to check them out as well. And give Hugh Maxwell a call — see if he can clarify the reason for the delay in opening the doors. It's probably nothing but let's check it out." Nicki headed over to the whiteboards, scanning them to see what else had been added during her absence. The second whiteboard had several crime scene photographs pinned to it depicting the discovery of the tongue on the roundabout, plus a photograph of the wolf and St Edmund. "What did you manage to get out of our skateboarder, if anything?" She turned around to focus on Darcie and Roy, who had just arrived back themselves.

Roy quickly got to his feet and joined Nicki at the whiteboard. "After we managed to rouse him from his bed, he didn't really tell us much more that we didn't already know. But . .

. there's something about him that doesn't quite ring true. I can't put my finger on it, but he was really nervous about speaking to us. And I don't think it was just because he'd stuffed a quantity of weed under his pillow before we arrived."

Nicki raised her eyebrows, but Roy shook his head. "Long story. Anyway. I just don't buy it. He claims he saw something odd when he came back from the skate park — thought there were spots of blood in the snow and went inside to tell his mum. But from what I can see at the scene, he wouldn't have been close enough to see anything. He said he was on his way home from the skate park — but he wouldn't have needed to go anywhere near the roundabout if that was true. Definitely not close enough to see spots of blood in the snow. The wolf sculpture is over the *other* side of the roundabout — wouldn't have seen it. But that's his story. He explained the delay in reporting it to us in that his mum was out at work, and he told her as soon as she got home." Roy paused and nodded at the whiteboard. "I've kept his name up there. I think we need to get him in for a formal statement. We both feel there's some-thing about his story that doesn't sit right."

Nicki pursed her lips as she eyed the whiteboard. "OK. I agree. Bring him in for a chat. And we also need to talk to the mum. I take it she wasn't in when you called?"

Roy shook his head. "No, out at work. Seems like the fourteen-year-old daughter, Kelsey, is running the house in the mother's absence."

"Keep at it. Try and pin the mother down and speak to her." Nicki scoured the rest of the board. "Who's following up on the St Edmund link for the tongue? And Sir Isaac Newton for the eyes?"

Darcie raised a hand. "Just on it now."

"OK, good. I doubt there's any significance in it. They're more than likely red herrings, so don't go falling down any historical rabbit holes. But we'll cover it just the same. And while you're at it, have a delve into Ernest Fisher's background. I don't think he was specifically targeted, but let's just tick that box."

Darcie turned her attention back to her screen while Nicki made her way back over to Matt's desk, taking hold of the list of theatregoers names once again. "The ones you've highlighted, Matt — are they the ones you haven't managed to speak to yet?"

Matt nodded, taking the biro out of his mouth. "Yep. Either didn't answer the phone or were unavailable to talk."

Nicki noticed that there were approximately a dozen names that Matt had highlighted. "OK, I'll take them with me back to my office — I'll give them another go. Keep doing what you're doing, guys. I'm going to speak to Caz at the mortuary — see if she has anything useful for us."

"I thought I'd head back and take a look at the alternative exit routes again." DS Fox reached for his coat and cane. "I thought about it when we called past today. I'll give Maxwell a call and get him to open up. Unless you need me here?"

Nicki shook her head. "No. You go — it's a good idea."

As Nicki made to follow Fox out of the incident room, Darcie caught her eye. In a low voice, she said, "Is he OK — Graham? To be back, I mean? Should he even be here?"

Nicki considered both questions before answering. "Whether he should be back or not is rather a moot point, Darcie — he's here. And we need all the help we can get. Anyway, you know what Graham's like. I think he's fed up of rattling around his flat on his own. We'll ease him in as gently as we can — he can do a lot of the desk work for us. Save his legs." Nicki paused. It was the other question that caused her issues. Was he OK? From what she'd seen of the detective sergeant yesterday, the old Graham Fox seemed to be back in full force, but . . . you could never quite tell. When something horrific and potentially life-changing happened, as it had to DS Fox just two months ago, you're never quite the same afterwards. Not entirely.

"He's doing OK," she eventually added.

* * *

4 Old Railways Cottages
Dullingham, Nr Newmarket

"Help your mother out, Adrian. She doesn't ask much of you." Larry Browning's face was taut.

"Why can't Mason do it? I've got to go to work in an hour." Adrian Browning grunted as he kicked off his trainers and headed for the stairs. "He gets away with murder."

Annette flinched as her youngest son stormed off upstairs, her face pinched, her eyes red.

Mason hovered in the kitchen doorway, then turned to start putting away the shopping. His brother always sneered at him for being the favourite, 'goody-goody' son — but all Mason wanted to do was keep the peace. His mother looked like she was about to cry — if she hadn't been already.

What was it with this family all of a sudden? Things had been tense ever since they'd left Wales.

Not long after moving he'd found two bottles of anti-depressants in the upstairs bathroom, in among all the pain-killers, both prescribed to his mother. It had shocked him a little. He knew she'd been upset at the move, but . . .

Hearing his brother crashing around in his bedroom upstairs, expletives ricocheting off the walls at regular inter-vals, Mason concentrated on putting the remaining shopping away. Adrian had such a temper at times, it was often best to just leave him alone until he calmed down.

He'd been told Adrian was the reason they'd uprooted from Wales — he'd got himself into a mess over some girl and managed to get himself thrown out of his flat. Apparently, he needed help to get settled again. But Mason didn't necessarily buy it. Adrian didn't look like someone who needed their help. And he certainly wasn't grateful.

With a sigh, Mason folded the empty shopping bags and put them under the sink and watched his parents disappear into the front room, the door closing behind them.

Something was up — he knew that much.

He just didn't know what it was.

CHAPTER ELEVEN

Bury St Edmunds Police Station

Outside, the late afternoon light was beginning to fade fast. Soon, everywhere would be plunged into an inky blackness with just the odd streetlight attempting to penetrate the gloom. With more heavy snowfall due overnight, it was a war that wouldn't be won anytime soon.

Nicki drew the blinds across the window and settled back down at her desk to continue ploughing through the list of theatregoers. She'd managed to speak to eight out of the dozen highlighted on the list, and had quickly ruled each of them out. As Matt had mentioned earlier, they were all pensioners and hardly fit the profile of the person they were looking for. That's not to say pensioners couldn't kill — far from it. But gut instinct went a long way in this job. Additionally, the majority of the theatregoers on the list were female — once again, an unlikely demographic for a sadistic killer.

Killer.

The word sent ice through Nicki's veins. Although they hadn't found any bodies — yet — she was increasingly certain they were looking for a killer. Maybe more than one. A quick Google search had confirmed it was possible for someone to survive after having their eyes gouged out, and even their tongue — but the situation didn't bode well.

Nicki shivered. Ever since Matt had shown her the CCTV of Ernest Fisher waiting outside the theatre, she'd been trying to connect the dots. Although they couldn't entirely dismiss the idea that the perpetrator was a member of staff, or the cleaning crew, there was still the chance that whoever it was had been outside waiting for the doors to open — slipping up to the Dress Circle while Ernest and his companions waited in the foyer. The timings were tight, but not impossible. Without CCTV inside the theatre, they were running blind.

Graham had just rung in — he'd managed to get back inside the theatre after a fashion, dragging Hugh Maxwell in to open up. He'd had a good look around, noting the available fire exits. Without a working alarm, the one closest to the Dress Circle appeared to be the most likely candidate. Nicki had told him to get off home and be in bright and early tomorrow.

Just as she was about to pick up the phone again to call the next person on the list, the handset began to trill.

"DI Hardcastle." Nicki tried to inject some enthusiasm into her tone. She felt exhausted and her head pounded. Apart from a couple of nibbles at the ham and cheese toastie DS Fox had given her earlier that morning, she hadn't eaten a thing all day.

"Hey," greeted the voice on the other end of the line. "Finally managed to track you down."

Nicki smiled, recognising Caz's soft Irish accent. "Hey, yourself. It's been a busy old day."

"Well, I've managed to take a look at both of your specimens." Nicki could hear Caz clear her throat before she continued. "I'll put it all in a report but essentially they were skilfully excised. Surgically, I would say. This was no amateur."

Nicki's stomach clenched. "A professional? You mean a doctor? A surgeon?"

"Who knows? But it's definitely someone who knew what they were doing. I've taken blood and tissue samples, and we're running a DNA profile. It could take a while."

"Without the DNA, can you tell me if it's the same person?"

Nicki knew the answer without really needing to hear it, and knew her friend would be shaking her head on the other end of the line.

"No. But I can tell you they have the same blood type — O positive. It's pretty common though, so doesn't really move you forward all that much."

"Thanks, anyway."

"No problem. Amy tells me we're having a wine night tomorrow?"

Nicki's stomach fell. Tomorrow. She'd forgotten. "Maybe," she managed to reply, rubbing her eyes at the thought of another late night.

"There's no maybe about it," continued Caz. "Doctor's orders. You're looking a bit peaky."

Despite her tiredness, Nicki couldn't help but give a small laugh. "And wine's the answer, is it?"

"One of them — it's very well documented."

Nicki gave a smile. "See you tomorrow."

* * *

The Farmhouse

He had slept late — a full twelve hours, which was unusual for him — waking up in the snug with the fire in the grate long since extinguished. After a long shower, he emerged refreshed, ready for the tasks of the day.

And today was going to be a good day — he could feel it in his bones.

Bones.

He'd been dreaming during the night — images of his father's body map flickering through his unconsciousness like an old 1920s silent movie. He could almost hear his father's booming voice.

'Carpals, boy! Carpals!'

Despite the pain from the crack of the leather-tipped cane that invariably followed, he welcomed the memory.

With a fresh mug of coffee in his hand, he continued on through to the pantry, spying the bloodied cloth containing Lucie's hand still sitting on the shelf. Remaining in the chilled pantry overnight, it had yet to start decomposing properly.

His smile widened behind his mug. Today would be Lucie's turn to take the stage.

Plucking his phone from his pocket, he logged on to his social media accounts and began to scroll. People were so careless these days — detailing their every move, their every meal. Even the thoughts inside their heads. Nothing was secret any more. Private lives had suddenly become so very, very public.

Which was what had led him to both Jacqui and Lucie in the end. And what would lead him to the others.

He chuckled beneath his breath as he took a mouthful of strong, bitter coffee. Both had been such clever girls in some respects — but oh so naive in others. They really did know how to make things easy for him.

Jacqui had been the easiest of the two to track — she posted constantly, every day, letting the world know her thoughts. Where she was, but also where she wasn't. Who she was with — and who she *wanted* to be with. Post after post — a constant stream, letting the world know everything about her.

It really was too easy in the end.

The estate agency website displayed photographs of all their employees — and Jacqui Massingham, senior negotiator, had instantly caught his attention. Or, at least, her eyes had. He followed up with a visit to the agency, intent on getting a glimpse of them for real — feigning interest in purchasing a three-bedroomed house in the town for his growing, non-existent family.

And Jacqui had been very obliging — smiling as she showed him a variety of properties that suited his needs.

It had taken all his strength and willpower not to just grab her there and then.

And once he had her name — displayed on the work badge pinned to her blouse — the real fun could begin.

She was everywhere — Facebook, Instagram, Twitter. Her entire life was a series of status updates, shared memes, and snapshots of homemade videos. Within a few minutes he felt like he knew her entire life history — a life that was about to be cut short.

* * *

Saturday 22 December 2018
Woodpecker Drive, Bury St Edmunds

Jacqui Massingham pulled up outside the front of her modest semi-detached house and expelled a huge sigh. It was her last day at work for two whole weeks — and she intended to spend a lot of it asleep. She'd been running herself into the ground over the last couple of months and it was starting to take its toll. But Christmas was coming, and she was intending to enjoy it for once.

Alone.

She'd been looking forward to it for weeks — marking the days off on the calendar and posting a countdown on her Facebook page. Time alone over Christmas and New Year with just herself for company. She could eat what she wanted, drink what she wanted, watch what she wanted on TV. She could stay up all night and watch cringe-worthy Christmas films. *If she wanted.* The mere thought made her shiver with pleasure.

Adrian had controlled her life for far too long — and the worst of it was, she'd let him. But now she was free — free of him and the hold he'd had over her for more years than she cared to remember. It felt invigorating.

As she exited the car, she quickly banished the face that popped unannounced into her head.

Slamming the car door shut, she took in a deep breath. The air was cold and, from the charred wood aroma on the wind, someone was having a bonfire nearby. The papers were saying the whole country was due a long, cold snap — something to do with the jet stream — and maybe even a white Christmas for once. Perfect. Holed up at home, snow falling and nowhere to be for a full fortnight.

And no Adrian.

Even better.

Smiling, she made her way towards the garden path that led around the back of the house. She always preferred to come and go through the back door — something she'd picked up from her childhood. She could vividly remember her grandmother's home back in Doncaster, where the front door was hardly ever used — in fact, she couldn't remember ever seeing it open. Instead, everyone came and went through the back — the door always kept 'on the latch' for people to come and go as they pleased.

The only time she recalled seeing anyone enter through the front door was on the night before her grandmother's funeral. She may have only been ten years old, but Jacqui remembered it like it was yesterday. The undertakers knocking on the front door and bringing her grandmother's coffin inside for one last night.

So now she did the same.

Except for keeping the door on the latch. Not in this day and age — she wasn't that stupid.

The garden path was narrow, but she knew her way around even on the darkest of nights. The moonlight above had been snuffed out by a blanket of low-lying cloud, pregnant with the promise of snow, but she easily picked her way along the gravel path until she reached the back garden.

The first inkling that something wasn't quite right struck her when the security light didn't come on. Usually it triggered as soon as she reached the end of the path and turned the corner — so sensitive that at various points during the night she would see it flash on and off, detecting an array of foxes, birds and cats prowling through her garden.

But not tonight.

Tutting, Jacqui felt for the side of the house with her hand to guide her — feeling the reassuring roughness of the brickwork beneath her fingers. She'd check the security light tomorrow — maybe it just needed a new bulb or something. All she wanted to do right now was sink into a hot bath with a generously sized gin and tonic.

The second inkling that something wasn't quite right was the figure standing by the back door. At least, she *thought* it was a figure — it was difficult to see for sure in the inky blackness.

Her heart sank. "Adrian? Is that you?" Maybe he hadn't quite got the message like she'd hoped.

Taking a hesitant step forward, her hand still on the brickwork, Jacqui felt her heart starting to race. "Just get out of the way, Adrian. Let me through."

The face advanced quickly out of the gloom. With a gasp, she took in the dark balaclava shrouding the figure's head and the pair of menacing eyes boring straight into hers.

"Adrian?"

But before she could even try to turn and run, her world turned black.

* * *

Friday 28 December 2018
The Farmhouse

Taking another mouthful of the now cooling bitter coffee, he trailed a finger over the body map pinned to the pantry wall.

Jacqui had been relatively easy — Lucie had been a little harder to crack.

He'd first seen her in the bakery, catching sight of her perfectly sculptured hand as she passed him his change. He remarked upon the tattoo, and got a coy laugh in response. He knew there and then that he wanted her — *needed* her for his collection.

For his map.

It hadn't taken long to find out who she was. Her badge said her name was Lucie and she was 'here to help'. All he needed to do was follow her home from work one night to get her home address, followed by a quick rummage in her wheelie bin for her surname.

Lucie Ballantine.

It sounded to him like 'ballerina' — which suited her petite and graceful hands.

His mother had been a performer. A dancer. And from what Laurence could remember, which wasn't much, she'd moved with elegance and grace — as if she were walking on air. He pushed the thought of his mother out of his head, and turned his thoughts back to Lucie.

Social media had, once again, done the rest of his work for him — and he soon found out that she was taking time off work over the festive period, just like Jacqui. Which slotted perfectly into his plans. No one was expecting her to show up for work and there was no one at home to miss her — he already knew she lived alone.

She posted enough about that every day.

The rest had fallen into place without much effort on his part.

* * *

Sunday 23 December 2018
Ravenwood Close, Bury St Edmunds

Lucie Ballantine's feet ached to within an inch of their lives — so much for the new pair of boots she'd bought for the winter. She couldn't wait to kick them off and sink her feet into the new plush pile carpet that had just been laid in the front room. She'd almost finished renovating the house — just one more room and then she was done.

Finished.

It had been a lot harder than she'd envisaged, taking on a house that needed so much doing to it. Fresh out of a relationship, she'd decided to buy a house in an area of the town she loved, but which was in need of some 'care and attention' — that was what the estate agent had told her. Just how much hadn't really dawned on Lucie until she'd moved in.

Thankfully, it was mostly cosmetic — the only major jobs had been a complete electrical rewiring, and then a new kitchen and bathroom. The rest had been decorating and laying new carpets — all of which was now coming to an end, the renovations entering their final stages.

And she now had a whole ten days off work in which to enjoy it. Maybe she'd tackle the spare room upstairs — but, then again, maybe she wouldn't. She needed a rest and some time to herself. She'd toyed with the idea of booking a spa week somewhere, time to really indulge and unwind — but it was Christmas and all the prices had shot through the roof. So, instead, she was going to spend the time at home. She'd stocked up on food and drink — treating herself to a few bottles of wine, a new flavoured vodka, lots of chocolate and festive shortbread. A few days of eating, drinking and Netflix was *exactly* what the doctor ordered. The spa week could wait for better weather.

The thought buoyed her as she pulled her scarf closer around her neck and continued along the alleyway that led to the rear of the house. The line of terraced houses had their own parking area and garages to the rear, with a narrow alleyway connecting to each of their back garden gates. It was one of the reasons she'd bought the house — off road parking was in short supply anywhere in the town, plus a large garage would be ideal for storage.

Another reason had been its close proximity to the pub. When the weather improved, Lucie could see herself becoming a regular.

The only problem with the alleyway was the dark. It wasn't lit at all at night and was some distance away from the nearest street light. Some of her neighbours had talked about clubbing together to get some security lights fitted, but that was all it had been so far. Talk.

But in all honesty, Lucie didn't really mind the dark. Even as a child, she'd never been scared. Never worried about monsters lurking under the bed, or the bogey man hiding in her wardrobe. Instead, she'd enjoyed plunging her room into near-total blackness, diving under the covers and reading by torchlight, munching on clandestine sweets and chocolate.

Lucie's house was the end terrace. Accessed via a tall wooden back gate, it led into a small courtyard garden which she hadn't yet tackled. That would be her job for the spring — she intended to sow herbs and vegetables in several of the raised beds. There was also a small brick outhouse in the corner that she planned to rip down and either replace with a greenhouse, or convert into a gym.

Tomatoes or dumbbells.

She hadn't quite decided.

Lifting the latch on the back gate, she stepped through into the enclosed rear garden, darkness immediately enveloping her.

She knew she should get a light for the garden — one of those motion sensor ones that came on when you stepped into range. Or maybe some solar powered garden lights to place in the flowerbeds. But winter had steadily crept up on her, and suddenly the light evenings were replaced with dark frosty ones.

Despite the dark, she knew where she was stepping, and soon skirted around the largest raised bed. With her eyes fixed on the back door, she felt for the key in her pocket.

She heard the sound before she saw anything move. It was soft and subtle, but a sound just the same. The Wilsons next door had a cat that liked to spend most of its time in Lucie's back garden, so she fully expected to see the sleek outline of the ginger Tom coming through the gloom.

But no cat emerged.

The hairs on the back of her neck began to bristle.

I can hear someone breathing.

And it's coming from behind me.

Frozen to the spot, key in hand, Lucie dared not move an inch.

Any thought that it would be next door's cat instantly evaporated, and Lucie lunged towards the back door.

Just let me get inside.

Just let me get inside.

But feeling the advancing breath on her neck, she knew it was too late. All she saw next was the hand in front of her face, then darkness.

* * *

Friday 28 December 2018
The Farmhouse

Finishing the dregs of his coffee, Laurence turned his attention to the contents of the pantry shelves. With Lucie and Jacqui safely tucked away inside the freezer, it was time to prepare for the next one to join them.

He certainly had enough ketamine to keep them sedated — and had even obtained a quantity of midazolam as a backup, both surprisingly easy to get hold of if you knew where to look. And he'd already prepared the concoction that would render his next victim unconscious — the bottle of diethyl ether was sitting patiently on one of the lower shelves. Held in front of the nose and mouth, unconsciousness followed in seconds.

Yes — he was ready.

But first he needed to deal with Lucie.

Her hand was still sitting on the shelving, wrapped in its bloodied cloth. Reaching for the cloth, he placed Lucie's severed hand inside a small, square plastic bag. He knew exactly where he was going to take her, and grinned at his own ingenuity. It would be difficult, risky even — maybe his riskiest yet. He'd need to be both quick and cautious. Rush in too fast and you risked drawing unnecessary attention to yourself — take it too slowly and, well, you might miss the opportunity altogether.

He felt a fluttering in the base of his stomach.

He remembered his mother telling him about first-night nerves — the feeling she got just before going out on stage for the first time. And how she channelled those feelings into something else — an inner calm, an inner confidence.

It was where he got it from, he supposed. His confidence. Certainly not from his father, that was for sure. Laurence Hemmingway Sr merely displayed arrogance.

And there was a whole world of difference between arrogance and confidence.

Arrogance could get you caught.

* * *

4 Old Railway Cottages
Dullingham, Nr Newmarket

Annette Browning shook the pills into the palm of her hand, her whole body trembling. She wasn't quite sure why she'd snapped at Larry earlier — it wasn't his fault. They'd both lived with this secret for more than twenty years now — it was the glue that bound them together — so why was today any different?

But today was different. And so would tomorrow be. And the day after.

Everyone was feeling the tension. Adrian was being his usual hot-headed self — flying off the handle at the smallest thing — and Mason . . . poor Mason was getting caught in the crossfire. She'd hated asking Mason to move back home: not when he'd got his own place and settled down with that nice girl. But she hadn't really asked him; he'd offered — saying that he and Olivia had split up anyway, and he could do with saving money on the rent. Larry did what he could for her, but it wasn't easy. Her body was so wracked with pain from widespread osteoarthritis that sometimes even getting out of bed was agony. The bathroom cupboard was stuffed full of any variety of painkillers, Annette was surprised she didn't rattle when she walked.

But none of this would have happened if they'd just stayed in Wales.

"Annette?" Larry's head appeared around the doorframe.

Annette quickly threw the pills into her mouth and dry swallowed. She turned on the tap and began to splash her face with cool water.

"Annie?" Larry stepped into the small en-suite. "What's wrong?"

Annette could feel herself bristle. How could he not know what was wrong? Ignoring him, she pushed past and headed into the bedroom. "I'm going to lie down for a bit. There are more sandwiches in the fridge for the boys if they're still hungry. I don't feel too good."

"It'll be all right, you know."

Annette felt herself tense. *It'll be all right.*

Hadn't those been her words to him all those years ago? That what they'd done — what *she'd* done — would be all right?

A wave of nausea started to engulf her as she reached for her dressing gown.

"Just give me some peace, Larry. Please."

CHAPTER TWELVE

Friday 28 December 2018
St Edmundsbury Cathedral

The snow from earlier had eased off and the congregation for Evensong was larger than Hettie Knox had expected.

"Come on, Len," she puffed, shuffling along the central aisle towards her chosen pew. "Stop dawdling. They'll be wanting to start soon."

Hettie never missed a Friday night Evensong. Well, hardly ever. The last time had been when she'd been housebound with a bout of shingles.

She reached the pew — *her pew* — always the same row, always the same seat.

Len had shown her to this particular pew when he'd first brought her to the cathedral some fifty years ago — and they'd kept the same seats ever since.

Slipping off her coat, she folded it up and put it on Len's seat to give him something soft to sit on — now he was getting on a bit, he found the hard wood a little unforgiving on his rear. Then she bent down to place her handbag on the stone floor, grimacing at her protesting joints as she straightened up.

The rows behind were quickly filling up and it wasn't long before the organist began playing. Hettie began to hum along to the haunting melody. She knew Len would be tutting good-naturedly by her side, and it made her smile even more. She glanced to the side and gave him a sly wink.

The choir were now filing in from the rear of the cathedral, each dressed in crisp, white robes. Once in the chancel, the first psalm of the service began — Psalm 32, one Hettie knew well.

Once the psalm was over, the dean began the first reading. Hettie settled back in her seat, listening to the dean's melodic tone as he read from Kings 4:25. She let her eyes close and soon the organist began again, the choir in perfect harmony as another psalm filled the cathedral.

Hettie's mind drifted as the dean's voice again wafted over the congregation — reading this time from Mark 3:19. In a state of pure contentment, it wasn't long before Hettie heard the beginning to the Apostles' Creed.

In days gone by, Hettie would have knelt on the cathedral floor to pray, but the arthritis in her knees prevented that these days. So, she stayed seated. But before bowing her head to pray, she leaned down to the side to pull out Len's hassock from underneath the pew.

Len was a kneeler — always had been. But even his knees needed something soft.

"Are you kneeling?" she whispered, tugging out the hassock. Glancing down, the smile very quickly slid from her face, replaced with one of wide-eyed horror.

It took several seconds for the scream to be released from her mouth.

* * *

4 Old Railway Cottages
Dullingham, Nr Newmarket

Annette stood once again by the window, masked from sight by the curtain. She'd only managed to doze fitfully, too restless for sleep. Her body ached but her mind refused to cooperate. He'd been in and out of the house that afternoon — the man from next door. She'd heard the door bang and the engine starting.

She wondered where he was going.

No matter how silly it sounded, she was still sure he knew something — knew something about them. *Their secret.*

She swallowed, her mouth feeling dry.

She'd also heard Adrian go out not long ago — the sound of his van roaring into life pulling her away from her quest for sleep. That meant it was just Larry and Mason home tonight — something she would usually look forward to.

But now all she could feel was a gnawing sensation inside — a creeping, sickening feeling that the world they had built so carefully was about to come crashing down around them.

They can never know, she told herself as she turned away from the empty window.

The boys can never know.

* * *

St Edmundsbury Cathedral

The call came in just as Nicki was about to grab her coat. Her heart sank. So much for getting away on time for once. She'd sent Darcie and Roy home not long ago — Matt and Duncan insisted on staying to trawl through yet more CCTV.

The journey to the cathedral took a matter of minutes — being literally around the corner from the station. When she'd heard what had happened, Nicki was surprised she hadn't heard poor Mrs Knox's screams for herself.

Nicki introduced herself at the main entrance and was quickly swept inside. The only people now in the cathedral were the crime scene investigators, who had already begun to set up the usual cordons and barriers, and DS Graham Fox. Fox had been passing the front entrance on his way back from the theatre when the commotion had first kicked off, and it was he who'd put the call through to the station.

She was guided along a set of stepping plates down the main central aisle, stopping at the tape marking the inner cordon. With no protective suit to hand, Nicki was forced to watch from afar. Fox arrived at her side.

"Graham. Tell me what's happened."

"From what I can gather, it seems our witness was sitting in her usual seat — or pew, if you want to call it that — just over there." Fox pointed to where two scene of crime investigators were processing the rows of wooden seating away to their right. "It was about twenty minutes or so into the proceedings — just when they were about to say a prayer. Mrs Knox doesn't kneel, her knees won't let her, but she pulled out a kneeler for her husband."

"Husband?" Nicki frowned. "I wasn't aware we had another witness. Where is he?"

"No idea," shrugged Fox. "Mrs Knox has been taken to a private room near the café for a cup of tea. I assume he's with her."

Nicki nodded. "Go on."

"Well, she pulls out one of the kneelers from beneath the pew — and when she looks down, she sees it."

"The hand?"

Fox nodded. "Yes. Severed just above the wrist."

Nicki craned her neck a little, but couldn't see past the first few pews. "I take it we're getting statements from anyone who was here? The rest of the congregation?"

Fox nodded again. "Happening as we speak. They're all in the café where we've got uniforms taking their details. I can see if we can blag some protective suits if you want to get closer?"

"No, let's give them some space to get on." Nicki stepped away from the cordon and surveyed the rest of the cathedral. "We need to find out how many people might have been in here during the day. When was the last service?"

"This one started around half five. But the whole cathedral's open to the public throughout the day, so I think we'll struggle to get much of an idea as to when it might have been deposited."

Nicki bit her lip in frustration. "You're right. It'll be hard to establish a timeline on this one. Let's go and see our Mrs Knox."

The room next to the café wasn't far away, and Hettie was sitting nursing a mug of strong tea when Nicki and Fox entered. Beneath the harsh overhead lighting, she looked every one of her seventy-nine years. Maybe a few more.

"Mrs Knox?" Nicki slowly approached, but the woman didn't seem to react, continuing to stare down at the stone floor beneath her feet. It was only when Nicki's own feet entered her field of vision that the woman flinched and looked up.

"Sorry. I didn't mean to startle you." Nicki pulled across a velvet footstool and sat down. "How are you feeling? It must have been a terrible shock for you."

"Oh, I mustn't grumble," replied Hettie, her lips trembling as she spoke.

"Well, you've had a shock." Nicki placed a hand on the old woman's forearm, feeling the tremor beneath her touch. "And I hope there's sugar in that." She nodded at the mug in Hettie's grasp.

The woman managed a weak smile. "I don't usually take sugar. My Len does — two and a half teaspoons. And he can always tell if you leave off the half."

"I'm Detective Inspector Nicki Hardcastle. Are you feeling up to talking about what happened here tonight?"

"Oh, yes." Hettie's pale green eyes took on a new ferocity. "I've never seen anything quite like it in my life."

"Tell me what happened. Start from when you first arrived at the cathedral."

The old woman took a sip of her too-sweet tea and began. "Well, I'd been looking forward to coming tonight — Evensong is one of my favourite services. I haven't been able to get out much lately, what with the cold weather and my knees. But everything seemed normal when we arrived. Len and I headed down to our usual pew — we always sit in the same place, you see. Always have done — ever since we first came here in 1968."

"Len's your husband?"

Hettie nodded.

"And what happened when you made your way to your seats?"

"Well . . . nothing. Nothing out of the ordinary, anyway. We shuffled along the pew and got ourselves settled. I took off my coat and folded it up on Len's seat. He likes something soft to sit on now, you see."

Nicki smiled. "And you didn't see anybody walking away from your pew as you arrived?"

Hettie shook her head. "No, not that I recall. But I don't suppose I was really looking. There were quite a few people coming in by that time — it's quite a popular service — and it was so cold outside."

"If you feel up to it, can you tell me how you made the discovery?"

A cloud crossed the old woman's features. "Well, it was all very shocking, as you can imagine. You don't expect to see something like that, do you? Not in a cathedral." Nicki gave Hettie's hand a squeeze. "It was just as we were about to say the first prayer. I pulled out one of the hassocks for Len — I can't get down there anymore but my Len likes to kneel." She gave a small chuckle but Nicki noticed the laughter was somewhat hollow. "So, I pulled out the kneeler for him."

"And?"

"Well, there it was — just sitting there. A hand."

Nicki nodded. "I'm so sorry you had to find it, Mrs Knox. Is your husband still here? Can we have a word with him before you go?"

Hettie held on to Nicki's gaze and eventually gave a sad smile. "Oh, my Len isn't here, Inspector. Well, he's here, but he's not actually *here* — if you get what I mean?"

Nicki frowned. She didn't. "I'm sorry, I'm not sure I understand."

"If you need to speak to him — my Len — you'll find him over in the cemetery these days. Two rows back from that lovely new rose bush they've planted."

Nicki stared open mouthed, unsure quite what to say. "Oh, I see . . . well . . ."

It was Hettie who now reached forward to squeeze Nicki's hand. "I'm not mad, my dear. I know my Len's dead. Has been for the best part of ten years now. But he's still with me in here." She tapped her chest, just above her heart. "And in here." She tapped the side of her head. "He used to love coming to the services here at the cathedral. Always in awe of the beautiful interior — no matter how many times he'd seen it. I do truly feel like he's here with me." She gave another squeeze of Nicki's hand. "But I'm not going doolally. Even when I pull out the cushion for him to kneel on, I know he's not really going to use it. But it's a comfort to me — I miss him so much. I guess it sounds silly saying it out loud."

Nicki felt a lump rise up inside her throat as she saw the raw grief still shadowing the old woman's eyes. Even after a decade she still felt the pain of her own loss.

Clearing her throat, Nicki got to her feet. "I know you're not doolally, Mrs Knox," she smiled. "Far from it. Grief never really leaves you, I know that much." Slipping out one of her business cards from her pocket, Nicki leaned down and placed it inside the old woman's trembling hands. "If you think of anything else, just give me a call."

Back outside, Nicki caught Fox's eye. "Let's leave the scene of crime guys to do their thing. They'll call us with any updates I'm sure." Pulling her coat around her, she headed out on to the street. She hadn't seen either Cassie or Faye inside and with this now being the third crime scene in twenty-four hours, she wondered just how far the department could stretch its finite resources before it snapped completely.

"What are you thinking, boss? Same person?" Fox followed Nicki across the street, his cane tapping on the ice.

Nicki shuddered as the ice-cold blast from the quickening wind outside hit her face. "I don't know, Graham. Eyes and tongue. Now this? I've no idea if we're looking at one victim . . . or . . ." She left the rest of the sentence unsaid.

"No hits on DNA I suppose?"

"Not yet. It'll be a long shot anyway. The chances of them being on the system are minute."

"I'll give the missing persons database another go — see if we've overlooked anyone. At least we can get fingerprints from the hand."

Nicki led them to where she'd parked her car. "Don't work late again tonight, Graham. This can all be done in the morning. None of the results will be in anytime soon." She pulled open the driver's door. "I'm taking you home. That's an order."

CHAPTER THIRTEEN

The Farmhouse

Slamming the van door shut, he tried to imagine what was going on inside the cathedral — the thought brought a lopsided grin to his face. Lucie would be found tonight, he was sure — it was a popular service. But if she wasn't, soon enough the maggots and flies would descend — followed by the smell. Decaying flesh had a particularly pungent aroma.

Placing Lucie's hand on the cushion had gone surprisingly smoothly. No one had taken any notice of him kneeling in the pew, head bowed as if in prayer. He'd been tempted to stay — join the congregation at the back and wait to see the show commence — but knew that would be inviting fate.

He wasn't stupid.

Pushing open the front door to the farmhouse, he made his way to the kitchen where he knew the range cooker would welcome him with warmth — even if everywhere else was cold and desolate.

But it hadn't always been that way. When his grandfather had been alive, the farmhouse was full of warmth and laughter — family mealtimes around the kitchen table; fresh bread on the worktop; a stew or pie cooling on the stove.

Laurence had been ecstatic when his father announced they were going to live permanently at his grandfather's farm. Not just for the odd weekend. Not just for the holidays. But *forever*. He could remember the day they moved in. Grandfather had been out on his tractor and Laurence had run the full length of the wheat field to greet him.

His grandfather was a hard worker — out in the fields long before the sun came up, often not finished until it sank back below the horizon. No one worked as hard as George Frederick Hemmingway.

Hating the time he had to waste in school, hankering to be back in the fields on the farm, young Laurence would play truant more times than he cared to remember. Much to his father's displeasure.

'There's no future in farming, boy,' a phrase his father would repeat on an almost daily basis. "The medical profession is where you're heading." But Laurence would sit at the window, enviously watching his grandfather toiling the fields day after day. There was always plenty of food on the table, fresh bread baked daily on the stove. Meat would always be hanging in the pantry. To him, watching from the window, farming seemed the idyllic lifestyle.

Laurence shook his head, stirring himself from his memories and flicked on the kettle.

He wished his grandfather was still with him now — he missed his sunny smile, his calm manner, the way he'd reach out and ruffle Laurence's hair before climbing aboard the tractor. Life had seemed so uncomplicated back then.

But the idyllic lifestyle didn't last long.

For one day in July, just over twenty years ago, life at the farm changed forever.

18 July 1997.

The day Laurence Hemmingway Jnr encountered death for the very first time.

Little did he realise, at eight years old, it wouldn't be the last.

* * *

It was a glorious summer's day — a cloudless blue sky that stretched for miles. The day that would be forever etched into his memory.

For at 3.22 p.m. on Friday 18 July, under the cloudless blue sky, little Laurence Hemmingway's grandfather died.

Death occurred from time to time on the farm, he knew that. His grandfather kept cattle, sheep and pigs — and every so often they would disappear in the back of the local abattoir's van. He might only be eight years' old, but he wasn't stupid.

But today was different. This wasn't an animal bred for slaughter. This was a person; a human being.

This was his *grandfather.*

Laurence had skipped school — again. His father had enrolled him in the local summer school to keep him busy during the holidays, and classes had just started — but Laurence hated every second, and played truant whenever he could. If his father found out, he knew he'd be whipped. Or worse. Apparently, he wasn't going to become a doctor if he carried on like that, so his father would shout at him as he lashed out with the leather-tipped cane. But Laurence didn't really want to be a doctor — or, at least, his eight-year-old head didn't think he did. There were far more exciting things to be.

An explorer. A racing car driver. *A farmer.*

Whatever the motivation, the morning of July 18 heralded the perfect day to skip school. He'd hidden in the hedgerow as the bus trundled down the lane, and stayed there until his father's car drove past on his way to London. After plucking the twigs and leaves out of his hair, he'd run as fast as his legs would carry him back towards the farm.

Grandfather didn't mind if he skipped school — he would merely put a gnarled finger to his lips and give him a wink. And sure enough, when George Frederick Hemmingway saw his grandson scampering over the field towards him, he tapped the seat on the rusting tractor and helped the young boy clamber aboard.

Much of the hay harvest had already been brought in, and all three hay barns were almost full to bursting. It had been a bumper crop and the farm would do well for animal feed through the coming winter. Today they would bring in the last of the bales, and then they could turn their attention to the barley fields.

It was backbreaking, sweltering work — and by lunchtime they were both sweating like pigs and sporting red foreheads. His grandfather had had the foresight to wear a cap, but Laurence could feel his own scalp tight and tender beneath his hair from the intense rays overhead.

They took a break in the shade of a tree, leaning up against the trunk beside a dried-up stream. The lack of rainfall had been good for the harvest, but not so good for the watercourses around the farm — or the wildlife that lived within them.

His grandfather had made a huge doorstep sandwich for lunch, thick with butter, cheese and pickle — and tore it in half to share. The bread had been freshly baked early that morning and tasted like heaven on earth. Laurence didn't know how his grandfather found the time to bake his own bread, as well as run the farm — whenever he asked, the old man merely tapped the side of his sunburnt nose and gave another wink. "There's always time in the day if you make it, sonny," he would say.

He'd never known his grandmother. She'd died before Laurence was born. There were pictures up in the main farmhouse, but nobody really spoke about her. Once or twice he'd catch his grandfather staring at one of the photographs, a tear in his eye.

At a little after two o'clock they made their way back to the farmhouse. His grandfather told him to go inside and get himself washed up, while he went to put the final bales in the barn.

Laurence wasn't sure precisely when it was that he began to think something was wrong. Maybe it was when his grandfather didn't come back from the barn — or maybe it was something else. Just a feeling that something wasn't quite right — that something had shifted in the ether.

Leaving the farmhouse, the young Laurence looked around the yard — but he still couldn't see any sign of his grandfather. Everything was quiet and peaceful. The old sheepdog, Dolly, was having a doze beneath the shade of the porch, and the chickens were inside the hen house, sheltering from the heat. An eerie stillness enveloped the yard as he made his way out towards the barns.

He could see the rusting tractor parked close to the first barn and his heart momentarily lightened. His grandfather must still be unloading the bales.

As he approached, the feeling that something was wrong intensified.

It was quiet.

Too quiet.

Something was wrong.

The first barn was stacked up to the rafters with thick hay bales, no room for anything else and certainly no room for his grandfather. Laurence moved across to the second barn and saw a mirror image of the first. It wasn't until he rounded the tractor and stepped towards the third barn that he saw it.

Several hay bales had spilled out into the yard, randomly scattered and coming to rest haphazardly across the tinder-dry, dusty ground. He felt a frown form on his hot brow. The bales shouldn't have fallen like that — not when they'd been stacked properly. And grandfather *always* stacked them properly.

The sense of disquiet grew the closer he got to the third barn. It became clear that it wasn't just a couple of bales that had become dislodged — a whole stack had collapsed inside the barn itself.

He found his grandfather's body at 3.22 p.m. He checked the time on his new digital watch.

Not knowing what else to do, Laurence merely sat there holding his grandfather's hand and waited for his father to come home. He'd known the old man was dead the moment he'd found him. His pale grey eyes empty and dulled, staring up towards the top of the barn and cloudless summer sky beyond. He tried to move the bales that had fallen, but they were far too heavy to shift.

So, instead, he sat.

And he waited.

As he did so, he began to ponder his grandfather's life — and for the first time in his eight years on earth, he began to think about death.

Had his grandfather known what was about to happen? Had he sensed it, in those final few precious seconds as the hay bales came tumbling down? What went through his mind in those final few moments of clarity? Panic? Fear?

His father arrived home from work at a little before nine-thirty that night, and found young Laurence still holding his grandfather's hand inside the hay barn.

His father's reaction surprised young Laurence. There was no sadness, no sudden rush to see if there was anything he could do. He'd merely told his son to go back to the farmhouse and get ready for dinner.

They'd sat in silence around the kitchen table, eating the ham hock pie that his grandfather had made that morning, along with the freshly baked bread. No words were spoken. No questions were asked. Once the meal was finished, Laurence was merely sent to bed.

And when he woke the next morning, his grandfather was gone.

Yes — Friday 18 July at 3.22 p.m. was firmly etched into Laurence Hemmingway's memory.

* * *

Friday 28 December 2018
The Farmhouse

Laurence splashed hot water into his mug and stirred.

His grandfather had had the last laugh though — leaving the farm in trust for Laurence until his eighteenth birthday, when the farm finally became his.

His.

Laurence looked around at the thick stone walls of the farmhouse kitchen and smiled. It wasn't everyone's idea of perfection. Crumbling walls, damp patches, broken and rotting window frames. But none of that mattered. Not even the birds slowly destroying the roof space and all manner of vermin inhabiting the outbuildings — it all still felt curiously like home when he stepped inside.

His father had been beyond angry when the will had been read. He hated the farm with a passion — hated the animals, hated country life. But he hated the fact that it was all left to his eight-year-old son even more. More whippings came Laurence's way from the leather-tipped cane, but Laurence didn't care. The farm would be his, and there was nothing his father could do about it.

Eventually, his father gave up, spending more and more time at his flat in London close to the hospital where he worked. By this time Laurence was twelve and would be left to fend for himself — a handful of ten-pound notes stuffed under the egg basket in the kitchen to keep him going. Laurence suspected there might be a woman involved, but he didn't care one way or the other. The farmhouse was a better place without his father in it — and, despite his tender years, young Laurence thrived on his own.

He weeded the herb garden and tried to grow vegetables in the patch close to the kitchen door. Although his father had got rid of all the animals by this time, and sold off all the machinery that was worth anything, Laurence had been allowed to keep the chickens to give him a regular supply of fresh eggs.

Spooning two teaspoons of sugar into his mug, he took his coffee over to the kitchen window. It was inky black outside, heavy clouds suffocating the moonlight. His thoughts returned to the cathedral.

A familiar thrill trickled through him as he stirred his coffee. With Lucie's hand now pinned to the body map, he needed to turn his attention to the next one.

* * *

The flats above the Arc shopping centre looked attractive from the outside. For some reason, Nicki had had it in her head that Graham had been stuck in a crumbling bedsit somewhere on the edge of town, damp patches on the walls, graffiti on the door. But these looked quite smart — chic, even.

"You coming up?" Fox jabbed his cane at the door that led to the flats above the mobile phone shop. "I might be able to rustle us up something edible if you're hungry — or we could order in?"

Nicki saw something in Fox's eyes that she hadn't seen in a long time. Not quite neediness, not quite desperation. But something close. After cutting himself off from everybody for so long, it finally looked like Detective Sergeant Graham Fox acknowledged he needed human company after all.

Nicki felt herself smile and followed him up the stairs.

The flat was just as impressive inside as it was outside, if not more so. Although there was just the one bedroom, it had a spacious living/dining area big enough to house a decent three-seater sofa, coffee table and TV stand in the corner. There was even room for a small bookcase beneath the window.

Nicki parted the curtains with a finger, noting the quiet and abandoned street below. During the day it would be full of shoppers, but at night it had a peaceful and serene feel — the thick, triple-glazed windows keeping out any noise.

Fox was busying himself in the small open plan kitchen, filling the kettle and putting it on to boil. Not big by any stretch of the imagination, the kitchen had all the essentials a young bachelor needed — a sleek-looking built in oven and hob, fridge-freezer and even space for a small washing machine.

"Coffee all right? I'm out of tea bags."

"Fine."

"And it'll have to be black. I'm out of milk, too."

Nicki smiled. "Also fine."

While the kettle boiled, Nicki took the opportunity to take a look around. The décor was simple — cream walls with pale grey carpet underfoot — a few simple abstract prints on the walls. A widescreen TV sat in the corner, and Nicki spied a PlayStation resting on a footstool. A simple chrome floor lamp sat in the corner, giving off a low-level light, while recessed lights on the ceiling gave the room a subtle warmth.

"I never knew these flats were so nice inside," she commented, as Fox brought through their coffee. "I'm quietly impressed."

Gesturing for Nicki to take a seat on the sofa, Fox removed the PlayStation and gently lowered himself on to the footstool.

"Yeah, they're not bad. I only lasted three months in my last place. Too small — not somewhere I could have the kids over to stay."

"How are the kids?" Nicki noticed a photograph of two grinning children on the window ledge. "You get to see much of them?"

Fox shifted his weight on the small stool, Nicki noticing another wince.

"They're good. Debbie lets me see them whenever I want. It's not easy with the job, but we're making it work. They're going to stay over one night, too — once we finish this investigation." Fox couldn't mask the smile that broke out on his lips, the sparkle returning to his eyes. "They're really excited. We're going to stay up late playing on the PlayStation and have pizza. It'll mean me kipping on the sofa, but I don't mind."

A flash of pain crossed Fox's face as he twisted slightly on the stool. Nicki noticed he'd managed the stairs up to the flat relatively well, but rested heavily on his walking cane when they'd reached the top.

"You should book some time off work, Graham. Get yourself back into shape." She sipped her coffee and nodded at the abandoned walking cane propped up by the door. "Spend some time with the kids."

Fox gave a slow shrug. "We'll see. I've only just got back to work. Too much time off does my head in."

We'll see.

Fox was nothing if not stubborn.

But stubbornness was a character trait Nicki often welcomed in her team.

"I couldn't have done it without you that night, you know." Nicki placed her coffee cup down but didn't take her eyes off Fox. "The Lucas Jackson case. You giving chase like that — as dangerous and idiotic as it was — we'd never have solved the case if it wasn't for you."

Fox brushed the compliment aside. "It was nothing. Anyone else would have done the same. Right place, right time."

Nicki wasn't sure that was necessarily true. Graham had put his life on the line that night, without hesitation. A life he'd very nearly lost. "I remember seeing you at the hospital," she added. "I couldn't believe you'd managed to get out of that wreck alive."

Another faint shrug followed. "I'm indestructible, me. You know that." Fox smiled through the steam wafting up from his mug. "Just a few scratches."

"A few scratches? You nearly died, Graham! The surgeon told me that if that gearstick had penetrated just a few centimetres more, it might've been goodnight, Vienna!"

"Like I said. Indestructible." Fox drank a mouthful of his black coffee. "So, what's your instinct telling you about our cases?"

Nicki acknowledged the discreet change of subject. "I really have no idea what we're facing, if I'm honest. But whatever it is, it's not good."

"I can't get my head around who'd do something like this. Killers we've dealt with before, even sadistic ones, but . . . why leave body parts strewn around the town?"

Nicki shrugged. "Shock value?" She didn't believe her own words but had nothing else to give. "We really need some IDs for our body parts, so we know what we're looking at. And who we're looking for."

"Displaying them like that . . . this goes way beyond just killing someone. He — or she — isn't just dumping them — they've thought about this. This is *staged*." Fox ended with a sigh. "If they're even dead, that is. You ever come across anything like this before?"

"No. Never. But I think you're right. This isn't just your usual murderer — *if*, as you say, our victims are dead. This is something more than that. Remind me tomorrow to get searching the database for any similar offences anywhere else in the country. It's a long shot but you never know. And, like I said, we need to get moving with some IDs."

"I'll go back through the missing persons' reports first thing. Somebody somewhere must be missing them."

CHAPTER FOURTEEN

Saturday 29 December 2018
Bury St Edmunds Police Station

The incident room lights came on long before the sun put in an appearance. Nicki hadn't had to ask her team to come in early — they automatically did it without thinking, each looking sleep-deprived but alert, nursing fresh coffees in their hands.

A new investigation could sharpen the senses like nothing else.

With an increasingly heavy heart, Nicki began to annotate a third whiteboard. After leaving Graham's flat she'd returned home, but sleep had evaded her — offering a fitful hour at best. She'd contemplated a run at 5.30 a.m. but instead stood beneath a scalding shower and let the jets pummel her skin. She'd called Caz a little after six, knowing the pathologist would be awake and most probably already on her way to the mortuary. Caz had informed her that she would be taking a look at the hand later that morning and would call with an update just as soon as she could.

The hand.

Nicki shivered as the thought of last night's find re-entered her head. She snapped the lid back on her marker pen and turned towards her team.

Before she could open her mouth, the familiar 'ping' of an incoming email cut through the air.

"Boss?" Duncan raised his hand, his eyes still glued to the computer screen. "You might want to come and see this. Email notification — we've had a hit on the DNA database for the eyes — and also the tongue."

Nicki's eyes widened. "Really? That was quick? Who've we got?" She headed towards Duncan's desk, the screen already angled in her direction.

"DNA for both specimens is a match for one person — a young woman by the name of Jacqui Massingham," replied Duncan. "Aged twenty-three."

Nicki squinted at the screen. "Jacqui Massingham. Find out what you can about her — current address, next of kin. And a recent photo, if possible. Try social media. And find out why her DNA is on the system."

"Will do." Duncan began tapping away at his keyboard while Nicki returned to the whiteboards.

Writing the name Jacqui Massingham on both the first and second whiteboards, Nicki took in a deep breath. "OK, so this is quite a big step forward. Knowing the ID of our first victim gives us something to work with. The fact that our eyes and tongue come from the same person is a relief — not for Jacqui Massingham, it has to be said, but one victim is better than two. We can now consolidate both investigations. As for last night's discovery at the cathedral . . ." Nicki paused, her gaze flicking to the third whiteboard. "The hand is being examined later this morning — we'll know soon enough if it belongs to the same victim. I'll let Caz know about the DNA."

Nicki turned back towards her team. "As Jacqui Massingham is the first lead we have, our first action has to be to dig into her background as much as possible. Something made her a victim. Trawl her phone records, social media accounts, work history, anything. Duncan as you're already looking into her, can I give that to you?" Duncan nodded, already tapping away at his keyboard. "And while you're at it, chase up the fingerprints for the hand. If we've got this Jacqui's DNA on the system, then we may well have her fingerprints."

Duncan nodded again and added the action to his list.

"Plus, I want all CCTV checked throughout the town for last night. This person can't have come and gone without being seen by someone. Matt? You happy to carry on with that?"

DC Matt Holland raised his coffee mug. "No problem. I'm already widening the time frame for the theatre and roundabout crime scenes."

"Why are they doing this?" Darcie shivered as she hugged her mug of hot coffee. "It's one thing to kill someone — take trophies, even. But they're not keeping the trophies for themselves — they're *displaying* them. Are they looking for some kind of reaction? Acknowledgment?" Darcie shivered again as she took a sip of her drink. "It's creepy."

"Graham and I were thinking much the same last night," agreed Nicki. "But there's some other motivation for our perpetrator. Can I get one of you to start checking the database for any similar sounding crimes, anywhere in the country? As bizarre as it sounds, they might have done this before."

"I'll take a look." Darcie put her mug down and pulled her computer keyboard towards her.

"And we still need to catch up with Tommy McCrae's mother. Roy? You went to see young Tommy before, so see if you can track down the mum. See if his version of events stacks up. Take Darcie with you." Nicki paused, facing the second whiteboard where Tommy McCrae's name had been written in capital letters. She frowned. "Why do I feel like I've heard that name before?"

Roy got to his feet. "I looked him up not long after we got back yesterday. Been in a few scrapes over the years, which is why you might have heard of him. Nothing too sinister. Some anti-social behaviour as a juvenile, possession of cannabis and criminal damage. Nothing for the last twelve months, though." Roy added the details to the whiteboard, plus a mugshot of the nineteen-year-old. "Maybe he's turned over a new leaf."

"Hmmm." Nicki frowned at the pasty-faced teenager's picture — noting the defiant look in his eyes, and two large silicone tunnels in each ear lobe. "Bring him in. I'd like a chat." Turning away from the board, she started to head towards the door, not having yet set foot in her office that morning. "In the meantime, a press release has gone out to the media — details of both discoveries at the theatre and the roundabout. It'll be hitting the online news headlines any time now. But we're holding on to last night's discovery for a while longer."

"Boss?" Duncan caught Nicki's eye as she passed. "Just put Jacqui Massingham's details into the system — looks like there are a couple of allegations of domestic abuse and harassment. First one in the summer of 2017, the next three months later. Then there's an alleged assault recorded in January of this year — that one's still open."

"Interesting. Find out what you can about them — especially the assault. In particular, who was she accusing? Is there an address for her?"

Duncan tapped the keyboard. "Last address we have is over in Moreton Hall. Her next of kin are down as her parents — Lionel and Audrey Massingham. They live out in Horringer."

Nicki paused by the door, her mind crunching the latest information. "Matt, concentrate on the CCTV. I know it's a drag but it needs doing. Plus, contact any theatre staff we haven't spoken to yet. Duncan, you keep digging into Jacqui Massingham's background. Graham?" Nicki turned towards the detective leaning up against the back wall, a mug of strong, black coffee in his hand, a pinched look on his face. Although he looked freshly shaven, Nicki saw the tiredness entrenched in his skin. She gave a wan smile. "How do you fancy a trip out to Horringer with me later?"

Fox gave a thumbs up.

"Give me a couple of hours to catch up on some paperwork — and I'll need to contact the Massinghams in advance and give them the news."

* * *

The Farmhouse

Laurence's jaw clenched as he scrolled through the rolling news headlines, stabbing at the phone screen. It was everywhere — in every newspaper, on every channel.

'Theatre Horror'

But it wasn't that headline that caused his nerves to grate. He already knew the eyes had been discovered — and had been expecting the media frenzy that would follow.

It was the next headline that made his blood start to simmer.

'Tongue found by local man'

That wasn't supposed to have happened yet; the boy had messed up.

Laurence gritted his teeth and scrolled through yet more news articles charting the horrific find on one of the town's busiest roundabouts.

The boy hadn't done as he was told — in fact, he'd done the complete opposite.

Laurence slammed the phone down and strode out of the kitchen, heading towards the pantry. He'd spent much of the previous evening making preparations — preparations for the next one. His eyes strayed towards the pantry shelves where everything was lined up, ready and waiting.

But now he'd have to put his plans on hold. First of all, he needed to deal with the boy.

* * *

Caz pushed the sliding door shut on freezer number four — little Milly Darkins was now awaiting permission to be buried. Yesterday's meeting with her parents had gone pretty much as Caz had expected — she'd been through it enough times to know the ritual. The box of tissues on her desk had been emptied — a second box making a subtle appearance soon afterwards. Caz knew there was little she could do or say that would make the family's heartbreak any easier to bear, but by the end she thought she saw a glimmer of something akin to relief in the eyes of the mother.

Caz turned her attention to the next job of the morning — there was little point in delaying. Nicki needed answers fast, and the clock was already ticking. A message had pinged to her phone not ten minutes ago, advising her that the eyes and tongue she'd examined yesterday belonged to the same unfortunate victim. The question now on Nicki's lips, along with everyone else's, was could the same be said for the hand?

Making her way through to the main examination room, Caz pulled on a fresh plastic apron and donned a set of gloves. Her hair was already tied back and hidden beneath the elasticated cap, her feet buried in white wellington boots.

The mortuary technician had already laid the specimen out on one of the steel examination tables. Beneath the harsh overhead lighting, the skin on the severed hand looked pale and stark.

As she approached, the first thing that struck Caz was the vivid colour of the woman's nail polish. It was such a striking colour — a vibrant red that warranted a name like Firebird or Volcano Cherry.

With the overhead microphone set to record, Caz began.

"Today — Saturday 29 December 2018 — we have the left hand of a Caucasian female. There are two outwardly distinguishing marks on the dorsal side — first there is a small birthmark measuring five millimetres by four millimetres just beneath the index finger. Then there is a superficial scratch measuring fifteen millimetres between the second and third web spaces."

Caz proceeded to take a swab of the skin surrounding the scratch, depositing it in a narrow plastic tube and handing it to the mortuary technician to label. It might be nothing, but it could turn out to be something.

"The rest of the dorsal side of the hand is free from obvious injury." Caz turned the hand over. "On the palmar side, there is a distinctive tattoo located on the inside of the wrist joint — a butterfly. Plus, a smaller tattoo of a rose at the base of the thumb." Caz stepped away as the mortuary technician leaned in to take a series of close-up photographs of each tattoo. Once finished, she resumed her examination. "The rest of the palmar side of the specimen appears free from any other markings."

Taking hold of a freshly sterilised scalpel, Caz began to take scrapings from beneath each of the fingernails. "No discernible tissue beneath the fingernails, but samples taken for analysis."

Straightening up, Caz took a long hard look at the severed hand. The feeling of disquiet she'd experienced yesterday when examining the eyes and tongue had returned. It was getting to be a familiar sensation.

"The site of the amputation is clean. Both radius and ulna have been severed with a fine-bladed saw. Faint grooves can be seen etched into the distal ends of both bones, but the severance is otherwise neat." Caz gently teased the exposed tissues with the end of her scalpel. "Similarly, the main extensor and flexor tendons of the forearm have been neatly cut with a sharp blade. Surrounding skin and subcutaneous tissue also cleanly cut." She paused for a moment. "This hand has been dissected in what can only be described as a surgical fashion."

Caz's thoughts flashed back to freezer number four next door. The contrast between the two examinations could not have been more stark.

Little Milly's legs and pelvis had been crushed on impact, her head catapulted against the windscreen of the speeding car. Her skull suffered thirteen fracture lines, her eye sockets smashed into pieces, her face so unrecognisable that Caz had had to arrange a silk cloth to be draped over her head when the family came to view her. No mother, no father, no brother or sister, should ever have to see carnage like that. The poor girl's body was broken beyond comprehension.

Contrast that to this morning's examination.

Cold. Clean. Clinical.

The only comfort Caz could offer the Darkins family was that Milly's life would have ended the instant her head hit the windscreen. The massive insult to her brain cut her young life short in seconds.

But Caz couldn't offer such cold comfort to whoever's hand this was. There was no telling what pain or suffering they might have endured, or what torture might have been inflicted upon them.

Continuing with the examination, Caz took blood and tissue samples for DNA and blood typing. It wouldn't take too long to cross reference the results and see if they matched those for the eyes and tongue.

Time would tell.

CHAPTER FIFTEEN

The Manor House

The village of Horringer was only just outside the town — a three-minute drive at most, even in the current wintry conditions. The Massingham family lived in a spacious, detached house at the end of a sweeping gravel drive, with surrounding leylandii trees obscuring it from the road outside.

Two double garages to the side were open, displaying two Aston Martins, a Porsche and a Range Rover.

DS Fox whistled through his teeth as Nicki brought her modest Toyota to a stop. "Jeez. They're not short of a bob or two, that's for sure."

Several inches of snow lay atop the expertly carved topiary hedgerows, and the sound of the gravel beneath their feet, instead of crunching and announcing their arrival, was somewhat muted and muffled.

But their arrival had not gone unnoticed completely, and the door to the Manor House was pulled open before they reached the top step. Before them stood a tall, thin man of indeterminate age, his hair swept back from his face, revealing an angular forehead and balding scalp. His hawk-like nose and protruding eyes gave him the look of a vulture.

A well-fitting, double-breasted three-piece suit covered his sinewy frame. Even his shoes shone.

Fox glanced down at his tatty brown loafers now sodden with melted snow. Brushing himself down, he pulled his Superdry jacket a little closer around him. Nicki stifled a smile as she stepped forward.

"DI Nicki Hardcastle." She held up her warrant card. "And this is DS Fox. I believe you're expecting us? We're here to see Mr and Mrs Massingham."

The man looked down his beak-like nose at both detectives, eyes flicking from one to the other. He then gave a curt nod and stepped backward, making a grand sweeping gesture with his arm.

"If you would like to step inside, I'll alert them to your arrival."

If the outside of the house had been impressive, it was nothing compared to the inside. Victorian-style black and white mosaic floor tiles stretched from one side of the vast entrance hall to the other. A huge mirror adorned one wall, and beyond that a grand wooden staircase swept towards the upper floor.

Nicki stood, mouth slightly agape, thinking she'd just stepped into a scene from Downton Abbey.

"Do people really live like this?" muttered Fox. "Butlers? Entrance halls? Chandeliers?" His eyes gravitated towards the ceiling where several crystal chandeliers hung above their heads. "And is that a Rodin?" He nodded towards a bronze sculpture sitting on a wooden plinth opposite the mirror. *The Thinker* — one of Rodin's finest pieces. "Do you think it's an original? Or a copy?"

Nicki could only shrug as she inched forward. Whatever it was, it was out of the price range of a detective inspector. But for all its obvious wealth and finery, the entrance hall felt cold and clinical — instead of a place to welcome guests, it felt like the exact opposite.

Less than a minute later, the bird-like butler returned. "Mr and Mrs Massingham will see you in the drawing room."

The drawing room was every bit as impressive as the entrance hall. Another hugely expansive room that opened out on to landscaped gardens at the rear. In better weather, Nicki could imagine the vast patio doors being flung open to welcome in the outdoors. But on a day like today, with just a sea of white outside, the outdoors remained firmly where it was.

After showing them inside, the butler gave a sweeping bow and departed. Mr and Mrs Massingham were seated on an uncomfortable-looking Chesterfield sofa in front of the patio doors. The maroon leather looked highly polished and distinctly unforgiving — as did the expressions on Jacqui's parents' faces. Pinched was the first word that sprang to Nicki's mind as she made her way towards them.

A small woman, Audrey Massingham sat perched on the edge of the hard sofa, her legs tucked demurely to the side. Dressed in a formal beige coloured twin-set, she looked as though she was about to attend a business function — not discuss the disappearance and possible death of her only daughter. Her greying hair was swept back from her narrow face up into a harsh bun on top of her head, her skin looking sallow beneath a layer of foundation and powder. A whiff of lily of the valley met Nicki's nose as she approached.

"Detective Inspector Nicki Hardcastle." Nicki neared the sofa and held out a hand towards the perfectly poised Mrs Massingham. "We spoke on the phone earlier?" The gesture was met with a frown.

"I know who you are." Audrey Massingham held her gaze in a cool stare, and Nicki immediately dropped her hand back to her side.

Next to Jacqui's mother, although there was more than six feet between them, sat Lionel Massingham. A mirror image of his wife, except for the twin-set and bun, he was a small, pinched man with an air of disdain about him. Dressed in an expensive-looking tailored suit and waistcoat, as if about to greet royalty, he also sat stiffly on the edge of the sofa, back straight and hands knitted together tidily in his lap. His hair was less grey than his wife's, just a peppering at the temples, but he sported the same cool expression.

Nicki had been in her fair share of bereaved families' homes over the years, where grief was expressed at its rawest. Sadness would cling to the air, squeezing and suffocating until it was hard to breathe.

But the feeling inside The Manor House was altogether different.

"I'm sorry to have to call in such sad circumstances," continued Nicki, standing by the edge of a vast glass-topped coffee table. They hadn't been offered a seat, and Nicki didn't want to presume to take one.

There was still no discernible reaction from either Mr or Mrs Massingham. Nicki felt Fox's presence at her side but didn't risk catching his eye. Instead, she took another small step forward and tried her best, sympathetic smile.

"When we spoke earlier, I informed you about the discoveries made in the town on Thursday evening. And how we have now forensically linked them to your daughter Jacqui?"

At the mention of their daughter, Nicki detected the first movement in Lionel Massingham's face. A slight twitching at the sides of his mouth; a slight flaring of his nostrils. Then nothing.

"Is there anything you wish to ask us, before we continue?" Nicki looked from Audrey Massingham's face to that of her husband. There was no interaction between them, no reaction at all to what had been said. Nicki could have been asking about the weather, or plans for the local church fete — not the suspected abduction and possible murder of their daughter.

"No, why would we?" Mrs Massingham's voice was cold and clipped. "Just say what you have to say and be done with it."

"Mrs Massingham." Fox stepped forward, his face contorted in disbelief. "You've been informed that your daughter's eyes and tongue have been found at two different locations in the town, and that in all probability she is no longer alive . . ." He raised his eyebrows and stared wide-eyed at both of them. "Surely you have some questions?"

"What exactly is your point, Detective?" Lionel Massingham fixed his cold, grey eyes on Fox. "We fully understand what you're telling us. We're not imbeciles."

"No, of course not," interjected Nicki, stepping to the side and placing a restraining hand on Fox's elbow. "Would it be all right if we asked you some questions about Jacqui? To help us try and build up a picture of her lifestyle? Her friends?"

Mr Massingham snorted. "Her lifestyle. Well, that's what would have landed her in this mess, you mark my words."

This mess? Nicki bit back the retort that was finely balanced on her tongue. She felt Fox bristle at her side, and gave his elbow another squeeze.

"Could you tell us a little more about that lifestyle, Mr Massingham? It could be very important in finding out what happened to your daughter."

A look was exchanged between Mr and Mrs Massingham, the first evidence of any interaction between them. One cold expression against another — iceberg against iceberg.

"Jacqueline was always a wilful child," began Lionel Massingham. "Even from a very young age we could see that we were going to have trouble with her. We had a succession of nannies, au pairs and home tutors but nothing seemed to work. At nine years of age, we enrolled her at St Hilda's in Berkshire. They have an excellent reputation for correcting waywardness and insubordination."

Nicki watched Fox whip out his notebook and begin to take notes. "And how long was she at the boarding school?" Nicki wondered how long the poor girl had had to endure it.

"She ran away when she was fifteen."

Good on her, thought Nicki, placing a neutral expression on her face. "And did she come back here to live?"

A look of abject horror crossed both Mr and Mrs Massingham's faces. "Goodness me, no — she did not." Lionel Massingham's nostrils flared once more. "We wouldn't tolerate her in the house — not after that display of sheer delinquency and disregard for authority."

Nicki raised her eyebrows. "At fifteen? Where did she go?"

"Some succession of lowlifes took her in, I expect." Mr Massingham smoothed down the feeble excuse of a moustache on his top lip. "Oh, she would get in touch with us from time to time, turn up on the doorstep, usually wanting money. She's brought all of this upon herself, you know. It's nothing short of what she deserves."

Nicki swallowed back yet another retort and cleared her throat. "And when was the last time you saw your daughter?"

A few moments of frosty silence filled the room — just the heavy tick-tock of an antique grandfather clock could be heard in the background. Eventually, Audrey Massingham broke the silence.

"It would have been sometime at the beginning of the year. She came here asking for a place to stay for a few nights, and some money. The usual excuses. Something to do with falling out with that good-for-nothing boyfriend of hers again."

Nicki's eyebrows twitched as she caught Fox's eye. "A boyfriend?"

"Adrian," continued Mrs Massingham, her face blanching at the mention of the man's name. "Adrian Browning."

"And the last time she came to see you, she was in trouble? With this boyfriend, Adrian?" Nicki thought back to the allegations of domestic violence and assault Duncan had mentioned earlier.

Audrey Massingham remained stony faced. "I know what you're trying to do, Inspector, but I refuse to be blamed for what may or may not have befallen my daughter. She chose her own path in life."

"But the boyfriend?" persisted Nicki. "What kind of trouble was she in? Did you know him well?"

Mrs Massingham angled her head upwards, her nose pointing towards the ceiling. "I wouldn't have him set one foot inside the house, if that's what you mean. He was bad news. Into drugs, violence. Most probably had a criminal record. But she chose him. She made her bed. She was old enough to make her own decisions. We cannot be held responsible for her lack of judgment."

Nicki could see Fox scribbling the boyfriend's name into his notebook out of the corner of her eye.

"Was she frightened of this Adrian, Mrs Massingham?" *Not that you would care*, she wanted to add, but bit the words back. Nicki's question was met with silence. "What about any other friends she may have had?"

"Look, Inspector. We know very little about our wayward daughter's lifestyle — we washed our hands of her a long time ago. And rightly so."

"Clearly." Nicki caught Fox's eye as they came to the same conclusion. They weren't going to get much more from either of Jacqui's parents — and every minute they spent here would be a waste of precious time. "I think we'll be leaving you in peace now," said Nicki, plastering a suitably forced smile on to her face. "If you can think of anything else that might assist us in catching whoever did this to your daughter, or anything else you might think relevant, then please don't hesitate to get in touch." Before turning away, Nicki slipped a business card on to the highly polished glass-topped coffee table.

As she and Fox reached the door, it opened before them and the butler from earlier stood to attention, a vacant expression on his face. Whether or not he'd been eavesdropping was impossible to tell. Without looking back, Nicki led Fox out of the front door and down the steps towards the car.

"I don't think I've ever experienced anything quite like that in my whole life," she exclaimed, pulling open the driver's door of the car. "I can't quite believe what I just witnessed."

"I take it we won't be offering them a family liaison officer for emotional support?" quipped Fox, lowering himself into the passenger seat.

"It's not top of my agenda," replied Nicki, slamming her door and shoving the keys into the ignition. "I wouldn't want to waste a penny of my budget on either of them."

"We did get one useful lead though. Adrian." Fox slipped his notebook out of his pocket and thumbed over a few pages. "Sounds like someone we need to speak to."

"He certainly does, Graham. He certainly does."

* * *

Southgate Street, Bury St Edmunds

The TV was blaring once again, and toddlers Kane and Kieran were sitting in the same place, eyes glued to the screen. A sea of toys still littered the carpet around them — a carpet that could no longer be seen beneath the carnage.

Fourteen-year-old Kelsey had once again answered the door, baby Freddie still clamped to her hip.

"Is your mother at home, Kelsey?" enquired Darcie, her eyes straying over the girl's shoulder into the hallway beyond. "We just need a quick word."

Kelsey McCrae stepped back and yelled up the stairs. "MUM!" She then turned and walked back towards the kitchen.

Accepting the unspoken invitation, Darcie and Roy stepped into the narrow hallway, closing the front door behind them. Although the sun was trying its best to break through the cloud and instil some warmth, there was a keen wind behind them.

It wasn't long before Maria McCrae appeared at the top of the stairs. "Who is it, Kels? If it's anyone wanting money, just shut the door."

Darcie stepped towards the bottom of the stairs. "Sorry to trouble you, Mrs McCrae. I'm DC Darcie Butler, from Suffolk Police. And this is DS Carter. Could we have a quick word?"

Maria McCrae paused before muttering something incomprehensible under her breath as she descended the stairs. "Thomas McCrae — if you've been getting yourself into bother again, I'll . . ."

"It's about the discovery your son made on the round-about on Thursday night," added Darcie, watching as Mrs McCrae came into view. Dressed in tartan pyjamas and her hair bundled up in a towel, she pulled heavily on a cigarette.

"Ah, yes. Nasty business. I saw it in the news this morning. Not sure there's much else I can tell you."

Roy joined Darcie at the bottom of the stairs, notebook in hand. "Just a couple of things we'd like to clarify, then we can let you get on with your day. Can you remember what time you arrived home that night, Mrs McCrae? Your son told us you'd been at work."

Maria McCrae nodded, exhaling a plume of smoke towards the ceiling. "That's right. My shift finished at eleven — it's only round the corner so I was home by ten past."

Roy nodded, glancing down at his notebook. "And what happened when you arrived back?"

Mrs McCrae frowned. "Not much. I went to make myself a sandwich and a cup of tea."

"Did you notice anything unusual when you arrived home? Anything out on the roundabout?"

Mrs McCrae shook her head. "No, but I wasn't exactly looking. It was snowing and I wanted to get inside quick."

"Quite. And how did you get to know about the tongue that your son had found?"

Mrs McCrae made a face. "Disgusting, that was. Fair turned my stomach."

"But how did you get to hear about it? And when?"

"Well, it was when I was in the kitchen making myself that sandwich. Our Tommy came downstairs."

"He told you about what he'd found?"

Mrs McCrae hesitated, drawing in another lungful of tobacco. "No, not exactly. I saw blood on the sleeve of his coat — at least, that's what it looked like to me."

Roy caught Darcie's eye for the briefest of seconds before turning back to face Mrs McCrae. "You saw blood on Tommy's sleeve?"

Maria McCrae slowly nodded. "Like I just said — I didn't know it was blood right away, but yeah. It's a brand-new coat — cost a fortune — so I was livid. Thought he might have been fighting again."

"And what did Tommy say?"

"Well, I asked him what it was — and then he told me what he'd seen. The tongue."

"Just like that, he told you about the tongue?" Roy's eyebrows hitched.

Mrs McCrae nodded. "I didn't believe him, of course — so I asked him to show me."

"He took you over to the roundabout?"

Mrs McCrae descended the final few stairs, stubbing out the remains of her cigarette in an ashtray that rested on the bottom step. "Showed me straight away what he'd found. Was a bleedin' tongue. Hanging out of that wolf's mouth, so it was. I couldn't believe it."

"And then what happened?"

"Well, I called you lot, didn't I? Didn't look right, that being there. I mean, I didn't know if it was human or nothing, but . . . it's not right, is it?"

"No, it's not right, Mrs McCrae," agreed Roy, closing his notebook and slipping it back in his pocket. "It's not right at all. Is Tommy here by any chance? Could we have another word with him?"

Before Maria McCrae could reply, Tommy thundered down the stairs, pushing his mother roughly to the side as he hurtled towards the front door. Both Roy and Darcie staggered backwards as Tommy McCrae yanked open the door and ran for his life.

CHAPTER SIXTEEN

Bury St Edmunds Police Station

The incident room was quiet when Nicki and DS Fox arrived back from visiting the Massinghams. Roy and Darcie were still out tracking down Maria McCrae, and Matt had gone to speak to the tech team about tidying up some CCTV images. Nicki sent Fox out to get them some decent coffee and found DC Duncan Jenkins alone, sitting at his computer.

"Duncan, what else have you managed to find out about Jacqui while we've been gone?" Nicki headed across the room to where the detective was hunched over his keyboard.

"She's worked at Prescott's Estate Agents for the last two years. I had a quick chat with the office manager. They told me she left work on Saturday 22 December at around five-thirty, and was due to have the next two weeks off as annual leave. That was the last they saw of her. Her work colleagues describe her as reliable, hardworking and dependable." Duncan nodded towards the whiteboards. "I downloaded a photo of her from the estate agents' website."

Nicki, perched on the edge of a nearby desk, looked up at the first whiteboard that now had a photograph of Jacqui tacked to it. "OK — our next job is to take a trip out and have a look around her home. See if she made it back there that night. It could even be our crime scene. I'll get a team out there as soon as I can. I'll get Matt to add her address to any CCTV trawling — see if we can spot her leaving work and her journey home that day."

Nicki grabbed a notepad and scribbled a note for Matt.

"Graham and I have just got back from seeing her parents, and to say they were unhelpful and seemingly unconcerned as to their daughter's fate is an understatement. By all accounts they washed their hands of her some time ago and haven't seen her in over a year. The only decent lead we got from them was the name of a previous boyfriend — someone the parents thought was trouble."

Nicki stepped over to the whiteboards and wrote Adrian Browning next to Jacqui's name.

Duncan glanced up from his computer screen. "Well, that's interesting — that's the name I found when I looked up the details for the domestic abuse allegations, and the assault. He was the one the allegations were made against."

"Let's do a full background check on him — find out who he is, and where he is. In the meantime, tell me more about those allegations."

"The details are a bit brief, but what I've got so far is that Jacqui Massingham made her first allegation of harassment against him in the summer of 2017 — stating that he was following her home from work, standing outside her home and repeatedly calling her mobile. Records show that uniform visited him on three occasions around that time regarding the harassment. No action was taken as it appeared it was an argument that had got out of hand, and they subsequently got back together. Then we have another allegation — this time of domestic abuse — this was about three months later — September 2017. Jacqui rang 999 to report Adrian had forced himself into her home and assaulted her. Officers turned up and found Jacqui alone in her house, with no sign of Adrian. She was taken to hospital for assessment and found to have some evidence of bruising and abrasions around the wrists, consistent with being restrained. There was a further abrasion to her scalp, where Jacqui described how Adrian had dragged her across the floor by her hair.

"Adrian was interviewed but denied being at the property. Jacqui later withdrew the allegation and the case was closed. In January this year, a similar call came in — this time Jacqui alleged that Adrian had broken into her house while she was at work, and lain in wait for her return. She claims he assaulted her — splitting her lip and pulling an earring out of her ear. Again, he'd left the property before officers arrived. She was taken to hospital for assessment — further minor injuries were noted.

"Adrian was brought in for questioning, again — and this is where it gets interesting." Duncan paused, tapping his biro against his chin. "He alleged that it was *Jacqui* who had attacked *him*. He claimed she bit him."

"Bit him?" Nicki's eyebrows shot up. "Really?"

Duncan nodded. "On examination, he did have a recent bite mark to his forearm. Jacqui was questioned about the incident, and DNA swabs were taken — which explains why her DNA was on our system. From the looks of it, the case is still open. No DNA was recoverable from the bite mark to prove it was her."

"Anything else we need to know about him?"

"Details are sketchy. After I'd seen his name on the system, I called the estate agents back — the office manager knew of him, but told me Jacqui had ended her relationship with him some time ago. Said that Jacqui had moved on, and felt she'd been the happiest they'd seen her in a long time."

Nicki shrugged out of her coat and headed for the door, in dire need of the caffeine Graham had gone to find. "Good work, Duncan. Has anyone from the mortuary been in touch about the hand?"

Duncan shook his head. "No, nothing."

"OK, I'll chase it up. Let me know when the others get back. As well as visiting Jacqui's home address we need to have a chat with our Mr Browning. Get his current address and we'll go and see him."

* * *

Abbey Gardens

Sitting on an icy bench in front of the aviaries, Tommy could see this part of the gardens was deserted. Just him — and the odd squirrel rummaging among the leaves.

He'd heard the police knocking at the door — and then he'd heard what his mother had told them about the tongue. Why did she have to drop him in it like that?

Now the coppers wouldn't leave him alone.

He was pretty sure they hadn't given chase — he'd caught them unawares and was gone before they realised what had happened. Running from the police was never a great idea, but what choice did he have? They might not have been interested in the contents of his ash tray when they called before, which was still stuffed underneath his pillow, but they would definitely be interested in the contents of his jacket pocket.

Tommy's eyes darkened and he checked the gardens once more — still deserted, he was still alone. He hadn't known where to run to — his blind panic taking him to the town centre and eventually the gardens.

Reaching into his pocket, he pulled out the bloodied piece of cloth. The man hadn't told him what he was supposed to do with it — so he'd just kept it. But he wasn't daft. Now the police were sniffing around, he knew he needed to get rid of it.

The story about the tongue in the wolf's mouth had been all over the news that morning. The police didn't know who it belonged to yet, but the statement they released confirmed it was human. The thought made him feel queasy. He never paid attention in science classes at school, so how was he to know?

He wished he'd stayed home now and smoked some weed in his bedroom, playing on his Xbox. None of his friends had showed up at the skate park — so it had been a complete waste of time.

And then he'd met the man.

Tommy shivered and pulled his fake Tommy Hilfiger padded jacket around him.

Giving him a hundred quid to put the tongue in the wolf's mouth had seemed quite cool at the time. Just a bit of harmless fun. And easy money. Who'd turn their nose up at a chance to earn a ton?

A ton could buy you a lot of weed.

The man had told him not to say anything to anyone. Which was fine by Tommy — he wasn't a grass.

'*I can cut out your tongue just as easily as I did this one*' — those had been the man's exact words.

Tommy wasn't sure if he believed him — but the look in the man's eyes was enough for him to keep his mouth shut.

But that was before his mother had seen the blood on his jacket. She was like a Rottweiler at times — once she got her teeth into something she never gave up. She'd been about to go through his pockets when he'd snatched the arm of his jacket out of her hands and decided to show her the tongue. He'd had no choice. How else was he meant to explain the blood?

So, he'd ended up telling a half-truth — or a half-lie, depending on your point of view. He pretended he'd found it while he was walking home. Surely that wasn't enough to get your own tongue chopped out, was it?

It wasn't like he was going to tell her about the man.

Tommy's eyes darted left and right once again, double checking that he was still alone. If he was going to do it, he needed to do it now.

Once the cloth was gone, the police could do what they liked — come back and look in his room all they wanted. There would be nothing to tie him to the tongue — or the man. He'd already scrubbed the bloodstain from his jacket sleeve using some of the bleach from under the sink in the kitchen. If anyone suggested he was lying, he could just deny it. They couldn't bang him up for something he didn't do, no matter what you saw on TV.

The thought that the man might come after him floated briefly into his head as he stuffed the cloth into a nearby dog waste bin.

But how could he?

He had no idea where Tommy lived.

* * *

Watching the boy make a hasty retreat from the gardens, Laurence slipped out from behind the row of aviaries.

He'd clearly been wrong to trust him. He should have walked away, taken Jacqui's tongue with him and chosen somewhere else.

Seeing the headlines that morning had instinctively told him he needed to keep an eye on the boy. There was no telling who he would squeal to next. And his sixth sense had been rewarded — he'd only just pulled up opposite the boy's house when he saw the two detectives knocking at the door. A few minutes later, the boy himself had bolted.

The detectives hadn't given chase — so Laurence thought he better had.

It was surprisingly easy to run in the snow if you knew where to put your feet, but the boy had been hesitant and wary of slipping. Which meant he didn't run very fast, if at all. Walking mainly — which made him easier to follow.

At first Laurence thought he might be going to meet those waste of space friends of his at the skate park to smoke their shitty little cigarettes. But instead, the boy had turned towards the Abbey Gardens and headed towards the aviaries. Using the trees to mask his presence, Laurence managed to hide behind the aviaries — and watch.

The boy sat for a while, looking furtively out through the trees. Eventually, he reached into his pocket and made his way over to a dog waste bin, ramming something inside before having it away on his toes.

A mixture of anger and fear rippled through Laurence as he reached into the bin and pulled out the bloodied cloth.

The boy really was as stupid as he looked.

He'd need to do something about that.

And soon.

CHAPTER SEVENTEEN

Arnold & Son Butchers Ltd

Arnold & Son Butchers stood on a side street, just off the Market Square. A small table outside was stacked high with packets of link sausages, pork steaks, marinated lamb cutlets and minced beef. The freezing temperatures acted like a chiller to keep them fresh.

Nicki and DS Fox entered the shop, a bell jangling overhead to announce their arrival. Meat hung from large metal hooks behind the counter, and the display case at the front showcased all the cuts available to be purchased. The unmistakable aroma of a butcher's shop greeted their nostrils.

"That looks like a nice bit of steak." Fox edged closer to the glass cabinet. "Love a juicy steak with chips on a Saturday night."

Just then, the blue and white beading that separated the shop from the back of the building swished open and a squat, red-faced man emerged.

"Afternoon. What can I get you?"

Seeing the name above the door on their way in, Nicki took a punt. "Mr Arnold?" she enquired.

The butcher hesitated for a split second before nodding. "Aye. That's me. What can I do for you?" A slight edginess entered his tone as he took in the appearance of his newest customers. Neither of them appeared to have a shopping bag and when Nicki brought out her warrant card, followed by DS Fox a moment later, his suspicions were confirmed.

Police.

"Do you happen to have an employee by the name of Adrian Browning working here today?" Nicki slipped her warrant card back inside her pocket.

Arnold nodded. "Adrian? Yes — he's out the back. What's this about?"

Nicki used one of her best and most practised smiles. "If we could just have a word with him. If that's not too much trouble?"

The bell above the door jangled once more, announcing a new customer.

"Perhaps you have somewhere a little more private?" Nicki gestured towards the blue and white beading.

Arnold considered his options for a moment, and then clearly decided that he didn't really have that many. Sighing, he turned towards the customer who was now hovering by the display counter.

"Be with you in two shakes, Mrs Cunningham. I've got some lovely fresh liver put by for you." He turned his attention back to Nicki and Fox. "If you'd like to follow me, I'll show you out the back."

Fox let Nicki lead the way, following her through the beading and out into the rear of the shop. The first space they entered was clearly a packaging area — stacks of polystyrene containers and other packing materials lined the worktop along one side.

Arnold pushed through a heavy steel door into another room. This one was temperature controlled, the air temperature dropping several degrees as they entered.

Adrian Browning was standing at a stainless-steel work-top, meat cleaver in hand, chopping a rack of lamb into cutlets

— the sound of the knife hitting the wooden chopping board beneath echoing around the chiller. Various carcasses hung from metal hooks all along one wall. Nicki brought a hand to her face to mask the thick aroma of raw meat that assaulted her nostrils.

"Adrian? Some people here to see you. Police."

Adrian had his back to everyone and continued slamming the meat cleaver down hard on to the rack of lamb. For a moment Nicki wondered if he'd heard his boss, but at the mention of the word 'police' she saw the man's shoulders tense.

Slowly, he turned, meat cleaver in hand, and eyed up the two visitors. A wariness entered his pale eyes as he stood, motionless, by the steel worktop. Nicki saw his grip tightening on the handle of the knife, the apron tied around his waist already smeared with blood.

"If you could just put that down, Mr Browning." Nicki nodded at the meat cleaver. "We have a couple of questions to ask, if you have a moment."

Adrian quickly shot a look at his boss, and received a discreet nod in return. "Take your break now, Adrian. I'll be out front." The butcher turned and disappeared back through the steel door, more than likely to go and serve Mrs Cunningham with her usual order of liver and bacon.

Nicki continued to fix Adrian with a cool stare, almost matching the chilled temperature of the room, and nodded once more towards the blade still in his hand. The muscles in Adrian's jaw tensed, but he slowly acquiesced and placed the meat cleaver down on to the chopping board, wiping his hands on his apron.

"What do you want?" he said, not even attempting to disguise the derision in his tone. "I'm busy in case you hadn't noticed."

"Are you still in contact with Jacqui Massingham, Mr Browning?" Nicki took a step closer, but kept herself out of meat cleaver range. "I believe you two used to be in a relationship?"

Adrian's face remained stony, his eyes blinking once before responding. "I knew her, yes."

"You *knew* her, Mr Browning? Why the past tense?" Nicki's eyes bore into Adrian's until she saw the man flinch and turn away. Although details of the eyes and tongue found in the town had now made the news, Jacqui Massingham's name was being withheld. For now.

"I haven't seen her for a while," he shrugged. "So yeah, I *knew* her. Once. Before."

"When was the last time you saw her, Mr Browning?"

Adrian made a show of puffing out his cheeks. "No idea. Ages ago."

"Is it correct that you made an allegation of assault against her in January this year?" Nicki cocked her head to the side, watching for a reaction. "Our files say you claim she bit you."

"She did," hissed Adrian, his teeth clenching. "But you lot still didn't take me seriously. She's a crazy bitch — look." Adrian angled the inside of his forearm towards Nicki. A pale pink, semi-circular scar could be seen nestling among the ink that otherwise decorated his skin. Even from this distance, Nicki saw it resembled teeth marks. "Glad to be rid of her."

"*Rid* of her, Mr Browning? What do you mean by that?"

Adrian merely shrugged. "Dumped her. She was too much like hard work."

Nicki and Fox exchanged a glance. "Did you know Jacqui's not been seen since last Saturday? She's not at home. Not at work. Nobody's seen her."

Another shrug. "Not my problem what she does anymore. Like I said — she's crazy. I couldn't care less about her."

"Our files also tell us you were convicted of common assault in 2016. Care to tell us about that?"

"Not really," grunted Adrian. "You already know the details — I'm not stupid."

"Indeed, we do, Mr Browning. Nasty little encounter outside a pub, no less."

"I just lost my temper, that's all."

"Do you lose your temper a lot, Mr Browning?" Nicki saw Adrian's jaw tense once more. She decided to change tack. "Where were you on Thursday 27 December, Mr Browning? The Thursday just gone?"

Adrian paused, his eyes straying to the meat cleaver on the worktop. "Not sure I can remember. At home, probably. Or here during the day."

"Probably?" Nicki paused before continuing. "What about during the evening? Where would you have been then?"

Adrian's eyes narrowed. "Why? What are you trying to say?" Standing squarely by the side of the worktop, he folded his arms across his chest and fixed Nicki with a sneer. "I don't have to answer any of your questions, anyway. I know my rights. If you want to ask me anything else, especially about that bitch, you'll need to arrest me." The muscles in Adrian's jaw clenched once again, and Nicki thought she could detect the hint of a smile playing on his lips.

Don't tempt me, she wanted to say.

Instead, she fixed him with a smile of her own. "In that case, we'll leave you to the rest of your day, Mr Browning." With that, she turned and headed back towards the steel door. Before pulling it open, she turned and caught the young butcher's eye. "But don't be going anywhere. I'm sure we'll need to catch up with you again soon."

* * *

Southgate Street, Bury St Edmunds

Tommy slammed his bedroom door shut and leaned against it, breathing hard. He'd taken a long, circuitous route back home — just in case. Just in case of what, he wasn't quite sure.

But just in case.

He felt better having got rid of the bloodied cloth — at least the cops couldn't pin that on him now. He'd had enough dealings with the law in the past, he didn't need any more aggro.

Collapsing on to his bed, he pulled off his jacket and flung it across the room to join the growing heap of clothing in the corner. His mother occasionally ventured into his room to gather his dirty washing, but only when things got desperate. By the looks of it, she hadn't been in for a while.

Letting out a pent-up breath, he felt his heart rate begin to slow. He hadn't counted on the police arriving on his doorstep again quite so soon — but now the evidence was gone he felt better. So much so, he reached down to rummage beneath his bed for his latest stash of weed. He'd managed to get a good batch this time — properly good stuff. And right now, it was exactly what he needed.

He already had a couple of joints rolled, so plucked one from the rusting tin and lit it with a disposable lighter. Mum didn't like him smoking in his room, but acknowledged there was little she could do to stop him. There was little she could do to stop him doing *anything*.

He grinned and rested his head back against his pillow, closing his eyes while the drug infiltrated his bloodstream. The hit would come soon: he could feel it. Taking another deep drag on the joint, he held the smoke inside for a fraction of a second longer than usual. As he released the smoke into the air, a satisfied smile spread across his face.

The police could come back as much as they wanted now — they had nothing on him. Not a thing. Not anymore.

He patted the back pocket of his jeans. The cash was still safe.

The volume of the TV downstairs rose a notch, and he could hear the familiar and annoying theme tune to SpongeBob SquarePants floating up the stairs. With the joint almost done, he grabbed his headphones and pressed the power button on his Xbox.

CHAPTER EIGHTEEN

Bury St Edmunds Police Station

"She says she saw blood on the sleeve of his jacket." Darcie took a marker pen and tapped it on Tommy McCrae's name. "His original story to us was that he just saw something odd in the snow. Spots of blood. Didn't go over to the roundabout, just went inside to tell his mum and they discovered the tongue together. Her version of events is that once she saw the blood on his jacket, he told her about the tongue and took her to see it." She glanced across at Nicki, who was perching on the corner of a desk. "Like Roy said, there was always something odd about his original story. He didn't need to go anywhere near that roundabout to get home, and he would have been too far away to see spots of blood in the snow. So . . ."

"He's lying," finished Nicki. "I think we know that now. We just have to work out why. What else did the mother have to say?"

"Her version was that she got home from work around ten past eleven and Tommy was upstairs. When he came down she saw he had what looked like blood on the sleeve of his jacket. She was annoyed because it was brand new. At which time he told her what he'd seen on the roundabout and took her outside to see it."

"Hmmm. But that doesn't explain how he got the blood there in the first place — if he claims he never went near it." Nicki pushed herself off the desk, her lips pursed. "We need to talk to him again."

"Currently AWOL, boss," said Roy. "Scarpered while we were talking to the mum. We went to follow him but he was long gone. We've asked her to let us know when he surfaces again."

"And will she?" Nicki's eyebrows hitched.

Roy could only shrug. "No idea. We've circulated his details — see if any patrols can pick him up. He's well known in the town — uniforms know where he usually hangs out."

"OK. Let's return to that later. Well, Graham and I went to see Adrian Browning at work. He admitted he used to know Jacqui, but claims not to have seen her in a while. Showed us a scar that could have come from a bite — but he didn't elaborate. He was evasive and clearly on edge by our presence. Couldn't really account for his whereabouts last Thursday so he remains a person of interest in the investigation. I want as much background information as possible on him before we talk to him again. Maybe a home visit this time. Duncan, get on to his social media — build up a picture of the man."

Duncan nodded and jotted several notes down on his notepad. "I dug a bit deeper while you were out. The common assault conviction in 2016 — he got off with a suspended sentence on the understanding he attended a drug rehabilitation programme."

"Once we have more on him, I want to pay him another — less friendly — visit. Matt — anything useful from the CCTV that hasn't already been covered?"

"I got the tech team to smarten up the images — managed to isolate a couple that I think must be her. The first one is her leaving work last Saturday." Matt got up from his seat and pinned two still images to the first whiteboard. The quality wasn't bad, considering some they had to deal with, but they were still somewhat grainy. He pointed at the first image. "This is her walking along in the direction of the main car park. The second is at the entrance to the car park. We lose her after that."

Nicki nodded. "OK, so we assume she made it to her car. We just need to know if she made it home. Let's check out her home address and see if her car's there. I'm told Faye and her team are heading out shortly to assess the scene, so I'll drop by a little later. Anything else?"

"I took the CCTV from outside the theatre back to the morning — this is at a little after eight o'clock on Thursday morning." Matt returned to his computer and angled the monitor towards Nicki. "These images are the cleaning crew arriving for their shift. Four employees were down to work that morning, but according to those we spoke to, only three showed up."

"Who was missing?"

"A guy by the name of Fernando Tavares. According to his work colleagues he never missed a shift. Except for that day."

"Do we have his contact details? Have you spoken to him?"

Matt nodded. "We do — but he's not picking up. Lives out in Thetford."

"We may need to pay him a visit. Does it show much of note?"

Matt tapped the keyboard. "There's no camera footage inside the theatre as we know, so all we have is the view from the street outside." He enlarged the image on the screen. "The three cleaning company employees all arrive together. See?" The camera played out the scene, showing three people approaching the front entrance. "They enter the theatre together at 8.12 a.m."

"And?" Nicki knew Matt well enough by now to know that something else was coming.

"And this." Matt fast forwarded the footage to 8.41 a.m. when another figure entered the frame.

Nicki inched closer. "And who is this?"

"No one knows. While you were out, I sent the footage through to Hugh Maxwell. The guy looks like he's wearing an ID badge, and has the cleaning company uniform on. Maxwell doesn't recognise him but acknowledges that he probably wouldn't recognise the cleaning crew anyway. I then downloaded the still and sent it to the supervisor over at Swift Cleaning. They have no idea who he is, but they're sure he isn't one of their employees. It's definitely not Tavares."

"Can you zoom in?" Nicki peered closely at the screen. The image wasn't great, and the man had his head down, a cap pulled firmly down over his head. "How can the supervisor know he doesn't work for them from this? It could be anybody."

"Apparently, they only have one male cleaner on their books — just Tavares. And it's not him."

"OK. Send it down to the tech guys — see if they can clean it up a little." Enlarging the image had lost some of its clarity and it was impossible to get even a vague impression of who they were looking at. "We might be able to get an approximate height and build. The hair looks dark coloured beneath that cap, but other than that . . ." Nicki didn't hold out an awful lot of hope that the image could be sharpened. It had been grainy to begin with, and whoever it was seemed to know there was a camera in the vicinity and was angling his head towards the ground.

"Will do."

"And get out to see this Tavares chap. See why he didn't make it into work. Take a picture of this CCTV with you. What about in and around the cathedral?"

"Just taking a look at that now."

Nicki turned away from Matt's desk, spying a large brown paper parcel sitting next to Roy. She caught his eye.

"Roy?"

A sheepish smile crossed the detective's face. "Sorry, boss. Nothing to do with the case. I've had a delivery from my grandmother in Nigeria."

"A delivery?" Nicki watched as Roy picked up some scissors and began snapping the string surrounding the parcel, ripping off the brown paper.

"If I'm not mistaken it'll be a food parcel." The smile on Roy's lips broadened. "She thinks I'm about twelve and I don't eat properly — that I can't possibly look after myself." Reaching inside, he brought out several plastic containers. Opening the largest one, he tipped it towards Nicki. "But, having said that, these are delicious."

Nicki peered inside. "And what are they exactly?"

"Chin chin," relied Roy. "Fried cookies, basically. They're really nice." He dipped his hand inside the container and brought a few of them out.

"*Fried* cookies?" Nicki's eyes widened as she patted her stomach. "As if normal cookies aren't fattening enough. They do look good, though."

"They're great. Try one." Roy handed one of the small, golden-coloured cubes towards Nicki. "Seriously. You'll be addicted. My grandmother makes the best chin chin ever."

Nicki's stomach growled in anticipation as she took hold of the small, fried biscuit. As she bit into it, she was surprised by the light and crunchy texture. A hint of both cinnamon and vanilla hit her taste buds as the sweet biscuit dissolved in her mouth.

"Oh, my word — that is actually pretty good."

Roy chuckled as he handed her another. "Wait 'til you taste these." He brought out two more plastic containers from the parcel. "Looks like we've got cake."

"Did someone say cake?" Darcie's ears pricked.

Roy pulled the lid off one of the containers and brought it up to his face to inhale the aroma. His eyes sparkled as he nodded. "This is my grandmother's famous rum cake. Lasts forever. And this one . . ." Loosening the lid from the other container, he broke out into another broad smile. "This one's a traditional Nigerian fried bean cake." He watched Darcie's face drop and laughed. "No, really. It tastes amazing. Just try it."

"Hmmm, well maybe some of the rum cake to go with my coffee." Darcie went to top her mug up from the hot water urn. "I took a quick look into Ernest Fisher's background when we got back, boss. Distinguished military career and seems to lead an uneventful retirement. I can't see him being targeted specifically." She returned to Roy's desk and accepted the slice of rum cake. "Same with the St Edmund and Sir Isaac Newton angles. I think they must be red herrings."

"I agree." Nicki headed towards the door, taking another couple of chin chin biscuits with her. "Focus on our known victim, Jacqui. Keep delving into her past, see what you can find. I don't think the parents are going to be much help to us. Once we have some more details on Adrian, we'll pay him another visit. Roy, keep trying to find this Tommy McCrae — he can't just disappear. And Matt, get that CCTV image down to the tech suite then keep trying that Tavares guy. I'll give Caz a call at the mortuary and see if we have any news about the hand."

* * *

4 Old Railway Cottages
Dullingham, Nr Newmarket

Adrian slammed the door of his white van and strode up the garden path. He was still seething. How dare they come to his place of work and question him like that? The boss hadn't been too happy, giving him sidelong glances and pulling him up for each and every mistake he made. Eventually, Arnold had sent him home. Adrian hadn't been in the job all that long and he really needed the money. Employers weren't exactly falling over themselves to offer him work with a history like his.

And it was all that bitch's fault.

Jacqui.

He'd been in a bad mood ever since her name escaped the mouth of that detective.

Two plastic carrier bags swung from his arm as he unlocked the front door. It didn't look like anyone was home, which wasn't a bad thing. At least he wouldn't have to explain why he'd been sent home from work. Kicking the door open, he stepped into the hall.

"Mason?" he called out, slamming the door shut behind him. "You here?" With the silence that greeted him, he guessed not. Where was that good-for-nothing brother of his? "Could do with a hand here, you know?"

Still nothing.

Sighing, Adrian made his way towards the kitchen, heaving the bags up on to the worktop. He saw his mother's coat hanging up behind the kitchen door, and her handbag on the side. But the house was in darkness and there was no sign of her.

Snapping on the kitchen lights, he picked the bags up and headed for the utility room. He'd managed to sneak out the back of the shop while the boss was serving; he hadn't seen Adrian stuff two carrier bags full of sausages, steaks, lamb cutlets, and enough minced beef to sink a ship.

He knew he was treading on thin ice — *very* thin ice — and he'd more than likely get caught one day. The law of averages said he would. But, until then . . . the temptation was too great.

And temptation was one of his many downfalls.

Take Jacqui, for example. She'd been bad news from the moment he'd met her, but . . . there was something about her that kept him coming back for more. When they'd first met, she'd needed him. She was young and naive, trying to get by on the streets, but she had a rebellious, independent streak. He'd liked that about her — in the beginning. But she grew in confidence and started telling him what to do. He hadn't liked that so much.

Pushing thoughts of Jacqui from his mind, he yanked open the door to the fridge-freezer. After rearranging the contents to make room, he filled it with his latest haul. He needed to cut back on the pinching — they already had more meat than they knew what to do with. Slamming the freezer door shut, he flicked the switch on the wall thermostat and heard the aged boiler clunk into action. He needed hot water for a shower. He stank of meat — like he always did.

Climbing the stairs, he paused outside his brother's bedroom door, pressing his ear up against the wood. Nothing. Not a breath. Not a sound. Pushing the door handle down, he nudged the door open and peered inside.

Empty.

Where the hell had he got to?

And where was Mum?

He closed Mason's door and headed towards his own room at the back of the house.

He knew he was the reason the family had moved back here. They'd given up their lives in Wales and come to his rescue — *again*. He hadn't wanted to move back in with them, but he'd had no choice. Thrown out of his last flat for not paying his rent, he didn't exactly have any decent references to get another. And he'd been in trouble with the police again when that bitch had bitten him. They didn't exactly say it, but he knew what they were thinking. *Here's Adrian — that useless waste of space.* A disappointment — the black sheep of the family. And Mason didn't help. He could do no wrong in their parents' eyes. He was the golden child, earning a fortune from just drawing pictures for a living — not like Adrian's job at the butcher's, slogging his guts out for minimum wage, coming home stinking of raw meat.

One day things would change. One day he'd leave it all behind and take off in his van; make something of himself. He'd been telling himself that for a good while now, but one day it would happen. It *had* to. It was the reason he'd got the van in the first place — maybe set himself up with house clearances, or a handyman service. Anything to get him away from here.

Reaching his bedroom, he snapped on the light and headed towards the window which overlooked the back garden. He could also see part of the next-door neighbour's garden — Benedict or something. He had no idea what the man did for a job, but whatever it was it kept him away from home a lot. Or maybe he had another house somewhere else. He looked the type.

As Adrian looked out of the window into the fading light, he saw movement from the bottom of the garden.

A frown crossed his forehead.

Why was Mum wandering around in the garden in the freezing cold?

After watching his mother disappear out of sight, heading for the back door, Adrian pulled off his jacket and tossed it on to the bed. He then pulled off his work shirt, instantly detecting the aroma of raw meat clinging to every fibre. He then pulled off the bloodstained T-shirt beneath and threw both garments across the room to land in the corner.

Sometimes he hated his job.

But right now, he hated Jacqui even more.

CHAPTER NINETEEN

Bury St Edmunds Police Station

Nicki slumped down behind her desk and rubbed her eyes. The grittiness told her she needed sleep — but the piles of paperwork that greeted her told her otherwise. Resting on top of the largest pile were the reports Caz had emailed over earlier that day — reports into the examination of both the eyes and the tongue that were now known to belong to Jacqui Massingham.

There was also a draft of her examination of the severed hand with a post-it note attached — '*Call Caz*'.

Swallowing the last of her chin chin, Nicki reached for the reports and settled back in her chair. She already knew what they said — her conversation with Caz yesterday had given her the low down — but she felt she needed to read them for herself just the same.

It wasn't long before various familiar words stood out on the page as she read.

Enucleation
Skilled
Clean
Neat

Whoever they were looking for knew what they were doing — Caz had said as much before. This wasn't a case of gouging out someone's eyes with an ice-cream scoop, or amputating a hand with several wields from an axe or cleaver.

This was different.

The thought of a meat clever instantly brought Adrian Browning to the forefront of Nicki's mind and the aroma of raw meat filled her nostrils once again.

Would he know how to remove an eyeball? He'd most probably know how to amputate a limb, and maybe cut out a tongue, but . . . The remnants of the chin chin churned uncomfortably in the base of Nicki's stomach.

She reached for her mobile and the call was answered almost immediately.

"Caz — what about a butcher?" Nicki heard rustling from the other end of the line and the scraping of a chair. "Would a butcher know how to dissect an eyeball, or whatever it was you called it?" She reached for the post-mortem report once again.

"Enucleation," replied Caz. "And yes, possibly. Whoever it is, they have surgical skills and knowledge of the human body. I guess that could translate to animals."

"And butchers do sell tongues . . ."

"They do indeed. Have you had a chance to look at my report on the hand?"

Nicki picked up the draft report. "I'm looking at it now."

"Well, the edited highlights are — definitely female, and once again, expertly dissected. The bones were neatly cut — the nerves, tendons and other tissues separated with a degree of skill."

"The same victim?" Nicki's thoughts turned to Jacqui Massingham. Could this be her hand?

"I've taken tissue and blood sampling. The DNA will no doubt tell you if you've got a match."

Or I could just show a photograph to Lionel and Audrey Massingham — see if they recognise the tattoos. Nicki didn't relish another trip to the frosty Manor House just yet. "We're searching for a fingerprint match as we speak. That may come back more quickly than the DNA." Nicki made a mental note to check how they were getting on with the fingerprint analysis. "Could someone still be alive, Caz? After having their hand amputated like that?" She shivered — the thought seemed incomprehensible.

"That would depend. Surgical amputations, if performed in a controlled environment with appropriate aftercare, aren't life threatening in themselves. So, given the right circumstances . . . yes, the person could still be alive. But done the wrong way, the blood loss could be catastrophic. And then there's the risk of infection, sepsis . . ."

"And if we're looking at it being the same person — Jacqui? Already missing her eyes and tongue. Would . . . *could* she survive losing a hand, too?" Nicki's stomach gave another involuntary jolt.

Caz paused on the other end of the line. "It would be asking a lot for the body to cope with something like that, I'll say that much. And then you need to factor in the shock . . ."

"So, unlikely then?"

"Never say never, Nicki. But . . . you haven't found a body yet, have you?"

"No, nothing."

Just then, Nicki's desk phone began to trill. "Sorry, Caz — I've another call to take. We'll catch up soon."

"We will indeed — it's wine night tonight, if you haven't already forgotten."

Nicki had.

"I'm not taking no for an answer, Nicki. I'm picking Amy up on my way."

Nicki cut the call and snatched up the desk phone. "DI Hardcastle."

"Hi, Nicki — it's Faye. Just to let you know we're here at the Massingham house. Just about to get suited up. Wondered if you wanted to join?"

"Good idea, I'll head down in a moment."

"I don't have much for you from the theatre, I'm afraid. Everything so far has come back clean, forensically speaking. The various reports will be heading your way soon."

Nicki nodded. She'd suspected as much.

"And I doubt Cassie has had much more luck at the roundabout, what with the elements being against us."

"No problem — it was a long shot anyway. Give me ten minutes and I'll be with you."

* * *

2 Old Railway Cottages
Dullingham, Nr Newmarket

Benedict watched as Annette Browning hurried back up towards the house in the fading afternoon light, pulling thorns from her cardigan as she went.

Had she been to see the headstone?

He let the curtains fall back into place and made his way back downstairs. The kitchen table was now strewn with photographs, printouts, emails and spreadsheets. Everything was falling into place, just as it had before. But now he was *sure*.

He'd give anything for the chance to get back inside next door's study again — he needed to see those cuttings. Their contents were embedded in his brain, but he just wanted to see them one more time.

To be absolutely sure.

But how he was going to get back inside number four was anyone's guess.

Sighing, Benedict picked up his phone and scrolled through the latest news headlines. The town was front page news again — details of the two gruesome discoveries dominating every tabloid and broadsheet.

And right there in the very thick of it was Detective Inspector Nicki Hardcastle.

Benedict looked once more at the array of evidence decorating his kitchen table.

He needed to get back inside number four — and soon. Glancing up at the kitchen window, an idea formed in his mind.

* * *

Woodpecker Drive, Bury St Edmunds

Although Nicki hadn't been along this particular street before, it was quite clear which house belonged to Jacqui Massingham. The blue and white police tape stretched across the front of number seven and a solitary uniformed officer on the doorstep gave it away.

Ducking beneath the tape, Nicki made her way up the garden path. After logging her details on the attendance log, and donning a white protective suit, both Nicki and DS Fox entered Jacqui Massingham's neat, semi-detached home.

Following the metal stepping plates, they headed towards a decent-sized front room. Muted shades of mocha and chocolate were interspersed with softer caramel and cream. An invitingly soft and comfortable looking corner sofa graced the far wall, covered in scatter cushions. Nicki could imagine Jacqui relaxing after a hard day at work, a glass of wine on the coffee table, warming herself in front of the wood-burning stove in the fireplace.

She experienced an all too familiar tinge of sadness that invariably made its presence felt when visiting the home of the deceased. An essence of whoever had lived there often still lingered — be it a coffee cup waiting to be washed in the sink, or freshly laundered clothes waiting to be ironed. Sometimes even a shopping list pinned to the fridge.

A life interrupted.

Not that Nicki knew for sure that Jacqui Massingham was dead.

But, after her conversation with Caz, it didn't look good.

Stepping out into the hall, Nicki briefly took in the rest of the ground floor. A downstairs bathroom and immaculate kitchen, both recently refurbished and tastefully decorated — whatever poor start in life her parents had given her, Jacqui had made something of herself, creating a beautiful home.

Heading upstairs, she left Fox to give the downstairs another look and to check outside for Jacqui's car. He seemed relieved not to have to negotiate the narrow stairs, leaning heavily on his cane as she disappeared from sight.

Upstairs, Nicki found a second bathroom and two bedrooms — all recently redecorated. A vase of wooden tulips sat on the window ledge on the landing, and several abstract paintings lined the pastel-coloured walls.

Visions of Lionel and Audrey Massingham looking haughtily down their narrow noses at the mere mention of their daughter's name made Nicki's skin prickle. How dare they say such derogatory things about their own daughter — a daughter they had systematically failed, abandoning her at the tender age of fifteen to make her own way in the world.

She couldn't quite square the picture painted by Lionel and Audrey Massingham of a disobedient delinquent with the person living in such a stylish and well cared for home.

Nicki shook her head to rid herself of the image of the Massinghams — not wanting to waste her thoughts on people who would never change. Heading along the landing, she recognised a familiar figure crouching down inside the bathroom.

"Faye." Nicki stopped outside the door, not wanting to crowd the investigations going on within. "Anything?"

Faye straightened up and shook her head. "Not really. We're taking a few random samples as we go around, but I don't see anything to suggest that this is your crime scene." She nodded back towards the bath. "There are a couple of spots of blood on the side of the bath, which we'll swab, and then we'll Luminol the rest — but otherwise the whole house looks clean. The house was locked when we arrived — front and back. We haven't located a handbag, car keys, mobile phone or purse anywhere."

Nicki thanked Faye for her work and went to head back downstairs. At the top of the stairs was the door leading into, what Nicki presumed was, Jacqui's bedroom. Nudging the door open with her foot, Nicki took in the clothes draped over the back of a chair; the dressing gown lying on the pillow; a half-drunk mug of tea sitting on the bedside table; a book lying face-down on the floor by the bed. It was as though she'd just stepped out and would be returning home soon.

Fox met her at the bottom of the stairs. He raised his eyebrows towards the ceiling, but Nicki shook her head. "Nothing. The place is immaculate. I seriously doubt she met her abductor inside these walls."

"Same down here. Nothing out of place. No signs of a struggle."

Fox lifted his cane and waved it in the direction of the front door. "That Renault Clio we saw on the way in — I checked and it's registered to Jacqui Massingham."

"I think we can be relatively confident she made it this far. I'll make sure Faye double processes the front and rear entrances — maybe she went round the back instead of coming in through the front door and he was waiting for her there. Never got the chance to get inside. That would fit with her bag, phone and keys being missing."

Net curtains twitched as they made their way back to the car in silence. With the sun now setting, darkness was descending. "We'll get house-to-house organised. See if anyone saw anything out of the ordinary. And Jacqui's name is being released to the media later this evening — we'll see if that throws up any leads." Nicki unlocked the Toyota and glanced across the roof at Fox.

"Let me drop you off at home, Graham. You look dead on your feet."

CHAPTER TWENTY

College Lane, Bury St Edmunds

Nicki pulled open the fridge and surveyed the damage. She hadn't been shopping since before Christmas, and the empty shelves spoke for themselves. There was, however, still an unopened bottle of wine and a jar of olives. Grabbing both of them, and the last of the cheese, she set about making a cheeseboard.

Luna jumped up on to the worktop, her nose twitching, sensing the aroma of her favourite cheese.

"You know you shouldn't eat this really," smiled Nicki, cutting a small chunk from the block and dangling it in front of the Russian Blue's mouth. Like lightning, a set of razor-sharp teeth swiped the morsel from Nicki's fingers. "It's bad for your digestion."

Luna ignored her and purred for more.

"This is your lot." Nicki gave Luna one more sliver of cheese then shooed her from the worktop and out of the kitchen. "Now leave me in peace to get ready."

She hadn't had time to run a bath or change out of her work clothes, but she knew the girls wouldn't mind. Although it was tempting to call it off, citing work pressure and tiredness, Nicki knew they all needed this little get-to-gether. Trying to fix a time when the three of them were all free was always a headache. Amy worked such long and odd shifts at the hospital and Caz — well, Caz seemed to *always* be working. Nicki reckoned they probably said the same about her.

Nicki had dropped Graham close to his flat, but they both knew he probably wouldn't make it through the front door. By now, she fully expected the detective sergeant to be back at his desk, slogging away at whatever jobs he could find to give him the excuse not to go home.

Finding a spare packet of tortilla chips in the cupboard, Nicki brought the wine and hastily prepared cheeseboard through to the living room, placing everything on the coffee table. She then found three clean wine glasses and some side plates.

Her stomach rumbled as she eyed up the meagre selection of cheese and olives. The chin chin biscuits from earlier were a distant memory now. Her gaze then flickered towards the framed photograph of Deano, sitting next to the clock.

Plucking the photograph from the mantelpiece, she slipped it beneath a copy of yesterday's newspaper and slotted both beneath the coffee table. Very few people knew about the loss of Deano — or her previous life as Nicola Webster. Despite Amy and Caz being two of her closest friends, she hadn't quite got around to filling them in on her past. She didn't really know why — but it wasn't exactly something you could casually drop into the conversation in between chatting about last night's TV and where they'd all go on holiday if they won the lottery.

Something always got in the way. And the longer she left it, the harder it became.

Turning away from the mantelpiece, Nicki reached for the wine bottle and began to unscrew the cap. A cool glass of wine was just what she needed right now.

Just as she finished pouring the wine, three short raps on the front door sounded.

"We've brought supplies!" Amy Butler thrust two bottles of wine at Nicki as soon as the door was opened, bustling across the threshold out of the cold.

"And because we know you detectives are shockingly bad at shopping, we've brought food, too!" Caz followed Amy inside, a bulging carrier bag in one hand. She kicked the door shut behind her. "And I'm starving!"

She immediately headed towards Nicki's tiny kitchen. "I've brought dips, samosas, mozzarella sticks and some fresh bread we can warm up in the oven."

Nicki smiled. "Thanks both." She glanced at the pathetic offerings on the cheeseboard. "I haven't got much in — I still need to go shopping."

"We know," chimed Amy and Caz in unison, both grinning.

Caz slipped the bread into the oven and brought the other items through to the coffee table. "Sit yourselves down — the bread won't take a minute."

Nicki didn't need telling twice and gratefully flopped down on to one end of the sofa. Amy handed her one of the glasses of wine. It was only just hitting her how tired she was — exhausted, even. It was always the same when a new investigation kicked off — days and hours running into each other, night and day blurring into one, sapping whatever energy she possessed.

Closing her eyes, she took a welcome gulp of cool, crisp wine. "I don't know what I'd do without either of you," she murmured, sighing contentedly as the wine slid comfortingly down her throat. She took another mouthful.

"Starve," commented Caz, loading a plate with samosas and olives and handing it to Nicki.

"But you might be more sober," added Amy, leaning over to top up Nicki's glass.

Caz returned to the kitchen to take the bread out of the oven, the enticing aroma following her back into the living room. She picked up her wine glass and held it aloft. "Here's to us, then."

"Here's to us," echoed Nicki, taking another mouthful of wine before tucking into her samosa, the flaky pastry dissolving on her tongue.

Amy settled back in her seat, tucking her legs beneath her and dipping a piece of warm bread into the sour cream dip. "So, how's things? Aside from work, of course," she added, hastily. "We all know how horrendous that must be right now. What else is going on in Nicki's world?"

Nicki hesitated, slowly chewing the remains of her samosa. What was going on in her life? She knew the answer was short and sweet.

"Not much. Just work — you know how it is."

"You not seen anything of Jeremy recently?" Amy's eyes sparkled over the rim of her glass. "You make a sweet couple."

Nicki smothered a laugh with another gulp of wine. "We're not a couple, as you well know. Sweet or otherwise. We're just friends." Jeremy Frost was a reporter with one of the local newspapers, and was a person Nicki knew well and trusted.

Amy continued to smile behind her glass. "If you say so."

"Faye says you're going to her martial arts class on Monday." It was Caz's turn to flop down next to Nicki on the sofa. "She says you're really looking forward to it." Caz popped another olive into her mouth as she grinned.

"I said I *might* go," warned Nicki. "It's not definite."

"Monday?" Amy reached for the remains of the wine bottle. "That's New Year's Eve. You haven't forgotten you're meant to be going to the pub with Darcie, have you? She's been banging on about it for weeks — someone's birthday?"

"Ah!" Nicki flashed a grin at Caz. "Prior commitment! It's Matt's thirtieth birthday — we're all going out for a drink to celebrate."

"Hmmmm." Caz held her glass out for a refill. "I'll let you tell Faye the good news. But she'll get you there one day. Resistance is futile."

Amy emptied the remains of the bottle and reached for a second. "What about you, Caz? How's your love life?"

Caz almost spat her wine out across the coffee table. "My love life? Well, since I spend about fourteen hours a day in the company of dead people, I think we can safely call it barren and unexciting."

"Looks like my little sister gets more dates than the three of us put together!" Amy reached for another chunk of bread. "I'll have to ask her what her secret is."

* * *

The Farmhouse

Standing in front of the body map, he let his fingers run lightly over the surface of the Polaroids. "Not long now, my beautiful girls. You'll soon have another friend to keep you company."

According to the boy's social media accounts, tonight was to be the night. Pulling his cap down firmly over his head, Laurence paused in front of the old pantry shelves, now stacked with his personalised range of sedatives and anaesthetic agents. Not exactly pickled onions or beetroot anymore. He smothered a small chuckle before letting his eyes wander towards the jar on the top shelf.

The jar that had started everything.

Laurence brought the jar down and tapped the lid with his finger.

Tap — tap — tap — tap — tap

Tap — tap — tap — tap — tap

The sound swelled his heart, announcing that death would soon be coming to the farmhouse once again.

Just like it had all those years ago.

It had been a hot summer's night, back when his grandfather was alive. Laurence couldn't sleep, the bedclothes sticking to his skin as he tossed and turned. Not a breath of air wafted through the open bedroom window.

He needed to cool down.

Creeping downstairs as quietly as he could, careful not to wake his father in the next room, Laurence Jr made his way to the kitchen in search of a glass of water.

The kitchen lay in semi-darkness — only a pale moon-beam filtering in through the window afforded any light. At the sink, he filled a glass tumbler full of water and drank deeply, the cool liquid soothing his parched throat. His skin felt hot to the touch, sweat lining his brow.

Making his way out of the kitchen, his feet relishing the cool of the stone floor beneath him, Laurence paused at the door to the pantry. The pantry was always cool — it had no windows and thick concrete walls. Taking another gulp from his glass, he stepped through the doorway.

It was then that he heard it.

To begin with, he wasn't sure what it was or where it was coming from. A strangely eerie sound that echoed as he stood barefoot by the pantry shelves.

Tap — tap — tap — tap — tap

Tap — tap — tap — tap — tap

Young Laurence held his breath, straining his ears to listen.

There it was again.

Tap — tap — tap — tap — tap

Tap — tap — tap — tap — tap

It sounded like it was coming from the boot room.

Tap — tap — tap — tap — tap

Tap — tap — tap — tap — tap

Mesmerised, Laurence followed the sound.

The boot room was dark — the only window set high towards the ceiling, out of reach of the pale moon. He paused in the doorway, letting his eyes adjust to the gloom. Soon he could see the familiar row of pegs by the back door, heavy jackets and dog leads hanging down from each. Discarded boots lay in a heap by the side of the butler sink, the smell of dusty earth still in the air.

Cautiously he edged further inside.

Tap — tap — tap — tap — tap

There it was again.

Tap — tap — tap — tap — tap

Suddenly, the sound was all around him, tapping incessantly, one after the other.

"All right, my boy. What are you doing awake?"

The sound of his grandfather's quiet tone made him jump and he spun around to see the old man in the doorway, already dressed for work. The working day began early on the farm, long before sunrise — and although it might feel like the dead of night to him, for his grandfather it was time to start the day's toil.

"I . . . I was thirsty," replied Laurence, his voice a scratchy rasp. "I couldn't sleep so I came down for a drink of water."

"Aye, it's a warm and sticky one, all right." His grandfather stepped forward to ruffle his grandson's hair. "And it'll be a warm one today, too. You mark my words."

The tapping sounds continued, increasing in intensity, and Laurence found himself turning towards the darkest corner of the boot room.

"What's that noise, grandfather?" he asked, the frown returning to his young brow. "That tapping sound. Over there."

He watched his grandfather's head tilt towards the noise and then up towards the rafters. "That, my boy, is what we call a problem."

The sigh that escaped the old man's mouth was deep.

"Problem? What kind of problem?"

His grandfather took him by the hand and led him towards the darkest corner of the boot room — as they did so, the tapping sounds intensified.

"That noise you can hear?" His grandfather nodded towards the oak timbers that made up the structure of the boot room. "That's hundreds upon hundreds of tiny beetles hidden inside the wood."

"Beetles?" Young Laurence Hemmingway's eyebrows shot up. "What kind of beetles?"

"Wood-eating beetles," grinned his grandfather. "Although that's not strictly true. It's the larvae that are burrowing through the wood, eating into it. The tapping sound you can hear is actually the mating call of the adult beetles. And on a hot, sultry night like tonight, it's perfect for them. They'll be out in droves."

Larvae? Mating calls? Laurence recalled something in his biology classes at school about how caterpillars turn into butterflies. But he'd never heard of wood-eating beetles. "They eat *wood*?"

His grandfather smiled and ruffled his hair once again. "The female beetle lays her eggs in the tiny crevices of the wood, and in there they grow into larvae. When they're big enough, the larvae start to burrow into the wood, eating it as they go." He sighed again as he turned to look up at the wooden rafters above. "They're slowly destroying all the wood there is in here, sonny — this whole room will need to come down soon."

"And that's what I can hear? The beetles?"

His grandfather nodded. "Deathwatch beetles, my lad. That's what they call them."

"*Death*watch beetles?" Intrigue flooded young Laurence's features, all feelings of tiredness evaporating in an instant. His eyes shone. "Why are they called that?"

His grandfather began to lead him by the hand away from the tapping sounds and back towards the kitchen. "Superstition has it that they're the harbinger of death."

"What's a harb . . . harbringer?"

"A *harbinger*. What they mean is that the sound of the deathwatch beetle announces the arrival of death. Maybe even the devil, if that's what you believe. If you can hear the beetles tapping, then death isn't far behind."

"Really?" Laurence's eyes widened in awe. "Someone's going to die?"

His grandfather's eyes crinkled as they made their way into the relative brightness of the kitchen, his mouth breaking out into a wide grin. "Of course not. It's just a silly story. All that tapping sound means is that I need to pull the boot room down and build another one."

Laurence smiled at the memory of his grandfather as he shrugged into his coat. Not long after that night, the boot room was razed to the ground. It didn't take long — the rotting timbers didn't put up much of a fight.

He'd been told to stay away — it being dusty and dangerous work — but had found a hiding place behind a tractor in the yard and watched from a distance.

His grandfather was right. It *was* dusty. And noisy.

The sound of the timber splitting as each one was pulled to the ground tore through the otherwise tranquil summer's afternoon. Cracked and rotten timbers were hurled into the back of one of the farm's carts and, once it was full, it was dragged into a neighbouring field, the contents ready to be burnt.

Young Laurence watched from his hiding place until every plank of wood had been pulled down. But before the cart was finally pulled away, he'd bolted from behind the tractor, glass jar in hand. Ever since he'd learned what was responsible for the tapping noises, he'd wanted to see one for himself. A deathwatch beetle! He had looked them up in one of his grandfather's huge collection of encyclopaedias in the snug — but it wasn't the same. They were only pictures. He wanted to actually see one in real life. Maybe even touch one.

Knowing he didn't have much time, he began turning over pieces of rotten and splintered timber in the back of the cart, the wood disintegrating into fine sand beneath his touch. The dust tickled his nose and made him sneeze.

Just as he was about to give up, he spied movement beneath a particularly rotten length of wood. He kicked it to the side and immediately saw several small insects scurry for cover. Taking his jam jar in a steady hand, he bent down and scooped them up, slamming the lid back on fast. With his heart thudding beneath his T-shirt, he jumped down from the cart and ran back to the farmhouse.

The jam jar sat proudly on the window ledge in his bedroom, and every day he would watch them. To begin with, the beetles scurried around the glass jar, searching for a way out. After a while, they began to slow down and eventually accept their fate — there was no way out. Not now. Not ever. And then they became still.

Death fascinated Laurence as much as life. In school, they learned about the life cycle of insects and plants — they were even moving on to how babies were made soon — but nobody mentioned death. It was all about *life*. How *life* was created.

But what about *death*?

He had asked the teacher one time but all he got in response was a quizzical look and an order to go and sit down.

Ever since his grandfather had told him how the death-watch beetles had got their name, the thought stayed with him, night and day. Even when his grandfather reminded him it was nonsense, just a silly superstition, he couldn't get it out of his head.

What if it *was* true? What if they really did herald death and disaster? An omen of bad things to come? How soon after their eerie tapping sound would death finally come knocking?

A day? A week? A month?

Laurence didn't have long to wait to find out.

After the new boot room was rebuilt later that summer, his grandfather's life was snuffed out beneath the hay bales.

Standing in the farmhouse now, some twenty years later, Laurence felt a strange shiver ripple through his bones. He had kept the jam jar, all these years, even though the tiny insects inside had long since ceased to exist. He remembered trying to research how to preserve dead insects, and even asked the same teacher at school again — which had earned him yet another quizzical look, together with a frown. So, he had tried his best. He hadn't got it completely right — the insects soon shrivelling at the bottom of the jar.

But he still kept it all the same.

He tapped the lid of the jar once again.

Tap — tap — tap — tap — tap

Tap — tap — tap — tap — tap

Death was coming tonight.

CHAPTER TWENTY-ONE

Saturday 29 December 2018
Bury St Edmunds Town Centre

Lee hadn't wanted to go to Barney's leaving do. He'd been steamrollered into it, unable to think of a decent excuse. He didn't even particularly like the guy, and wouldn't miss him once he was gone. But Lee being Lee, he'd acquiesced and agreed to meet them in the centre of town.

That was forty-five minutes ago.

He'd already had one text message asking where he was — which he'd ignored. And then there was the phone call. He'd switched his phone off after that and headed home. The house would be empty so he could do exactly as he wanted and no one would be there to see.

There was the batty old lady next door, but she hardly popped her head outside her own door these days — not now the bad weather had arrived. He was supposed to go round and check on her tonight — orders left by his parents before they had left for their ten-day break in the sun. He'd do it when he got home — *if* he remembered. Or maybe he'd do it in the morning instead.

He took a left and headed along Churchgate Street. Who had a leaving do in December anyway? Right after Christmas when no one had any cash left? The tenner he'd felt compelled to put in the kitty for a leaving present had stung his wallet. And the rest of the night was likely to cost a pretty penny, too. They'd chosen one of the most expensive places in town to meet. A couple of pints in there and that would be his budget blown.

Decision made.

He grinned to himself as he headed away from the centre of town. Snow was in the air once again, tiny snowflakes starting to settle on his nose. There was leftover curry in the fridge which would do him for tonight — and Mum had left the cupboards so full he had enough food for a month. Plus, there was beer — his dad leaving several boxes in the utility room.

Curry and beer. Perfect.

And there was boxing on the TV tonight.

Even more perfect.

The town had been quiet for a Saturday night. No doubt the adverse weather was keeping people indoors. He had loved snow as a kid. When they'd lived up north they'd used tea trays as makeshift sledges to race down the hill at the back of the house. He missed those days. When you were a kid, you had nothing more important to worry about other than what sweets you could afford to buy with your pocket money that week — and whether it was chips for tea that night.

Now he was meant to be a grown-up, things weren't quite as much fun anymore. And everything cost so much money. Take his trainers, for example. He glanced down at his feet, already able to feel the ice-cold snow chilling his feet. So much for paying over two hundred quid for them — you'd at least expect them to be waterproof. Or snow proof.

He upped his stride and pulled his phone from his pocket, switching it back on. Immediately he noticed status updates from his work colleagues, even tagging him into photos when he wasn't even there. He decided to put a status on for himself and see if anyone noticed.

'Heading home for the boxing!'

He 'checked into' a restaurant as he passed by — sending a photo of a deserted street as he continued his journey. With the thought of the boxing on TV and the curry in the fridge, Lee quickened his step.

The snow underfoot muffled his footsteps.

And those following behind.

* * *

College Lane, Bury St Edmunds

"I know we shouldn't talk shop tonight but . . ." Caz opened the third bottle of wine and topped up everyone's glass. "But the blood results came back on your severed hand. I checked before I left the mortuary this evening."

Nicki took a gulp of wine. "And?"

"Different blood group." Caz mopped up some olive oil with the remains of the bread on her plate. "Your first victim was O positive. This one is AB positive — it's pretty rare. But you're looking at a completely different person."

A second victim.

The words hung uncomfortably in the air as Nicki swallowed her last mouthful of samosa. If the hand didn't belong to Jacqui, then who did it belong to? And how would they find them? "We're releasing Jacqui's name to the media tonight. No doubt it'll hit the headlines in the morning. But now we know the hand belongs to someone else, we're back to square one with that one."

Caz reached for a mozzarella stick. "I've got some pretty good images of the tattoos. They're very unusual — especially when viewed together. Someone might recognise them if you made them public?"

Nicki knew that was the next logical step. But one she wasn't looking forward to taking. "I've got to go and see the DCI in the morning — I'm sure that's what he'll suggest."

Amy shivered. "Imagine recognising it as someone you know — a close friend, a sister, mother. I can't think of a

185

worse way of finding out — seeing it splashed across the front pages like that."

Nicki chased a lone olive around her plate, her appetite waning. "Me neither. But I'm not sure we've got much of an alternative."

"Right, no more shop talk, it's depressing." Caz pulled a bottle of elderflower gin from her handbag. "Who fancies some of this to end the night with?"

Nicki groaned, knowing that with an early start in the morning she should really say no — but Caz was already getting the glasses together. Very soon, a generous serving of gin with a splash of tonic landed in her hand.

"Is Darcie still seeing that porter from the hospital?" Caz asked. "What's his name? Ryan, or something?"

Amy gave a shrug as she took a sip of the gin. "I don't think so — I think they're just friends now. Nice lad, though. She keeps her private life just that — private. Not even her big sister gets to know the juicy gossip! But I do think she might have a bit of a crush on our new lodger."

"Lodger?" Nicki felt the gin entering her bloodstream. "Since when have you had a lodger?"

"For a few weeks now. We've got an attic room that we don't use and to be honest we could do with a bit to help towards the mortgage and bills. I put an ad up at work and had one of the doctors apply. Oliver. He's nice. He lives out in the sticks somewhere, so I think he was interested in having a base in town for when he's doing late shifts. To be honest, we hardly see him."

"Ooh, a doctor!" Caz joined in the teasing. "Is he good looking?"

Amy dissolved in a fit of gin-infused giggles, narrowly missing sloshing the contents of her glass over herself. "I told you, he's rarely even there! But he is rather easy on the eye!"

Caz finished her gin and held the bottle up for refills. Both Amy and Nicki shook their heads. "Well, if he pays the rent on time, you can't complain. Does he have anything else going for him? Is he single?"

"Well, he's an amazing cook! We might not see much of him, but we often find a lasagne, or a pasta bake, in the fridge. He bakes, too."

"Well, he sounds too good to be true, if you ask me." Caz poured herself a shot of gin. "Good looking. Good job. Pays the rent. Likes to cook. And hardly there to get under your feet. People like that surely don't exist."

Amy's cheeks coloured a little. "Well, I was going to get him to pick me up tonight, but he had to go out. Maybe next time."

The evening continued with more food and gin being consumed — eventually Luna slunk down the stairs to see if there were any worthy leftovers, which was the cue for Amy and Caz to ring for a taxi. Once they'd left, Nicki barely managed to climb the stairs to bed before falling asleep.

* * *

Sunday 30 December 2018
The Farmhouse

He stood for a moment by the side of the steel trolley, Lee's unconscious form still quietly slumbering. It would be a shame, in a way, to wake him and disturb the peace, but there was no fun in death if it wasn't witnessed.

Anyone could die in their sleep — many hoped that would be the way they exited this world, painlessly and without fear. But what a missed opportunity that would be. To miss that final transition — the last journey anyone, anywhere, would ever make. Thoughts and feelings from your final seconds on this earth — who wouldn't want to experience that?

He had already washed and sterilised his instruments and set them out in the steel tray.

He was ready.

He had set up the infusion pump, as he had with both Lucie and Jacqui, and spent the last few hours just watching the boy's chest rise and fall.

Time was on his side. It was still early — dawn yet to break on the new day. He could keep the boy in a perpetual slumber for as long as he wanted — within reason. He'd kept both Jacqui and Lucie for several days before deciding to bring them round and enjoy the fun. But this time he felt different — he could feel the spark of impatience growing inside him. Now the map was taking shape, he didn't want to delay things for too long.

There was so much more still to do.

He'd strapped Lee down in the same way as the ones before — a leather strap around each ankle, and one around each wrist. He'd added an extra strap around the middle of the boy's torso, securing it in place, but didn't attach the homemade head restraint this time. The focus of his attention wasn't going to be on the head. Not for Lee.

He stopped the infusion pump, halting the continuous infusion of ketamine that was keeping Lee from this world. And then he waited — watching night turn into day as the minutes ticked by. A familiar thrill began to build — he wondered what expression might be on the boy's face when he finally stirred. Whatever it was, he would capture it on camera — just like he had all the others.

He'd already checked the video camera was switched on, seeing the reassuring red light out of the corner of his eye.

He wouldn't gag this one, either. He wanted to *hear* how death felt this time — not just see it.

When he was sure that Lee was starting to come round, he reached towards the equipment trolley and selected a particularly sharp scalpel. The first incision was met with a grunt and a slight stiffening of both legs beneath their straps. Lee's eyes were still closed, but his eyelids were beginning to twitch. The second incision brought more twitching, and both eyes began to peel open. The grunting got louder.

It was the third incision that rendered Lee fully awake — his eyes snapping open as wide as saucers as a scream bubbled inside his throat. Pausing with the bloodied scalpel in one hand, Laurence leaned across the boy's incapacitated body and grinned.

"You're awake!"

The scream that erupted and echoed around the roughly hewn farmhouse walls, brought a satisfied smile to Laurence's face. Turning to the side, he reached for his phone and selected his favourite, haunting melody. *Danse Macabre* filled the room, drowning out the terrified yells emanating from the pathology trolley.

He smiled once more, feeling that familiar tingle embrace him — and continued with his work.

CHAPTER TWENTY-TWO

Sunday 30 December 2018
Bury St Edmunds Police Station

"The hand definitely doesn't belong to Jacqui Massingham."
Nicki sipped her strong, black coffee and willed the headache
crashing at her temples to retreat. Although the three bottles
of wine and gin they had managed to get through last night
probably hadn't been a good idea, not in the middle of a
complex investigation, it was exactly what Nicki had needed.

Apart from today's headache.

"Caz has confirmed the blood type is different, backed
up by the confirmation we've just had that the fingerprints
don't match those we have for Jacqui on the system. We are
looking for a second victim."

Nicki let the information sink in while she took another
mouthful of hot coffee. She winced as it hit her tongue. "It
doesn't need saying, but we need to get an ID for this poor
woman as quickly as we can. Her DNA profile is being processed, but we won't hold our breath on that one — and her
fingerprints aren't on the system.

"Once again, the hand was amputated with surgical
expertise. We are looking for someone with at least some

basic medical training." Nicki couldn't help seeing a vision of Adrian Browning — the image of a surgical scalpel replaced with a meat cleaver.

"Are you going to go public, boss? With a picture of the hand?" Roy voiced what had been on everyone's lips as soon as they heard the words 'second victim'. "See if anyone recognises the tattoos?"

"As unpalatable as it might sound, I think we have no option." Nicki paused. "The DCI wants to see me, and I think that's probably top of his agenda. We went out to Jacqui's home last night — I'm convinced that wasn't the crime scene, but it's being processed just the same. There's no sign of Jacqui's mobile phone, handbag, coat or house keys." With her coffee in one hand, she added the details to the whiteboard. "We need to find these as soon as possible. In the meantime, trace her phone. With her car parked outside, it looks like she at least made it that far before she met her abductor. They either followed her home, or were waiting. Further house-to-house enquiries are being undertaken this morning to see if anyone in the vicinity saw anything unusual. On top of that, Jacqui's name will be released to the media this morning and we'll see what that brings."

"I've been taking another look at the CCTV around the cathedral." DS Fox nodded towards his computer screen. Nicki noticed the dark circles beneath his eyes, and the stubble gracing his chin, and wondered if he'd been at his desk all night. "Nothing definite, but there is someone who enters the cathedral at the front entrance at around four-thirty — but doesn't seem to come back out."

Everyone crowded around Graham's desk while he loaded up his computer screen with the CCTV image. "There he is — 4:31 p.m."

On the screen was a grainy image of a man entering the cathedral.

"And you say he doesn't come back out?"

Fox shook his head, then brought up a series of different images. "I wondered if he had slipped out the rear exit instead. You can get into the cathedral grounds through the corridor near the café. No cameras out there, but I did find a similar looking guy walking through the town at around the right time."

Three images filled Fox's computer screen.

Dressed for the cold weather in a hat and scarf, which covered most of his face — the man looked exactly like countless others bracing the wintry weather.

"It's not much to go on, I know."

Nicki sighed. "Maybe not, but it's progress. The tech guys haven't been able to do much with the image we got from outside the theatre, but see if they can do anything with those. It certainly looks like it could be the same guy."

Various grunts echoed around the incident room.

"Widen the search area around each location. The theatre, the roundabout and the cathedral. Let's see if we can't follow him somewhere. Maybe find a vehicle. The guy can't just disappear into thin air. Roy and Darcie — give Matt and Duncan a hand with that. Are you going out to see our friend Fernando Tavares this morning, the missing cleaner?"

Both Matt and Duncan nodded. "He's finally answered his phone and says he'll talk with us." Duncan gave a shrug. "His English isn't great but it's probably better than my Portuguese."

"What else have we got?" Nicki drained the rest of her coffee and began to feel the effects of the caffeine. "What about our friend Adrian? We still need to go back and see him again."

"Ah, well — here's where it gets a little bit more interesting." Duncan tapped his computer screen with the end of his biro.

"Interesting how?"

"He's not a prolific user of social media, except for Twitter. Goes on there most days." Tapping a few keys, Duncan brought up Adrian's Twitter feed. He waited a few moments while Nicki skimmed the contents, watching her eyebrows hitch.

"When were these sent?" Nicki tapped the screen. "That last one in particular."

"Two days before she went missing." Duncan enlarged the screen. "It was the last in a series that day. He seemed to have a right bee in his bonnet about something."

Nicki reached for her coat. "Print those out for me. I think we need to go and have another chat with our Mr Browning. Get his home address. Graham? Be ready to take a little trip out just as soon as I get back from the DCI's office. While we're gone, keep an eye on the house-to-house coming in from Jacqui's street — flag up anything we need to follow up."

"Maria McCrae called in half an hour ago," added Darcie, helping herself to the last of the chin chin biscuits. "Says Tommy arrived home yesterday afternoon."

"OK — well, maybe go and see him later. Before that, help Matt with the CCTV and carry on the social media trawls for both Adrian and Jacqui. I want to know how much they've interacted recently."

* * *

The Farmhouse

He had to hand it to him — the young lad was tough. Now, even minus both feet at the ankles, he was still alive.

Just.

The tourniquets around each leg had minimised the blood loss which had been useful on two fronts. Firstly, he didn't want the lad to go into shock and slip away too quickly — not before he was ready. That would have made the whole endeavour a pointless waste of time. And secondly, he didn't want the mess.

The familiar trickle of excitement began to build once again.

The boy had slipped back into unconsciousness soon after Laurence had started the process of amputating his feet just above the ankles. Laurence couldn't really blame him. He'd reconnected the infusion pump and allowed Lee a little extra slumber time while he carried on with his work.

There was plenty of time for waking later.

The bones of the ankle were much thicker than those of the wrist, so Laurence had used an electric saw this time. There was still the same delicious sound of grating bone when the blade came into contact. With the tibia and fibula now neatly cut, all muscles and ligaments dissected cleanly, Laurence needed the boy to be awake.

Now the fun could start.

Once again, the infusion pump had been disconnected and Laurence waited for Lee to rouse.

The anticipation was almost too much to bear.

Eventually Lee's eyes flickered open as consciousness started to return. It didn't take long for them to widen in seemingly equal measures of fear and pain — but maybe fear just edged it.

"Hello, sleepyhead." Laurence snapped on a fresh pair of gloves and smoothed down his surgical scrubs. "How are we feeling now?" Ever the doctor, he chuckled at his own bedside manner. "Would you like me to make you more comfortable?"

Lee's eyes stretched open even more, if that were humanly possible.

"Are you in pain?" Glancing back down at the bloodied stumps, Laurence saw that the tourniquets had done their job well. The worst of the blood loss had been stemmed, keeping the blood supply circulating to the boy's vital organs, but there was still a gentle ooze trickling from the wounds. He itched to remove the tourniquet completely and watch the resulting cascade — but he needed to be patient. A catastrophic blood loss such as that would still the boy's heart in seconds. And he didn't want that — not yet.

Instead, he pulled a wooden stool to the side of the steel trolley and sat down. With a gloved hand he stroked Lee's damp forehead.

"There, there. Let's take the rest of the journey together, shall we?"

Lee's eyelids blinked rapidly as if he were fighting to comprehend where he was; what nightmare he'd woken up in. His throat made a faint gurgling sound.

With one hand still on the boy's sweating forehead, Laurence reached down and gently released the clasp on the right-sided tourniquet. The blood had started to clot, but with the removal of the tight tourniquet the recently severed arteries opened up once again, with a little help from Laurence's scalpel.

He detected a shudder from the boy, noting his chest rising and falling in panicked bursts. Placing a finger to the side of the boy's neck, he felt the blood pumping faster and faster, no doubt as his fear level rose. A smile flickered on to Laurence's lips as he watched — a faster heart rate meant a faster blood flow. The end would be coming soon.

Laurence leaned forward on his stool and stared deeply into Lee's panic-stricken eyes — waiting for that delicate moment between life and death. All he needed to do was keep watching. The time would come soon.

Without taking his eyes from the boy, he stretched across and released the other tourniquet, his excitement building. What was the boy feeling now? Pain? Fear? Terror was probably high up on the list. Would he know the end was coming like his grandfather had?

The boy's eyelids fluttered, his whole body beginning to shake.

Lee was going into shock.

Laurence held his breath, not wanting to miss a single second of the transition. This was what it was all about.

Life.

And death.

Every time he witnessed life leaving a human body, he thought of his grandfather. He hadn't been there that time — not when it truly mattered. He hadn't been able to see or hear what his grandfather's final moments had been like

— all he'd been able to do was sit with the old man in the aftermath of death . . . and imagine.

Death was almost here now; he could see it. Lee's face had taken on a pale, pallid look as the blood continued to exit his body. The flow was lessening — but not enough to stem the eventual destination of death. Any moment now, his heart would stop the fight to stay alive. The boy's breathing pattern was changing — breaths coming out in short, sharp gulps, his lungs desperately seeking the elusive oxygen they needed to survive.

But the effort was futile and would soon pass. No amount of oxygen could save him now.

And then he saw it.

That precious moment, hovering between life and death.

Not quite one, not quite the other.

Then, as quickly as he'd seen it, it was gone.

CHAPTER TWENTY-THREE

Bury St Edmunds Police Station

"I'm worried, Nicki." DCI Malcolm Turner gestured for her to take a seat. "This case seems to be spiralling out of control."

"It might be spiralling," acknowledged Nicki, "but we're not out of control yet." An edge entered her tone, one she instantly regretted.

The DCI's face softened. "It's not a criticism. I'm just worried the department will be unable to cope if things continue. You've only got a small team on this — there's only so much you can do."

"I'm using extra bodies to do the grunt work — house-to-house around the three locations, and I'm getting fresh eyes to look at the CCTV and fixed camera footage. We're coping."

"I'm not saying you're not coping, Nicki. I just wouldn't be doing my job properly if I didn't express my concern. I see the identification on the first victim has reached the newspapers this morning."

Nicki nodded. "Yes. Her name was released in a press statement last night. We had no grounds to keep it under wraps any longer. Next of kin have been notified."

"But there's nothing on the second victim yet?"

Nicki shook her head. "Not yet. Just confirmation it definitely isn't Jacqui Massingham."

"No leads on why she might have been targeted?"

Another shake of the head. "Not at this stage. We do have a cranky ex-boyfriend — there is a history of domestic disputes between them, plus an outstanding assault case. And there's definitely no love lost between them. We're going back to see him this morning."

"Keep me posted. How do you feel about going public? With the hand?"

Nicki had been prepared for the question, already acknowledging there was no other course of action open to them. They were in a corner and needed to get out of it — and fast. "I think we're going to have to."

Turner pulled his diary towards him. "I hoped you'd say that. I feel you need to strike while the iron is hot, as they say. No sense in delaying matters. I'll schedule a press conference for midday. Make sure you have everything ready and liaise with the press office for a suitable statement I can read."

"Yes, sir," Nicki replied meekly. It wouldn't be easy. Displaying the image of a severed hand and asking the public if they recognise the woman's tattoos would be a shocking way of finding out a loved one's fate.

But what else could they do?

The killer — if he *was* a killer — was leading them down a blind alley.

And the only way to catch him would be to turn around and face him head on.

* * *

The Farmhouse

Lee's feet were sitting on a piece of polythene sheeting next to the pathology trolley. Laurence had taken a particularly good photograph and now pinned it to the body map.

The map was taking shape.

The thought excited him in a way that was difficult to explain.

What would be next?

There were many fascinating parts of the human body that were completely hidden from view. The liver. The kidneys. The stomach. Then there was the intestines — about fifteen feet of deliciousness, when stretched out end to end. All just waiting to be discovered and made a part of this living, breathing, human body map.

Well, maybe not living and breathing anymore.

The thought made him smile.

He could feel the hidden flame inside igniting once more.

Leaving the boy lying on the pathology trolley, life now deliciously extinct, Laurence padded through to the kitchen, his stomach rumbling. He'd cleaned up the majority of the blood and changed out of his scrubs. Now he was hungry. The range had made the room warm and inviting, and he soon had a saucepan of boiling water on the go for some boiled eggs to go with his toast, and the kettle for a pot of tea.

He fancied eggs this morning. Boiled eggs with a nice runny yolk.

As he popped three eggs into the boiling water, and the tea brewed in the pot, he settled down at the table to scour the headlines on the online news outlets. It didn't take long for a contented smile to flicker on to his lips.

Jacqui Massingham.

So, they'd managed to find out her name. He was quietly impressed.

The article was short, giving merely the poor unfortunate woman's name and the briefest of summaries as to her background. They didn't seem to know all that much about her. The thought intrigued him.

He skimmed the rest of the front-page article — there was nothing about Lucie. He wondered how long it would take them to pin a name to the hand.

Reaching across the table, he poured himself a mug of tea, adding a dash of milk. He returned his attention to the news reports — selecting a different news article this time. As he read, the contented smile on his lips froze.

Maria McCrae.

Ignoring the eggs that were now ready to be taken out of the boiling water, he read on.

Maria McCrae had given an exclusive interview to one of the newspapers lead reporters, detailing how her son had made the shocking discovery of Jacqui Massingham's tongue on Thursday night. There was even a picture of her standing by the side of the wolf, a suitably disgusted look on her face.

Not only had the boy blabbed — his mother had, too. To the press.

Laurence knew the boy had told the police, but he didn't realise he'd spilled the beans to his mother. So much for telling him he needed to keep his mouth shut if he wanted to keep a hold of his own tongue. The boy clearly hadn't believed him.

Pushing his mug of tea to the side, he stood up. Suddenly, his appetite for breakfast deserted him. He grabbed the saucepan from the range and hurled it into the sink, the eggs cracking against the ceramic sides, the boiling water hissing as it met the cool basin. Steam billowed up towards the ceiling.

The little runt couldn't be trusted to keep his mouth shut. What else did he tell his precious mother?

When Laurence had made mistakes, his father dealt out his punishment with the leather-tipped cane.

Striding back towards the pantry, he stood in front of the growing body map.

Maybe young Tommy could make amends in another way. He certainly needed to be taught a lesson.

CHAPTER TWENTY-FOUR

4 Old Railway Cottages
Dullingham, Nr Newmarket

Getting out of Nicki's Toyota, shutting the car door behind
him, DS Fox followed Nicki as she walked along the garden
path. The house looked neat and well-kept from the outside — a trellis with a rambling rose climbing the wall next
to the front door. Now pruned back, the plant was lying
dormant, waiting for the warmth of the sun to return and
reawaken it. The windows were clean, the front step swept
free from snow. Outwardly, number four looked like a normal, respectable family home.

Nicki rapped on the door using the brass door knocker
in the shape of an eagle. The sound reverberated along the
quiet lane. The sky was a dull grey, but at least no more snow
was forecast. The worst was over, according to the news, and
the country was gearing up for the big melt.

Looking through the frosted side panel, Nicki could see
movement within, and soon heard a key turning in the lock.
She took a step back as the door was pulled open. Before
her stood a timid looking woman, approximately in her late
fifties, with a tired yet kindly looking face. She wore plain

clothing, a simple cashmere jumper with a pair of linen trousers, and a silver chain bearing a cross around her neck. Her greying hair was swept away from her face in a loose bun.

"Yes?" she enquired, holding the door half open, half closed.

"Mrs Browning?" Nicki stepped a little closer, holding her warrant card out in front of her. "I'm Detective Inspector Nicki Hardcastle, from Suffolk Police. And this is my colleague, Detective Sergeant Fox. I wonder if it would be possible to have a quick word with your son, Adrian? If he's at home?"

Nicki had experienced many a reaction to her unannounced visits in the past, but she'd never quite witnessed such a rapid change in composure as displayed by Mrs Browning. The softly spoken, kindly faced woman instantly looked horrified, her eyes widening in shock. A hand flew to her mouth and she swayed unsteadily in her stockinged feet, grabbing the door frame for support.

Nicki leaned forward to place a hand beneath the woman's elbow, feeling it tremble beneath her touch. "I'm so sorry, Mrs Browning. I didn't mean to startle you." She nodded at Fox to take the other arm and help the woman back inside the house. "Everything's fine. It's nothing to worry about. We'd just like a few words with Adrian. Nothing more than that, I promise."

Between them, Nicki and Fox managed to guide Mrs Browning back along the hall, closing the door behind them to keep out the morning chill. As they passed the stairs, the door beneath flew open and a man Nicki presumed to be the woman's husband emerged.

"Annette?" The man rushed to his wife's side. "What on earth's happened?"

"I'm so sorry," said Nicki, taking her hand from Mrs Browning's elbow. "I think I may have unintentionally given your wife a fright." She held up her warrant card again. "I'm Detective Inspector Nicki Hardcastle from Suffolk Police. I was hoping to have a quick chat with your son, Adrian? Is he here?"

Once again, Nicki watched the colour drain out of another human being's face at the mention of her name. She thought she caught a fleeting look of what could only be described as panic or even fear being exchanged between the couple — but as quickly as it had appeared, it was gone.

"Mr Browning?"

Suddenly, Larry Browning's face broke out into a smile — but one that definitely didn't reach his eyes. "Of course, yes, come on through. Sorry. You just took us by surprise, that's all." He motioned towards the kitchen. "We don't get that many callers out here, you know. And my wife here suffers with her nerves, don't you, Annie?"

Larry Browning looked pointedly at his wife; another look exchanged.

Annette Browning stiffened, but a weak smile followed. Still visibly pale, she cleared her throat before speaking. "Yes, do forgive me. I can be a little melodramatic at times." A faint chuckle. Another forced smile. "Adrian, you said?"

"If that wouldn't be too much trouble," replied Nicki. "It shouldn't take long."

"He's upstairs, isn't he, Larry?"

"No doubt with those infernal headphones on," smiled Mr Browning. "Be a pet and go and fetch him for these kind officers?"

Mrs Browning seemed to find renewed strength from somewhere and darted back towards the stairs, while Mr Browning herded Nicki and Fox into the kitchen. "Kids, eh?" he smiled. "Always some drama or another. Cup of tea while you wait?" He nodded towards the kettle.

Nicki shook her head as she glanced around the country-style family kitchen. "No, thanks, Mr Browning. We won't be here that long." In the centre of the room was a large wooden table, housing a teapot and a selection of the morning's papers. Nicki saw Jacqui Massingham's name emblazoned across each one.

Before long they heard the tell-tale sound of footsteps on the stairs, one set distinctly heavier than the other. Mrs

Browning entered the kitchen, her face showing a little more colour than it had before. Her eyes darted nervously towards her husband. Adrian skulked in behind her, a look of annoyance on his face.

"Sorry to disturb you, Adrian," began Nicki, getting straight to the point. "We just have a couple more questions for you about Jacqui Massingham. If you don't mind?"

Unless it was her imagination, Nicki noticed the anxious looks on both Mr and Mrs Brownings' faces relax somewhat.

"I don't have anything else to say," replied Adrian, picking at his fingernails. "You asked me everything yesterday."

"You don't know what my questions are yet." Nicki felt her irritation rising. From their brief chat yesterday afternoon, she thought Lionel and Audrey Massingham's assessment of him was fairly accurate. Although not particularly likeable characters themselves, she had to admit the Massinghams had got that bit spot on. The small amount of background they'd managed to unearth didn't paint a particularly rosy picture: the man had a temper, particularly where women were concerned. Swallowing her increasing dislike, Nicki pushed on. "Did you happen to see the headlines in the newspaper this morning, Adrian?" Her eyes flickered towards the folded copies on the table.

"Which one?"

"Doesn't really matter. They're all reporting on the same thing." Nicki paused. "The body parts found in the town last Thursday night have been confirmed to belong to Jacqui Massingham — your ex-girlfriend."

Adrian flinched. "Well of course I saw that. It's everywhere. Can't get away from it."

"And how do you feel about that, Adrian?" Nicki tried to catch his gaze, but failed. He remained staring towards the linoleum floor. "How do you feel about that being Jacqui?"

The question earned the merest of shrugs as Adrian continued to examine his nails. In his line of work, Nicki shuddered to think what might be buried beneath them.

"What do you mean?" he eventually replied. "I don't feel anything. Why would I? She's my *ex*. I told you that yesterday."

"So, no feelings at all then?" Nicki darted a look towards Mr and Mrs Browning who were standing side by side at the sink. Their expressions were hard to determine.

Adrian shook his head, and eventually looked up, his eyes hot with anger. "No. Why should I? She was a daft cow. Glad I got rid of her when I did."

Nicki's eyebrows hitched. "Got rid of her? In what way did you *get rid of her*, Adrian?"

The sigh that escaped Adrian's mouth filled almost every inch of the kitchen. "You know what I mean. When I dumped her." Exasperation filled his tone. "Stop putting words in my mouth, I know what you lot are like. Is there actually a point to any of this?"

"I'm coming to that." Nicki pulled a sheet of paper from her pocket. "We have a series of tweets printed out here — tweets that we believe came from yourself? And, in them, you're a little less than polite about Miss Massingham."

"It's a free country, I can say what I like."

'I wish the bitch stopped breathing.' Nicki detected a very slight change in Adrian's demeanour. The abundance of cockiness now replaced with more than a little caution. "What exactly did you mean by that, Adrian?"

Adrian's jaw tensed.

"And then we have '*She needs putting in her place — permanently.*' Followed by '*no one would miss her if she dropped down dead.*'"

"I don't have to say anything, do I?" Adrian flashed a look at his parents, both still standing by the sink, but neither said a word. He then turned back to Nicki. "I don't have to answer any of your stupid questions unless you take me down to the station."

"You don't have to say anything at all, Adrian, that's quite right." DS Fox, who'd been hovering by the kitchen door watching the show, stepped forward. "Station or no station. That's your right. But all we're doing is asking a few friendly questions, asking for help in finding out what happened to Jacqui. Surely you want to help?"

Nicki stepped forward, hand outstretched. "Would you mind if we took your phone, analysed a few of the social media sites you may have been on recently, and looked at your calls and messages?"

All cockiness now disappeared from Adrian's tone. "My phone?" His face began to colour. "What do you want with my phone?"

"It's standard procedure in investigations such as this. We're just trying to build up a picture of the victim — who she'd been in contact with, that kind of thing." Nicki stepped a little closer, hand still held out in front of her. "It's your call. You don't have to. It's purely voluntary."

Adrian shot another look towards his parents, but didn't get much in return. "They can't make me, can they?"

Fox stepped closer and shook his head. "We can't make you. As Detective Inspector Hardcastle rightly said, it's your choice. Giving us your phone is entirely voluntary."

"And I'm not under arrest?" Adrian's eyes widened.

"No, you're not under arrest," confirmed Fox. "This is all very informal. We're talking to everyone who knew Jacqui — trying to get to the bottom of what happened to her."

"Oh, for goodness' sake, Adrian, hand it over," hissed Mrs Browning. "What have you got to hide?"

Adrian tugged his phone from his back pocket and reluctantly placed it into Nicki's outstretched hand. "When do I get it back?"

"As soon as we're finished with it," replied Nicki, dropping it into the plastic evidence bag Fox had open ready.

"Well, I want it back soon."

"Of course, as soon as we're done." Nicki gave him a plastic smile. "Thank you for your cooperation. We'll leave you in peace now." She turned her smile towards Mr and Mrs Browning, still standing side by side at the sink. "Let you get on with your day. Sorry to have disturbed you on a Sunday."

Mr Browning sprang into step beside Nicki and walked the two detectives to the front door. Adrian merely grunted and disappeared upstairs, muttering under his breath. Nicki could only guess at what expletives might be being aimed in their direction as they stepped outside and headed for the car.

"I want that phone analysed pronto. Let's see what else the delightful Mr Browning had been saying about our victim."

Fox slipped into the passenger seat. "Did you notice the looks on the parents' faces when we rocked up? Something inside that house isn't right."

Nicki switched on the ignition and pulled away from the kerb, nodding. "Let's try and find out if it has anything to do with Jacqui Massingham."

* * *

Bury St Edmunds Police Station

Roy took a slice of his grandmother's rum cake back to his desk. With Matt and Duncan out visiting Fernando Tavares, and Nicki and Graham having another chat with Adrian Browning, the incident room was quiet. After the identification of a figure exiting the rear of the cathedral not long before the severed hand was discovered, Roy had decided to take another look at the CCTV from around the Southgate Street roundabout.

Darcie was sitting next to him ensconced in reviewing yet more images from around the town, searching for the elusive man in a hat and scarf. It was like looking for the proverbial needle in a very large haystack. He noticed the thickly cut slice of fried bean cake sitting next to her mug of tea and smiled.

Good old Grandma.

Roy focused his attention back to his computer screen. The main camera angle wasn't ideal — showing only two of the entrances and exits from the roundabout. But it was better than nothing. He lengthened the timeline — the teenager's story was so full of holes the original timespan could be miles out.

As the grainy images played out, Roy took down the registration numbers of vehicles that passed through, together with the time stamp. Predictably there weren't many; traffic was light. After half an hour, the time on the screen approached the vague time Tommy McCrae said he'd arrived home, Roy sat up straight, ignoring the painful twinge from his ribs, and focused intently once more on the screen. He'd watched this particular section before — they all had — but this part of the recording was particularly poor. It wasn't just grainy and blurred, like a lot of CCTV, it was jumpy too. The images repeatedly froze on the screen and then unfroze. By looking in the bottom corner and the time stamp, Roy could see that several seconds were lost in-between frames.

More than several seconds in fact.

Roy rewound the images and played them again. The same jumping. The same blurred outlines. The same annoying pixelating.

The same vital seconds lost.

Thirty seconds, in fact — thirty seconds where the cameras lost all focus.

"Darce? Take a look at this." Roy tilted his computer screen towards Darcie and tapped the time stamp in the bottom corner. "Keep your eye on this."

He rewound and played the images again.

"That's a decent chunk of time lost," mused Darcie as the images froze and skipped. "Anything could've happened."

"My thoughts exactly." Roy jumped up from his chair, wishing he hadn't when his ribs protested once again. "I'll see if the tech guys can take a look."

* * *

In exchange for some rum cake, the tech team had accommodated Roy's request to look at the CCTV images and had quickly worked their magic. Loading the frames on to his computer once again, Roy immediately noted the improvement. The pictures were still grainy, still blurred in parts, but they weren't jumping quite so much and most of the vital thirty seconds had been restored. He fast forwarded to the time in question and settled back to watch the missing thirty second gap.

He didn't have to wait long before something caught his eye.

Inching his chair closer, his eyes gravitated towards the bottom right-hand corner of the screen where a blurred figure moved into shot. The figure seemed to hesitate briefly, maybe for a second or two, before heading towards the roundabout.

The image started to pixelate and jump, time standing still. The figure was then lost from view.

Roy swore under his breath. About to hit rewind and try the footage again, his finger hovered over the keyboard as the pixelating screen began to settle. He decided to let the images play on, and what happened next caught him by surprise.

The figure in the bottom right-hand corner came into focus once more, and headed directly towards the roundabout. They stopped by the wolf sculpture for several seconds, back towards the camera. Then they turned and jogged back round towards the houses just out of shot, the camera jumping and pixelating all the while.

Roy froze the screen and took down the time stamp.

The picture might be grainy and out of focus, but he knew exactly who that person was.

The skateboard tucked under their arm was the perfect giveaway.

CHAPTER TWENTY-FIVE

A14 Suffolk

"Roy?" Nicki put the call onto the hands-free system as she pulled the car on to the A14. Roy sounded breathless and she could hear what sounded like raised voices and slamming doors in the background. "What's up?"

"It's Tommy — Tommy McCrae," he replied. "I got that CCTV from the roundabout cleaned up — noted there was about thirty or so seconds missing as it was so jumpy and distorted. Anyway, short story is, the boy's lying."

"We already know that." Nicki swung the car into the outside lane to overtake a lorry.

"Yeah, but I mean *really* lying." Roy paused. "He's there, bold as you like, going on to the roundabout at ten-thirty — which is *before* his mum came home from work. He heads over to the wolf, stays a few seconds with his back towards the camera, then heads home. It's in complete contrast to what he told us."

Nicki swung the car back into the left-hand lane. "You think he saw the tongue then?"

"My guess is yes. There was always something wrong about his story. Maybe he even put it there."

The thought that the spotty nineteen-year-old could be responsible for cutting out Jacqui Massingham's tongue didn't sit easily with Nicki.

"OK, we're on our way back to the station — we'll be fifteen minutes or so. But I've got this blasted press conference to do." Nicki flashed a look at the dashboard clock. She'd only just make it in time, and even then she'd have to put her foot down. "Who else is there with you?"

"Just me and Darcie."

"Head out to Tommy's — the pair of you. If he's there, pick him up. Take some uniforms with you, too — in case he tries to do another runner."

"Will do."

Nicki cut the call and glanced across at Fox in the passenger seat. "Are we really thinking Tommy McCrae is our man?"

Fox braced himself against the door panel as Nicki swung the car on to the slip road. "Nothing surprises me anymore."

* * *

4 Old Railway Cottages
Dullingham, Nr Newmarket

Adrian Browning slammed his bedroom door behind him and took a half-hearted punch at the side of his wardrobe. Although a cheap flat-pack model, it withstood the punch and left Adrian nursing swollen knuckles.

"Bloody bitch!" he swore, deciding against a second punch.

Jacqui.

Some days he wished he'd never laid eyes on her — she was nothing but trouble.

Seeing the police in the kitchen made him think of being banged up in the cells again. It hadn't been a pleasant experience the first time around. And he didn't care to repeat it.

But the cells weren't a patch on prison.

Prison.

He wasn't sure what they'd find on his phone, but it would have been useless to refuse — only making him look more guilty than he did already. His parents had sported unnervingly jovial looks on their faces when the police had departed, but he knew they'd be seething inside.

Adrian in trouble — *again*. How many times did they have to bail him out? Not like Mason . . . butter wouldn't melt in his brother's mouth, not where their parents were concerned. Always the favourite, no matter what.

But he wished he hadn't sent those tweets now. He wasn't even sure why he had. For some reason she'd got under his skin again — and it was so easy to let off steam on Twitter and have a rant. No one had even reacted to it — so as far as he was concerned no one had even seen it.

Except the coppers.

Adrian felt the anger rising once again.

Jacqui.

The bitch.

He took another swipe at the wardrobe, his knuckles cracking on impact.

* * *

Mason quietly shut the door to the study behind him. The drama of the police showing up at the door had eventually subsided — Adrian had sworn at the top of his voice and thrown things around in his room for a while, but even he was silent now. Mum and Dad had shut themselves away in the front room, talking in hushed voices, and Mason got the distinct impression they were not to be disturbed.

Settling down on a stool by the window, he turned his attention to his latest sketch. He knew Dad didn't really like him sitting in the study to work — but the light was so much better in here than upstairs in his bedroom. His drawing board didn't take up too much space, so he wasn't really sure what Dad was grumbling about.

He'd preferred the house in Wales if he was honest, it was bigger and the countryside around them was stunning — but maybe they'd get back there some day. Right now, Mum needed him. He knew she put a brave face on most days, hiding the chronic pain she suffered. But he always knew when she was having a bad day — he could see it in her eyes.

Dad did his best, but he couldn't be around all the time. And Adrian? It was no use asking him to do anything. His temper always got the better of him, more and more often it seemed, and he had no patience at all. So, Mason hadn't minded moving back in with the family to help out while Mum waited for her operations. It wouldn't be for long — although the NHS waiting list was growing by the second.

Reaching for a charcoal pencil, Mason turned his attention to the drawing board. He needed to take advantage of the quiet times — who knew when all hell would break loose again.

* * *

Southgate Street, Bury St Edmunds

Tommy had nodded off with his headphones still clamped to his head. The remains of a second joint had long since been snuffed out, the butt squashed into the already overflowing ashtray next to his bed. He could still smell it in the air, though — and it made him crave another. He had one left — but he also had a pocket full of cash with which to buy another stash. He'd text his dealer mate later — maybe round up the guys and go down to the skate park for a smoke. He'd charge them a fiver a joint — make a bit on the side.

Pulling the headphones from his ears, Tommy stretched. He felt hungry. As he considered hauling himself to his feet and making his way down to the kitchen for a sandwich, he paused — legs dangling over the side of the bed.

Bang! Bang! Bang!

He knew that sound without needing to look.

Police.

Fear quickly replaced the hunger coursing through his veins — the relaxing effect of the weed now a long and distant memory.

Calm down.

They had nothing on him.

Nothing.

Now he'd got rid of the cloth there was nothing to worry about. All he'd done was tell a little white lie about how the tongue had got on to the roundabout. What difference did it make in the end anyway?

Despite his own reassurances, Tommy felt the agitation build. What if the cops planted something on him? Miraculously 'found' something buried in a drawer in his room. He knew it happened — he'd seen it on TV.

Planting his feet on the floor, he scoured the carnage that covered the carpet. Scooping up his tobacco tin and the solitary joint resting inside, he shoved it into the pocket of his hoodie.

Bang! Bang! Bang!

He could hear Freddie wailing downstairs, over and above the TV theme to some annoying kids' programme. Kelsey was shouting about someone going to answer the door.

Knowing he didn't have long, he jumped on top of the bed and wrenched open the window. Grabbing his skateboard, he flung the board out ahead of him, watching it land on the snow-covered grass below. It barely made a sound.

With one leg over the windowsill, he glanced once more around the room. He could hear more voices now. Someone must have opened the door.

They've got nothing on me, he repeated to himself as he edged further out of the window. *Nothing.*

Nothing except his jacket.

His eyes fixed on the discarded baseball jacket over in the far corner of the room where he'd tossed it earlier. A sickening sense of disquiet started to spread. He might have got rid of the cloth, but what about the blood? He'd tried his best to clean it with bleach but . . . the police could do tests and things, couldn't they?

Why hadn't he tried washing it again? He looked around the rest of his bedroom, at the piles of dirty, unwashed clothing that covered the floor. Who was he trying to kid? He never washed anything.

The voices were getting louder now, and it wouldn't be long before he heard footsteps on the stairs. Police footsteps. Booted footsteps.

His heart rate raised another notch.

With one last look around the room, he jumped.

CHAPTER TWENTY-SIX

Bury St Edmunds Police Station

Nicki pulled on her coat and followed DCI Turner downstairs. She felt fortunate to have him to hide behind — she hated press conferences with a passion, and disliked nothing more than having to speak at one. Words would instantly tangle inside her mouth, her tongue running dry.

Slipping her phone into her pocket, she noticed a missed call from an unknown number. There was no message. Deciding they would ring back if it was anything important, Nicki continued down the stairs.

"Ready?" Turner half-turned as they negotiated the double doors that led out into the foyer of the station. She merely nodded in reply, feeling anything but.

Although only a little past midday, the temperature was already dropping. Not that it had been all that high to start with. There would be a bitter frost tonight. The DCI's and Nicki's breath billowed out in front of them as they stepped outside the station.

The weather clearly hadn't deterred an army of reporters from gathering to hear the latest on the current investigation gripping the town, with several groups already clustered outside. It was a grisly and unprecedented situation — but one that made for fantastic headlines.

Nicki could almost see the occupants of various newsrooms around the local area rubbing their ink-stained hands with glee at such a story breaking on their doorstep. They knew their circulation figures and website visits would triple overnight — if not more. It was a side to the job that sickened her, but she also recognised how important the press could be at times like these.

DCI Turner cleared his throat and looked out over the heads bobbing in front of him. An array of bobble hats and anorak hoods greeted him.

"Good afternoon, ladies and gentlemen," he began, his voice steady and calm. "Thank you for coming. I'll keep this brief. You will all now be aware of the current investigation based here at Bury St Edmunds. Over the last three days, several body parts have been located around the town. On Thursday evening, a pair of eyes and section of tongue were discovered — which we have now positively identified as belonging to a twenty-three-year-old woman by the name of Jacqui Massingham. We do not yet know the fate of Miss Massingham, but her next of kin have been informed of any developments.

"On Friday, a severed hand was found beneath a pew at St Edmundsbury Cathedral during Evensong. As yet, we do not know to whom this hand belongs. And that is where myself, and the team here at Bury St Edmunds, need your assistance."

Turner shifted his weight slightly and caught Nicki's gaze. Stepping out from the shadows of the front porch, she opened the folder she was carrying and extracted two sheets of paper which she passed across. Turner held up the first sheet.

"This is a photograph of a tattoo — a butterfly. I would ask that anyone who recognises this tattoo — who knows of anyone who has a similar tattoo — to please get in touch. Please look carefully. The tattoo is of a butterfly and was on the victim's inside left wrist."

The DCI let the first description and image sink in before holding up the second sheet. "This second image is of another tattoo — this time of a rose. This tattoo is at the base of the thumb. Please think carefully — do you know someone who has both tattoos on their left hand? If so, please contact us on the special hotline number."

Turner handed the sheets of paper back to Nicki. She was itching to get back inside and continue with the investigation. DS Fox had taken Adrian's phone back to the incident room for analysis and she wanted to be present the moment they found something. Fox had been right about one thing — something inside the Brownings' house wasn't right. Both Mr and Mrs Browning had looked horrified at the police turning up on their doorstep. More than would be expected.

Thankfully, the DCI started to wind up the press conference. "May I thank you all for coming out today and please don't forget to circulate the hotline number. Good afternoon." After answering some heated questions from the gathered journalists, Turner took Nicki's elbow and guided her back inside the station. "That went as well as could be expected," he began, heading for the double doors that led back upstairs.

Nicki followed the DCI through the doors. "You think someone will recognise the tattoos?"

Turner headed for the stairs. "We'll soon see. I've organised a team to answer the hotline number — and another to sort through the chaff. You'll only get passed the decent stuff to deal with. I'm no expert but I think they're fairly distinctive tattoos — especially together on the one hand. Someone, somewhere, must recognise them." Once upstairs, they reached the corridor leading to Nicki's office. "Anything further from today?"

"We've got the phone from Jacqui's ex-boyfriend. Not exactly a pleasant individual, so we'll see what that throws up. And we're about to pick up Tommy McCrae — the lad who found the tongue." Just then, the door to the incident room opened and DC Duncan Jenkins' head popped out.

"In here, boss. It's about Tommy McCrae."

Nicki's heart sank.

"He's gone AWOL again."

* * *

4 Old Railway Cottages
Dullingham, Nr Newmarket

Larry Browning was glad to find the study empty. He could see Mason had been in — he could see there was a new sketch on the drawing board, and several rough drafts pinned beneath. Heading across the room, he took a closer look. He had to admit it, the boy had talent.

Turning away from the drawing board, Larry felt his gaze drawn towards the mahogany desk. Nothing looked out of place, everything as it was. Annette told him he worried too much — that the boys wouldn't be interested in what was in the desk.

Which was probably true. But Larry still had that churning feeling in his stomach every time he knew Mason had been sitting at his drawing board. What if he needed a pen, or a pair of scissors? What would stop him rummaging in the drawers and possibly seeing what had really brought them back to this part of the world?

Larry felt like slapping himself around the face. *Get a grip, Browning.* Mason had his own art supplies and wouldn't go near the desk. And Adrian — Larry was pretty sure he'd never even set one foot inside the study since they'd moved in.

He was worrying about nothing. Again.

Despite his own reassurance to himself, Larry went behind the desk and made sure the drawers were shut tight.

They were.

Maybe he should get a lock . . .

He frowned at himself. The visit from the police had clearly shaken him more than he'd expected — and not just because they wanted to question Adrian. He'd felt it — and he knew Annette had, too — the minute he'd seen her. He knew exactly who she was even before she'd announced her name; he'd seen her picture so many times it was imprinted on his brain.

Annette had been a bag of nerves afterwards and gone for another lie down.

Larry gave the drawers one last look before heading out of the study.

* * *

Bury St Edmunds Town Centre

"Get in."

Tommy McCrae looked warily at the open van door.

"You have any better options right now?"

Tommy snatched a look over his shoulder, in the vague direction of his house. He'd run for his life — again — not caring in which direction he headed. Anywhere would do — anywhere away from *them*. They'd be in his bedroom by now, searching through his stuff. They'd find his ashtray full of joint butts — and then they'd find the jacket.

"But I haven't done anything."

"Then you've nothing to worry about." Laurence pushed the door of the van open a little more. "But I'm leaving in precisely five seconds — with or without you."

Tommy didn't need asking twice, diving into the passenger seat just as the van pulled away from the kerb. Slamming the door shut, he eyed the man behind the wheel. "Where are we going?"

"Somewhere they won't think of looking."

"How come you're here?"

"Never you mind."

Tommy's gaze landed on a plastic bag wedged up on to the dashboard in front of him. It was see-through — one of those bags you used to put things in the freezer. Even from the passenger seat he could see the contents clearly. The bloodied cloth he'd discarded in the bin yesterday.

His throat constricted while his eyes widened. The look didn't go unnoticed.

"That was an incredibly stupid thing to do — dumping the cloth like that in a public bin. What were you thinking?" The man's cold stare bore into him as he took his eyes off the road for a second. "You lost your mind or something?"

"I . . . I . . ." stammered Tommy, his mouth opening and closing like a fish. No matter how hard he tried, no words formed.

The man merely shrugged and switched his attention back to the road ahead. "No matter — I've fixed it."

"None of this has got anything to do with me," wailed Tommy, finding his voice at last. "None of it. I didn't ask to get involved."

"Well, you *are* involved. Whether you like it or not. I told you to go home, and not tell a soul. But what did you do? Squealed to your mummy at the first available opportunity." The man didn't try to hide the scorn in his tone. "Now it's all over the papers."

"I had no choice! She saw blood on my sleeve — she wouldn't let it go until I told her how it got there. I had to tell her. But I didn't say anything about you — I swear!"

"You didn't need to. Your place is crawling with police now. They won't give up until they find what they want."

Tommy looked out of the window, noting they were heading out of town. "Where are we going?" he repeated, trepidation entering his voice.

"Like I said. Somewhere they won't think of looking."

Tommy's face paled, his stomach tightening as they turned down a B-road. The weed from earlier was now making him feel sick. "You can just drop me off anywhere. I'll wait a while before going home. Or I'll go and stay with a mate."

The man stayed silent and carried on driving.

As the van slowed for a corner, Tommy made a grab for the door handle. Whatever damage he did to himself by jumping from a moving vehicle, it was a whole lot more attractive a proposition than what might be in store for him if he stayed where he was.

The door lock clicked into place before his hand reached the handle.

A cruel smile crossed the man's face as he tightened his grip on the wheel. "Not so fast, sonny."

CHAPTER TWENTY-SEVEN

Bury St Edmunds Police Station

The press conference had had the desired effect. After the image of the tattoos went online, and every news outlet filled their front page with the chilling pictures, calls started trickling in to the hotline. Only the most credible were being filtered through to the incident room, but even those were bogging the team down in extra work.

"House-to-house isn't giving us much — uniforms have spoken to most of the residents along Jacqui's street." Nicki rubbed her eyes, feeling the grit beneath her fingertips. "No one saw anything out of the ordinary. By all accounts Jacqui was a quiet neighbour, kept herself to herself."

"We've been tracking her mobile, boss." DC Matt Holland picked up a sheet of paper from his desk. "The last time it pinged was around the time she left work on the Saturday. Nothing since. Phone was switched off soon after. We're just accessing her calls and messages."

Nicki gave a tired smile. "Thanks, Matt. See who her contacts were, who she was in touch with. Emails too, if there are any. And Graham — keep working on Adrian's phone."

"Fernando Tavares wasn't much help in the end." DC Duncan Jenkins edged towards one of the whiteboards. "There was a bit of a translation issue, but I think we got the gist of what he was saying. He phoned in sick on Thursday because he was offered cash by an unknown male. He gave us a description, but to be honest it could be anybody. Male. Tall. Dark hair. Tavares is in debt up to his eyeballs by all accounts, has two other jobs working cash in hand. He says this guy followed him back to his car after work earlier in the week — offered him money to hand over his work uniform and pass. Threatened to tell the authorities that he was working illegally. It didn't take much to persuade him."

"You think he was telling the truth?"

Duncan nodded. "I think so. He's clearly dodging tax and working under the radar, but I don't think he had a clue about what was going to happen at the theatre. We can go back with a translator if you think we should"

Nicki shook her head. "No, let's leave that one. We need to focus on the credible leads we have. Roy, what's the latest on our good friend, Tommy McCrae?"

"Missing in action once again. I can't imagine he'll stay hidden for all that long. Despite the swagger, he's not all that streetwise and scarpered without his phone. His mum reckons he'll come home when he's hungry."

"Keep me posted." Nicki pushed herself up from the table she'd been perching on, intent on catching up with some long overdue paperwork. She hadn't reached the door when Darcie piped up.

"Boss, you might want to take a look at this." Darcie nodded towards her computer monitor. "Hotline calls. Just had another put through, but this one looks more credible than the others."

Nicki headed back towards Darcie's desk, peering over her shoulder at the details on the screen.

Lucie Ballantine.

"Says here — her sister called in half an hour ago. Positive ID on the tattoos. Has both the butterfly and rose on the left hand. Hasn't seen her in a while and she isn't answering her phone."

* * *

The Farmhouse

Tommy had been easy enough to overcome when the time came. Fear could paralyse you just as swiftly as any one of the concoctions Laurence had on his pantry shelves. But always prepared, like the good boy scout he never was, Laurence had brought with him the bottle of diethyl ether and quickly rendered the boy unconscious so he could get him inside the farmhouse.

Tommy now lay on one of the pathology trolleys, strapped securely at the wrists and ankles. Laurence had set up the infusion pump, unsure how long he intended to keep the boy sedated, but the ketamine would keep him quiet while he decided.

Entering the boot room, Laurence felt calmed by the contented hum coming from the freezers. Heading over to the first freezer, he lifted the lid and smiled. He'd left Lee on a trolley by the side, and now lifted the boy up in his arms and deposited him on top of Lucie and Jacqui.

"Enjoy, ladies," he murmured as he closed the lid on the frozen tomb.

The freezer was filling up nicely — maybe room for one or two more then he'd need to move on to freezer number two.

A third freezer was set a little way apart from the others — an older model, installed inside the boot room conversion not long after his grandfather had died. Laurence made his way across to lay a hand on the lid.

This freezer had been occupied for some time — long before Jacqui and Lucie put in an appearance; and long before any of the others.

Laurence's heart swelled at the memory flooding his thoughts.

With his hand hovering over the freezer lid, he pulled it open.

"Hello, Father."

* * *

Saturday 4 October 2008
The Farmhouse

He'd been planning his father's death for some time — maybe ever since his grandfather died on that hot summer's day when Laurence was eight — but that was all it had been. *Planning.*

But today was different.

He was home for the weekend — meant to be research-ing the cholecystectomy procedure for Professor Ferguson's class the following week. But instead, Laurence Hemmingway Jr had been researching anaesthesia.

The university library had many excellent textbooks, and Laurence had maxed out his permitted number of bor-rowed books, lugging them home in a holdall back to the farmhouse. He'd stayed behind after class one day to ask Professor Ferguson about the effects of anaesthesia — what the best drugs for sedation would be, how long someone could be anaesthetised for, and how to induce muscle paral-ysis. The professor had answered his questions, albeit with a mild hint of concern. His final question on embalming had resulted in Laurence being sent on his way, the professor citing an important meeting he needed to get to.

But Laurence didn't care what the professor or anyone else thought of him. Right now, all he cared about was end-ing his father's life.

Laurence Hemmingway Sr was a creature of habit. If he was at the farm — an increasingly rare occurrence it had to be said — then every evening without fail, he would sit in the snug with a large glass of port. Eventually he would nod off, head lolling forwards, chin resting on his chest. Whatever medical journal he'd been reading would lie abandoned by his side. All Laurence had to do was wait.

It really was that simple.

But Laurence wasn't exactly the patient type. Before dinner, he'd crushed up a handful of sleeping tablets and slipped them into the half-empty bottle of port in the snug. With any luck that would accelerate the process and Laurence could get on with the next stage of his plan.

At a little after ten-thirty that night, he peered around the doorframe of the snug and saw his father slumped in his chair, head to the side, snoring softly. Clutching a generous handful of cotton wool in his hand, Laurence wasted no time. Tipping an equally generous measure of ether on to the cotton wool, he approached his father's chair.

"This is for you, grandfather."

In one swift motion, Laurence covered his father's nose and mouth with the cotton wool and pressed down hard. The man barely grunted. There was a momentary flickering of his eyelids, a slight tensing of his neck muscles, before unconsciousness overwhelmed him.

Dragging his father's unconscious form from the snug to the boot room was slightly more problematic. The man was heavily built — evidence of one too many lunches with hospital bigwigs — but Laurence was determined and managed to heave him on to his shoulders. Staggering through the narrow passageway that led to the pantry and then the boot room, he may have hit his father's head a few times on the doorframes as they passed, but he didn't much care. And neither did his father.

Depositing the surgeon's unconscious body on to the tiled floor of the boot room, Laurence was again unconcerned when the man's head hit the ground first. The dull thud was somehow comforting.

Laurence then asked himself the next question.

How shall I kill him?

As painfully as possible was the conclusion.

He'd read somewhere that certain medications given during anaesthesia can temporarily paralyse the body — and his father had been especially pleased when young Laurence had asked to spend the day observing him in theatre before heading off to university. Laurence had shown little interest in his father's surgical career up to that point but when he finally feigned enthusiasm, Laurence Hemmingway Sr had proudly brought him along to his surgical theatre one August morning.

That had probably been his first mistake.

The second was when the anaesthetist turned his back for a moment – but that was all the time that young Laurence needed.

Despite a thorough search and subsequent investigation, they never did find the missing anaesthetic drugs — eventually putting it down to an administrative error.

Laurence turned the vial over in his hand, feeling the excitement build. He wasn't sure how much of the drug to use. He only needed it to work for a short time — for a short time was all that his father had left.

He carefully selected a vein, having taught himself the elements of phlebotomy in the university library, and with a rock-steady hand, Laurence successfully gave his father a small, measured amount of the anaesthetic agent — and waited.

He used the time effectively — securing his father's ankles and wrists with strong cable ties, and making sure he had his selection of medical instruments to hand.

And then he waited some more, enjoying watching his father's incapacitated form — wondering what thoughts would go through his head when he woke.

Time inched by agonisingly slowly, but eventually the anaesthetic agent began to wear off and Laurence Hemmingway Sr's eyelids flickered open. Confusion was the first expression to cross the surgeon's features — quickly followed by panic. He instinctively started trying to move, but the cable ties held firm. He tried rocking from side to side on the cold tiles, his legs bent beneath him to try and get some purchase on the floor.

It was a futile effort.

Laurence watched his father's chest rise and fall, rapidly. He needed to work fast if he was going to achieve what he wanted.

"Laurence?" His father's words slurred as though he'd drunk more than the three glasses of port that evening. "What . . . What're you doing?"

Laurence leaned in closer, a mixture of hatred and joy etched on to his face. "Hello, Father. Today is a good day — because today you are going to die."

His smile widened as he brought his lips close to his father's ear and whispered.

"And I'm going to watch you."

* * *

Sunday 30 December 2018
The Farmhouse

Laurence Hemmingway Sr's body had lain in the freezer for the last ten years.

But to Laurence Jr the memory of what happened that day was still fresh.

Initially, he'd chosen to cut him — superficially, at first, just to watch the blood trickle. Then he cut him more deeply, seeking out the larger vessels. At first, the eminent surgeon's eyes had bulged in their sockets — a heady mixture of pain and fear. Although maybe there was no pain — maybe the effects of the anaesthetic agent were still working. Laurence would never know, because his father wouldn't live to tell him.

The floor tiles became thick with blood, but all the while Laurence merely sat and watched; oblivious to the crimson blood soaking into the knees and ankles of his jeans. Nothing could take his attention from the life slowly ebbing away from his father's body.

He started to tap his fingers on the tiled floor.

Tap — tap — tap — tap — tap

Tap — tap — tap — tap — tap

Death was coming.

The beetles said so.

And then the light was gone — as if merely flicking a switch and cutting the power. One minute he was there, the next he was not.

Laurence had placed a hand in the space above his father's open mouth, wondering if his soul was still within him. Or had it already escaped, making the journey to its final destination? Would it be heaven, or would it be hell?

Laurence knew which one was more appropriate for his father.

He slammed the lid of the third freezer back into place and made his way towards the back door.

He needed some air — and to think about what to do with Tommy.

CHAPTER TWENTY-EIGHT

Ravenwood Close, Bury St Edmunds

Nicki led DS Fox towards the front door of number six. Outwardly, everything appeared to be normal. A quiet house on a quiet street. A lone robin hopped across the snow-covered front garden, its head cocked to the side, perusing the new visitors. Nicki glanced up and down the street — no curtains twitched, no doors cracked open. Nothing stirred.

Rapping on the front door, Nicki heard the echo reverberate along the row of houses as Fox stepped across the front garden to peer inside the downstairs window. He cupped his hands around his eyes, his breath fogging on the glass.

"Can't see anything inside. No lights on."

Nicki knocked again, louder this time. Still nothing.

"Can we force entry?" Fox hopped back over to the garden path, pointing his walking cane towards the door.

"I don't think that'll be much use to us," replied Nicki, noting the sturdy UPVC front door before them. "And I don't think either of us are built for a shoulder charge."

"Next best thing then." Fox bent down and picked up a ceramic toadstool, plucking a silver key out from beneath.

"Wha . . . ?" Nicki stepped back as Fox unlocked the door. "Do people still do that?"

The door swung open. "Apparently so. And thankfully, for us, they do. I don't fancy adding the cost of a replacement door to the investigation expenses, do you? You know how expensive these things are?"

Nicki conceded the point and stepped across the threshold into Lucie Ballantine's front hall. A smattering of letters sat on the carpet and, from a quick glance, several looked to be Christmas cards. The lamp at the bottom of the stairs was unlit — as was the rest of the house. The air inside felt chilled — as if the heating hadn't been on for a while.

"Lucie?" called Nicki. "Lucie Ballantine? It's the police."

There was no reply. Fox nudged a door to their right with his walking cane, revealing a pleasantly spacious front room, a plush carpet under their feet. Soft pastel shades greeted them as they peered through the doorway. A leather sofa, small nest of tables and a neatly kept bookcase filled the room. They refrained from touching anything — right now, they had no idea if they were stumbling across a crime scene or not.

The kitchen at the end of the hall was a small, galley-type affair. Compact, yet practical. The granite worktops were free from clutter, the sink without limescale. Just a few items sat in the rack on the draining board waiting to be put away.

Nicki touched the side of the kettle with the back of her gloved hand. Stone cold. She then tried the back door. Locked.

They made their way upstairs. Two bedrooms and one bathroom showed no signs of life. Lucie Ballantine was clearly a tidy person: her room was immaculate. The bed was made, no clothes littered across the floor. Even the contents of her dressing table were neatly arranged.

The second bedroom looked as though it was in the process of being redecorated. A pot of paint sat on top of a wooden stepladder, the final coat of Ocean Mist waiting to be applied. A pair of curtains were folded up inside a

dry-cleaning bag, a curtain pole resting against the wall waiting to be fixed.

The bathroom between the bedrooms had been recently
refurbished too — the white ceramic basin and sparkling
stainless steel taps gleamed. Nicki peered into the sink —
dry. The towels hanging on the towel rail also looked dry.

As they padded back downstairs, Nicki couldn't help but
think it was a carbon copy of Jacqui's house — deserted with
no sign of life. But no sign of death, either. Nicki doubted
Lucie had met her abductor here.

"Let's take a look outside, see if we can find her car."

Nicki led the way around to the back of the row of terraced houses, immediately noticing the narrow alleyway that
connected the rear of each property. Nicki would bet her last
pound that Lucie used this entrance rather than the front
door. A quick glance over her shoulder told her that they'd
located Lucie's car — her sister had given them the make and
model, and, sure enough, a Mini Cooper sat in front of one
of the garages.

"You thinking what I'm thinking?" Fox followed Nicki
back to their own car parked on the road out front.

"That Lucie's our second victim?" Nicki unlocked the
driver's door. "Almost certainly. No coat, no bag, no phone,
no keys. Same as Jacqui." She paused, looking back over her
shoulder at the neat row of terraced houses behind them.
"It's like he just plucks them out of the air and disappears."

* * *

The Farmhouse

Lee's feet were still sitting on top of the plastic sheeting, the
blood drying and congealing around the exposed bones.
Laurence prodded the flesh around the amputation stumps,
prompting a little more blood to trickle out. As he wrapped
the rest of the polythene around them, he glanced over at the
body map hanging on the wall.

Eyes
Tongue
Hand
Feet

His lips quivered at the thought of what was yet to come.

Tommy was lying motionless on the pathology trolley, still slumbering in his artificial state of sleep. The infusion pump was slowly treating his body to a steady stream of ketamine, but Laurence knew he would disconnect it soon.

Tommy's time was coming.

He just needed to deal with the feet first.

With the feet now securely wrapped in their polythene shroud, Laurence placed them carefully inside a large holdall and headed for the door.

CHAPTER TWENTY-NINE

Bury St Edmunds

Amy Butler was meant to have finished her shift an hour ago. But the freezing temperatures had brought on a spate of accidents, and A&E had been full to overflowing for most of the evening. Eventually managing to leave a little after 9.30 p.m., she made her way across the town. She knew she was lucky to live within walking distance of the hospital — meaning she didn't have the headache of finding a car parking space, or paying for a ticket — but on a night like tonight she'd give almost anything to be able to slip into the warm comfort of a car.

She'd fleetingly contemplated calling Darcie to come and give her a lift home, but knew her baby sister was working, too. With several particularly nasty cases on the go at the minute, Darcie was rarely home at all.

Amy pulled the collar of her coat firmly around her neck and readjusted her scarf, then turned in the direction of home. The ice and impacted snow underfoot made her progress slow. Although it was dark, she headed down the narrow alleyway towards the meadow, squinting through the gloom. Every so often she would glance back over her shoulder — just in case.

A shiver rippled through her as she quickened her step, careful not to slip on the ice beneath her feet. She always told herself not to take the isolated shortcut home alone in the dark, but the longer, colder route wasn't enticing.

Before long she came out on to Cullum Road and headed up towards the roundabout, thankful to at last see some street lighting. She turned down Westgate Street and began to lengthen her stride. The gritters had been out and there was a layer of salt and grit scattered across both the road and pavement.

She ploughed on with her head bowed, tucking her chin beneath her scarf and her hands thrust inside her pockets against the chill. The street lights gave off enough light to cause the impacted snow and ice of the pavement to glisten, like diamonds scattered in the rough.

It was then, just past the entrance to the school, that she saw it.

Or, more accurately, *them*.

Amy froze to the spot. The chill air made her teeth tingle as she drew in a sharp breath.

She could see they were a pair of trainers but, as she edged closer, she felt warm bile bubbling at the back of her throat.

Someone's feet were still inside.

* * *

The Farmhouse

Leaving the trainers on the pavement had only taken seconds, but there were still plenty of windows along Westgate Street — and windows meant curtains: curtains with nosy people behind them. He knew it was a risk, but something inside him told him it was a risk worth taking. He was becoming bolder — he liked the way it felt.

He'd swapped the registration plates on the van again — something he did regularly to evade detection by the many cameras today's society seemed to be obsessed with. Each plate cloned from a vehicle many miles from home. So far, it had served him well.

And if anyone did see him from behind their twitching net curtains, he was pretty sure he looked like anyone else out on a freezing December night — hat, scarf, face obscured from the chill.

Entering the boot room, Laurence crossed towards the third freezer and lifted up the lid.

Still there.

Still cold.

Still dead.

Unlike Jacqui, Lucie or Lee, his father's body was naked. There was no ulterior or perverse motive behind this decision — it was something borne purely out of necessity. Because his father's death had been different; the man had served a purpose.

He'd killed his father quite early on in his medical training — at the beginning of his second year — and quickly his body began to develop numerous perfectly placed incisions.

Useful.

More useful in death than he ever had been in life.

In essence, Laurence Hemmingway Sr's death, however barbaric it had been at the end, had helped light the touch paper to his only son's career and turn him into the man he was today.

* * *

December 2009
University Medical School

He'd named his cadaver Sebastian — his father's middle name. When the cadaver was presented to him at the beginning of his third year, a cadaver he would work on throughout the next twelve months of his studies, Laurence felt an all-too-familiar ripple of excitement.

They'd bonded instantly.

Some of the other students hadn't wanted to name their cadavers — preferring the anonymity of the deceased to be preserved. They were never told the real names of those who had given the ultimate gift to help them through their university career, those who had signed on the dotted line to donate their body to medical science after they died. All the students were told was their age, sex and the cause of death.

The rest was a glorious mystery.

Laurence stared down at the cadaver lying peacefully on the examination table. Dissection was his favourite class — finding his way around a real human body gave him a thrill like no other. They'd performed several different dissections over the last few months, but despite that Sebastian still looked at peace with the world. He'd died of a heart attack at just fifty-six — cut down in his prime before he'd really had a chance to fulfil his dreams. Laurence could already tell from the rest of his body that he'd had no other underlying health conditions — life was so fickle. And death, too.

Today's task was a simple appendicectomy — and Laurence knew he could do it in his sleep. On the third weekend of every month, he took the train back home to the farmhouse and practised his skills on his father.

The irony.

Laurence Hemmingway Sr had had his appendix removed almost a dozen times already.

Laurence reached for his scalpel and leaned in close by the cadaver's side. The extra practise would no doubt mean he would be top of the class again today. Before making his first incision, Laurence considered the life that had once coursed through the man's veins before his heart had finally given up.

Did his life flash before his eyes as people said? With the crushing central chest pain and shortness of breath — had he known what was coming? Had he known the end was approaching fast? That death had chosen him?

"Is everything all right, Oliver?"

Professor Gordon Ferguson's deep baritone voice cut into Laurence's thoughts, jolting him back to the present. He still found it odd when people addressed him as Oliver — but Oliver was the person as whom he had chosen to spend his medical school days. *Oliver Harper.* Not Laurence Hemmingway.

Laurence Hemmingway had too much baggage.

Glancing around, Laurence was aware that he was the only student in the room who hadn't yet started the dissection task. Most had at least made the first incision, others progressing further. He blinked and smiled, nodding towards the professor. "Yes, absolutely." He stepped a little closer to the cadaver and raised his scalpel. "I'll begin now."

Without further delay, he ran the sharpened scalpel along Sebastian's lower right abdomen, inhaling the beautiful scent of embalming fluid as he did so. The sweetness filled his senses and quickened his heart.

Professor Ferguson stepped away and returned to the front of the room, the look of concern etched on to his face hidden from his students.

Oliver Harper was a brilliant student, there was no denying that. Every once in a while, one came along — someone who had a natural-born ability and flair for medicine. He supposed there must be an element of genetics involved too — the boy's father had been an outstanding surgeon. The world-class surgeon, Laurence Hemmingway. But Oliver had enrolled in the medical school programme using his middle name and his mother's maiden name — seemingly not wanting to be suffocated by the millstone that the Hemmingway surname might present. Professor Ferguson had no opinion either way — the boy was good, whatever name he chose to go by.

Oliver didn't like talking about his father — visibly flinching at any mention of his name. The professor suspected a family rift of some sort, but let the matter ride. When asked what his father was doing these days, his name noticeably absent from any number of medical papers and journals, Oliver merely said that his father had retired to write his memoirs.

Professor Ferguson couldn't blame him. Retirement couldn't come soon enough for him. At fifty-nine he felt every one of his advancing years. Tiredness engulfed him most days; a feeling of permanent exhaustion. That and the dull ache in his side, coupled with nausea and bloating. He'd seen a doctor and there was talk of a biopsy. He pushed the thought from his mind.

Standing at the front of the room, he surveyed the third-year students before him. They were a good bunch this time around — with some very talented and hardworking individuals among them. He had no doubt that each and every one would make an excellent doctor in some shape or form. Some might end up specialising in surgery, who knew? There was at least one who was destined for neurosurgery — they had a steady hand and an accurate eye. Several others would make excellent trauma surgeons — they were confident and quick-thinking, not afraid to take control.

And then there was Oliver.

Professor Ferguson's frown deepened.

Oliver Harper bothered him.

Because Oliver Harper was different.

* * *

Sunday 30 December 2018
The Farmhouse

Laurence looked down at his father's battered body at the bottom of the freezer. Almost every inch of his torso was covered in a criss-cross pattern of surgical incisions and suturing. The gallbladder had been removed and replaced more times than he could remember, as had sections of his colon. The liver had been lacerated and re-sutured like a patchwork quilt.

And with each incision, with each suture, Laurence's surgical skills had improved, sending him to the top of

Professor Ferguson's class each time. Maybe his father would be proud in a macabre kind of way, helping his one and only son even in death. The thought made Laurence chuckle as he slammed the lid and turned away from the freezer, heading for the pantry.

Tommy was ready and Laurence now knew exactly how the boy would contribute to the body map. A smile touched his lips as he ran his fingers over the trays of prepared instruments sitting on the pantry shelving. This was one he was looking forward to.

But as much as he looked forward to making Tommy his next show piece and embarking on the boy's final journey, Laurence knew he needed sleep.

CHAPTER THIRTY

Westgate Street, Bury St Edmunds

Nicki arrived at the scene within fifteen minutes of receiving Amy's distressed call. She had requested a full forensics team to join her, plus extra patrol cars to block off the road.

Westgate Street was now a crime scene.

Again.

The forensics team arrived quickly, securing the scene and creating an inner cordon around the trainers. The victim's feet had been severed just above the ankle — leaving a short section of visible bleached white bone.

"Nicki." Caz made her way across the street towards her. "I was just driving through the town after a late session at the mortuary, heard the commotion and the sirens. My pathologist's nose brought me here." She glanced across to where the trainers, and the embedded feet, were still sitting on the pavement. A mixture of emotions crossed her face. "You're kidding me, right?"

Nicki shook her head. "I wish I was. Amy, over there, discovered them about half an hour ago. Walked right up to them."

Amy Butler was sitting in the back of a patrol car, her hands wrapped around a takeaway cup of coffee that someone had magically conjured up from somewhere. A tartan rug was draped around her shoulders.

Caz looked around, up and down the deserted street. "Someone must have seen something. This is quite a busy road. CCTV surely?"

"Let's hope so." Nicki stamped her feet on the ground, trying to get some circulation back into her frozen toes. "But you know what I'm going to ask, don't you?"

Caz glanced back towards the trainers. "Same body — or new body?"

Nicki nodded.

Caz noted a series of metal stepping plates had been placed at strategic intervals. She edged as close as she could, careful not to get too near to contaminate the scene. "From what I can see, which isn't much to be fair — they look like male feet to me. I can see hairs on the lower portion of the leg. The style of trainers, and the size, all look male. But I'll be able to tell more once I give them a proper look." Caz returned along the plates towards Nicki. "I'll take blood samples, DNA — yada yada. You know the score."

Nicki nodded again. She did. With the eyes and tongue confirmed to belong to Jacqui Massingham, and the hand Lucie Ballantine's, tonight's discovery now looked to bring the victim tally to three. The thought made her stomach swirl. Raising a hand, she caught the attention of Darcie who was hovering by the side of the patrol car next to her sister.

The white-faced DC hurried across the street.

"Get yourself home, Darcie." Nicki gave her a sympathetic smile. "And Amy, too. Pour yourselves a large brandy. We'll talk tomorrow."

After remaining at the scene a while longer, talking things through with the forensics team, Nicki headed towards home herself. The feet, together with the trainers, would be bagged up and shipped over to Caz to examine them first thing in the morning. Rubbing her eyes, she stifled a yawn.

Someone was playing games with them — but only they seemed to know the rules.

Heading up Whiting Street, she turned towards College Lane. Inside her pocket her phone vibrated. As she approached her front door, she pulled the phone out and frowned. The call had gone straight to voicemail but the caller had declined to leave a message.

Again.

Another unknown number.

Shoving the key in the lock, Nicki slipped the phone back in her pocket. She was dog-tired and random scam calls she could do without.

* * *

Maynewater Lane, Bury St Edmunds

Darcie took the front door keys out of her sister's hand and unlocked the door. The warmth of the narrow hallway hit them both as they stepped inside. Kicking the snow from her boots, Darcie yanked each one off and wiggled her frozen toes. Amy merely stood, white-faced, on the doormat, still wrapped tightly in the tartan travel rug.

"Come on, let's get you inside and warmed up." Darcie took hold of her sister's elbow and guided her towards the living room. A small step led them down into a sunken floor space, the hardwood floorboards sanded and polished to a visible shine. Two sagging sofas and an armchair faced a low-rise wicker coffee table, multicoloured throws flung across each.

There was a small wood burner in what had once been a rather ornate fireplace — they'd chosen to keep the fireplace intact to give the room some character, and not brick it up like many similar house renovations along the street had done.

And tonight they were glad of it. Darcie led Amy towards the armchair, and as her sister sat down, she gently pulled the boots from her frozen feet. "They might want these later — to eliminate your footprints from any they recover — but I don't really hold out much hope of them finding anything useful. Footprint evidence is difficult at the best of times, but in those conditions . . ." She shook her head and placed the boots by the side of the sofa.

"Thanks, Darce." Amy managed a thin smile. "I don't know why I'm being such a wuss." She shivered once more, pulling the rug more closely around her shoulders.

"You're not being a wuss. You've just seen something horrific." Darcie got to her feet and headed in the direction of the galley-style kitchen. "It would have shocked anyone."

"I know but, as I told Nicki, I've seen worse at work. Far worse. I've seen people mangled beyond recognition from road accidents, burnt in fires, multiple stab wounds and broken bones. This was nothing in comparison, really."

"It wasn't nothing," Darcie called back over her shoulder as she disappeared into the kitchen to make some tea. "Don't be too hard on yourself." Switching on the kettle, she headed back to the living room, grabbing a bottle of Jack Daniels on the way. Tea was good, but tonight called for something a little stronger. "You've just seen someone's feet hacked off at the ankle. Cut yourself some slack."

Amy accepted the large measure of whisky and sunk a mouthful almost immediately. "I know, but . . . I'm a nurse. I should be able to deal with these things."

"You *are* dealing with it," countered Darcie, flopping down on to one of the sofas, her own shot of whisky in hand. "As soon as you realised what it was, what did you do? Did you scream and run? Did you faint? Did you collapse into a complete mess and sob incoherently?" Darcie fixed her older sister with a stern gaze. "No, you didn't. You called Nicki — clearly and calmly telling her what you could see. You preserved the scene and waited. You dealt with it, Ames. You dealt with it."

Amy gave a deep sigh and then a shrug. "OK, I take your point."

Neither felt like sleeping so Darcie flicked on the TV and they started to watch some old episodes of the *Great British Bake Off*. There was nothing like a perfectly whipped meringue or an expertly baked Swiss roll to take your mind off seeing a pair of freshly severed feet.

After a while, Darcie turned towards her sister. "You hungry?" She hadn't eaten all day, except for a quick sausage roll from Greggs around midday, and some of Roy's grandmother's fried bean cake. Despite the night's gruesome events, her stomach was beginning to rumble. Maybe it was all the chocolate and fondant icing they were seeing on the TV.

Amy was nursing her second JD, mixed with a little lemonade this time — they'd left the kettle to boil and go cold in the kitchen. She laid her head against the back of the armchair and nodded. "Kind of, I guess. But I don't fancy cooking."

Darcie prised herself off the sofa and padded back through to the kitchen. She noted the empty sink and spotless surfaces — and all the washing up that been on the draining board that morning seemed to have found its way back into the cupboards. She smiled to herself as she pulled open the fridge, bathing the narrow kitchen in a bright, white light.

"What d'you fancy?" she called out, perusing the contents of the fridge.

"Something quick," came the reply. "And not too much."

Darcie moved a few packets and jars around on the shelves before spying a casserole dish wrapped in cling film and a post-it note taped to the top. Frowning, she pulled it out.

'For you both! Enjoy!'

Through the cling film, Darcie could see the dish was full of chicken curry and after lifting up the side and taking a sniff, her eyes sparkled.

"How do you fancy some homemade chicken curry?"

"Perfect! How come we've got curry?"

"Ollie," replied Darcie, slamming shut the fridge door and removing the rest of the cling film from the casserole dish. "He's left us a note."

Darcie popped the dish into the microwave and then rummaged around inside one of the cupboards for some microwavable rice. She grabbed a packet of Uncle Ben's. It wasn't long before the sisters had plates full of steaming curry on their laps. The food didn't last long, the thick curry sauce mopped up with wedges of naan bread Darcie had found in the cupboard.

As she placed her empty plate on the floor, Darcie looked across at her sister, noticing the cloudiness returning to her eyes. The shock of the night's events was still raw.

"You OK, Ames?"

Amy nodded and tried a smile. "I'll be fine. Just need my bed, I think." She made a move to push herself out of the armchair. "Oliver did us proud with that curry. I'm guessing he's not coming back here tonight?"

Darcie helped her sister to her feet and picked up the plates. "Doesn't look like it. I'll do the dishes, then I'll head for bed, too. I've an early start in the morning."

Darcie listened to her sister's footsteps climbing the creaking stairs as she trekked back into the kitchen. She ran a bowl of hot water and began to rinse the plates clean. Stacking them up on the draining board, she left the casserole dish to soak in water overnight.

Although she knew she needed to go to bed — the night's revelations would more than likely keep her awake into the small hours.

CHAPTER THIRTY-ONE

Monday 31 December 2018
Bury St Edmunds Police Station

Another whiteboard.

More body parts.

Nicki's stomach clenched, the early morning coffee swirling uncomfortably within.

A stark photograph of the trainers — with feet in situ — had been pinned to the middle of the board. It was all they had.

Nicki had rung Amy a few minutes ago to see how she was. *'OK'* came the reply. Nicki knew it was Amy's brave face talking — it would take a while for last night's events to fully sink in, but her friend was tough. Darcie had insisted she wanted to go out with the team doing the house-to-house along Westgate Street, and Nicki knew it would be foolish to try and persuade her otherwise.

Both Roy and DS Fox had come in early and were already wading through the CCTV of the area. Their initial euphoria at seeing a nondescript white van in the vicinity of Westgate Street around the time the trainers would have been deposited, soon evaporated.

The van's registration plates were cloned — the image of the driver only seen from behind and useless.

"Keep looking for that van," urged Nicki, as she headed towards Matt and Duncan who were hunched over their computer terminals. "I want to know if it's been anywhere else in the town — we may be able to track where it goes even if we don't know who it belongs to."

She pulled a chair across next to Matt's desk. "What have you got for me?"

"OK, so Duncan and I have been raking through both victims' social media accounts."

Victims.

Nicki couldn't help but shudder. Although they had yet to find any bodies, she knew that with each passing hour the likelihood of finding anyone alive was getting more remote. Not inconceivable, but remote.

"The most prolific user was Jacqui." Matt tapped the keyboard and brought up the Facebook account for Jacqui Massingham. "Mostly Facebook. An occasional tweet. Hardly ever on Instagram, though." He used the mouse to scroll through the most recent posts. "Nothing too outrageous in the days leading up to her disappearance. Just the usual — looking forward to a break from work. Wishing her friends a Merry Christmas. What she was watching on TV. That kind of thing."

"Anything from Adrian?" Nicki squinted at the screen.

Matt shook his head. "No, she blocked him some time ago."

"Sensible girl," muttered Nicki. "So, there's no contact between her and Adrian?"

Another shake of the head. "Not on social media. Last interaction was back in January which would fit in around the time they finally split — and the alleged assault. There were a few nasty messages back and forth, then nothing. Then of course we have his tweets about her a couple of days before she disappeared."

"OK, is there any indication that he was acquainted with Lucie?"

"Unfortunately not." Matt minimised Jacqui's Facebook page and brought up the one belonging to Adrian. "He does use Facebook on occasion, but is more of a Twitter man. We can't find any interaction between him and either of the victims — except the Twitter outburst we already know about."

"What about Lucie?"

Lucie Ballantine was next up on screen. "Lucie used Facebook and Instagram. Quite a regular user, posting every day at various times. Prefers photos to text — lots of images of cats, food and books — and checks into a lot of places when she's out and about."

"Anything that stands out?"

Another shake of the head, accompanied by a sigh. "Not really. Quite standard stuff these days, telling everyone and his wife what you're doing and where you are. But nothing to suggest she knew Jacqui. Or Adrian for that matter."

Nicki matched the detective's sigh. Often social media gave up useful leads, or at least opened avenues you hadn't considered before. But the fact that neither of the victims seemed to have any kind of connection to each other, virtual or otherwise, was a blow to the investigation. A link, no matter how small could have been all they needed.

"You think he's just picking them at random?"

A random killer was dangerous — more so than any other. If there was no rhyme or reason to his selection of victims, no pattern or explanation for who he chose, then the job of tracking him down was made infinitely harder. No pattern often meant no clues.

Nicki shuddered at the thought and got to her feet. "I don't think so. He puts too much thought into his victims, and what he does to them. He's a planner. No way is this some random nut-job."

"Do we need to go back and speak to Adrian? Ask him about Lucie?"

Nicki considered it for a moment but shook her head. "Not right now. Let's concentrate on what we've got. Keep looking into both Jacqui and Lucie's social media accounts, plus phone calls and text messages."

"Jacqui's phone records are in." Matt tapped the keyboard and brought up the most recent report. "Currently switched off. The last time it pinged was on Saturday 22nd around the time she left work. It went quiet soon after."

"Do the same with Lucie's phone records. There has to be a link somewhere — no matter how tenuous. We just haven't spotted it yet."

Getting up from her seat, Nicki headed towards the door. DCI Turner had requested a meeting, and Nicki wasn't looking forward to it. "We're going to be circulating images of the trainers as a priority this morning. I'm told those are the latest model — limited edition — and worth upwards of two hundred pounds. I wouldn't expect that many people to own a pair, not around here anyway. But, in the meantime, find out who stocks them. We need to know who bought some recently. They looked brand new to me."

As she continued towards the exit, Nicki felt the sinking feeling return as she glanced at the whiteboards. They'd reached an unhappy stalemate where the investigation risked slowing down and grinding to a halt completely. The renewed energy they'd all felt at getting positive identifications for both Jacqui and Lucie was petering out.

And now they had a third victim to find.

And all the while they were heading towards the unenviable position of possibly knowing *who* their victims were — but not *where* they were.

With a sigh, she headed in the direction of the DCI's office.

* * *

4 Old Railway Cottages
Dullingham, Nr Newmarket

"Sorry it's taken me so long to get it properly sorted." Benedict gave an apologetic look and nodded towards the fence panel. "Work's really busy at the moment."

Mason nodded and gave a half shrug. "Dad said it's no problem. What is it that you do? For a job, I mean?"

Benedict hesitated, busying himself hauling the new fence panel into place and chucking the battered old one to the side. "Oh, you know. This and that." He decided to deflect the conversation. "Your mum tells me you're a bit of an artist." He leaned up against the fence post. "What kind of work do you do?"

Mason nodded. "Yeah. I'm a freelance illustrator — magazines, a few books. That kind of thing. I used to work for a design company but I've been working for myself the last few years. It means I can travel, work from home. I've just landed a deal to illustrate an author's science fiction series — ten books' worth."

Benedict gestured for Mason to hold the new fence panel in place while he fished around for the nail gun. "Congratulations, that sounds really good. I know your brother works in the butcher's shop in town, but what do your parents do?"

Mason braced himself against the fence post as Benedict fired in the first set of nails. "Dad's an accountant. Has his own business and works from home. Mum's never really worked — not since I can remember anyway. Always been at home with us."

Benedict motioned for them to swap ends, brandishing the nail gun at the opposite fence post. "You said you moved around a lot. Where were you before coming here?"

Mason held the panel firm as Benedict fired in more nails. "Wales. It was nice there, I liked it."

Twenty minutes later, the new fence panel was securely in place. Benedict couldn't help his gaze drifting towards the bottom of the Brownings' garden — and the headstone he knew lay beyond. His thoughts were interrupted by Mason handing him his tool box.

It had started sleeting while they were working on the fence and Benedict could feel the icy dampness seeping through his jumper to his shirt below. "Thanks. Any chance of a coffee? I've run out and my fingers are like icicles." It sounded like a feeble excuse, and he hoped Mason didn't see right through him.

Mason merely nodded and led the way to the back door, pushing it open with his boot and gesturing for Benedict to step inside. The kitchen was pleasantly warm — the oven switched on and what looked like a pot of stew bubbling away on the hob.

After switching on the kettle, Mason headed towards the hallway. "While that boils, I'll pop upstairs to get out of these wet things. Mum'll go ape if she sees me like this."

And then he was gone.

Without wasting a second, Benedict followed. He knew he wouldn't have long. All he could hear were Mason's footsteps reaching the top of the stairs, the rest of the house appeared to be in slumber. Having no idea where the rest of the family were, he decided it was now or never and headed for the study beneath the stairs.

Once inside, he went straight over to the desk and pulled the top drawer open.

They were still there — dozens and dozens of newspaper cuttings. But this time there seemed to be even more — including cuttings from yesterday's paper, and the day before. He pulled them out and began to take photos with his phone. Everything was slotting into place. There really could be no other explanation.

The most recent cuttings showed Detective Inspector Nicki Hardcastle — one was a still from the press conference yesterday, and another showed her standing by a section of 'police — do not cross' tape by the cathedral. The headlines accompanying the images all concerned the recent gruesome finding of body parts in the town.

But it was the cuttings beneath these that had originally stirred Benedict's inquisitive nature.

The oldest cuttings — the ones he'd first seen back in October after the request to fix the Brownings' Wi-Fi — were still there. Benedict snapped more photos with his phone.

'FEARS GROW FOR MISSING BOY'

'BOY ABDUCTED FROM FAMILY FAIRGROUND TRIP'

'FAIRGROUND HORROR'

Once again, he skimmed the articles. Five-year-old Dean Webster had disappeared from a fairground in November 1996. Last seen with his sister — ten-year-old Nicola Webster — he literally disappeared into thin air.

Over the years, various theories were batted around concerning his fate — most favoured was that he'd been the victim of a paedophile — but no trace of the youngster had ever been found.

But now Benedict knew better.

Hearing the floorboards creaking above him, Benedict hurriedly took the rest of his photos and stuffed the newspaper cuttings back inside the drawer.

On his way to the door, he passed the drawing board displaying Mason's artwork, with the selection of framed family photographs hanging on the wall above. Stopping to look once more at the Brownings and their two young boys, he quickly snapped a couple more pictures.

Everything now made sense.

Stepping back out into the hallway, he just about made it to the kitchen before Mason returned, dressed in a grey marl tracksuit, a towel around his head.

"Coffee? Or tea?" He gestured towards the kettle which had finished boiling.

Benedict's gaze gravitated towards the window and the headstone that lay beyond. "Anything is fine," he murmured, distracted by the thoughts tumbling through his head. "Whatever you're having."

While Mason busied himself with mugs and getting the milk from the fridge, Benedict continued to look out into the garden. Now, more than ever, he was sure he knew exactly what had happened to little Dean Webster.

Now he just needed to tell the boy's sister.

* * *

"We're coping fine. We just need that one breakthrough, that's all." Nicki could taste the lie on her tongue as she spoke.

"That's as may be . . ." DCI Turner gave a sigh and nudged the mug of freshly ground coffee across the desk. "But you're all running on empty — I can see it with my own eyes. All I'm suggesting is drafting in some help."

Nicki took hold of the mug but didn't drink. "No," she repeated, her tone a little harsher than the DCI deserved. She softened. "I appreciate the thought but we've got this. All we need . . ."

"Is that one break, I know." Turner tapped his biro against his keyboard. "But I've got people above me, carefully watching what's going on. The powers that be are getting restless. I've just come out of a particularly strained budget meeting — it wasn't pretty. With each new find . . ." He broke off, another sigh closely following. "I have to give them something. A plan at least."

"Give us the rest of this week. If we're no further forward by Friday . . ."

"Forty-eight hours, Nicki." The DCI fixed her with a kind yet firm gaze. "You've got forty-eight hours to get me something solid. Then it's out of my hands."

Before Nicki had a chance to retaliate, the office door swung open. A breathless Royston Carter stood in the doorway.

"Apologies for barging in, but you need to see this." He flapped an A4 sheet of paper in the air. "We've got three names for the possible owner of the trainers."

CHAPTER THIRTY-TWO

4 Old Railway Cottages
Dullingham, Nr Newmarket

"Who's been here while we've been out?" Larry Browning eyed the two used coffee mugs on the draining board as he entered the kitchen.

Annette Browning gave a nervous shrug as she lifted the shopping bags on to the kitchen worktop. "I . . . I don't know. I think the man from next door might have put the new fence panel up." Her gaze travelled through the kitchen window to the newly repaired fence. "Maybe Mason invited him in?"

A thunderous look crossed Larry's face, his eyes darkening. "Someone's been in my study. I don't like people messing about in my study."

"I don't think anyone would . . ."

"Someone's been in there, I know it." Larry joined his wife at the window. "The papers in one of the drawers have been moved."

"Calm down. I'm sure it's nothing. You've been on edge ever since the police came to speak to Adrian."

Larry's neck muscles tensed. "Can you blame me? Seeing that woman, in the flesh, standing in our kitchen? You weren't exactly thrilled yourself."

"What did you expect? *You* made us move here." Annette didn't try and hide the cut to her words.

"I didn't expect her to be calling at my bloody house!" Larry dragged his gaze away from the window. "And we had to move here — for Adrian. You know that."

"No, we didn't. He could have come to us — in Wales. It might have been better for him that way. We certainly didn't need to come *here* — of all places. You knew she worked here — all those newspaper cuttings you collect, following her career like some obsessed fan. What were you thinking?" Annette was surprised at the defiance bubbling up inside her. She'd never spoken to Larry like this before. But now she'd started, it was like the floodgates had opened. She couldn't stop. "It's like you *want* us to get found out. Like you want them to know what we did."

"What *you* did, you mean." Anger flashed in Larry's eyes. The words he usually kept inside spat from his mouth. "All I've ever done is try and pick up the pieces, Annette. None of this was my doing."

Annette felt the familiar hot tears prickling at the corner of her eyes. She avoided her husband's simmering gaze and once more stared out towards the bottom of the garden. Eventually she shuddered. "So, what are we going to do?"

* * *

Bury St Edmunds Police Station

"Out of the three names we've been given, the Tennant family live here in the town." Roy highlighted the name Lee Tennant before passing the A4 sheet across to Nicki. "He's got to be top of our list. Call came in from someone he works with — said he definitely has a pair. Passed us his mobile number but it's switched off."

The media had been having a field day with the new information divulged early that morning. Details of the find on Westgate Street, and then the pictures of the trainers, had been all over the online news portals.

"Agreed." Nicki passed the paper back to Roy. "Let's get a team out to that address sharpish. Check with the neighbours who lives there. Take Graham with you."

Nicki stared at the name Lee Tennant. She didn't hold out much hope of anything coming from a search of the house, if it did turn out to be the victim's home. Both Jacqui and Lucie's houses had drawn a blank. But it needed to be done just the same. "Has anything come through from last night's scene?"

"We've looked at the CCTV again from Westgate Street. Nothing other than the white van with the cloned plates." Matt angled his screen towards Nicki where the grainy images were playing. She watched again as the van stuttered into view; a man exiting the driver's side, back to the camera, depositing something on the pavement before getting back into the van and disappearing from view. The scene took less than fifteen seconds. "Cameras are being checked for other sightings of the van, but nothing so far."

"Darcie? How about the house-to-house?" Nicki turned towards the detective constable sitting by her computer.

Darcie shook her head and sighed. "Nothing useful. No one saw or heard anything."

"And how is Amy? Has she said anything more about last night?"

Darcie gave a wan smile. "She's OK. Shocked, obviously, but she says she's seen worse. And she's pretty sure there wasn't anyone else around when she found them — no cars were passing, no one else on the street."

"OK — well if we do think our feet belong to this Lee Tennant, do we have any details as to next of kin? Family?"

Roy took a look again at the A4 sheet of paper. "He's not on our system, but the home address is registered to a Brenda and Frank Tennant. I'm assuming they're the parents."

"Head out there and see what you can find out. Next door neighbours and the like. But keep it subtle. We don't want to cause any unnecessary panic." Nicki glanced down at her watch. Time was ticking.

Forty-eight hours wasn't long.

CHAPTER THIRTY-THREE

West Suffolk Mortuary

The creamy whiteness of the freshly severed bones gleamed under the intense beam of the overhead lights. With a deepening sense of foreboding at what might still be to come, Caz reached for the left trainer. Ice-white, it had a distinctive gold flash on the side with a designer logo beneath. The gold laces were still tied in a carefully executed bow.

Caz let the pathology technician take a series of close-up photographs of the feet in situ, still wondering just who would spend over two hundred pounds on a pair of shoes.

Photographs complete, Caz proceeded to take samples and swabs from the outside of the trainer — noting a collection of tiny abrasions on the heel.

"Fine scrapings observed at the back of the left trainer — possibly consistent with being dragged along a rough surface." Taking a sample, she then turned the trainer in a full 360-degree arc. "Otherwise, the trainer is in a brand-new condition, no visible wear to the outside." She repeated the same examination for the right-hand trainer, noting identical scrapings on the heel.

With the external examination of the trainers complete, Caz then slowly began to unlace them and ease each foot out on to the examination table.

An uneasy silence descended. Caz and her team had witnessed many a horrific and often stomach-churning scene within the four walls of the mortuary — late last night she'd completed the unenviable task of conducting the post-mortem on the victim of a collision between a pedestrian and an articulated lorry on the A14. The pedestrian understandably had come off worst — his body all but scraped off the tarmac.

But this was different. This made no sense at all.

Outwardly, both feet had nothing by way of distinguishing marks. The nails were intact, neatly clipped, with slight evidence of a healed blister on the right hallux valgus. Caz measured each foot — 27.8 centimetres consistent with a size eight shoe. Turning the rim of the left trainer towards her, the 'UK size 8' tag confirmed the measurement.

With nothing else of note visible to the naked eye, Caz proceeded to take scrapings from beneath the toenails and swabs from the skin surface. She then turned her attention to the amputation stump.

"Evidence of recent haemorrhaging is seen." Caz teased away some of the coagulated blood with the tip of her scalpel. "But the wound looks clean. No jagged edges — skin and subcutaneous tissues have been dissected with a sharp bladed instrument." She ran a gloved finger over the exposed bones. "Similarly, both the distal tibia and distal fibula have been amputated cleanly — I suspect an electric or motorised hand saw has been used. The amputation is precise. No fragments or splintering."

Once finished with the left, Caz continued with the right foot — with almost identical results. Just as she was concluding the examination, taking one last look at the trainers, something caught her eye. Taking a fresh scalpel in her hand, a frown began to form beneath her elasticated cap.

"Well, well, well — what do we have here?"

* * *

Phone calls with the next of kin in any investigation were difficult to deal with — but in this case it was even more so. Nicki leaned back in her chair and rubbed her temples, where the mother of all headaches was brewing. Roger and Cindy Ballantine were understandably distraught, and Nicki had immediately mobilised the local force in Cumbria to pay them a visit as a matter of urgency.

Lucie's parents insisted they would make the journey south as soon as they could, despite Nicki urging them not to. There was nothing she could tell them in person that she hadn't already told them over the phone, but she understood them wanting to be as close to Lucie as possible; whatever the outcome. Nicki had rung off after giving them a list of local bed and breakfasts.

A stack of messages sat next to a half-drunk cup of cold coffee — the latest batch of hotline calls. Nicki's heart sank. Calls had flooded in within minutes of the details being released to the media that morning — the overtly crank ones had been weeded out at source, but the rest were passed through to the team. Any promise of more bodies to help with ploughing through them had yet to materialise.

Nicki pulled the stack towards her — it was possible the answer they were looking for could be there. Glancing up at the clock, she could almost visualise the forty-eight hours the DCI had given her slipping through her fingers.

Just as she picked up the first message, her desk phone began to trill. Momentarily, she thought about ignoring it — in case it was DCI Turner checking up on progress — but with a sigh she grabbed the handset.

"DI Nicki Hardcastle."

"Nicki." Caz sounded breathless. "I've just finished looking at the feet."

"And?"

There was a brief pause before Caz continued, her voice hitching slightly. "And I think I've found something."

* * *

Laurence could still picture the look in the boy's eyes as he made the first incision, the homemade head guard working well to keep him still. He'd let the boy scream — the sound of his blood-curdling cries echoing around the stone walls of the pantry. No one would hear him.

Blood trickled down the side of the boy's face

Maybe you should've kept your blabbering mouth shut.

Laurence felt a chuckle bubbling at the back of his throat. If he hadn't already taken the tongue from Jacqui, Tommy would've been the perfect choice. Teach him a lesson about keeping quiet.

He left Tommy's sedated body on the pathology trolley — he'd enjoy bringing him round later to watch his soul finally depart this earth. Adjusting the infusion pump, ensuring a continuous level of ketamine kept him quiet, Laurence made his way over to the pantry shelving.

He was on a roll now — he needed to prepare for the next one.

He'd already decided what was to be next. The crowning glory — he chuckled once more at his own joke.

He'd seen her in the town on several occasions, eventually following her back to her home in the shadows. It was her jet-black hair that had first caught his attention — it framed her already perfect face. He'd scalp her, to preserve that beauty forever on the map — just like the Native Americans did.

Hair.

The thought excited him.

He'd seen the headlines that morning — urgent calls to trace the owners of the trainers were flooding every news portal. The discovery had sent everyone into a head spin — everyone except Laurence that was. The police were clearly chasing their tails — dutifully following the merry dance he was leading.

Well, tonight they would dance some more.

* * *

A sticker.

At least, part of one. Curled up and stuck to the sole of the right-hand trainer. Caz had carefully teased it out and flattened it as best she could — sending Nicki a photo.

It wasn't much — but it was more than they'd had five minutes ago.

"All we can see is part of a word — maybe it's part of an address." Nicki tacked the photo to the fourth whiteboard next to the one of the trainers. "It may mean nothing — may have nothing to do with any potential crime scene — but it's something."

"Could be farmhouse," volunteered Duncan. "Of which there are literally hundreds around these parts."

"Agreed. Like I said, it may be nothing." Nicki turned towards Roy. "What did you manage to find out at the Tennants' family home?"

Roy edged towards the whiteboards. "Not a lot. Place was locked up, everything in darkness. Neighbours on one side confirmed that Mr and Mrs Tennant went away a few days ago, leaving their nineteen-year-old son, Lee, home alone. When asked, they confirmed they hadn't seen him for a couple of days. Gave us a mobile number for the mother — so far she's not picking up."

Nicki nodded. "OK, keep trying them. As far as forensics are concerned, results are now in from both the theatre and the roundabout. No prizes for guessing that both sites have drawn a blank. Nothing there to assist us. Caz has sent the sticker from the trainer to the lab to see if we can get anything from it — but don't get your hopes up." She glanced up at the wall clock and then towards the closed door.

DCI Turner was in the building but had yet to make an appearance in the incident room. Nicki, for one, didn't want to be there when he did. She reached for her coat.

"Keep doing what you're doing — keep trying Mrs Tennant and also see if we can't find the lad on CCTV anywhere in the town in the last forty-eight to seventy-two hours. If he's wearing those trainers, he should be identifiable. I'm going to pop out for some air."

"What time are we meeting tonight?" Roy settled back down at his computer. "Don't want to leave it too late or we won't get a table."

Tonight.

Nicki's heart sank. The last thing she needed was a night out — not when the investigations were on such a knife edge — but she couldn't let the team down; not when it was Matt's birthday. But New Year's Eve? She couldn't remember the last time she'd gone out on New Year's Eve. The thought made her shudder.

"How about seven-ish? That OK with everyone?"

A smattering of 'OKs' trickled around the incident room as Nicki made her way out. She glanced again at her watch.

7 p.m.

She just needed to keep out of the DCI's way until then.

* * *

2 Old Railway Cottages
Dullingham, Nr Newmarket

Benedict wasn't a fan of New Year's Eve. He'd enjoyed it many years ago in his youth, but now — now it was just an excuse to be charged an entrance fee to a pub, or if you stayed home you just got woken up at midnight by a raft of fireworks thudding over the rooftops.

Slipping on his jacket, he scoured the mass of papers still littering the kitchen table. He didn't know what to bring. Maybe nothing? Maybe the paperwork could come later. Maybe for now he just needed to talk to her.

He'd tried to call her a few times, but the call was never picked up. He didn't blame her. Who answered a 'no caller ID' number these days? Next time he wouldn't disguise the number.

Making his way out of the front door, he noticed the Brownings looked like they were still up — lights were on in the downstairs living room. The van was gone though — which may mean the younger lad was out partying somewhere.

The journey wouldn't take long, and there was no guarantee she'd be at home. But if he had to wait, he would wait.

He'd waited this long — another few hours wouldn't make any difference.

CHAPTER THIRTY-FOUR

The Moreton Hall Pub, Bury St Edmunds

Nicki hauled herself to her feet. No one had really felt in the mood for a drink that night — the pallid, washed-out faces in the incident room told that story well enough. But it was Matt's thirtieth and they'd all promised to put on their happy faces and make an effort — even if just for a couple of hours.

DS Fox had cried off, citing that he was going to drop in to see his kids that evening — Nicki had a strong suspicion that the dogged detective was back at his seat in the incident room, trawling once more through the evidence. Such as it was.

Amy had been invited, but understandably wasn't in the mood for a celebration. Nicki had wavered herself — the lure of a hot bath and glass of wine at home almost too much to resist — but Darcie had insisted, not taking no for an answer.

And it had been a good night, despite the team's weariness and preoccupation with the investigation clouding their thoughts. Darcie had been on good form and Matt had liked his tickets for a stadium tour of Old Trafford. He was staying behind to welcome in the New Year but, even though the clock had yet to strike midnight, everyone else had decided to call it a night.

"Where's Darcie?" Roy shrugged into his coat, his eyes sweeping the bar area. "You think she needs a lift?"

Nicki grabbed her bag. "Maybe she's already left? Duncan got into a taxi about ten minutes ago — maybe she went with him?"

Waving their goodbyes to Charlie and Sylvia behind the bar, promising to return again soon — maybe for one of the legendary Wednesday quiz nights — Nicki and Roy headed outside. Roy had offered to drive, for which Nicki was thankful. The mother of all headaches hadn't subsided one bit. What she craved right now was a lie down in a darkened room.

"Isn't that Darcie over there?" Roy pointed across the pond towards the car park.

Darcie's distinctive purple puffa jacket stood out beneath the muted street lights. Roy waved to catch her attention, making a driving gesture with his hands and pointing back towards the car park behind them.

Darcie waved her own hands across her face, and gestured towards the car idling by her side. With another wave, she pulled open the passenger door and slipped inside.

"Looks like she's sorted for a lift," remarked Nicki, burying her chin in her scarf and turning away. "Come on, let's get going before the fireworks start. I'm freezing."

* * *

Darcie watched Roy's car pull out of the pub car park. She gave a brief wave as they passed by, unsure if anyone inside could even see her through the misted-up windows. She'd enjoyed the night — toasting Matt's milestone birthday — but her thoughts were never far away from her sister.

Amy hadn't felt like joining them in the pub, instead planning an early night as she had a shift in A&E the next morning. Darcie had given her a hug before she left — feeling

268

her sister tense beneath her touch. Amy was tough, but the events of last night had clearly rocked her.

Darcie smothered a hiccup. She'd drunk a little too much prosecco, she knew that. Her vision was a little hazy, her legs a little wobbly — but the alcohol was also numbing her from the cold, so it wasn't all bad. All she could think about right now was her bed and a mug of hot chocolate.

"You OK?" The voice startled Darcie from her hot chocolate dream.

She turned towards the driver. "Yes, sure. Sorry. It was good of you to come out. It's freezing out there!"

"No problem." Oliver smiled. "I wasn't busy. You ready to go?"

Darcie nodded as the car pulled out of the car park. "Can I put the radio on?"

"Of course."

As Darcie fiddled with the radio, she glanced out of the window and noticed they were heading in the opposite direction to what she expected. A frown crossed her forehead.

"Ollie? Where are we going?"

* * *

College Lane, Bury St Edmunds

Nicki wasn't at home — he could tell. The place was in darkness.

He could break in — but he didn't want to scare her.

Not this time.

Benedict stamped his feet on the frozen ground and leaned up against the wall opposite. He'd heard a few early fireworks being let off while he waited, but midnight was still a few minutes away. Nicki didn't strike him as someone to go out partying on New Year's Eve — but then again, he didn't know her. Not really. All he knew was what he'd managed to read online.

As he waited, he pulled a packet of cigarettes from his back pocket, along with a bundle of business cards showing a variety of names and occupations. Tapping one of the cigarettes out, he flicked through the cards. Most were out of date now and he should probably toss them.

One caught his eye in particular.

Caspar Ambrose — Private Investigator

Caspar had been one of his favourite creations.

He was never quite sure what he should call himself. Private investigator came close — but it often went way beyond that. Hired muscle was also accurate — there wasn't much Benedict wouldn't do if the price was right. He could have taken the more legitimate route — set up his own investigation agency, everything above board and legal; and he'd probably make a decent living out of it, too. But there was something that appealed to Benedict about floating just beneath the radar — sailing a little bit too close to the wind.

The first time he'd met Detective Inspector Nicki Hardcastle, back on that cold November evening, he hadn't exactly handled things well. No doubt she thought him cocky and self-assured — most probably even a conman or charlatan. She'd got the wrong idea about him — he knew that now.

He had planned to tell her everything he knew about her brother's disappearance back then in November, but things hadn't gone as he'd hoped. He'd been dragged away on an overseas assignment — an assignment that he couldn't refuse; not if he valued his legs still being attached to his body. So, he had kept his findings to himself.

The resulting silence from his end must have spoken volumes — Nicki no doubt thinking the worst of him. In her shoes, he would have thought the same. He just hoped he hadn't burnt all his bridges in one go. She deserved to know the truth, as painful as that might be.

* * *

Roy dropped Nicki at the bottom of Whiting Street — the short walk up to College Lane wouldn't take long. She muttered a hurried goodbye from beneath her scarf before striding quickly towards home.

It was dark — no moonlight to be seen behind the heavy clouds above. As she turned into the narrow close, she was already rummaging in her bag for her house keys. With her head down, chin buried in her scarf, she didn't see the figure waiting in the shadows.

It wasn't until the key was in the lock that she sensed movement out of the corner of her eye. Startled, she pulled the key from the lock, turned around and held it out in front of her, feet planted firmly to the ground. Fight or flight, which should she do?

The figure advanced out of the darkness, and Nicki's heart rate sky-rocketed. "Don't come any closer!" she yelled, her words swallowed by the gloom. "I'm warning you. I'm a police officer!"

The figure took no notice and moved closer. Wishing she'd taken Faye up on her offer of martial arts training, Nicki considered her limited options, Run or scream? Run *and* scream?

"I'm not here to hurt you." The stranger's voice was unusually calm. "I promise."

"Stop right there!" Nicki backed up towards her front door. "I can get a car full of police officers here in seconds!" It was a lie, but she wasn't quite sure what else to say. She wished she had finished opening the front door — at least she could then have dived in and slammed it behind her.

The stranger took another step forwards and came into view. He held his hands out in front of him, in an unusually calm gesture. He was wearing dark clothing, but nothing to obscure his facial features. Nicki felt a flicker of recognition ignite.

"I'm here to talk about Deano."

It was then that it hit her. Those eyes, that thin face.

Caspar Ambrose.

"You've got to be kidding me." Nicki continued to brandish the key in front of her. "How you have the nerve to . . ."

"I know, I know." Benedict held both hands up in surrender. "But I can explain. *Really,* I can. Just give me ten minutes — five, even. Then I'll go."

Nicki felt herself hesitate. Ready to shout and scream her loudest, her blood pulsating in her veins, she faltered.

Deano.

So, she gave Benedict his five minutes — which turned out to be fifteen in the end. The pair of them stood on her frozen doorstep, fireworks exploding in the sky all around them, while he first explained who he was, then explained who Caspar Ambrose had been — eventually following on with recounting what he suspected — no, what he *knew* — had happened to her brother.

"Wow." It was all Nicki could think to say.

"I know it sounds beyond belief, but I swear to you it's the truth. I've done all the checks. I have the evidence. I can show you . . ."

Nicki's mobile trilled through the icy night air, making her jump. She let it ring — her head still swimming with what Benedict had just told her about Deano. The caller gave up and the phone silenced. A few seconds later, it trilled again.

Nicki fished the phone from her pocket, seeing '*DS Graham Fox*' on the screen. She glanced at the time. Phone calls this time of night could never be good news. She hit the accept button.

"Graham? What's happened?"

CHAPTER THIRTY-FIVE

Tuesday 1 January 2019
Bury St Edmunds Police Station

After taking the call from DS Fox, Nicki rushed back to the station leaving Benedict with a vague promise to be in touch.

"She hasn't seen him since yesterday." Fox handed Nicki his scribbled notes together with Maria McCrae's phone number. "She was hysterical. She's just seen the headlines about the trainers — and although she doesn't believe they belong to Tommy, she's understandably concerned about him. None of his friends have seen him and he didn't take his phone."

Nicki took the note, rubbing her eyes. Her head was full of Deano and Caspar Ambrose — and now this? "Get another alert put out. See if anyone's seen him at his favourite haunts."

"Already done. You don't think it could be him then?" Fox nodded towards the whiteboard where the image of the trainers with the amputated feet inside was pinned. "We still think that's Lee Tennant, not Tommy?"

Nicki considered it for a second, then shook her head. "From what you've all said about Tommy McCrae, he's unlikely to be able to afford a pair of two hundred quid trainers."

"Could've nicked them?"

Nicki slumped down into a vacant chair and held her head in her hands, the pounding at her temples intensifying. "Graham — see if you can find me some paracetamol and a black coffee. I think this is going to be a very long night."

* * *

Nicki lifted her head off her hands and winced as pain shot through her neck. A squint at the clock on the wall told her it was quarter to eight. By the looks of things, she'd fallen asleep at her desk. Someone had been thoughtful enough to lay a tartan blanket over her shoulders as she slept.

Gingerly pushing herself to her feet, she ran a hand through her tangled hair and took a sip of water from the glass by her computer. An open packet of paracetamol sat by the side. Rubbing the blurriness from her eyes, she headed out into the corridor and towards the incident room.

She was greeted by a gentle hum of activity. A mug of fresh coffee soon found its way into her hands. Standing by the whiteboards, she willed her brain to re-engage and take in what they had so far.

Forty-eight hours, Nicki.

The DCI's words echoed painfully inside her throbbing head.

Well, they were now down to just twenty-four.

So many pieces of the jigsaw didn't fit together. They had two confirmed IDs — a possible third with Lee Tennant — but still no idea how they were connected. *If* they were connected at all. The tech team were still deciphering mountains of data from Jacqui and Lucie's social media accounts — plus the obligatory phone trawls. Matt had made a start on looking at Lee's social media accounts too — just in case. And then there was Tommy McCrae, reported missing by his mum.

Maybe the lead they so desperately needed was coming — but it needed to hurry up. Nicki was acutely aware that time was running away from them.

Forty-eight hours, Nicki.

Swallowing a mouthful of coffee that stung her lips, she looked around the incident room. Fox was sitting at his computer, drumming his fingers lightly on the desk. Matt and Duncan were sat together analysing the technical data that was streaming in. Roy, she was told, had gone in search of some breakfast for them all.

"Anyone seen Darcie this morning?" Nicki addressed the question to the whole room. It was still relatively early, but it was unlike her colleague to be the last one in when they had such a high-profile investigation running, despite the late night they had all had. Everyone gave a shrug or shake of the head. "No matter. Graham? Have you spoken with Maria McCrae again yet this morning? Any sign of Tommy?"

Fox pointed towards the phone at his ear. "On it now, boss."

Nicki headed towards the door, intending to swallow some more paracetamol before tackling the morning's actions. As she reached the corridor, her phone began to buzz in her pocket. Pulling it out, the display told her it was Benedict Thatcher.

Again.

He'd already left three text messages since last night, and now a voicemail.

The messages were all the same. All about Deano.

'I need to tell you where Deano is. Today. Call me.'

Nicki slipped the phone back into her pocket — she couldn't handle this right now. She had twenty-four hours to make a breakthrough otherwise the case would be taken away from her. And anyway, her misgivings about Caspar Ambrose — or whoever it was he called himself these days — were still there. *She still wasn't sure she trusted him.*

Heading along the corridor in the direction of her office, still toying with whether to return Benedict's call, she saw a

PC coming towards her, a large brown paper parcel in their hands. Nicki's thoughts instantly turned to chin chin and rum cake. Despite her tiredness, she felt her stomach start to rumble.

"Parcel for you," said the PC, thrusting the parcel towards her.

"Thanks." Nicki took hold of the package and made to turn back to the incident room. "I'm guessing this is for Roy."

"No, I think it's addressed to you."

Nicki stopped and frowned at the parcel. She'd been convinced it would be another food package from Nigeria, but on closer inspection it, did, indeed seem to be addressed to her.

No postmark.

No stamps.

Hand delivered.

She nodded her thanks to the departing PC and continued on to her office. She placed the parcel on the desk and reached for a pair of scissors. Snipping the parcel tape that was holding the box together, caution suddenly kicked in. She had no idea who the parcel was from, or what was inside. Placing the scissors down she reached for a pair of protective gloves and snapped them on — just in case.

Slowly pulling apart the flaps, she peered into the box.

Her stomach gave an uncomfortable jolt.

There were no chin chin biscuits sitting at the bottom; none of the rum cake that had gone down so well with the team. As she placed a steadying hand on the back of her chair, the office door flew open and DS Fox breezed in.

"Just spoke with Maria McCrae — still no sign of Tommy and . . ." Fox stopped, mid-sentence, noticing Nicki's pale cheeks and the wide-eyed look on her face. "Are you OK? You look like you've seen a ghost."

Nicki let out a shuddering breath. "Not far off, Graham. Take a look." She gestured towards the open box.

Fox approached the desk, a look of trepidation on his unshaven face. "I'm not sure I follow . . ."

"I think there's a very good reason why young Tommy McCrae isn't at home, Graham." She nodded again towards the box. "That look familiar at all?"

* * *

Maynewater Lane, Bury St Edmunds

Amy snapped the kettle on and reached for the teabags. She had phoned work to swap her shift to later — she just couldn't get her head together right now. As she waited for the kettle to boil, she noticed that the hot chocolate sachet she had left out for Darcie was still sitting by the mug, unopened.

Frowning, she pulled her dressing gown around her and padded back upstairs. "Darcie? You up yet?" Her words were met with silence as she reached the upstairs landing. Gently knocking on her sister's bedroom door, Amy nudged it open and peered around the door frame.

Her frown deepened. The bed didn't look like it'd been slept in — unless Darcie had risen early and made it before she left. But now she thought of it, Amy didn't think she remembered hearing Darcie come in last night — and Amy was a very light sleeper. Stepping further into Darcie's bedroom, Amy noticed the coat her sister always wore to work was still draped over a chair, plus her police ID and warrant card were on the dressing table.

Pulling her phone from her dressing gown pocket, Amy scrolled through Darcie's messages from last night. There were several — including a selfie with a bottle of prosecco. Her last message was sent at 11.25 p.m.

'*Ollie coming to pick me up. Home soon. Happy New Year! xxx*'

A sickness began to spread through Amy's stomach as she hurried out of Darcie's room and headed towards the second set of stairs that led to the attic bedroom. Hesitating briefly, Amy tapped on the closed door. There was no reply, no sound from within. She tapped again, a little harder.

"Ollie? Are you there?"

More silence.

Amy tried the door handle. It was unlocked. Pushing the door open, Amy saw the room was empty.

No Ollie.

No Darcie.

Just where the devil had they got to?

CHAPTER THIRTY-SIX

Nicki downed two paracetamol tablets, feeling herself shudder. It wasn't like her to feel this rough in the mornings — she'd survived on less sleep than last night many times before, and she'd only had a couple of gin and tonics in the pub. The scratchiness at the back of her throat told her she was probably coming down with something. *That's all I need,* she thought as she gulped down the rest of the coffee.

The revelation that Tommy McCrae was, more than likely, their fourth victim sat uncomfortably in the pit of her stomach. She had left DS Fox with the unenviable task of phoning Maria McCrae back and informing her of the latest development. It was passing the buck — she knew that — but Graham had been more than willing to shoulder the responsibility. He had also offered to go and see Maria in person, just as soon as he'd spoken with her, which was an enormous weight off her own shoulders.

Despite what was going on around her, Nicki couldn't get Benedict Thatcher or Deano out of her head.

Why couldn't he just tell her what he knew?

Why was he choosing to play games again? Because that's what it felt like — *playing games*. And she had enough of those with the current investigation. Her finger hovered over the screen of her phone — she should call him back, get it over with.

Before she could decide one way or the other, Nicki's phone began to ring. It was Amy.

"She didn't come home last night." Amy's voice sounded faint. "Darcie. Has she turned up for work?"

The disquiet in Nicki's stomach grew. "Darcie? Well, no — no she hasn't arrived yet. I assumed she was just having a late start." Nicki glanced at her watch. It wasn't like Darcie to be this late and not to have called in. "Have you tried calling her?"

"Several times. It just goes to voicemail." Amy broke off. "I'm a bit worried, Nicki. It's not like her not to tell me where she is. Her last message to me last night sounded like she was on her way home. Ollie was picking her up."

"Ollie?"

"Our lodger. The doctor I told you about." Nicki heard Amy take in a sharp breath. "Oh God, you don't think they've had an accident, do you? I need to go — I need to ring the hospital, see if anyone's been brought in."

"OK, let me know what you find out. And Amy?" Nicki was already heading for the door, swiping the packet of paracetamol up as she passed. "Try not to worry."

Amy's voice began to crack. "I'm going to ring work. See what I can find out."

"We haven't been told of any serious accidents here at the station, so . . ." Nicki reached her office door. "I think she's just stayed out all night and she's running late. It was New Year's Eve, after all. In the meantime, keep trying her phone."

Nicki headed to the incident room. Another whiteboard now bore Tommy McCrae's name, plus a photograph of the contents of the parcel.

An ear.

It was undoubtedly his — Nicki could see the same silicone tunnel in his mugshot pinned to the first board.

Roy had arrived back from the baker with breakfast — a variety of greaseproof bags were scattered around the desks — but Nicki waved hers away.

"Boss?" Duncan waved at Nicki from the other side of the incident room. "We're getting some interesting data coming in about Jacqui and Lucie's social media contacts. And Lee Tennant, too." Nicki headed in his direction, pulling up a chair. "They may not know each other, but all three of them had one mutual contact."

Duncan tapped his keyboard and the screen was filled with the profile page for a 'Sebastian O'Conner'.

"Sebastian O'Conner?" Nicki pulled her chair in a little closer. "And all three are friends with him?"

"Well, not exactly. It's a little more complicated than that, which is why we didn't spot it earlier. On paper, they don't have any mutual contacts at all. None. But the tech team have been digging further and found these additional profiles." Duncan again tapped the keyboard and two further profiles populated the screen. He split the screen to show all three at once and angled the monitor towards Nicki.

"Sebastian O'Conner, Sebastian Conner, and Sebastian Connelly." Nicki frowned. "I'm not sure if I understand. Two *more* mutual friends?"

Duncan shook his head. "No. It's the same person — or, at least, that's what we think. Just different profile names. Different surnames."

"Same person, different names. You're sure?"

Duncan gave a hesitant shrug, "Not a hundred per cent, but the tech guys seem convinced. They all have the same profile image."

"You can have more than one Facebook account?"

Duncan nodded. "You're not meant to — Facebook says it's against their rules but if you have more than one email address then it's easy enough to do. And let's face it, email addresses are a piece of piss to get hold of these days."

Nicki scanned the three profiles, her head still throbbing dully. Duncan was right — the three names might be different, but the profile pictures were identical.

Duncan continued. "The tech team are looking into the email addresses used to set up the accounts — but don't hold your breath. Chances are they'll be sent on some high-tech, virtual-reality merry-go-round."

"Anything on the profiles that tells us more about him?" Nicki already knew the answer to that from the look on Duncan's face.

"None of the profiles have any personal information at all. No pictures. No posts. No nothing."

"So, how come they all accepted him as a friend?" Nicki wasn't on Facebook, but knew enough about how it worked to know how risky it was to accept a friend request from someone you didn't actually know. Scammers were everywhere.

"No idea."

"And what *is* that, exactly?" Nicki peered closely at the profile pictures on the screen and wrinkled her nose. "Some sort of insect?"

"Looks like a beetle to me."

Nicki was no fan of creepy-crawlies at the best of times. "Why would someone want a beetle as a profile picture?"

"Again, no idea. Someone who doesn't want to be seen would be my guess."

Nicki got to her feet just as her mobile began to vibrate in her pocket. "Run those three names through the system. See what pings." Pulling out her phone she saw Amy had sent a message.

No accidents.

Darcie still not picking up.

Her concern began to grow as Nicki made her way towards the door, intending to head back to her office. She wanted to keep her head down in case the DCI was about.

Forty-eight hours, Nicki.

As she passed Matt's desk, she saw Lee Tennant's social media pages on his computer monitor. "Have we managed to get hold of Lee's parents yet? Anyone picking up the phone?"

Matt shook his head. "Still no answer. I've left a message."

Nicki massaged her temples and headed for the door. She needed to ring Amy.

CHAPTER THIRTY-SEVEN

Nicki took up her position next to the fourth whiteboard containing Tommy McCrae's details.

"Although no formal identification can yet be made, we're pretty certain that the ear sent to the station this morning belongs to Tommy McCrae." Nicki's gaze flickered over the whiteboard's scant details. "Last seen fleeing his home address on Sunday. No sighting of him since then."

"I can't find him on any social media platforms, boss." Duncan frowned at his computer screen. "Graham brought his phone back from the mother's house, but I can't see any connection to either Jacqui, Lucie or Lee. And no connection to any of these Sebastians — all of which, by the way, have shown up squeaky clean on the system."

"Let's hope there's some CCTV somewhere showing what's happened to him, or a witness comes forward with a sighting. Basic details are being circulated to the media as we speak." Nicki cleared her throat and turned back to her team. "But, right now, I have some rather more worrying news about Darcie. She hasn't shown up for work and according to her sister she didn't come home last night. Her phone goes straight to voicemail. The last time anyone saw her was when she got into a car outside the Moreton Hall Pub last night."

"A car? Do we know who it was?" Concern flooded Roy's face.

"We do. Well, at least we think we do. Ollie — Oliver Lomax — is a doctor at the hospital and rents a room in Darcie's house. I've just spoken to Darcie's sister and she tells me Ollie is only at the house sporadically. He has a family home somewhere else — somewhere local." Nicki paused, watching the shock circulate the room. "While I don't want us to panic — there's nothing that points to anything untoward happening to Darcie — it is most unlike her not to phone in if she's going to be late. Or tell her sister where she is."

"A doctor?" Roy's eyes widened. "Aren't we looking for someone with surgical skills?"

Nicki gave a slow nod. "It's no secret that our perpetrator has medical training of some sort. But let's not make a huge leap and start panicking everyone."

"What about that sticker?" persisted Roy. "We thought it could say farmhouse. Maybe this doctor lives in a farmhouse in the middle of nowhere."

Nicki's mind started connecting dots that she didn't want. She turned to Matt. "Run him through the system — Oliver or Ollie Lomax. Then try and find out where his family home might be."

While Matt grabbed his keyboard, Nicki continued.

"We've been concentrating on getting as much information and background as possible on our known victims so far — I think we need to change tack and try and understand what makes our perpetrator tick. Caz is sure he has surgical skills that go beyond watching YouTube and that we're not just looking for a cack-handed butcher." Nicki paused, her eyes straying to the whiteboard displaying Adrian Browning's name. Despite him popping on to their radar early on and being a particularly unlikeable character, there was nothing further to suggest he was their man.

"He's local — or at least has somewhere to stay in the area. He has to be a car driver."

"He knows how to obtain cloned registrations plates," added Roy. "Probably changes them every time he goes out."

Nicki nodded. "He's clever. He somehow worms his way into his victims' lives — whether they realise it or not. Social media could play a big part in that — we've seen that one link between Jacqui, Lucie and Lee. That may mean he's relatively young — not a technology dinosaur at any rate. As we've no time or budget for a forensic profiler, this is all we have to go on."

"Nothing showing up for Ollie or Oliver Lomax on the system," said Matt, leaning back in his chair. "He's certainly not troubled the police before."

"See if you can find him on social media — and look for that address." Just then, Nicki's phone vibrated in her pocket. Instantly, her stomach clenched, visualising yet another message from Benedict about Deano. Instead, it was Amy.

'He's here at work. Ollie. What should I do?'

Nicki stood still for a moment. Oliver Lomax. Was he really who they were looking for?

Nicki felt the familiar trickle of fear start to spread. What if this Oliver *was* their man, and Darcie was in trouble? He certainly had the medical background — and he was local, with another place to stay in the area.

Farmhouse.

Nicki started striding towards the door, tapping out her reply as she went.

'Nothing. I'm coming.'

As she reached the door she turned. "Graham — you're with me. The rest of you — track down Tommy McCrae's and Lee Tennant's last movements. There must be a camera somewhere that catches them. And keep looking into Oliver Lomax."

CHAPTER THIRTY-EIGHT

They'd found him in the hospital library, head bowed in deep concentration. The textbook open in front of him — *'Skin grafting and skin flap techniques'*.

Although desperate to begin questioning him there and then, Nicki knew she needed to play things by the book — in case matters progressed to more than just casually checking on the whereabouts of a work colleague. The thought sent waves of nausea through her stomach.

Ollie had been surprisingly amenable to accompanying them back to the station, although his face was fixed with a permanent frown. They settled into one of the interview rooms, Nicki ensuring the recording equipment was running and the caution had been repeated before introducing the occupants of the room.

"My name is Detective Inspector Nicki Hardcastle, and this is my colleague." Nicki looked sideways at Fox.

"Detective Sergeant Graham Fox."

"Please state your own name for the tape."

Ollie's expression continued to exhibit a mixture of fear and confusion. "Ollie . . . Oliver Lomax. What's this all about?"

"This is a voluntary interview, Mr Lomax. You are not under arrest and free to leave at any time."

Ollie nodded. "But I still don't . . . ?"

Nicki cut in and got straight to the point. "When was the last time you saw Darcie Butler?"

"Darcie? This is about Darcie?" Ollie's eyes widened.

"If you could just answer the question, Mr Lomax."

"Last night. I mean, this morning."

"Well, which is it Mr Lomax? Last night or this morning?"

"This morning. I picked her up from the pub last night about half eleven I think, maybe just after. Then I took her home."

"Her bed hasn't been slept in, Mr Lomax. Her sister says she didn't arrive home."

"I mean *my* home. I took her to my family home." Ollie's cheeks began to colour. "She slept in my room. I took the sofa downstairs. My parents are still a bit old-fashioned."

"I'm not interested in your sleeping arrangements, Mr Lomax. But where is she? Where is Darcie? She didn't arrive for work this morning and nobody's seen her. Apart from you, it appears."

Alarm now crossed Ollie's face. "She didn't arrive at work? Is . . . is she all right? Has there been an accident?"

"That's what we're trying to establish, Mr Lomax. You say you saw her this morning. When exactly?"

Ollie shook his head, eyes widening further. "I don't know the exact time — around half six, I guess. She said she needed to get into work early. I was still half-asleep so she took my car."

"Where is your family home, Mr Lomax?"

As Ollie recited the address, Fox scribbled it on to a notepad and rose from his seat.

"DS Fox leaving the interview room." Nicki gave a discreet nod as he left. "Why drive all the way to your family home when you have a perfectly good house here in Bury?"

Ollie gave the faintest of shrugs. "I don't know . . . my parents are away and I'm meant to be looking after the place while they're gone. It seemed like a good idea at the time . . ."

"How did you get into medicine, Mr Lomax?"

Ollie frowned at the change of questioning, confusion descending. "It's in the family. My dad's a doctor. So was his dad. Why?"

Nicki ignored the question. "And which university did you attend?"

"Nottingham."

"Do you know how to . . ." Nicki frowned as she searched for the correct word. "*Enucleate* an eyeball? Or maybe cut out a tongue?"

The confusion on Ollie's face intensified. "Well, yes . . . I suppose. In theory. But why would I need to? What's this got to do with Darcie?"

Nicki changed tack once more. "Do you use Facebook at all, Mr Lomax?" She nodded towards the laptop Fox had left behind, loaded up with the three profiles for the mystery 'Sebastian'. Nicki touched the mouse and woke up the screen.

Ollie shook his head. "No, it's not my thing."

Nicki was about to comment how strange that was now, when just about everyone was on social media, but then realised she wasn't on it either — and let it slide.

"Do you recognise the names Sebastian O'Conner, Sebastian Conner, and Sebastian Connelly?"

A blank expression met Nicki from across the table.

"What about Jacqui Massingham and Lucie Ballantine? "

"Who? No . . . hang on. That Jacqui was in the news, wasn't she? In connection with the body parts . . ." Realisation hit Ollie square in the face. "Wait, you think *I* had something to do with that?"

Nicki paused, the tension in the room escalating. "Well, did you?"

"No!" spat Ollie. "That's absurd!"

"Where were you on the evenings of the twenty-second and twenty-third of December?"

A flicker of anger began to ignite in Ollie's eyes. "I have no idea! I'd have to check my work diary but . . ."

"What about last Thursday? You go to the theatre much, Mr Lomax? Or how about Friday night? You a regular in the cathedral?"

Defiance now joined the anger bristling across the table from Nicki. "Look, I came here to help you regarding Darcie . . . this is . . . do I need a solicitor?"

"I don't know, Mr Lomax. Do you?"

The door to the interview room opened, and DS Fox stepped inside, the relief evident on his face. "It's Darcie. She's just rung in — car broke down and then her phone battery died. She had to walk twelve miles before she could find somewhere with a phone."

The sickness that had been swelling inside Nicki's stomach began to subside. She briefly closed her eyes and said a silent prayer. "Thanks, Graham. We'll be wrapping up in here soon."

Fox closed the door behind him and Nicki turned her attention back to the man sitting across the table. Did she really think he was their abductor? Potentially their killer? She'd got a little carried away pressing him about his movements — he seemed genuinely shocked at the suggestion. But then again . . . the man they were looking for was clever.

"That's great news that Darcie's OK. You had me worried there for a moment." Ollie's face relaxed a little, the defiance he'd shown earlier somewhat lessened. "Can I go now?"

Nicki sighed. She didn't have anything to keep him here — and she certainly couldn't arrest him just because he was a doctor. And now Darcie had been found safe and sound — what else was there? There was nothing else to suggest he was their man. She nodded and got to her feet, switching off the recording devices. "You're free to go, Mr Lomax."

Ollie rounded the table, glancing down at the open laptop screen as he passed. It was still showing the three Facebook profiles of the mystery Sebastian. Pausing by the side of the table, the frown returned to his brow.

"Tell me those names again — the three that had the first name Sebastian."

Nicki repeated the three surnames. "Why?"

Ollie edged closer to the table, peering more intently at the laptop screen. "And that's them, is it?"

"Are you telling me that you *do* know them?"

Ollie frowned harder. "That image there, on all three — that's a deathwatch beetle."

"It's a what?"

"A deathwatch beetle. They eat wood or something, I'm not really sure." Ollie paused and pulled the laptop towards him.

Nicki glanced at her watch. Time was running away from them — she could almost feel the DCI's breath on the back of her neck.

Time's up, Nicki.

They'd wasted precious hours this morning sidelined by Darcie's disappearance and needed to get back on track. "Mr Lomax," she sighed. "I think we're done here."

"No, you don't understand. Those three names . . . and this beetle. I think I have a good idea what connects them. I think I might know who you're looking for."

CHAPTER THIRTY-NINE

Bury St Edmunds police station

"Tell me what you know." Nicki passed the vending machine coffee across the table and gestured for Ollie to continue.

"I was at university in Nottingham, like I said. I shared a room with him in halls during the first year. He was odd — definitely odd."

"Define odd."

"Just odd. Weird. Clever — *really* clever. Obviously naturally talented in medicine, he was the top student every year — especially in the anatomy classes. His dissections were *perfect*. We all used to joke that he must be digging up dead bodies in his spare time and practising on them." A small chuckle lodged in Ollie's throat. "And his wardrobe was stacked full of books on anaesthetics, embalming and taxidermy. Like I said — odd."

"And what connects him to the three names we have here?" Nicki nodded towards the laptop screen still showing the three profiles.

"Some of us used to give our cadavers a name — the dead body we used to practise our techniques on during dissection classes. He called his Sebastian. And that surname there — Connelly? There was a girl in our class — Alicia Connelly — who couldn't think of a name — so he chose one for her. He chose Conner. I'm not sure about the other one though — O'Connor."

"And the relevance of the beetles?" Nicki was beginning to think the link was tenuous at best.

"He was obsessed with them. Deathwatch beetles. Even had a jar of dead ones that he kept by the side of his bed. Like I said, he was weird. Creepy. I moved out in second year."

"What else do you know about him? Where is he now?"

Ollie shrugged and sipped his coffee. "I don't know. We never kept in touch, as you might imagine. After university we all went to different hospitals for our foundation training. I did hear a rumour though."

"What kind of rumour?"

"That he didn't finish his foundation training — left in second year, if I remember. Apparently, he had an unhealthy interest in 'end-of-life' care patients. More interested in the *end* than the *life*, if you get my drift. That was the rumour anyway."

* * *

7 November 2014
East Midlands Hospital

"I assure you, he'll be in safe hands. I'll call you if anything changes." Dr Oliver Harper smiled at the grieving and exhausted family, hoping he looked and sounded sincere. It was becoming much harder to get rid of family members now that open visiting for the relatives of terminal patients was hospital policy. It made his work — his research — all that more difficult.

But the Ferguson family had eventually fallen for it.

He would watch them sitting by the bedside, holding hands and crying — day after day, night after night. But the human body could only withstand so much, and he knew that at some point or other they would break.

And, today — luckily for him — they did.

Closing the door to the ward behind the departing family, he strode back towards side room three. He did his best to hide the emerging smile on his face as he passed the nurses' station, slipping back inside the side room and clicking the door shut behind him.

The man lay on the bed, his hospital gown barely covering the emaciated form beneath, the thin hospital blanket unable to mask the fact that he was clearly dying. Pallid, translucent skin stretched across his angular features.

Death wasn't far away.

Dr Harper tapped lightly with his fingers on the bedside table as he sat on the edge of the bed.

Tap — tap — tap — tap — tap

Tap — tap — tap — tap — tap

He'd been a little economical with the truth to the relatives — he'd told them that there was 'no change' in the patient's condition over the last twenty-four hours, and that he was 'holding his own'. The lie had been accepted without too much debate — the family were run ragged, barely an ounce of energy between them.

Death was tiring.

With the light now fading outside, he leaned across to snap on the bedside light, bathing the man's face in a harsh, white light.

The man stirred at the intrusion.

"It's just me, Professor. You can lie back and rest now."

Professor Gordon Ferguson's eyes snapped open. With the sclera tinged yellow, evidence of the advancing metastatic deposits in his liver, he peered out from beneath hooded eyelids. His dry lips paled but nothing more than a whisper emerged.

"Don't try to speak, Professor." Oliver edged closer towards him, taking the man's frail hand in his. "You remember me, don't you?"

The look on the man's sunken face told Oliver that he did.

"Laurence . . ." the man whispered — that one word seeming to require an exorbitant amount of energy to produce. "Laurence Hemmingway."

Oliver smiled and patted the man's hand. "Now, now — you know I don't use that name anymore, professor. My name is Oliver. Oliver Harper. Just like at medical school. Surely you remember that?" He gave the professor's hand another squeeze, feeling the man's bones beneath his fingers. Cancer was very efficient at ridding the body of unnecessary flesh.

Although a shadow of his former self, Gordon Ferguson wasn't stupid — the cancer cells hadn't yet reached his brain. He knew the end was near, but he didn't think it was quite *this* near. There had been talk of a hospice for his final few weeks, somewhere for him to be surrounded by his family when the time finally came. For him to go in peace and dignity.

Not here.

Not now.

Warily, he watched Oliver reach into the pocket of his scrubs and pull out a syringe. Fear entered the professor's jaundiced eyes, and he shifted slightly in his bed, trying to reach the call button.

Oliver chuckled. "Now, now, Professor. Let's not spoil the fun." He nudged the call bell further away from the professor's trembling hands.

* * *

Tuesday 1 January 2019
Bury St Edmunds police station

"I heard there were a few complaints flying about towards the end — how he always seemed to be there when patients passed away. More than could simply be explained by chance. Relatives found it unnerving." Ollie drained the rest of his now cooled coffee. "But he left before they could fully investigate. Just walked out. Never seen again as far as I know."

DS Fox's head appeared around the interview room doorframe once again. "Nothing on the system for an Oliver Harper, boss."

Ollie looked up. "I don't think Harper was his real surname — not his birth name, anyway. We all knew he came from a medical family — his father was a surgeon. I remember something about him not wanting to follow in his father's footsteps, didn't want his father's name to map out his career. Something like that."

"And what was his father's name?"

"I guess he must have told us, but I don't recall. Sorry."

"Try and think." Nicki already had two urgent messages to go and see the DCI, presumably to give her the good news that the case was being taken away from her. She was ignoring them for the time being, but knew she couldn't avoid the man indefinitely. "This is really important."

Ollie frowned, followed by another shake of the head. "Sorry. But his father was quite well known back in the day. Made *The Lancet* and everything. Pioneered a new cardiology procedure when he was barely out of training — I think they named it after him. It's been superseded by more innovative techniques now, but . . . it'll still be referenced somewhere, I'm sure."

Nicki grabbed the laptop and turned it toward Ollie. "Show me."

Ollie began typing into the search bar while Nicki watched the clock. "Anything?" she enquired, conscious of the impatience in her tone.

Ollie held up a hand while scrolling with the other. "Bear with me."

Fox grabbed a spare chair and sat down, his face pensive. "We've found a few images of Tommy McCrae in the town on the day he went missing — but nothing helpful. He just seems to vanish into thin air."

Nicki was about to reply when Ollie almost leapt from his seat.

"The Hemmingway Patch!" Ollie looked up from the screen, eyes shining. "Guy's name was Laurence Hemmingway."

Fox sprang from his chair and headed for the door.

* * *

2 Old Railway Cottages
Dullingham, Nr Newmarket

Benedict stood staring out of the kitchen window, a mug of cold coffee in his hand. He'd heard muffled shouting through the walls from next door on and off all morning — and the occasional thud. The Brownings were usually a quiet family — not so much as a raised voice or the TV on too loud — and when he'd got back home last night, their house had been in darkness.

But this morning, things were different. They'd been out in the garden a few times — both of them.

First, Annette Browning — then her husband.

Benedict put the mug into the sink and pulled on his jacket. Nicki still hadn't replied to any of his messages.

Grabbing a selection of the paperwork still strewn across the kitchen table, he stuffed it into his pocket and headed for the door.

If the mountain won't come to Muhammad . . .

CHAPTER FORTY

The Farmhouse

"You know we should wait for backup and tactical support?" DS Fox knew his words were falling on deaf ears but he said them anyway.

"Like you did last year, you mean?" Nicki scrambled out of the Toyota. They'd parked at the side of a single-track lane that led to the rear of the farmhouse. "I'm not sitting here when Tommy could be in there, still alive maybe. And God knows who else he's got."

Fox hurried after her. "You think he has more? More victims?"

The sharp wind whipped through Nicki's hair as she headed towards a battered wooden gate. "You heard Ollie. He left his medical training under a cloud in his second year. That would have been around five years ago. You think he just magically started doing this now?"

Nicki pushed the gate open — it didn't give up much of a fight. "If we come from this angle, we'll be shielded from the main building. If he's home, less chance he'll see us." Without waiting for a response, she headed towards the yard.

As soon as Ollie had given them the name Laurence Hemmingway, it hadn't taken long to find a property registered in that name some fifteen miles away in the middle of nowhere. Further checks confirmed the owner to be Laurence Oliver Hemmingway.

It was him.

Using his cane, Fox jogged over the uneven ground to catch up. They passed three hay barns, now empty — an old rusting tractor sitting idly in front. In its heyday, Nicki could imagine the yard being a hive of activity — tractors ticking over, dogs barking, a family of chickens running amok searching for grain. But now it looked nothing short of desolate — long forgotten and uncared for.

"Are you sure anyone even lives here anymore?" Fox squinted up at the side of the farmhouse looming into view. "The place is falling down."

"Utilities are still connected." Nicki slowed down, putting an arm out to stop Fox in his tracks by her side. "And the lights are on — so someone's home. We need to be careful."

"And wait for backup," added Fox, looking warily towards the farmhouse.

"We don't have time." Nicki scoured the building. "I'll try the front entrance. You make your way around the back, see if we can get in that way?"

Fox hesitated, but knew resistance was futile. "Sure. Yell if you need me." *For all the good it'll do*, he wanted to add as he set off towards the back of the stone building.

As she watched him disappear around the corner, Nicki took in a deep, shuddering breath before heading for the main entrance.

It felt almost as cold inside the farmhouse as it did outside, the thick stone walls keeping the chill locked in. The front door had been unlocked, sweeping open with minimal noise. A deep, penetrating silence lay heavily on the air as Nicki edged into a narrow passageway. With the stone floor beneath her feet, she crept as quietly as possible further inside the farmhouse, holding her breath.

The first room she came to was a kitchen — empty yet warm from the heat of the range cooker. Continuing along the passageway, she thought she heard music; soft at first, coming in waves. Standing still, she strained to listen above the sound of her thudding heartbeat. Definitely music, coming from deeper inside the farmhouse. With another deep breath, Nicki inched forward, each step as soundless as the last.

The music was getting louder — louder and clearer. Recognition tugged at the back of her mind — it was something she recognised, but couldn't place. Something classical. As she made her way towards it, the thought crossed her mind once again of just what would she actually do if Hemmingway was there. She'd mulled it over on the car journey — and, not for the first time, Faye and her martial arts lessons flooded her thoughts. She'd done some basic self-defence classes many moons ago — but the only exercise she did these days was running.

Maybe running would be a good option right now.

Despite the chill of the farmhouse, her palms felt slick with sweat.

What am I doing? Just what am I doing?

Feeling her heart thud, threatening to explode, Nicki contemplated turning around and heading back the way she had come; waiting for backup like she knew she should. The moment passed and she continued, her breath caught in her throat as she approached an open doorway.

And there he was.

Hemmingway.

Ice chilled her veins in an instant.

He was standing with his back to her, dressed in what looked like hospital scrubs, a large knife in one hand. In front of him was a steel trolley, bearing the body of who she could only assume was Tommy McCrae. Was he moving? Nicki couldn't see from where she was standing.

The sound of the music filled the room, masking her approach and rapidly rising heartbeat. Her feet glued themselves to the floor, her legs starting to quiver like jelly.

Reaching to the side, she placed a shaking hand on the door-frame to steady herself.

Maybe it was that movement which alerted him to her presence. Or the soft cry that lodged in her throat.

She saw his shoulders stiffen, then his head tilt slightly to one side.

What happened next flew past in a blur. He came at her like lightning — turning on the spot in one seemingly graceful move, then lunging across the tiled floor towards her. Before she had a chance to react, his cold hands were around her wrists, dragging her further and further into the room. The scream in her throat loosened but died, suffocated by an overwhelming sense of terror. He was strong, so very, very strong, and made short work of dragging her across to the side of the steel trolley.

Tommy McCrae was lying motionless beneath a white shroud, blood crusted around the side of his head where his ear had once been. He looked pale and lifeless.

But Nicki's gaze soon gravitated to something else — something equally sickening.

The knife Hemmingway still held in his hand.

* * *

The Farmhouse

Nicki. Nicki. Nicki.

Just what have you done?

DCI Malcom Turner sat in the passenger seat of the black Mondeo, his usual calm manner evaporating by the second. He had known there was something brewing — Nicki had been avoiding him all morning despite several attempts to catch her attention. In fact, she had been avoiding him ever since he gave her the ultimatum.

Forty-eight hours, Nicki.

Turner looked at the dashboard clock, then turned to the sergeant in the driving seat. "How long?"

"Almost there, sir. And backup are two minutes behind."

That was something at least.

Turner bit his lip as the car bounced over the rough ground of the farm track. The garbled message he had eventually received told him that Nicki and Fox had gone on ahead, without protective clothing and without waiting for backup. And currently there was radio silence from them both.

If their intelligence was correct, then this farmhouse was the epicentre — the place where they were most likely to find the person who had been terrorising the town for the last few days. And Nicki and Fox were heading right into the thick of it.

She had her father's spirit, that was for sure. Hugh Webster had been a fine officer, and an inspiring detective superintendent. Certainly not afraid of getting his hands dirty when the need arose.

More bumps in the road and more unease spread through Turner's stomach. If only she had waited until the backup had been arranged — but waiting wasn't part of Nicki's mindset. Not when she believed someone's life may be in danger.

"Approaching target property, sir." The sergeant slowed the Mondeo, pulling up next to Nicki's Toyota.

The car was empty. Nicki and DS Fox were nowhere in sight. Turner let out a shuddering breath.

Shit, Nicki. Where are you?

* * *

The Farmhouse

Hemmingway had his arm locked around her neck; the stranglehold so tight Nicki thought her bones would almost certainly snap. Her body started to convulse as panic gripped her. She knew what this man was capable of.

The grip around her neck tightened.

302

More screams died in her throat as she watched Hemmingway's free hand rise up in front of her, the gleam from the silver blade glinting in the half-light.

This is it.

This is the end.

In that split second, Nicki found herself thinking of her work colleagues — Darcie, Roy, Graham. And then Amy and Caz. Each one of them like family to her these days. Then she thought of Luna and her heart almost burst.

Then there were her parents — and Deano.

The blade of the knife turned towards her and Nicki closed her eyes.

What happened next, she couldn't quite comprehend, but she found herself falling, crashing to the ground, her head striking the cold hard tiles with a thundering crack. She heard the knife clatter to the floor by her side, then Hemmingway's body thudded on top of her, punching the air from her lungs.

Eyes now wrenched open, she looked up to see DS Fox standing over the pair of them, wielding his cane.

CHAPTER FORTY-ONE

The Farmhouse

Support had arrived not long after DS Fox's cane had cracked across Laurence Hemmingway's skull. Knowing the blow would only momentarily stun him, Fox had been quick enough to leap on top of Hemmingway's body to pin him to the ground. Still somewhat groggy, Nicki found a bag of cable ties next to Tommy and secured the man's wrists and ankles.

They'd then found Tommy McCrae was still breathing, a flicker of consciousness returning to his pallid face — dried blood where his ear should be.

With Hemmingway now safely stowed in the back of a police van, and Tommy McCrae on his way to hospital under blue lights and sirens, Nicki felt the adrenaline finally leave her body. She reached for the side of a wooden worktop to steady her shaking legs.

It was only now that she could fully take in the bizarre room they were standing in. What appeared to be an old-fashioned farmhouse pantry had been kitted out to look like an operating theatre. Surgical scrubs and masks hung from hooks on the wall; several IV stands stood close by; rows upon rows of jars and bottles lined the pantry shelves.

"When will the crime scene lot get here?" Fox headed towards the door that led into Hemmingway's boot room.

Nicki dragged her gaze away from the pantry shelving and shook her head — then wished she hadn't as a bolt of pain stabbed her between the eyes. "Soon. I guess. We just need to lock this whole place down until they get here."

Fox reached into his pocket and threw a pair of protective gloves at her. "Well, I for one want to know what's inside those freezers." He nodded towards the boot room. "Coming?"

Nicki exhaled a long pent-up breath and pushed herself away from the worktop. "I think we already know what we'll find, Graham." But she followed him anyway.

Fox was already by the side of the first freezer. "Ready?"

Nicki arrived at his side and gave a nod.

Lifting the lid of the freezer, they peered inside. The contents were as expected — but not any the less brutal. The frozen bodies of who they assumed to be Jacqui Massingham, Lucie Ballantine and Lee Tennant lay entwined at the bottom.

Fox closed the lid and moved to the next. Nicki turned away, not wanting to know what they might find.

"This one's empty." Relief edged Fox's tone and Nicki's stomach began to unclench. An empty freezer was good news. Fox then headed over to the third freezer and popped the lid. Nicki could see from his expression that this one wasn't empty.

"Male. Naked. Older. Seems to be covered in lots of surgical cuts. Lots of stiches." He frowned towards Nicki. "You think this could be our long-lost Hemmingway Sr?"

It wasn't really a question.

Nicki heard her phone ping with an incoming message. "It's Faye," she said, squinting at the screen. "They're just pulling up outside."

Making their way out of the boot room and through the pantry, they paused by the body map pinned to the wall. The had both already taken a good look at it after Laurence Hemmingway had been escorted from the premises, and the

305

images had sickened them. Jacqui's eyes and tongue; Lucie's hand; Lee's feet. And now Tommy McCrae's ear graced the macabre map.

"I don't think I've ever seen anything quite so grotesque," murmured Fox. "You?"

Nicki shook her head. "Never."

About to follow Nicki out to meet the forensic team, Fox hesitated once more by the map, his eyes trained on the top right-hand corner. The map was tacked to the pantry's stone wall, but the corner was starting to peel away. Reaching up, he tugged at it a little bit more.

"Graham? You coming?" Nicki hovered by the door. "Faye and her team will want to get in here."

Fox continued to pull the corner of the map, his eyes widening by the second. "Jesus, Nicki. There's another one."

* * *

The Farmhouse

"I want this whole place taken apart — brick by brick." Nicki's breath billowed out in front of her as they congregated in the yard. Faye and her team, suited up and carrying their equipment towards the front entrance, nodded in response. "Leave absolutely nothing behind."

The discovery of a second body map, hidden beneath the first, had given the investigation a new focus.

"If he's done this before, then where are they?" Fox blew into his hands and began stamping his feet to ward off the encroaching chill. "They're not in the freezers."

"I don't think we need to pretend that Jacqui was his first. Or Lucie. He's done this before — no question about that. Like we said earlier — he dropped out of his medical training some five or so years ago. My guess is he's been doing this a lot longer than we think." The thought made Nicki shudder; she pulled her coat close around her.

"We hanging around much longer or . . . ?"

"Let's get out of here. I need to defrost."

"And you need to get that head injury looked at."

Nicki had refused to be checked over by the ambulance crew when they had turned up to take Tommy to hospital, promising to take herself to A&E if she felt unwell. Her head had hit the tiles heavily, and she could feel the lump swelling beneath her hair — but there was no blood, and she felt fine other than a headache.

The DCI had congratulated her on cracking the case, although she detected an element of concern in his voice. Maybe even a hint of irritation. She *had* gone against procedure, she knew that. Placed herself, and a colleague, in danger. But it looked as though Turner was going to let that slide — for now.

"Maybe," she muttered, knowing she probably wouldn't. "Come on. I'll buy you a hot sausage roll when we get back to the station."

The journey back was less tense, with Fox taking over the driving. As they approached the town, Nicki's thoughts turned back again to the second body map. It had chilled them both to the bone, seeing numerous other polaroid snaps of an array of body parts taped to the wall. Nineteen — Nicki had counted them. Nineteen victims.

The missing.

Her thoughts naturally turned to Deano.

He was missing too.

As Fox pulled the Toyota into a space in front of the station, Nicki glanced out of the window and immediately recognised the person waiting for her.

Benedict Thatcher.

CHAPTER FORTY-TWO

Dullingham, Nr Newmarket

"I could have driven myself." Nicki fidgeted in the passenger seat of Benedict Thatcher's VW Golf.

"I know." Benedict's face was taut as he concentrated on driving.

"You think I've dismissed you as a crackpot."

"And have you?" Benedict half-turned in the driver's seat, eyebrows raised.

"Jury's still out on that one." Nicki cast a glance out of the passenger window, her head throbbing. "I can't be gone long. I've got a major development breaking in one of my investigations."

"I won't keep you. But you really can't delay this any longer."

Benedict had thought long and hard about how he would tell her — how he would break it to her exactly what had happened to her brother all those years ago. Should he sugar-coat it? Skirt around the unpleasantness? Or should he just confront her with the evidence and let her see for herself.

Whichever way he chose, Detective Inspector Nicki Hardcastle was in for the shock of her life.

Pulling into the village, Benedict took the Golf down the narrow lane that led to his house — and that of the Brownings' next door. He noticed the frown forming on Nicki's brow as they got closer.

"Wait, I've been here before." Her frown intensified as they came to a halt outside number 2 Old Railway Cottages. "What's going on? You said this was about Deano."

"It is." Benedict killed the engine and got out of the car, gesturing for Nicki to follow. Silently, she obeyed, unsure of what other option she had — other than ringing Graham to come and rescue her. Benedict grabbed her by the hand and pulled her towards the gate that led to the back garden of the Brownings' house.

Nicki tried to snatch her hand away. "You need to tell me what's going on. This isn't funny."

"No," replied Benedict, pushing open the Brownings' gate and pulling Nicki down the side of the house and into the garden. "It really isn't."

With increasing disquiet, Nicki found herself crossing the frosty lawn. This was Adrian's house — she recognised it as soon as they pulled up. What could Adrian and his family possibly have to do with Deano?

The garden narrowed towards the bottom and Benedict guided her through the tight mesh of brambles and over-grown bushes. Thorns ripped at her trousers as she almost tripped over her own feet on the rough grass.

"I told you I knew what had happened to your brother. And I do. And it all begins with this."

Before her, Nicki saw a freshly dug plot of earth in the middle of the frosty ground. At the side was a discarded garden spade.

"No, no, no, no!" Benedict released Nicki from his grip, his face paling. "This can't be happening!"

The confusion that had swamped Nicki up to now was swiftly turning to anger. "Just what the hell is this?" She gestured to what could only be described as a freshly dug grave.

"Why am I here? And what has it got to do with Deano?" As the words escaped her mouth her heart pounded.

Surely not?

A grave?

"This." Benedict pulled out his phone and scrolled through his photos until he found the image he needed. "Look." He thrust the phone towards her. "Yesterday there was a headstone there."

Nicki's face froze.

'Precious son and brother — taken too soon'

Five years old — RIP

A hand flew to her mouth just as an agonising wail started to form. "You can't be telling me this is Deano! You just can't! What kind of animal are you?" Nicki's legs buckled beneath her and she landed on the chilled grass, her knees sinking into the freshly dug earth. Her head thumped and nausea started to swell. "Not my Deano! Please, not my Deano!" Tears were coursing down Nicki's frozen cheeks, pain etched into every corner of her being.

Benedict grabbed her arm and pulled her to her feet. "No, no — that's not what I mean at all. Look."

* * *

A1 motorway

"You've overreacted." Larry Browning pressed hard on the accelerator and pulled the van out into the fast lane. "None of this is necessary."

Annette Browning sobbed quietly into her handkerchief in the passenger seat.

"It makes us look suspicious — running like this."

Annette shot a withering look at her husband. "I'm not overreacting and it's entirely necessary! I told you this would happen one day and you completely ignored me."

Larry kept his eyes on the road ahead. "I never ignore you, Annette. Far from it. Everything would have worked out fine if you didn't panic so much. I had everything under control."

"You said someone had been in your study — seen your newspaper cuttings."

Larry nodded. "Yes, I did. But maybe I was mistaken. Maybe it was one of the boys instead, or my imagination." He knew it wasn't the boys and he knew it wasn't his imagination. He knew exactly who it had been. "But even if it was someone — I could have handled it without us needing to run away like this." Benedict Thatcher would have been no pushover, but he was sure he could have found a way to ensure the man kept his trap shut, without them needing to run like this. Running made you look guilty.

Which, of course, they were.

"Adrian should have come with us." Annette rubbed her wet cheeks with the sleeve of her cardigan and stared out of the window at the passing traffic. "It's wrong to just leave him behind like that."

"Adrian will be fine." Larry's teeth clenched. "And he's the least of our concerns right now. He's got a job and he needs to stay in the house. We can't just abandon it."

"You plan on going back?" Annette couldn't keep the horror out of her tone. "Back there?"

Larry ignored the question and pulled the van back into the left-hand lane. "We can't run forever, Annie. You know that." His tone softened and he flashed a hesitant smile in his wife's direction. "I'm tired of running."

Annette nodded, feeling a fresh spate of tears starting to well up. She was tired of running, too.

* * *

2 Old Railway Cottages
Dullingham, Nr Newmarket

"I stumbled across the headstone by accident — last October." Benedict considered going into the whole underpants story,

311

but decided they didn't have time. "Obviously an odd thing to have at the bottom of your garden, but that wasn't what concerned me." He paused, nudging the hastily made mug of instant coffee across the kitchen table. "I was inside their house one day soon after, fixing their Wi-Fi. That was when I noticed all these family photos on the walls. I managed to get some snaps when I went back in yesterday." He scrolled through the images in his phone and selected a few for Nicki to view. "Two boys — the usual pictures in the park, on holiday, Christmas and so on. Naturally I assumed them to be the Brownings' two sons — Adrian and his older brother Mason.

"And they're not?" Nicki's voice sounded faint. She grasped the hot mug of coffee but didn't drink.

"Well, this is where it gets kind of complicated. One of the brothers — the older one from the look of the photos — has a very distinctive birthmark on his face. You can see it in the photos." Benedict tapped one of the larger images on the phone screen to enlarge it. "One of those port-wine stains, I think they call them. But neither Adrian nor Mason has a birthmark."

"I'm not sure I follow . . ."

"Bear with me." Benedict pulled his laptop towards them both. "When I showed you the photo of the headstone earlier — I didn't show you the one with the full inscription. And the name on the headstone confused me." He scrolled through the catalogue of images, pulling up one that showed the full inscription.

Precious son and brother — *taken too soon*
Five years old — *RIP*
Mason Douglas Browning

Nicki peered towards the screen. "Mason?"

Benedict nodded. "It's a headstone for Mason Browning. So, I ran a search looking for the death certificate. There isn't one. Nothing. Birth certificate, yes. Death certificate, no."

"But Mason Browning isn't dead. That's Adrian's older brother — you just said." Confusion battered Nicki's head alongside the increasing ache from the earlier injury.

"I know. Like I said, bear with me. Now, I managed to speak with Mason yesterday — and he told me something very interesting."

* * *

Monday 31 December 2018
4 Old Railway Cottages
Dullingham, Nr Newmarket

Benedict gestured for Mason to swap ends and hold the fence panel in place as he fired a fresh round of nails into the wood. His hands felt red raw from the cold, the air temperature barely above freezing.

"Thanks for helping me." Benedict aimed the nail gun at the fence post. "Much quicker job with two pairs of hands."

"No worries," replied Mason, bracing himself against the post. "I wasn't busy."

"You're older than Adrian, right?"

Mason nodded. "Just over three years between us."

"I remember when my baby brother was born — I must have been about the same age as you were, I reckon. About three? I remember I wasn't very impressed — I'd wanted a dog."

Mason smiled as the next round of nails thundered home. "I wasn't around when Adrian was born. This isn't my real family — we're not real brothers. I was adopted when I was five."

Benedict paused, nail gun in hand. "Adopted?"

Mason nodded. "It's no big deal. This is the family I've grown up with — all I've ever known really. My real parents and my sister died in an accident."

"I'm sorry to hear that." Benedict straightened up, looking at his handiwork. "That must have been difficult."

Mason shrugged. "It's a long time ago now. Mum and Dad — Annette and Larry — they've been good to me. I couldn't have wanted for a better family."

Except your real one, thought Benedict, his mind beginning to race.

With the fence repairs now complete, Benedict returned the nail gun to his toolbox, eyeing Mason across the grass. "This might sound like a strange question, Mason, but — have you ever had a birthmark on your face?"

* * *

Tuesday 1 January 2019
2 Old Railway Cottages
Dullingham, Nr Newmarket

"No birthmark." Benedict watched more colour drain from Nicki's face, the look of confusion still prevalent. "Mason — the boy who's meant to be Adrian's older brother has no birthmark. And never had. The boy in the photos in the Brownings' study *isn't* him. It can't be. It was another brother." Benedict paused. "A brother that's no longer here." Holding up his phone, Benedict once again found the image of the headstone. "The boy with the birthmark is the *real* Mason Browning. And this Mason Browning died in October 1996. According to the headstone." Benedict angled the image of the headstone towards Nicki.

"And?" Nicki's voice was barely a whisper.

"And *this* Mason Browning . . ." Benedict scrolled to a different image on his phone. "Is your brother."

CHAPTER FORTY-THREE

2 Old Railway Cottages
Dullingham, Nr Newmarket

"He told me himself. Mason. The Brownings aren't his real parents. His own parents died in an accident when he was five."

Nicki's bottom lip began to tremble. She tightened her grip on the mug of coffee.

"It's my belief, Nicki — my *strong* belief — that the Brownings' son Mason died in 1996. And your brother — Dean — was snatched to take his place."

Nicki began to shake. She abandoned the coffee mug. "No," she whispered. "No, no, no . . ."

Benedict persevered.

"I've a contact at the GRO — the General Register Office — who owes me a favour or two. He looked for any record of the adoption — there isn't one. Not with this family. Of course, there could be many reasons why there isn't a record, but what is clear to me is that the Brownings' son Mason died in 1996. Why else give him a headstone? Looks like they dig the poor boy up and take him with them wherever they go. They never registered his death, Nicki."

Nicki looked up, her face awash with shock.

"And then there was what I found in the drawer . . ."

"Drawer? What drawer?"

"Inside the study. When I was fixing the Wi-Fi. Newspaper cuttings — hundreds of them." Benedict pulled up another bank of images on his laptop. "See for yourself."

Nicki scanned the images, her mouth opening slightly. "They're all about me — and Deano," she breathed.

Headlines from the *Daily Mirror*, the *Daily Mail*, the *Express*, and the *Telegraph* instantly filled the laptop screen. Countless articles and reports on the disappearance of five-year-old Dean Webster in November 1996. Then there were the more recent cuttings — ones of Nicki's investigation into the abduction of little Lucas Jackson last year, and also the current investigation. Pictures of her. Close-ups of *her*.

"Why? What . . . ?"

"There's more. I did a search of where the Brownings were living around the time your brother went missing. They lived in Warcester from April 1993 to the end of 1996."

"Warcester. That was just five miles from us — from where I grew up." Nicki's voice wavered, her head swimming. "But . . .But how did you find out about me? I'm not Nicola Webster anymore."

Benedict had anticipated the question. "The Webster family were big news back then. The story into your brother's disappearance ran for weeks, months even. It sparked a huge debate on the tracking of known paedophiles when they were released from custody. As each anniversary passed, there would be the odd article mentioning the case — but no one mentioned the sister — no one mentioned *you*. It was as if Nicola Webster had also disappeared that night." He paused. "It wasn't hard to make the link. I managed it, so I'm sure the Brownings would have, too. Your name was splashed across all the papers last year with the Lucas Jackson case — I'm sure that opened up some very old and painful wounds.

"The more I dug — the more I found. Your mother — from what I can gather, she's an ardent supporter of the local WI — she set up a charity for underprivileged children a couple of years after your brother disappeared. Named it Dean's Club."

Nicki nodded. "Yes, she did. She said it helped her — helped her cope with the loss."

"It got me thinking — what did Mrs Browning do after losing her son? Surely her pain was no less — the chasm left behind just as deep? But they didn't even register the poor lad's death — let alone give him a proper burial."

Benedict hesitated once more, closing the lid of his laptop. "Here we have the death of the Brownings' five-year-old son, however that occurred, at much the same time your brother goes missing. They lived only a matter of minutes away from your family home and have an almost unhealthy fascination with Dean's case. And you." Reaching for his phone, he showed Nicki one last picture, taken from the Brownings' study. "Then there was this."

The image was one of Mason's drawings.

An intricate, pen and ink drawing of a funfair ride — a caterpillar.

Benedict leaned across and grabbed hold of Nicki's trembling hand. "You don't need to be a private investigator or a detective inspector to see what's gone on here."

Tears trickled down Nicki's cheeks. "Deano's alive." She tried a smile. "My Deano's alive."

Then the smile faltered, replaced by pain once more. "But where is he?"

* * *

A1 motorway

Mason found himself wedged into the corner in the rear of the van, several holdalls and a suitcase the only things preventing him from sprawling across the floor when his father pulled the van around a corner too sharply. Adrian still had a variety of old boxes stacked up in the back of the van too

— there hadn't been time to get rid of them. Mason just hoped they weren't full of stolen meat, slowly going rotten.

The thought churned his stomach.

Once he'd found out they were moving on — again — he'd asked to stay behind at the house with Adrian. Then he'd seen the look on his mother's face and immediately knew he couldn't do it to her; couldn't abandon her. Dad did his best, but Mason knew it was him that his mother needed. And he could do his illustrating work anywhere. Maybe once they were settled — wherever it was they were headed — he would come back.

With the van on a seemingly straight section of road, Mason stretched his legs out in front of him. He'd thought better of asking where they were going when he'd seen the looks on his parents' faces. Mum looked like she'd been crying, Dad just looked worried.

They hadn't brought much with them — just a few holdalls and a suitcase — although there was still plenty of room in the back. A lot of the space in the middle of the van was taken up by a large slab of stone and a curious wooden box. Dad had heaved both of them inside, sweat peppering his forehead and a grim look of determination on his face. Mason had hung back, having no idea what they were but knowing better than to ask.

But after a few hours in the back of the van, his curiosity was returning. The slab of stone and box were tucked beneath a large tarpaulin, but he could easily lift up one of the sides. He edged closer, the aroma of freshly dug earth filling his nostrils.

CHAPTER FORTY-FOUR

Tuesday 1 January 2019
A1 motorway

Annette watched another signpost flash past the window as they continued heading north. She hadn't asked Larry where they were headed — hadn't wanted to know. Anywhere was good. Anywhere was better than where they'd come from.

Mason hadn't said much, but Annette knew he wasn't happy about moving again. Or leaving Adrian behind. But there was no way she was letting Mason out of her sight — not for one second. They'd all been through too much — *she'd* been through too much — for them to give up now.

Mason.

Everything she'd done was done out of love — love for the little boy she had lost.

* * *

Thursday 7 November 1996
Little Wynham Fair

She'd seen him the very moment she'd entered the fairground.

He was perfect — just like Mason. Even down to the cheeky dimples on his cheeks. Dressed in a yellow anorak, yellow boots and a bobble hat on his head, Annette Browning followed the boy through the fair, keeping out of sight of the family.

She knew it was wrong — *of course* it was wrong. Every bone in her body screamed at her how utterly wrong it was. But she batted the thoughts away like they were just annoying, harmless flies. She *had* to do this. She had to do this for Mason.

He'd been such a sweet little boy — perfect in every way. No one could have wanted more from their son. A bundle of energy, and cheeky with it. Mason had been the apple of her eye.

But then there had been *the accident.*

It was all still such a blur. Sometimes she didn't think it had even happened, not really. It couldn't have happened, could it?

But then she saw, in her head, his beautiful yet lifeless tiny body tucked up in bed and knew it was real.

Larry had been away for work — leaving her alone with two young children. She should have been able to cope — other mothers coped, didn't they? She saw them at the local park, and in the community centre for the weekly toddler group. All coping perfectly — with their perfectly manicured nails and styled hair; their perfect bodies, toned at their twice-weekly gym sessions: and their perfectly behaved children.

So why did she feel so different? Why did she find everything so difficult?

Mason had been the most beautifully behaved baby — giving her no trouble at all. Sleeping through the night and leapfrogging the 'terrible twos'.

So why couldn't she cope when Adrian came along?

It was all her fault, she knew that. It had to be. It could be no one else's.

The night it happened played on her mind constantly. Mason had been feeling unwell for a few days — grizzly and clingy, which wasn't like him. He'd complained of a headache and feeling sick. He was off his food and looked quite pale. Annette had put it down to a virus going round the nursery school where he had just started going two days a week. Children picked up all sorts of things when they started school, so she had been warned.

She had tucked Mason up in bed with a dose of paracetamol for his temperature, and told him he'd feel better in the morning.

Adrian was still teething by that time and was also grizzly and unsettled. Annette was at the end of her tether without Larry.

The doctor had prescribed her some sleeping tablets and antidepressants some months previously after having a bad couple of weeks, eventually dissolving in a flood of tears in the doctors' waiting room. She didn't like to take them — seeing it as 'failing' — but on the evening of 21 October 1996 she'd decided to take both.

It was a decision she would regret for the rest of her life.

She had found him the next morning — cold in his bed.

Mason.

She hadn't been sure what to do — who should she call? Larry wasn't due back for another week. In the end, she decided to call no one. Social services would have a field day — they'd been called to the Brownings once before — an anonymous caller had informed them that a toddler was being left alone in the garden for considerable lengths of time without a parent being present. They were worried the child might do themselves an injury if they got into the unlocked shed at the bottom of the garden.

The social worker had been nice enough — reassuring Annette that she wasn't alone in sometimes not feeling able to cope. But gently reminding her that children, especially mobile and inquisitive children like Adrian, could find danger in just about anything if left to their own devices. She was the one who'd urged Annette to visit her GP for some support.

So, Annette had done just that — and now look what had happened.

With a black mark already against them, surely social services would come down hard this time? Maybe even the police? Was she a criminal? She had taken some tablets — she couldn't remember how many — and fallen asleep. The alcohol probably hadn't helped much.

When she had finally awoken half way through the morning of the next day, Adrian had been screaming the place down, his nappy soiled. And Mason was dead in his bed.

When Larry came home a week later, he found Annette a quivering mess and Mason still lying cold and rigid in his bed, dried vomit around his mouth. After the initial shock had sunk in, he had put a comforting arm around her shoulders and told her that everything would be all right.

That was her Larry — he always made things right.

They decided to bury Mason in the back garden — taking his tiny body out under the cover of darkness. The delay in reporting his death would have raised so many eyebrows at social services that Annette was on the verge of a breakdown. They would take little Adrian away from them and the family unit would be no more. Annette may well go to prison for neglect.

Larry had told her he would never let that happen.

Larry — her saviour.

Annette continued to watch the child as he queued up at the caterpillar ride with his sister, a huge grin on his face.

Oh Mason, she breathed. *My dear, darling Mason.*

It had happened so quickly in the end — over in a heartbeat. And he had come surprisingly easily.

The initial wariness on his face disappeared when Annette brought out the sticky toffee apple and told him what a big, brave boy he was. Before she knew it, Annette had led the boy out of the fairground.

Annette missed Mason like crazy, but now she had someone else to love.

Larry would understand, wouldn't he?

Annette dragged her thoughts back to the present, seeing yet more signs for northern towns and cities flash past the window.

"I'm sorry," she murmured, her voice so faint she wondered if she'd even said the words out loud.

"What was that, love?" Larry flicked the indicator to pull off at the next junction.

"I said, I'm sorry. For all this. It's all my fault."

Larry managed a sigh. "It's not all your fault."

"But it is — you know it is. If I hadn't . . ." Annette felt the words catch in her throat. She swallowed, her eyes momentarily flickering towards the rear of the van. "If I hadn't taken him . . . none of this would have happened."

Larry gripped the steering wheel, his face taut. "I should never have left you alone. I knew you weren't coping. I should have been there."

"But . . ."

"No buts, Annie." Larry flashed her a look, his face softening. "I should have been there. Maybe I wouldn't have been able to save Mason, but . . . I could have been there for you."

Annette tried a weak smile but it looked more like a grimace.

She would never forgive herself, even if Larry had.

CHAPTER FORTY-FIVE

Friday 11 January 2019
The Nutshell

Nicki made room on the small table for her gin and tonic and Roy's pint of IPA. For the first time that week, she felt she could relax. A little.

Laurence Hemmingway had been charged with four counts of murder — those of his father, Jacqui, Lucie and Lee — plus one count of the kidnapping of Tommy and wounding with intent. He was now languishing on remand in prison, unlikely to see a trial until the end of the year.

He'd given very little away during any of his interviews, his solicitor repeatedly advising him of his right to silence. The farmhouse remained sealed off, still in the process of being taken apart piece by piece to see what other gruesome discoveries could be revealed. The second body map threw up all sorts of horrific connotations — and checks were being made countrywide as the possibility of further victims became a reality.

The second freezer in the farmhouse had now been processed — showing some evidence of human blood and tissue at its base. DNA was being extracted, but it would be a long haul. A search of the surrounding fields had found several fire pits which looked to have recently been in use — whatever charred fragments that remained had been bagged up and sent for analysis.

Nicki shivered. "What makes someone do something so grotesque?" She nudged Roy's pint glass towards him. "No matter how long I do this job, I don't think I'll ever get to the bottom of it."

"I think we had a similar conversation after the Lucas Jackson investigation. Is a person born evil — or do we, society, make them that way?"

Nicki shuddered again, sipping her gin and tonic. Although the conversation was about Laurence Hemmingway, she couldn't help but visualise the Brownings at the same time. Were they evil too? For what they did? Benedict Thatcher was working on tracing the family, but so far no trace had been found. The van had been tracked travelling north as far as Carlisle, but then disappeared. Adrian, still living in the family home, knew nothing. Or, at least, was saying nothing.

Nicki had held back from telling her parents what they'd discovered — '*not until we know for sure*' had been her response to Benedict's question. There was a part of her that still didn't believe it could be true — that Deano was still alive. She wouldn't fully believe it until she saw him for herself, standing in front of her, able to touch him with her own hands.

"But, there's definitely more, yes? More victims?" Roy took a mouthful of his IPA, dragging Nicki away from her thoughts of her brother.

"There has to be. The other body map — it shows far too many body parts for it to be anything else. We just don't know who they are — or what he did with them."

"So, what made him start displaying the trophies now?" Roy wrenched open a bag of salted peanuts. "If he didn't do it before?"

Nicki pondered the question — one which had been playing on her mind ever since they'd discovered the second body map.

"Maybe it wasn't about the killing anymore. Not for him. If it ever even was. Maybe it was more about the shock value this time. Perhaps he got a thrill from showing the world what he could do, searching for some kind of adoration or respect in what he'd managed to achieve. Lots of killers take trophies — but not many make the effort to display them like Hemmingway did. It's as though he saying '*look at me*', '*look what I did*'.

"But to kill his own father like that and mutilate his body over and over." The post-mortem on Laurence Hemmingway Sr had taken place two days ago. Caz had concluded that the man had been preserved with embalming fluid, then repeated dissections had taken place on his body over an extended period of time before he was eventually frozen.

"Fathers can be hard to impress." Roy took another mouthful of his beer to wash down the peanuts.

"Maybe." Nicki eyed the detective sergeant across the rim of her glass. "Your parents are proud of you though, I'm sure."

Roy gave a nod, albeit a hesitant one. "I guess so. I still think they wanted me to be a teacher, or an architect or something. I'm not sure the police was what they had in mind."

Several minutes passed by in companionable silence. The pub, already full to bursting with six people inside, was beginning to mist up at the windows.

"How are your injuries now?" Nicki nodded towards Roy's healing face. There were only one or two faint markings now from where Marcus Jackson's fist had landed some two months previously.

"All good." Roy tossed the rest of the peanuts into his mouth and avoided Nicki's penetrating look.

She could tell his ribs still gave him trouble — the way he sometimes sat down gingerly, or rose from a chair. The way he winced at sudden movements.

"Honestly, you and Graham are as bad as each other."

Roy grinned and finished his pint. "Another?"

Nicki glanced at her watch. Another gin would definitely be welcome, but she had places to be. And people to see.

"Another time. I need to be somewhere."

Leaving Roy to order himself another pint, Nicki stepped out into the chill of the evening and headed for home. Benedict had messaged with an update on the search for the Brownings. A trip to Carlisle had been mentioned. The thought made a strange sensation ripple through her stomach.

Carlisle.

Would that be where she finally found her brother?

All Nicki knew was she would never give up looking.

THE END

MESSAGE FROM THE AUTHOR

There are many people I need to thank for helping get *The Trophy Killer* on to the shelves.

First, I must thank Detective Inspector Steve Duncan for being on the end of my often weird and vague-sounding questions. Your help is much appreciated! If there are any remaining procedural inaccuracies, then I can assure you that they are mine and mine alone!

Huge thanks must also go to both Dr Clive Duke, Consultant Anaesthetist at West Suffolk Hospital in Bury St Edmunds, and Mr David Sapsford, Consultant Pharmacist at Addenbrookes Hospital in Cambridge — the help you have both given surrounding sedation and helping my killer overpower his victims is gratefully received. And I take full responsibility for any questions raised concerning your internet search history as a result of investigating the street availability of ketamine!

My good friend Sarah Bezant always deserves a special mention — you have the most amazing hawk eye when it comes to plot holes, typos and missing words! I really appreciate everything you do for me.

And, of course, I must thank everyone involved at my publishers, Joffe Books — and especially Kate Lyall Grant for believing in me and making my writing the best it can be.

Although Cambridge-born, Bury St Edmunds has been my home since 2008. It is a lovely place to live and if you ever get the chance to visit then it's well worth it! I use many real locations in and around the town in this series, one of which is the roundabout near Southgate Street. The wolf sculpture on the roundabout is real — created in 2013, the 7ft wooden sculpture depicts the animal that, according to legend, guarded the head of King Edmund after he was killed by the Danes in 869. It is said that the King's men found Edmund's decapitated body, only later discovering the head in a nearby forest being protected by the wolf.

Although a small market town, Bury St Edmunds is home to St Edmundsbury Cathedral which is also featured in this book. Thanks to Sarah Friswell, visitor experience manager, for answering my cathedral queries, and also Ian White for help in all things ecclesiastical.

I must also thank Sharron Stowe from the Theatre Royal for my guided tour.

Thanks must go to Charlie Dorner and Sylvia Smith from the Moreton Hall Pub for always making me feel so welcome (and for making sure I always get the best table). Your support of my writing and offering to host book signings is very much appreciated.

And, finally, it is you — the readers! Without you, none of these books would ever see the light of day. I thank each and every one of you.

To keep up to date, there are various ways to get in touch:

www.michellekiddauthor.com — join my author newsletter for information on future releases and special offers. I also give away free downloads, content not available anywhere else!

www.facebook.com/michellekiddauthor

Twitter @AuthorKidd

Instagram @michellekiddauthor

THE JOFFE BOOKS STORY

We began in 2014 when Jasper agreed to publish his mum's much-rejected romance novel and it became a bestseller.

Since then we've grown into the largest independent publisher in the UK. We're extremely proud to publish some of the very best writers in the world, including Joy Ellis, Faith Martin, Caro Ramsay, Helen Forrester, Simon Brett and Robert Goddard. Everyone at Joffe Books loves reading and we never forget that it all begins with the magic of an author telling a story.

We are proud to publish talented first-time authors, as well as established writers whose books we love introducing to a new generation of readers.

We have been shortlisted for Independent Publisher of the Year at the British Book Awards three times, in 2020, 2021 and 2022, and for the Diversity and Inclusivity Award at the Independent Publishing Awards in 2022.

We built this company with your help, and we love to hear from you, so please email us about absolutely anything bookish at: feedback@joffebooks.com.

If you want to receive free books every Friday and hear about all our new releases, join our mailing list: www.joffebooks.com/contact

And when you tell your friends about us, just remember: it's pronounced Joffe as in coffee or toffee!

www.ingramcontent.com/pod-product-compliance
Lightning Source LLC
Chambersburg PA
CBHW031118210626
46816CB00016B/1623